MOMO ARASHIMA

BREAKS THE MIRROR OF THE SUN

Also by Misa Sugiura

Momo Arashima Steals the Sword of the Wind

MOMO ARASHIMA

BREAKS THE MIRROR OF THE SUN

Book 2

MISA SUGIURA

 LABYRINTH ROAD | NEW YORK

Text copyright © 2024 by Misa Sugiura
Jacket art copyright © 2024 by Vivienne To

All rights reserved. Published in the United States by Labyrinth Road,
an imprint of Random House Children's Books,
a division of Penguin Random House LLC, New York.

Labyrinth Road and the colophon are trademarks
of Penguin Random House LLC.

Visit us on the Web! rhcbooks.com

Educators and librarians, for a variety of teaching tools,
visit us at RHTeachersLibrarians.com

Library of Congress Cataloging-in-Publication Data
Name: Sugiura, Misa, author.
Title: Momo Arashima breaks the mirror of the sun / Misa Sugiura.
Description: First edition. | New York: Labyrinth Road, 2024. |
Series: Momo Arashima; book 2 | Audience: Ages 8–12. |
Summary: When kids begin to disappear, Momo teams up with the
magical fox spirit, Niko, and her friends to confront a dangerous enemy
from Shinto legend, Tamamo-no-mae, and embark on a quest to the
Sky Kingdom to steal the legendary Mirror of the Sun to save their world.
Identifiers: LCCN 2023033443 | ISBN 978-0-593-56410-3 (trade) |
ISBN 978-0-593-56411-0 (lib. bdg.) | ISBN 978-0-593-80853-5 (int'l ed.) |
ISBN 978-0-593-56413-4 (ebook)
Subjects: CYAC: Fantasy. | Shinto gods—Fiction. |
Japanese Americans—Fiction. | LCGFT: Fantasy fiction. | Novels.
Classification: LCC PZ7.1.S845 Mm 2024 | DDC [Fic]—dc23

The text of this book is set in 11.3-point Adobe Garamond Pro.
Editor: Liesa Abrams
Cover Designer: Michelle Cunningham
Interior Designer: Jen Valero
Copy Editor: Barbara Bakowski
Managing Editor: Rebecca Vitkus
Production Manager: Tim Terhune

Printed in the United States of America
10 9 8 7 6 5 4 3 2 1
First Edition

For Kaoru Sugiura, who taught me to be proudly, fiercely, stubbornly myself.

You regretted it sometimes, but I will always be grateful.

8 More Children Disappear: Feds Stymied

WINNETKA, IL, December 17—Local police and federal investigators are searching for clues leading to the whereabouts of 58 children who disappeared on Wednesday morning. All 58 were students at Hubbard Grove Elementary School in Winnetka, Illinois, a suburb of Chicago.

The children were on a field trip to the Skokie Woods when they vanished without a trace. According to witnesses, the group was last seen entering the forest preserve at 9:50 a.m., led by their teachers, Jestonia Price and Connor Chen. Ms. Price and Mr. Chen emerged without the children at 10:30 a.m. Both appear to be in a state of deep shock and remain under medical observation at Evanston Hospital.

"They were just staring into space. Wouldn't say a word. It was spooky," said one witness.

This is the latest in an alarming series of unexplained mass disappearances of children that began two weeks ago, bringing the total of missing children to 737. In each case, a group of children has gone missing, with no clues as to where, how, or why. No one has claimed responsibility for any of the disappearances. Beyond this common factor, law enforcement officials have been unable to establish a plausible connection between the events, nor have they identified any motives or suspects.

A Creeping Phobia of Giant Inflatable Snow Wizards

What am I doing here?

No, that wasn't me waking up from a coma, or pondering the meaning of life. It was me regretting my life choices. Specifically, my choice to show up unannounced to *this* party, at *this* house.

Let's start with the house, which was more of a mansion than a house, with its rich brown iron-studded wooden door, its crisscrossed wooden beams set in white plaster walls, and its sharply peaked roof and gabled third-floor windows. It was probably supposed to look like it had been transported directly from Merrye Olde Englande—if houses in Merrye Olde Englande had ye olde swymming pooles in the backyard, a giant two-story blow-up of an old white guy on the front lawn, and a herd of SUVs and minivans in the driveway. I wondered who the guy was supposed to be: the spirit of winter? Father Time? Gandalf from *The Lord of the Rings*?

"Friends call me Snow Miser—whatever I touch . . . turns to snow in my clutch! I'm too much!" the wizard sang from somewhere near his left armpit, and I almost jumped out of my skin.

But the forbidding oak-and-iron door and the giant singing

3

snow wizard weren't the only reasons I was hesitating on the front step. The other reason—the real reason—was much smaller. And scarier.

The real reason was the host of the party: Ryleigh Guo, the evil power behind the throne of her BFF, Kiki Weldon. I know it doesn't make sense: I was a half-kami who'd escaped an army of ghost crab samurai, fought a seven-foot-tall scorpion to the death, and defeated Shuten-dōji, the most powerful demon in the world. Why would I be afraid of a couple of seventh-grade girls?

But anyone asking that question would be severely underestimating the power of seventh-grade girls to make you feel like garbage.

According to a now-famous list that Kiki had made back in September, she and Ryleigh were the two most popular seventh-grade girls at Oak Valley Middle School; according to the same list, I was the least popular. And while Kiki was the one who'd *written* the list, rumor had it that it was actually Ryleigh's idea. Not only that, but after my friend Danny and I got back from defeating Shuten-dōji on the Island of Mysteries in October, Danny had confessed to me that Ryleigh was the mastermind of a prank that had ended up with me getting fruit punch thrown in my face at the back-to-school dance.

And here I was, about to crash her party.

Ryleigh had been bragging for weeks about how cool it was going to be: the cookie-decorating table, the wrapping-paper *Project Runway* contest, and (drumroll, please!) a "very special guest appearance" by Ryleigh's mom's cousin's best friend's husband's nephew, Jin Takayama—hands down the cutest member of the hottest boy band of the year, Straight 2 Tha Topp. Or SttTop, if you were a true SttToppie.

Wait, what's that—can you hear it? Oh, yes. It's the combined voices of a million fangirls, boys, and everything-in-between-and-beyond shrieking, "OMG, JIN TAKAYAMA? *AHHHH!!!*"

Was I one of them? No.

Okay, maybe.

Okay, fine, yes. But I wasn't here for Jin Takayama.

I was here for Danny.

Danny and I had been best friends who'd drifted apart over the years, and after our defeat of Shuten-dōji, I'd thought I finally had my old friend back. And I did, for a while. But then he'd started eating lunch with his bro-bot buddies every now and then—and I was *not* going to eat with those monsters. And after Thanksgiving break, he'd sat with Ryleigh when she waved him over on the bus. And he'd done it again last Friday. And now he was at Ryleigh's party and I needed to . . . to . . . well, I wasn't sure what I needed to do, exactly. Something.

As I stood under the watchful eye of the winter wizard, chewing my lip and trying to ignore a growing anxiety stomachache, it began to dawn on me that crashing this extravagant, invitation-only birthday-slash-holiday bash attended by the most popular seventh graders at Oak Valley Middle School—without a plan of action—might have been a very bad decision on my part. Even if I had a good reason.

Danny and I had been planning all week to watch a movie together, but he'd shown up about an hour ago and said casually, "Hey, I know it's kinda wack to do this last-minute, but I was thinking I'd go to Ryleigh's party tonight."

I could hardly believe my ears. "But—but you said—we planned—"

"I know, I know. I'm sorry. Really. But I was thinking . . . you and I hang out all the time. And this is, like, a special occasion, and—"

"You mean we *used* to hang out all the time," I corrected him. For a few weeks after our return from the Island of Mysteries, usually at dusk, when people were less likely to see us, we'd gone searching for local yōkai, practiced with our weapons (Danny with his magical bow and arrow, and me with Kusanagi, the powerful sword given to me by my grandfather, Susano'o, god of the sea and storms), played with magic origami bunnies, and even ridden a magic origami crane over the valley a couple of times. But all that had dropped off quite a lot lately.

"You say that like it's *my* fault," Danny protested. "But I wanted to hunt for kappa in the creek last Thursday after school, remember? And you said no."

"My *mom* said no. Just 'cause your parents were out of town doesn't mean I can do whatever I want, too."

"Yeah, but you can't blame me for that. That's your mom."

I let out a long, frustrated breath; he had a point. It was all those kids going missing. Mom was sure the culprit was an evil demon sent by Izanami the Destroyer to drag me down to Yomi, the land of the dead, to join her as her spirit daughter. And despite exactly zero of those disappearances having occurred anywhere near us—the last one had been two thousand miles away—she had forbidden me from leaving the house without her. And lately, even some regular human parents had been doing the same with their kids.

6

"But here's the thing—my mom's not here! She had to go somewhere, and Niko's staying with me. We don't have to watch a movie. I could—I could fold a flying crane, and the three of us could go for a ride!"

Mom had left that very afternoon, in fact. Before she left, she'd summoned Niko—the hundred-year-old magical fox spirit who had pulled me into the kami-verse in the first place—to be my babysitter. She'd given us very clear instructions and nothing else: "Do not leave the house until I come back. Niko, do not let Momo leave the house."

"Where are you going?" I'd asked. She never went anywhere.

"Nowhere. It's, er, just a quick errand. Nothing important." She cleared her throat and tucked her hair behind her ear—a dead giveaway that she was lying.

I decided to ask Niko to check his magic mirror later—the one that allows the viewer to see the activities of anyone they choose—but Mom must have read my mind, because she snatched it up and tucked it in her sleeve.

"Mom, seriously, what's going—"

She silenced me with a stern look and a kiss. "I'll be back before you know it. Stay inside until I return. I love you," she said, and—*poof!*—she was gone.

I was always low-key worried about Mom disappearing. Dad's death three years ago had turned her into an empty shell, and those three years had been the loneliest in my life. I'd felt so sad and lost without Dad, but I couldn't lean on Mom for comfort because she just . . . wasn't there. Since my adventures in the kami-verse, it was like her spirit had returned and she'd gone back to being the mother I'd missed so much: present, caring, and worried about my safety—maybe even too worried. So why would she just pick up and leave, after all that fuss she'd made about protecting me from whatever demons might be trying to deliver me to Izanami? Had she stopped caring about my safety? Was *she* in danger? Was she about to disappear for good?

"Oh, she cares, you big baby," Niko had huffed. "She summoned me to stay with you, didn't she? I bet she'll be back before bedtime."

Now I was glad I'd been left with Niko, because Niko was much easier to sway than Mom was. If Mom *really* hadn't wanted me to go out, she shouldn't have left me here with him.

I looked hopefully at Danny—he liked Niko. "So what do you think? Wanna go on a crane ride?" When Danny still looked unconvinced, I added irritably, "What's so special about that stupid party, anyway?"

He looked over his shoulder at his parents, who were waiting in the car in the driveway, then kicked the doormat with his toe. "I mean, it's gonna be huge—with a special celebrity guest and everything. And I was *invited*."

"Well, I *wasn't* invited."

Danny's face fell. Then, after a moment of hesitation, he said slowly, "You could come with me, if you want. You wanna come?"

Ugh. Please. "I don't want your pity," I snarled.

"What?" Danny looked confused. "That's just . . ."

"It's so obvious! You're only inviting me because you know I'll say no," I accused him. "You don't really want me to go."

"But why—"

"'Cause I'm not cool enough for you," I said bitterly. "Or maybe it's because you want to flirt with Ryleigh."

"What are you even talking about?" Danny spluttered.

"Oh, come on. You know." Lately, all anyone could talk about at school was how Ryleigh had a huge crush on Danny and how Kiki had told Jenny to tell Brad to tell Danny that he should kiss Ryleigh under the mistletoe tonight. It made me want to barf. Which is a mean thing to say—but also, it really did make me feel sick. If Danny and Ryleigh started being (ugh) boyfriend-girlfriend, where did that leave me?

But it felt weird to say all that out loud. So when Danny insisted again that he didn't know what I was talking about (*Yeah, right*), I said, "You know what? It doesn't matter. Go. Go have a *great* time at your *cool* party with your *cool* friends."

Danny gaped at me. "Seriously? Come on, Momo," he said. "Why are you being like this?"

"Just go!" I said.

When he didn't move, I shouted, "I said, go!"

This time, he drew himself up and said, "Okay, fine! I will."

"Okay, fine! Go, then!"

"Fine! I'm going!"

"Fine! Go!"

Danny turned and stomped back to the car, and I slammed the door, hard. My heart pounded and I squeezed my eyes shut to keep the tears from coming. I thought I'd banished the nightmare vision that Shuten-dōji had shown me on the Island of Mysteries about Danny abandoning me for his old friends—but here it was, happening in real life. What if I'd just slammed the door not only on him but on our entire friendship? Inside me, my rage monster—my connection to Susano'o—raised its hackles and argued back. *You didn't do anything wrong! It's Danny's fault for having terrible friends. Shuten-dōji was right—he's a jerk. We should never have trusted him.*

"Momo! Was that Danny at the door?" Niko's voice floated toward me from the kitchen, where he was devouring a large pepperoni pizza.

"No," I lied. "Just someone trying to sell something." I slouched off to my room and looked in the mirror. What was it about me that made it so easy for other kids to leave me out? Was it my hair? My clothes? I wasn't hideously ugly or anything—and even if I were, that would be a terrible reason. I was just like everyone else inside. Except for my spiritual connection to Izanami and Susano'o, anyway. Ha. Maybe that was it. Maybe people could sense it. I wished I could go into the mirror, like Alice in *Through the Looking Glass,* into a world where I wouldn't be such a loser.

Or maybe I should just let my rage monster take over. I sat on my bed for a while, fantasizing about showing up to the party and unleashing my power like the evil queen in "Sleeping Beauty." *You think you're so cool,* I'd say. *But look who you forgot to invite! Mwa-ha-haaa!* Then I'd pull Kusanagi out of my backpack, swing its blade through the air, and bring down a lightning bolt. It wouldn't hit anyone, of course, but it sure would make people pay attention.

Oh, who was I kidding? Even if I had the guts to do something like that, regular humans always misinterpreted what they saw when it came to the spirit realm. They'd probably think I was brandishing a giant stuffed panda instead of a gleaming sword, and they'd never connect it to the lightning bolt.

Maybe I really could *go, though.* The thought lit up and flitted through my brain like a firefly. Maybe I could fold Mom's magic origami into a crane and ride it to Ryleigh's house and . . . and . . . do something—just something small—to remind Danny who his real friend was. (*Me*, duh.)

I grabbed the bottomless backpack that Hotei, the god of contentment, had given me. I never left home without it. It was a portal to the Aum, which contained everything in the universe, and it was supposed to give me everything I needed. I folded an origami crane, snuck out the window, and set the crane gently on the ground. I sat down on it, and just like always, instead of getting squashed flat, it grew to the size of a giraffe. I gripped its silver feathers and we flew to Ryleigh's house, leaving Niko to munch on a bag of Flamin' Hot Cheetos that he'd poured on top of his second pepperoni pizza as he watched his favorite movie, *Fantastic Mr. Fox.*

So there I was, faltering on the doorstep of Ryleigh's Merrye Olde Mansion with a stomachache, a backpack, a terror of Ryleigh and her minions, and a creeping phobia of giant inflatable snow wizards.

If only Danny hadn't ditched me for this party. Then I wouldn't be in this situation. A tiny burst of resentment sparked at the base of my skull. Ryleigh was probably planning to spend the evening flirting it up with him, and he'd probably fall for it.

I ground my teeth. Who did she think she was, anyway? I had every right to be here. I was just as good as Ryleigh or any of them—better, even.

Maybe.

Good enough, anyway.

The point was, Danny was *my friend*, and Ryleigh had no right to steal him from me. The spark flared up and became a flame—just a tiny one, just enough for a birthday candle—but it got me through the door. I'd defeated monsters and demons! I was a fierce warrior demigoddess who wielded one of the most powerful magical swords in the history of the world! I'd literally faced death and lived to tell the tale, and I wasn't going to let a bunch of mean girls intimidate me!

As I entered, another creepy wizard voice boomed, "What ho! Another guest has arrived!" and everyone turned to see who it was.

"What's *she* doing here?" someone whispered not quite softly enough. Ryleigh and Kiki, who were standing at the center of a knot of girls at the foot of the stairs, stared at me, and then at each other, as if they couldn't quite believe what they were seeing. They made their way slowly across the front hall, followed by their minions, and stopped in front of me. I felt like a mouse at a party full of cats.

Kiki cocked her head and wrinkled her brow, like she was stuck on a difficult math problem. She turned to Ryleigh and asked incredulously, "Did you invite Momo?"

I'm, Like, Totally Freaking Out!

"Of course not! I only invited friends." Ryleigh's voice got syrupy sweet as she turned to me. "No offense."

My cheeks flamed. "It's okay," I said, even though it was definitely *not* okay. Where, oh where had my fierce warrior energy gone?

"So, like, what are you doing here?" Ryleigh sounded genuinely curious—or maybe it was shock.

"I was just . . . I mean, I was wondering if . . ." I looked around desperately for any sign of Danny.

"Oh, there you are!" I followed Ryleigh's gaze to see Danny sauntering into the room, modeling a brand-new Warriors jersey. Ryleigh clapped her hands. "Ooh, it fits perfectly! Do you like it?" Then, "Look who's here, Danny. It's Momo. Did you know she was coming?"

I managed a smile with my mouth, but I was murdering him with my eyes. I probably should have been trying to murder Ryleigh with my eyes instead, but I didn't have the courage to face off with her. Her eye-murder game was much stronger than mine.

Danny's eyebrows lifted in surprise. "Hey! What are you doing here?"

"That's what *I* said," said Ryleigh. Then to me again, "No offense."

Offense taken, you viper, I wanted to say. *Danny, I'm here to rescue you from Ryleigh's evil clutches.* But of course all I could actually say was "Um."

Then Ryleigh announced, as if I weren't even there, "She can stay if she wants. But this is boring. Come on, Danny, let's go." She grabbed his arm and flounced off. With a shrug and a guilty half smile at me, Danny allowed himself to be towed away.

The sensible thing for me to do at this point would have been to leave. I was obviously not welcome, and I definitely did not fit in. But my rage monster flared up inside me again and dug in its heels. *We are not giving her the satisfaction of seeing you leave in disgrace,* it said. *If we leave now, the princess wins.*

The princess in this scenario was clearly Ryleigh, so that meant I was . . . the evil queen?

That couldn't be right. *I* was the good person and *Ryleigh* was the bad one.

Are you sure? whispered a little voice in the back of my head. *Who is spiritually bound to Izanami the Destroyer and Susano'o the storm god? Who has an internal rage monster that, when un-leashed, nearly killed her two best friends and destroyed an entire island?* With a shudder, I smashed down that train of thought as hard as I could.

All alone now, I slunk into the living room and stood miserably against the wall, watching Ryleigh and Danny at the center of a swarm of minions and bro-bots. No one motioned for me to join them. No one even looked my way. I felt my stomach clench. If I hadn't been worried about getting lost in the dark and endless space inside, I would have crawled into my magic backpack. Instead, I decided to stick it out until nine o'clock; it would be good practice for if I was ever captured and tortured by real demons.

Through the doorway, I could see a bunch of grown-ups drinking wine and eating cheese in the dining room. Like I said, parents these days were extra protective; Ryleigh's party had probably only been allowed to happen if parents were also invited. I could practically hear Mrs. Guo saying, "Don't worry, honey, we'll stay out of the way and drink fancy wine and talk about the news." In fact, there she was—the elegant, lithe Asian woman chatting with Danny's parents, Mr. and Mrs. Haragan. Mrs. Meade, our new principal, was there, too—she'd just started a week ago, after our old principal had gotten sick and announced she was taking the rest of the year off. Mrs. Meade was tall and lean, with silky silver-white hair, and eyes that looked almost gold in certain lights. Her skin was wrinkled, but pale and unblemished, like she'd never been out in the sun. It was rumored that she'd once been a famous fashion model. Ryleigh was always bragging about how her parents knew all the important people; maybe Mrs. Meade was one of them.

I was just turning away when Mrs. Haragan saw me and called out to me. "Momo! I see you decided to come after all! I'm so glad. Is your mother here? I haven't seen her in ages!"

"Oh, uh." I cleared my throat. "She went . . . somewhere."

"You mean she let you come here all alone? With that awful kidnapper on the loose?" Mrs. Haragan looked horrified, and then pitying. "You poor thing. We should have insisted you come with us. Do you need a ride home?" It reminded me of the days after Dad died, when I'd had to take care of Mom instead of the other way round and grown-ups were always so sorry for me. Why did Mom have to be like this, even now that she was healthy and happy? It was so embarrassing. And then, unexpectedly, I felt a wave of loneliness for Dad. If he were alive, he'd have been the parent who'd driven me to this party.

"No, I have a babysitter," I said to Mrs. Haragan. "Anyway, it's just for the evening. She'll be back tonight."

Mrs. Meade had joined Mrs. Haragan now. "That's a very short trip indeed! Well, if she doesn't make it back before the party's over, I'll be happy to drive you home." She smiled, her perfectly painted crimson lips parting to reveal a row of gleaming white teeth.

"Thank you," I murmured, edging away. "I think I'll go decorate a cookie." If there was one thing worse than being seen alone at a party, it was being seen chatting it up with the school principal at a party.

I checked my watch: forty-seven minutes left.

I gritted my teeth and stood in a corner of the living room, away from the other kids. I could do this. I would stay for every one of those forty-seven minutes even if it killed me. But four minutes later, Mrs. Guo entered and clinked a fork against a glass. "Attention, everyone! I've just received some amazing news. Someone very special has arrived!"

The room erupted in squeals and shrieks as Ryleigh and Kiki and their posse of minions clutched each other and jumped up and down. "That's right, kids! Put your hands together for the one! The only! *Jin! Takayamaaaaa!*"

The lights flashed and a stereo boomed out the opening beats of Straight 2 Tha Topp's latest hit, "Imma Fight 4 Ya." A floor-to-ceiling mirror at the end of the room rotated to reveal possibly the handsomest boy in the world—even handsomer than Danny. The squealing got louder. Out of nowhere, a bouncer appeared and fended off the herd of girls who would have stampeded and probably suffocated *Jin! Takayamaaaaa!* as he strutted forward and sang the first verse of the track:

Hey, girl, you rock my world
Even though you didn't know . . .

There was no denying Jin's star power. I was spellbound. And when a roving spotlight found me and I saw Jin pointing and beckoning in my general direction, I nearly fainted.

I can tell you're shy, 'cause you're tryna hide
All the way in the back row

I checked behind me and around me, but I was standing all alone. So I looked at Jin and mouthed, *Me?*

In response, he twirled and planted his feet, pointed straight at me, smiled, and nodded. He launched into the chorus:

Doncha know, doncha know, Imma fight for ya . . .
Gonna light the night for ya . . .
Climb the highest heights for ya . . .
'Cause it just feels right . . . with . . . ya . . .

A pair of enormous hands landed on my shoulders and guided me gently through the crowd and toward the stage. I knew that everyone was going, *Momo? Really?* But it didn't matter. For once, I was the star of the show, and in a *good* way—in a dancing-with-an-internationally-famous-pop-star way, and not in a getting-an-entire-cup-of-punch-spilled-all-over-me-and-freaking-out-and-attacking-someone-and-tripping-over-my-own-feet way. Not that I still held a grudge about that or anything.

When the song ended and *Jin freaking Takayama gave me a hug,* I decided that sneaking out and coming to this party might have been a good decision after all—possibly one of the best decisions I'd ever made in my whole entire life.

Jin released me with a dazzling smile, and I was getting ready to thank him when someone pushed me aside.

"Um, excuse me, hi! Hi, Jin! I'm Ryleigh!" Ryleigh's voice was high and fluttery and loud. She opened her eyes wide, tossed her ponytail, and slid herself in between me and Jin, making sure to jab me in the ribs with her elbow.

"Omigosh, I'm, like, totally freaking out! Like, I'm, like, aaahhhh!" She squinched her eyes shut and did fangirl hands. "Seriously, this is, like, the best birthday present ever!" Ryleigh turned to the crowd and shouted, "Thanks, Mom and Dad! I love you!"

Then she turned and flung her arms around me. "It's my birthday," she hissed in my ear under the applause. "Take a hint and get off the stage."

I opened my mouth, but nothing came out. As I struggled to pull myself together, Ryleigh waved at the bodyguard, and within seconds those heavy hands landed on my shoulders again and steered me back into the shadows. Jin began singing "Happy Birthday" and gazing at Ryleigh like he was thinking of making her his next girlfriend. With a sinking heart, I realized what a fool I'd been. How could I have let myself believe that Jin Takayama might actually fight 4 me? The whole thing had been an act from start to finish.

I walked out of the room, through the front hall, and out the front door without looking back. Weird Winter Wizard sang gleefully, "Friends call me Snow Miser . . ."

"Lucky you. At least you have friends," I muttered. I reached into my backpack, where I'd carefully stored the crane so it wouldn't get squashed—but it wasn't there.

I reached deeper and felt around with increasing anxiety, but all I felt was empty space: the Aum. Which is to say, a space that contained everything—and nothing. Hotei claimed that the backpack was supposed to give me whatever I needed, whenever I needed it, but unfortunately, the Aum and I seemed to have very different ideas about what I needed and when I needed it.

What was I supposed to do now? I didn't know the way home from here, and I did *not* want to send a message to Niko to tell him I'd snuck out and I needed him to rescue me. He'd be furious—and what if he told Mom? She'd make me live in my room forever. (Though to be fair, she would have had a good reason.) But there was no other choice. I sighed and reached for the magic letter paper and calligraphy brush that Mom made me keep in my jacket pocket for emergencies because, unlike me, she wasn't foolish enough to trust my backpack.

But before I could write anything, Danny burst through the

front door. "Hey, why'd you leave? What're you doing out here? Are you okay?"

He'd noticed I'd left, and come looking for me! He was still my friend! Part of me wanted to fling my arms around him in gratitude. But part of me was still angry about getting shoved off the stage by his—ahem—other friend. "I'm fine. I'm just not having fun anymore, that's all."

"Aw, come on, don't leave yet. Jin Takayama's taking a bathroom break." Danny paused to snicker. "But then they're gonna do fireworks in the backyard. Look—Ryleigh and I each snagged a few little ones to set off later." He dug in his jacket pocket and proudly pulled out a few strings of firecrackers. "And then there's the cake. At least stay for the cake! Ryleigh said some world-famous pastry chef made it custom for the party."

Ooh, Ryleigh and her fireworks and her fancy cake. Yay, Ryleigh. Not.

"Daaannyyy!"

I almost groaned. Speak of the devil—literally. Ryleigh had always had a way of sneaking up on you out of nowhere, at the most inconvenient moments.

"Danny, I've been looking all over for you! Come on, the fireworks are about to start and I want you to—"

BOOM.

Whoa, Bruh. Chill!

The sky flashed white, then blue, then white again: *BOOM. BOOM. BOOM.* Shouts and screams rose from behind the house. Then everything went black.

"WHAT." Ryleigh was furious. "They started *without* me?"

But it only took a second to realize that something was off. The night was completely dark—even the house lights had gone out: the uplights that had illuminated the wizard, the porch lights, the lights that had been pouring from the windows, everything. The screams stopped as abruptly as they had started. And in the dark and eerie silence, a blue-white light glimmered to life at the back of the house.

We crept through the house to find the kids gathered on the grass, surrounded by a bunch of bobbing orbs that gave off that blue-white light we'd seen from the front. The adults stood on the deck, empty-eyed and slack-jawed. None of them moved a muscle or even blinked as we approached.

"Mom!" Ryleigh cried, running to Mrs. Guo. "Dad! What's wrong? Wake up!" But they wouldn't—or couldn't—respond.

Mr. and Mrs. Haragan were the same. Danny gave up on

his parents and called out to the kids, his voice cracking with desperation. "Hey! What's going on? Come back here!"

But there was no answer. Instead, the kids began shuffling away from the house in a silent, amoeba-like mob, following a line of more flickering blue lights spaced a few feet apart across the lawn. A long chain of those same lights led down the steep hill at the far end of the yard, into a thicket of manzanita bushes, poison oak, and blackberry brambles. As the human amoeba progressed, each little flame on the chain joined a sphere of lights that was slowly forming itself around the group.

"Danny, I'm scared," I said. "Those lights . . . They feel—"

"Evil," Ryleigh said. Her face looked ashen in the eerie blue glow, and her voice trembled a little. "They're onibi. It's a trap. This must be how all those kids have been disappearing."

My jaw dropped as I stared at her in shock. How did she know what they were called? For that matter, how was she seeing them? And why wasn't she freaking out that *I* could see them?

Danny's mouth fell open, too. "You can see the lights?" he asked.

Ryleigh stared back at him. "*You* can see the lights?" She turned to me. "I'm not surprised about you—you're always talking about the kami-verse. But how does Danny—"

"You *knew* about the kami-verse? And you *never told me?*" I felt like my life was turning inside out and upside down—like I had stepped through the mirror at home and into a whole other reality.

Jin Takayama's golden voice came from behind us. "Hey,

everyone! What'd I miss?" He stepped onto the deck and gasped audibly.

"A lot," Danny said.

"You should get inside the house," Ryleigh added.

Jin's mouth was open now, too—I was beginning to feel like I was part of a human cornhole board. "But . . ." He pointed at the zombified grown-ups and then at the glowing sphere surrounding the rest of the kids, who were shuffling ever closer to the woods at the edge of the lawn. "Those lights."

"*You* can see them?" I asked. This was getting out of control. First Ryleigh admitting that she'd *known all along* that we'd had the kami-verse in common. (*What???* And again—why had she pretended not to? Why had she ridiculed me for saying things she knew were true?) And now Jin?

"You know what? I don't care who can see them. We have to do something. I'm getting my bow and arrows," Danny said to as he rushed toward the house. "You take Kusanagi out."

Right. Of course. But first, I bent over and flattened the letter paper—which I was still clutching in my hand—and wrote, *NIKO! HELP!* I hastily folded the note into a slightly lopsided paper airplane and hurled it into the air, where it vanished through a little wormhole.

Danny came bounding back out of the house almost immediately, brandishing his bow and shouting, "All right, Momo! Let's gooo!" I couldn't help smiling. As frightening as this was, it felt good to be partners—and friends—again.

Ryleigh gave him an incredulous look. "What is *that*?" She waved her hand at the bow.

Jin stepped forward, his face set in a serious expression that had launched a viral meme ("Jin says SttTop") on social media.

"Bro. Get back inside with that thing. It's not safe out here."

"Oh, ya think?" Danny said, immediately defensive and sarcastic. "Listen, *bro,* I know what's going on here better than you do, and trust me, it's waaaay beyond what you could understand. So how about *you* go inside and call 911 and let me and Momo take care of things? Come on, Momo, whatever demon is behind this, we're not letting it get our friends."

Without waiting for a response, he rushed off the deck and across the yard, and I sprinted after him. As I ran, I reached into my backpack, and my hand closed around Kusanagi's hilt. At least Kusanagi was always there for me. I felt the familiar buzz of its power calling mine. *Let's go!* it seemed to say to me, echoing Danny. *Let's do this!*

Apparently Jin had the same idea, because he came right with us.

"Jin, seriously! Go back to the house!" I shouted, but he ignored me and dashed around the kid-amoeba. He planted himself in front of it with a slightly wild-eyed smile, and called, "Hey, everyone, it's Straight 2 Tha Topp's biggest hit! Sing it with me! One! Two! Three! Four!" He launched into a frenzied version of the band's breakout song, "Have Some Fun":

Hey, everyone, let's have some fun
Gonna dance and sing, gonna do our thing!

"What the heck is he doing?" Danny asked me.

I shook my head. "I have no idea."

But even with its panicky edge, Jin's voice seemed to cut

through the pale blue haze around my classmates, and a few kids blinked and focused on him. "That's right, that's right!" he continued. "Let's go all night!"

Don't care if you're the quiet type!
Hey pretty lady, come on, come on,
Come on out and dance, baby, all night long!

Jin looked just as sparkly and bright as he did in his music videos, like he was dancing in his own personal spotlight—which was odd, since the only lights I could see were the orbs encircling the party guests. He did one of those boy band "come hither" moves: right arm outstretched, left hand on his heart, head tilt, shoulder dip, Prince Charming smile. A few more kids inside the loop paused and smiled back for a moment, as if considering going thither—but then their eyes glazed over again and they turned and rejoined the amoeba.

"What? Why isn't this working?" Jin suddenly stopped smiling and started begging, "Please, everyone, listen to me! You need to turn around!"

"Jin! Back off and let us through," Danny said.

Jin turned to see me and Danny standing with our weapons drawn, and his eyes widened. Ryleigh, who had just caught up to us, looked equally shocked.

"Who—what—" Jin stammered.

Ryleigh pointed at Kusanagi, which was humming and glowing. "Is that—are you—?"

How do you explain that you're the granddaughter of Susano'o, Lord of the Seas and Master of Storms, and that he gifted you with his legendary magical sword? And that Izanami the Destroyer had a claim on you as well? I didn't exactly love that I was so closely connected to two of the most destructive powers in the kami-verse, and I didn't need any more judgment from Ryleigh. I decided to stick with the bare minimum.

"I'm half kami," I said. Ryleigh's eyes practically popped right out of her head. I didn't know what she'd thought my kami-verse connection was before, but she clearly hadn't expected this. It was kind of gratifying.

Okay, okay. It was *extremely* gratifying.

"You too?" Jin said.

"*You?*" I turned to Jin, who nodded. "Is that why you were glowing back there? When you were singing?" I wouldn't have thought it was possible, but Ryleigh's eyes got even bigger.

He nodded again. "When I sing . . . I mean, you saw what happens. But what about bow-and-arrow guy here?" he asked, looking down at Danny—Danny wasn't *short*, exactly, but he wasn't as tall as Jin, either.

"I got this from Susano'o, so you can just back all the way off," said Danny. He stepped forward and squared up to Jin, who took a step back, smiling.

"Whoa, bruh. Chill! I was just asking."

"Wait, so what's *your* deal?" I asked Ryleigh. "You never told me you could see the spirit realm."

"I'm a ninja."

"A *what?*" I shrieked. Though come to think of it, ninja were sneaky, double-crossing spies whose mission was often to seek out and exploit their enemies' greatest weaknesses. So that made sense.

"Sick!" said Danny. His eyes practically sparkled with admiration.

"So why didn't you ever—" I started to say.

"Because being a ninja means you don't go blabbing about it to everyone. Duh."

I turned away so she couldn't see the hurt on my face.

Danny was nodding slowly. "So, is your whole family, like, a ninja family, or—"

"Listen, I have a ton of questions, too, but we have more important things to think about right now," Jin interrupted. He pointed at the crowd, which was now making its way into the woods.

"Yeah, you're right," Ryleigh and I said together, which— super annoying.

Jin headed into the woods, with Danny on his heels, probably determined to prove that no pop star was braver than Danny Haragan.

"We need to be careful," I warned them. "We don't know what's down there."

But they were already committed, and now Ryleigh was right behind them. After a moment's hesitation, I hurried after Ryleigh, wishing I'd moved sooner—it would have been more demigod-like.

I lost track of her almost immediately, so I hurried to catch up to Jin and Danny. A minute later, she dropped out of nowhere, in front of all three of us, and Danny let out a squawk that he quickly turned into a cough.

"Shh! There's something waiting down there," Ryleigh

whispered. "We should stop and figure out a strategy. We need to use stealth."

As if I hadn't said basically the same thing a minute ago. Ugh.

"You've already been down there and back? How?" Jin asked incredulously.

"I'm a ninja," she said simply.

"Is that why you can walk so quiet like that?" Danny asked.

"Uh-huh. I can teach you, if you want." She flipped her ponytail and smiled at him.

"Um, *yeah*. Hey, did you hear that, Momo? Ryleigh can—"

"*Shhh!* Are you *trying* to announce our presence to the entire state, or are you just that clueless?" I snapped. "And by the way, *I'm* walking quietly, too, and I'm not a ninja. Watch." I took a few very quiet steps. "See? It's not that hard if you pay attention to where you're go— *Ahhhh!*"

My foot slipped on some loose dirt and I slid downhill on my butt, dislodging rocks, branches, and leaves as I went. I bowled right into the tail end of the slowly moving people-amoeba-bubble, which knocked a few of them off *their* feet, which caused a domino effect that sent the entire group flailing—quietly, without a yelp or a scream—down the hill, picking up more and more of those flaming bluish onibi as they went.

"Omigosh, are you okay?" Jin was helping me up, brushing leaves and dirt off my jacket.

"I'm fine," I mumbled. My body was fine, anyway. My ego was definitely in tatters.

"Hey, sorry, I missed that last thing you said." It was Danny, sounding smug. "Something about paying attention to where you were going?"

Unfortunately, it was too dark for him to see me shooting imaginary laser beams at him with my eyes.

Then, as if whatever-was-down-there had heard me, a cloud of bluish light rose up from the darkness and hovered in front of us. The blank-faced kids bobbed gently inside the cloud, still trapped in their onibi bubble, and a strangely familiar voice floated on the air.

"Why, *hello,* students. Are you here for your classmates? How very sweet."

My Head Is Exploding

"So much for stealth," grumbled Ryleigh, with a dirty look at me. I cringed inwardly and pretended not to notice.

Meanwhile, the glowing cloud formed itself into a sort of stage, and onto the stage stepped . . . Mrs. Meade?

Mrs. Meade was a demon?

"I *do* love seeing my students outside of school. Unfortunately, this isn't a very good time—unless you'd care to join your friends?" Her eyes glowed an unnatural blue, and her teeth lengthened into fangs right before our eyes.

Mrs. Meade was a demon.

I wish I could say that I bravely stepped forward and demanded that Mrs. Meade release the people she'd trapped in the bubble. But I didn't, because, well . . . it felt weird to argue with the principal, even if she *was* a demon.

"We got this," muttered Danny. "Come on, Momo, you've taken on worse. And I'm right beside you."

"Okay. Let's go." This was how we were supposed to be. Ready to fight and even die for each other.

I gripped Kusanagi's hilt and opened myself up to its buzzing energy, just a little.

"No!" I heard Ryleigh hissing behind me. "Danny, no! Stop! There's no way we can beat this thing. We need to hide!"

That was all I needed.

I felt my resentment flow up from my belly and through my arms to meet the energy of the sword, and we became one crackling, glowing being. *So you're a ninja, huh?* Kusanagi and I thought. *Sneaky, snobby, backstabbing, friend-stealing weasel is more like it. You have no idea what I can do.*

"No offense, guys, but I'm with Ryleigh. I'm sure you're powerful, but there's no way you can win."

Danny nocked an arrow and gave Jin a withering look. "Ooh, is the big singing star too scared to fight?"

"Um, yeah? And you should be, too, if you want to get out of here alive!"

"You'd think your dance moves would be enough to chase a demon away."

"Danny, stop!" I said. He knew how I felt about making fun of people for being scared. Besides, Jin was right. This *was* scary.

Still, I had to do something.

I took a step forward and raised Kusanagi in front of me. "We know you're a demon, and we're not here to join our f— Our f—" I couldn't help stumbling over the word. "Our friends." It felt strange to say that about people who I knew did not feel that way about me. I imagined Ryleigh rolling her eyes in disgust.

Okay, whatever. *Focus!* "We're not here to join them. We're here to rescue them."

"Oh, sweetie, you need to work on your listening skills. It's very nice of you to offer to engage with me, and I do wish I'd been able to collect the four of you along with the others, but as

I just told you, I don't have time to tussle. So I'm going to have to decline."

At that moment, Danny let one of his split-into-eight arrows fly. "No, you're not!" he shouted.

Mrs. Meade screamed and waved her hand, and a whole bunch of blue onibi flared out of nowhere and shielded her. With another wave of her hand, she sent a volley of fiery blue cannonballs at us. Danny shot at them, and I swung Kusanagi, which managed to deflect most of them. The rest exploded at our feet, throwing up dirt and stones in bright flashes of light.

"Fools!" she shrieked. "I waited a thousand years, trapped inside a boulder, until the Prince of Darkness released me last month. Do you have any idea how cramped it is inside a boulder? I will *not* let a few self-important little mortals get in the way of my return to power! YAAAHHHH!"

Something about what Mrs. Meade said rang a bell, but long, glowing ropes of fire unfurled from behind her shield and began hissing and snapping around us like angry snakes, and I didn't have time to think. I slashed them as they tore through the air, and they fell in ashes to the ground—but not before one of them nearly took Danny's arm off.

"Momo! You have to dig deeper!" Danny gasped. "You can't fight her at half power!"

It was tempting. But I couldn't risk a full connection with Kusanagi. I glanced at Danny, and at Jin and Ryleigh, who were crouched behind me. I didn't want to drown everyone in the ravine or crush them under a falling tree.

Meanwhile, Kusanagi trembled, reaching deep into my soul. I could feel it calling to all the angry energy I kept hidden away, and my rage monster clawed and clamored in response, begging to be let out to fight: *Lemme at that demon. Let's hurt her before she hurts us.* My whole body shook with the effort of blocking the connection.

And then I heard another voice—one I hadn't heard in weeks: *Stop fighting your power, you foolish, foolish girl.*

My blood ran cold. All around me, everything froze. It was like time had stopped—just like at the Island of Mysteries. This was why Mom hadn't wanted me to leave the house: my connection to Izanami the Destroyer, Queen of Death. She was physically trapped in Yomi, the land of the dead, but she had enough power to reach me in my dreams and thoughts.

"Go away," I whispered.

Izanami laughed softly. *Don't worry, child. I'm not here to collect you. I'm only here to help.*

"No." I barely managed to get the word out. I sounded scared and weak.

She continued as if she hadn't heard me. *Let me tell you a secret about anger. Anger is your friend. It is your ally. Anger hears the call of the weak, the frightened, and the injured, and rushes to defend them. It is your protector and the source of your power. It is your legacy.*

"No," I said again, louder this time.

You need only ask me, and I will teach you to wield it.

"I won't."

I think you will.

"I won't!" I insisted, my heart pounding. "I will never ask you for help! I will never—"

Ah-ah-ahh, Izanami sang. I knew she wasn't here, and yet

I saw her wave her hand, and suddenly my mouth was sealed shut. *I can't abide backtalk. I must admit I'm a little disappointed in your attitude. But I have faith in you, my child. Just call for me when you realize you need me, and I will come to your aid. Good luck denying your true nature!*

Ponk.

I opened my eyes to see a pebble—the one that had just hit my forehead—plunk to the ground. I hadn't realized my eyes were closed. From far away, I heard Danny's voice calling me: "Momo! MOMO!" and in front of me, Jin and Ryleigh shifted into focus, looking terrified. Behind them I could now see Danny, who had thrown the pebble. Just behind *him* was Niko, swooping down on a giant origami crane and yipping his head off.

"No, Momo!" he was yelping. "It's too dangerous! Get out! Get out now!"

The crane landed, and Niko ordered a very surprised-looking Jin and Ryleigh to get on; Danny scrambled up behind them as Niko nipped my heels, herding me toward the crane as well.

A huge *BANG BANG BOOM* made me jump, and the sky exploded with a fresh volley of glowing cannonballs and fire whips. I swung and slashed with all my might, even as I felt myself being dragged onto the back of the crane. It staggered to its feet and lurched into the air—four kids and a fox seemed to be a bit more than it was comfortable with. We'd barely gotten going when it veered to avoid a flaming blue orb—but not in time. The tip of its wing caught fire, and we crashed to the ground as choking blue smoke filled the air. I rolled off the crane's good wing and rose to my feet, coughing and holding my sword out in front of me—but the night had gone dark and winter-silent except for the burning crane; all I could hear was the sound of the flames and all of us breathing hard. There was no demon, no fire. And no other kids.

Then, through the smoke, I heard Jin's voice shouting, "Hang on, I got you!" followed by a hiss of steam.

"Nice. Now it's drowned," muttered Danny.

I blinked my eyes and squinted through the smoke. It looked like Jin had tossed the crane into a little stream, and now that no one was riding it, it had returned to its original size—which is to say, small enough to fit on your palm. It looked soggy and forlorn.

"I was trying to save its life," Jin retorted. "How was I supposed to know it was going to shrink?"

"Be quiet, you bickering bozos," Niko muttered as he herded the four of us back through the woods toward Ryleigh's house. "Just when I thought I was done with adolescent arguments."

"You're a talking fox!" Jin said, unnecessarily. But I couldn't blame him. He'd probably never met one before.

"Obviously. You may call me Niko."

"We really need to discuss what's happening here." Jin shook his head. "This is just . . ." He made an exploding noise and did that thing with his hands that's the universal sign for *My head is exploding.*

Ryleigh nodded her agreement, then glanced around us. "Did she take everyone?" she asked in a low voice. And then, "Are we safe?"

"I do not sense any imminent threat to our lives in the foreseeable future," said Niko. "Though frankly, that does not extend as far as I would like."

As we emerged from the woods onto the lawn, we could see the grown-ups still standing in slack-jawed silence exactly where we'd left them. "What happened to them? Why are they like that? My dad couldn't even see me!" Jin asked, his voice breaking.

His dad? The guy I'd thought was his bodyguard?

We walked faster and faster. I could see the worry growing in Ryleigh's, Jin's, and Danny's faces as we got closer to the grown-ups.

"They seem to have been cursed," Niko said. "Just like all the other grown-ups who witnessed their children's disappearance."

"We need to call 911. We need to get help," Ryleigh said. Her voice was sharp and urgent as she looked first into her mom's empty eyes and then her dad's.

Niko nodded. "Yes. But—"

"But if they're cursed, the police and the paramedics won't be able to help them," Danny said. He was squeezing his mom's hand. I could tell he was fighting back tears. "We have to get help from the kami."

"What about your mom?" Ryleigh spun to face me. "Didn't you say you were half kami? Is your mom a goddess? Where is she? Can she help us?" she demanded.

Izanami's cold, cruel voice suddenly rang in my head. *Wherever she is, she's not protecting you. But you can trust me, my dear.* I shivered and shook my head to clear it. Izanami couldn't harm me here, up in the land of the living. At least, I hoped so.

Shaken by Ryleigh's barrage of questions and by the thought of Izanami, I could only say in a small voice, "I don't know where she is." I turned to Niko, hoping maybe he'd been holding back some information, but he only shook his head.

Ryleigh took a deep breath in through her nose, then sighed, hard, like she should have known I'd be useless, like it was somehow *my* fault that Mom was MIA, or else that something was seriously wrong with Mom.

My heart contracted painfully, and I was suddenly furious with Ryleigh for judging Mom like that—what did she know, anyway? Or maybe I felt ashamed of Mom for being the kind of mom even kids would judge, because really, how *could* Mom have just run off like that if she thought there was a demon out to get me? Or maybe I felt scared and alone and worried that something awful was happening to Mom, even worse than being zombified. Or maybe I felt all of it, all mixed up together.

I saw Ryleigh glance back at her own mom, and I noticed that her next big breath was kind of shaky. She was scared, too. She took her phone out and started texting someone, biting her lip and blinking her eyes hard.

"What?" she snapped at me when she'd sent the text, and I realized too late that I'd been staring. But I didn't have time for a witty comeback because she immediately turned to Jin and asked, "What about *your* mom? You said you're half kami, too, right? I'm guessing your dad's a regular human, since he's over there."

Jin swallowed. "Can we *please* take a second," he said, "and, like, talk about this? I don't even know you guys. And you all seem to have a connection to the kami-verse, which is blowing my mind because I thought I was the only one. And maybe once we've got all the facts, we can figure out what to do next."

"Well said, young man," Niko said approvingly.

I was still feeling a little too starstruck to do anything but nod, but Ryleigh seemed to have recovered enough to smile brightly and say, "Great idea!"

Even Danny muttered a begrudging "Fine, whatever."

As if inspired by Jin's leadership, Ryleigh kept going. "I'll call 911 so the grown-ups can at least go to the hospital or something, and then we can go inside and talk."

"No, wait," I said. "If we're here when the emergency people arrive, we'll have to stand around and answer questions and go to the hospital. That could take forever."

"Okay, so what are we gonna do—hide?" Ryleigh demanded.

I reached into my backpack and—lo and behold, thank the kami-verse—my crane fluttered into my hand. "Sweet!" Danny exclaimed. He turned to Ryleigh. "Just trust her on this, okay? Call 911, and then we'll get out of here." It wasn't my favorite thing that Danny seemed to think that Ryleigh would listen to him and not me, but he was probably right, so I let it go.

So Ryleigh made the call, and once we were all settled on the crane's back, I whispered, "Home!" and off we flew, just as the police squad cars and ambulances pulled up in front of the giant winter wizard.

People Skills, Not Great

We sat in my kitchen while Ryleigh, who had nominated herself to be captain, began interrogating us. "We need a list of everyone's assets and liabilities," she announced. "Danny, could you write everything down?" She batted her eyelashes at him and handed him a sheet of notebook paper.

You'd think Ryleigh would have given me a *little* more respect after seeing me wield a legendary magical sword. But you'd be wrong. As we sipped our instant hot chocolate and I told her how Mom was the guardian of the Island of Mysteries, and how Susano'o was my grandfather, she only went, "Hm." To Danny, she said, "Write that down, I guess." She took a long, slow look around her and went, "Anyway," as if to say, *Your mom might be a goddess, but whatever, let's move on. Also, this place is not very nice.*

Then she said, "Liabilities?"

I didn't say anything. I figured telling her about my superhuman capacity for total destruction would pretty much kick me off the team, and besides, I really didn't feel like listing my weaknesses to someone who would probably like nothing better than to exploit them.

"Anxiety?" Danny offered.

What? Had he just . . .

He saw my expression and looked confused. "What? It's not a *bad* thing."

"You literally just said it was a liability."

"Yeah, but . . ." His forehead wrinkled. "I just meant that it gets in the way sometimes, like you get all anxious and you think you can't do stuff, but you actually can. It's not a big deal."

He wasn't wrong. I knew anxiety was nothing to be ashamed of—I needed a little extra moral support sometimes, was all. Still, I felt exposed and betrayed.

"Write it down," Ryleigh commanded him.

Danny wrote it down.

"And, oh, I know! Anger management," Ryleigh added.

Danny murmured as he wrote: "An-ger . . . man-age-ment."

"Oh, and people skills. Write 'people skills, not great.'"

"Not . . . great," said Danny. "Got it." I glared at him. He caught me glaring and smiled apologetically, like, *It's true, though, right?*

"Thanks!" Ryleigh looked around, smiling. "Okay, who's next?"

We went through Danny (*Assets: great athlete, great attitude, great interpersonal skills, magic bow and arrows; Liabilities: impulsive*—I wanted to add *is a traitor,* but I didn't have the nerve) and Niko (*Assets: limited telekinetic powers, shape-shifting powers, knowledge of kami-verse; Liabilities: tends to be pessimistic*). Danny gave me a long look, and I knew he was thinking about how Niko had accidentally let the demons onto the Island of Mysteries, and how he'd deliberately put me in danger so he could save me and earn his magic back. But I didn't say anything. That was between Niko and us.

Then we did Ryleigh herself (*Assets: can perceive spirit realm; master tactician, spycraft skills, leadership skills, expert in martial arts, excellent acrobat, can hold breath for five minutes; Liabilities: none*—though I would happily have added *sneaky* and *mean*). I wished I had the nerve to ask her why, if she was an expert fighter, she hadn't helped us fight the onibi. Though it wasn't like you could karate-chop an onibi.

It turned out that one of Ryleigh's ancestors on her mom's side was Mochizuki Chiyome, a female ninja who led a band of women ninja hundreds of years ago. Danny found this fascinating, and asked her question after question, like, "Can you walk on water?" and "Can you vanish into thin air?" which Ryleigh, back on her flirting game, answered with a lot of completely unnecessary eyelash fluttering and ponytail flipping ("No, don't be ridiculous!" *flips ponytail*; "Wouldn't *you* like to know!" *flutters eyelashes*).

I could have told him that advanced ninja draw energy from nature to do stuff like cause fires or create pockets of air underwater. But first they have to perfect their combat skills and learn human spycraft. Very few ninja have access to the spirit realm; I bet Ryleigh thought she was pretty special because of it.

I had questions, too, though I wasn't brave enough to ask them: *Why have you always made fun of me for seeing the spirit realm? Why have you pretended you can't see it? Why do you go out of your way to make me feel like a loser?* Instead, I asked Jin who his kami-parent was.

"Benzaiten."

Benzaiten, the goddess of water, music, and poetry? No wonder he was a pop star.

"Can she help us?" asked Ryleigh, finally back on task.

Jin looked away, then shook his head. "I'm not really in touch with her."

"Have you ever met her?" I asked.

He shook his head again.

"Then how do you know she's your mom?" Danny demanded.

"My dad told me. I guess they were a thing for a little while, and then she took off. But you know, whatever. It's fine. I don't care."

It looked like he cared a lot, actually. But it felt awkward to say anything, and Jin obviously didn't want to talk about it.

Danny didn't seem to notice. "How do you know your dad wasn't lying?" he said. "How do we know *you're* not lying?"

"Why are you acting like such a jerk? We just saw what Jin can do with his voice!" I snapped.

"Okay, okay, I'm sorry," Danny grumbled. "I was just curious, that's all."

"Nah, I get it. You don't know me—why should you trust me?" Jin said. "Anyway, my voice is probably an asset."

Danny muttered, "Sings . . . and . . . dances," as he wrote. "Nothing else?" he said, looking up. "No weapons or anything?"

Jin shook his head. "I've never needed them."

Danny bent his head to write again. "Lia . . . bil-i-ties. No . . . weapons."

42

"His voice is powerful enough!" I said. "I don't see *you* in-fluencing thousands of people with *your* voice."

Danny shrugged. Then he grinned and said, "But I can do this." He took a big breath, opened his mouth, and belched the alphabet.

Ryleigh made a face and smacked his arm. "Eww, Danny! You're so gross." I hated agreeing with Ryleigh, but . . . yeah. Gross.

Danny stood up and took a bow. "Thank you."

Jin looked at me and asked, "Is he always this way?"

"Pretty much," I said. Danny responded with another belch, so I knew he was mad. Well, too bad. He was being a jerk and he deserved to be called out.

Ryleigh's phone rang. "It's my brother," she announced. "I'm just gonna . . ." She pointed toward the living room and left.

Without Ryleigh to order us around, we sat in silence for a minute, which made it easy to overhear her conversation with her brother. "I *tried*," she was saying. "I—I didn't have the right weapons, that's all."

Even from the kitchen, I could tell she was lying.

"No, you don't understand, Tommy. You weren't there!" she continued. "No, I'm *not* trying to make you feel bad, I—No, I'm with some other kids right now. Because! Just . . ." She hesitated before saying in a small voice, "Can you please come home?"

Danny, Niko, Jin, and I looked at each other across the table. I felt guilty, like I'd just heard something I wasn't supposed to hear. Which I guess I had. To cover up my discomfort—and the

43

rest of Ryleigh's phone conversation—I said a little too loudly, "Isn't Benzaiten one of the Seven Lucky Gods? What if we contact them? Do you think they'd help us?"

"Not likely," said Niko. "They're especially busy this time of year."

"But what if we tell them Benzaiten's son is part of our group now? She'd help us if she knew, I bet. I bet Ebisu'll help, too," I insisted.

I watched Jin's face carefully. His expression was neutral, but I could tell he was holding his breath.

But Niko only shrugged. Jin's face didn't change, but he seemed to shrink into himself.

Danny looked discouraged, too, but only for a moment. "We could still try, right?" he said. "Do you have any airmail?"

I got out a pad of magic letter paper. Danny wrote to Ebisu, his spirit dad and the kami of luck, and Hotei, the kami of contentment. I wrote to Bishamon, the kami of warriors and war, and Daikoku, the kami of farmers, merchants, and time. I showed Jin how the letters worked and had him write to Benzaiten. We didn't have connections to the other two gods, but I figured five out of seven was pretty good odds.

I also sent another note to Mom. I wished I had time and space to write everything I was thinking: *Did you know that Benzaiten has a son who's just a little older than me? Are there other kami with human children? Did you know about this? Why didn't you tell me? Were you ever going to tell me?* But we didn't have much space or time, so instead I said what was most important: *Mom, where are you? I need you!*

We launched our paper airplanes into their wormholes just

44

as Ryleigh came back, looking suspiciously puffy around the eyes. Danny immediately got up and gave her a hug and said, "Wanna talk about it?" and the two of them retreated to the living room. How rude. And when did Danny become Ryleigh's shoulder to cry on?

Still, Ryleigh was obviously upset, and I felt my heart squeeze a little in spite of myself. I got up and started pacing around the kitchen table to work off all the uncomfortable feelings I was having. Meanwhile, Niko began grooming himself, and Jin hummed quietly to himself and scribbled something in a little notebook. I wondered what he was writing: Song lyrics? Homework? Personal thoughts? I wished I had the nerve to ask. I bet Ryleigh would. Ugh. I hated Ryleigh.

At that moment, a paper airplane sailed out of nowhere and landed gently on the table. I grabbed it, unfolded it, and read:

We cannot help you at the moment.
Please do not try to fight the demon;
you are not properly equipped or trained.
If anything changes, we will let you know.

—DAIKOKU

Her Nickname
Should Be Roll-Eye

"That's it?" I thought I might levitate with outrage and panic. I looked at Danny, who'd come back with Ryleigh when he heard me shout. "We're facing a full-on emergency with a demon holding kids hostage, and her response is *Sorry we can't help you, sit tight until further notice?*"

"Gimme that." Danny snatched the paper from my hand to read it for himself. I watched his eyebrows go up and then furrow as he scanned the note. "What the—" He shook the paper at me. "What is she thinking?"

"I know!"

"Can I see?" Jin held out his hand, and I took the paper from Danny and passed it to him. He looked at it and bit his lip. "Maybe we better do what she says. She is a kami, after all."

"Are you sure that's it? There has to be more. Maybe it's a code—does it look like it's in code? Here, give it to me."

It was Ryleigh, fully recovered and back in her new role as Ninja Boss Girl. She took the paper from Jin and turned it over a couple of times, examining each word and mumbling to herself. She folded it like a little fan, then unfolded it and curled it into a tube. She held it up to the light and squinted at it. Finally, she brought it over to the stove and turned on the gas.

"Hey! Give that back!" I shouted, rushing toward her.

"Omigosh, I'm just holding it over the heat to see if there's invisible ink or something. Stop freaking out, okay? Jeez." She rolled her eyes and gave Danny a smirk that said, *Wow, what is wrong with her?*

"Ryleigh." Why was my voice shaking? *You are the daughter of Takiri-bime and the granddaughter of Susano'o, Lord of the Seas and Master of Storms!* my rage monster fumed. *Get it together!* But I couldn't. Ryleigh's eye roll and smirk had drained all my self-confidence and left me nervous and unsure of myself. "The, um, the kami are magic. If they, um, I mean, if they wanted to give us a secret message, they'd put a spell on it so that only we could read it." Ugh! No wonder she didn't take me seriously.

"Okay, whatever." Ryleigh looked like she was about to roll her eyes again, but she stared at something behind me instead. I turned to see another paper airplane land on the table.

Danny got to it first this time, and unfolded it. *"PS Benzaiten sends her regards to Jin."* He looked up at Jin, who gave a stiff smile.

"Maybe that's just Daikoku's answer. None of the others have written back yet," Danny said hopefully. "Like, what about Hotei? I bet he'll want to help. And Ebisu's my spirit dad. I'm sure he'll write back."

"I wouldn't wait on him," said Niko. "He's the most unreliable kami of them all."

A third plane materialized, and Danny snatched it out of the air before it could even land, nearly tearing it in his haste to unfold it. But when his gaze fell on the message, his shoulders sagged. He didn't even bother to read it out loud—just tossed it on the table. I picked it up.

"You will not receive another message. Go home, stay safe, and wait." It was signed, D.

"But . . . but that's . . . they can't just *leave* us here!" Ryleigh protested. She probably wasn't used to people ignoring her.

"They can and they have," said Niko gloomily.

"How hard would it have been to write *Hi, son, how are you?* I didn't even get any crappy regards," Danny said.

Jin flinched, but I knew Danny hadn't meant to insult him. Danny cherished his relationship with Ebisu, and he must have felt really disappointed that his spirit dad hadn't bothered to write even one line.

The last time we'd had an emergency like this, we'd been left on our own because of Kami-Con, the annual conference that all the kami were required to attend. But now? I didn't see why a single kami couldn't take five minutes out of their day to help us vanquish a demon who was clearly getting ready to do a lot of damage.

No one said anything for a while. Then Danny said, "They said they wouldn't communicate with us. But what if we went to them?"

Niko's ears and nose twitched and his eyes narrowed. "Danny," he said in a warning voice.

"What if we went to the Sea of Heaven? What if we boarded the *Takarabune*?" Danny looked at me, his eyes sparkling with renewed hope. "They wouldn't let us hang out there all by ourselves, right? Someone would have to come."

"No. I won't allow it," Niko said.

"The Sea of Heaven? You can go there?" Jin looked at us, his own eyes shining.

"Well. Some of us can." I glanced at Ryleigh—I didn't mean it as an insult, but she was human, after all. Could she make it through?

"Seriously?" Ryleigh stared at me like she couldn't believe a little loser like *me* had the nerve to imply that *she* might not be able to do something. "Not only can I see everything you can see, but I'm a trained ninja and I'm going to figure out how to fight that demon, and you and your little attitude are not going to stop me. And I have these." She shook the little black designer bag that she carried everywhere with her. I could only blink. What did she have in there? All I could think of was the gold gel pens she always used to write her name on all her schoolwork. "Shuriken," she said. "I'm deadly with them."

Attitude? Shuriken? I could only blink and hope she didn't decide to prove her point by hurling her collection of ninja throwing stars at me.

"Yeah, Momo, that's kinda mean," said Danny quietly. "Probably anyone with a connection to the spirit realm can get through the portals." Darn it. It felt unfair for Danny to stand there and accuse me of being mean to Ryleigh when she was *always* mean to me, but here we were. And he was right—he'd made it to the Sea of Heaven, hadn't he?

I took a deep breath and said, "Danny's-right-I'm-sure-that-anyone-who-can-connect-to-the-spirit-realm-can-travel-

through-a-spirit-portal-That-was-mean-of-me-to-say-you-
might-not-be-able-to-and-I'm-sorry."

"Whatever." Ryleigh rolled her eyes. *She rolls her eyes so
much, her nickname should be Roll-eye,* I thought. So much for
being the bigger person.

Niko barked to get our attention. "You harebrained hiccup-
heads have all *missed the point.* You are *not.* Going. To the *Takarabune!*"

"Well, I, for one, do not want to sit around doing nothing
while my friends and family are being held hostage," Ryleigh
said. As if she hadn't heard what he'd just said, she turned to
Niko and declared, "I say you take us to the Sea of Heaven so we
can meet the Seven Lucky Gods and get them to help us."

Niko's eyebrows went up. "And you may not order me
around like some kind of pet."

Ryleigh opened her mouth but then shut it and said nothing.

As much as I enjoyed seeing Niko put Ryleigh in her place,
I had to admit that I agreed with her. We couldn't just sit and
wait for help that might or might not come. "Please, Niko?" I
wheedled. "We promise we'll be good. We'll bow and be re-
spectful and everything. What if that demon ends up killing all
those kids? How would we feel, knowing that we hadn't done
everything we possibly could to save them?"

"Have you all eaten each other's ears off? I said no!" But his
voice lacked conviction now. I think he knew he was fighting a
losing battle.

Then Jin and Danny joined in, and when Niko continued to
refuse, I said, "Fine. Danny and I still know how to get there, so
if you won't take us, we'll take ourselves." I got a chair from the

50

kitchen, went to the hall closet, and took down the box of magic origami from the top shelf.

"Here," I said, and handed everyone a piece. "All we have to do is—"

"Oh, all right, all right, you win!" Niko burst out. "I will accompany you to the *Takarabune,* you miserable monsters!"

"Thank you, Niko," I said, and put my arms around him.

"You're not welcome," he grumbled. "I am only going in order to keep you safe, and so your mother won't be angry with me when she returns. Hopefully she'll be angry with *you* for your disrespectful disobedience."

If that meant we all returned safely, I was okay with it. But I couldn't worry about her or us right now.

"I told you, we'll be so good," I said.

"Hmph. In that case, put three of those back. We don't have an unlimited supply, you know," Niko said.

I put away the extra origami while everyone else got their bags and jackets. Danny offered to share his crane with Ryleigh, evidently so the two of them could have a private conversation about her brother. Whatever. *I* got to ride with Jin Takayama, international pop star. So there.

There was a squeaky little whistle behind us as we launched into the air, but none of us paid attention to it. I thought it was a bat, myself. If any of us *had* bothered to look, we would have seen a little blue orb spiraling into the sky. And maybe we would have been better prepared for what happened next.

What Would a *Real* Friend Say?

We had just cleared the Presidio at the north end of the city and were closing in on the Golden Gate Bridge when the first attack came. I heard Danny and Ryleigh yell as their crane banked hard to the right to avoid the shining projectile. At first, I had the ridiculous thought that a star had fallen out of the sky. My next thought was that they had accidentally hit a drone. But then another one narrowly missed hitting me, Jin, and Niko, and a third barely missed Danny and Ryleigh again. We were being attacked by onibi.

"I knew it!" wailed Niko, cowering between me and Jin. "I *knew* we were heading into trouble!" He lifted his head up long enough to bark, "Take evasive maneuvers immediately! Head for the portal! Everyone hang on!"

Even as he shouted the words, three more onibi popped into view and streamed toward us. The cranes wheeled and dipped and zigged and zagged. Ours even did a couple of barrel rolls, and I found myself hanging underneath it for a second before it turned right side up and its back was solidly underneath me again. I didn't dare take Kusanagi out of my backpack; it was all I could do just to clutch the crane's silver feathers so I wouldn't plummet to my death. As we flew, more onibi whizzed and crackled past us and exploded above, below, and once just inches from my face. They sizzled and buzzed on the bridge's suspension cables, which must have looked to the people below like the cables were being struck by lightning and electrified.

Luckily, the fog wasn't too thick, so our cranes only had to deal with the onibi—which was plenty. As the first tower of the bridge loomed ahead of us, an onibi struck our crane's beak, and my nose was filled with the odor of sulfur and smoke. At the same time, Danny's voice came from just behind us. "We've been hit! We've been hit!"

I looked over my shoulder. Danny's and Ryleigh's faces were white with fear, and the tail of their crane was smoking.

"Just a little farther!" Niko urged our crane. To us, he shouted, "We're going to have to jump through!"

Jin and I looked at each other—Jin in confusion and me in horror.

"What does he mean?" Jin asked.

Niko explained: "I'll open the portal as we get close to it. As we pass, we'll all jump through."

"Niko, we'll never make it!"

"You should have thought of that before you insisted we embark on this expedition!" Niko shouted as the crane spiraled upward. He gave it a couple of firm pats and said, "Almost there! Climb! Climb!"

"Can't we just fly through?"

"Too risky! The onibi are following the cranes. If the cranes fly through the portal, the onibi could come with us. It's safer to jump!"

"Jumping off the back of a flying crane is the *safe* option?" Jin said.

"What about Danny and Ryleigh?" I asked, glancing over my shoulder.

"They'll figure it out. That Ryleigh's a smart girl, and brave, to boot." I didn't even feel jealous. I just hoped he was right.

Dodging one last volley of onibi, we sped toward the portal. Niko stretched out a paw and murmured a few unintelligible words, and a rectangle of light appeared next to the top of the first bridge tower.

"Whoa," I heard Jin say next to me.

"The crane will fly under the portal. We will jump through on the count of three," said Niko. "One!"

I got into a wobbly crouch.

"Two!" I grabbed Niko's tail in one hand and Jin's hand in the other.

"Three!"

I squeezed my eyes shut and jumped. I had just enough time for one thought to cross my mind as I flew through the portal to the Sea of Heaven: *Danny can't swim.*

The impact of hitting the water broke my grip on Jin and Niko. I kicked hard to the surface and saw each of them bob up next to me. The little wooden rowboat I remembered from last time floated a few feet away.

"Swim!" Niko panted.

I hadn't taken two strokes when Ryleigh and Danny splashed down right in front of me.

Ryleigh popped up almost immediately. "Where is he?" she demanded.

"I—" I looked at the spot where Danny had gone under, and when I looked back at Ryleigh, she was gone.

"Danny! Ryleigh!" I shouted frantically—and pointlessly, really, because how could they hear me if they were underwater? Where had they gone? What should I do? What if—

The water boiled and bubbled around me, and something pushed me toward the boat. A moment later, Jin was pulling me over the side, and then I was sitting next to him, dripping and spluttering.

"Danny!" I gasped. "He can't swim! He disappeared! We have to rescue him!"

"I'm right here."

I spun around. Sure enough, there he was—and Ryleigh, too—sitting right behind me, dripping wet and looking a little dazed.

I tried to hug him, but as I stood up, the boat rocked and I staggered and fell and ended up hugging Ryleigh's knees instead.

I pushed myself off her, too embarrassed to complete my hug attempt. "What—how—"

"One of the dragons kinda scooped us up," said Danny. "I guess they knew I don't really swim."

Ah, of course. I smiled. I loved those dragons.

"I'm just glad Danny's okay," Ryleigh said, and gave him a squeeze and a faceful of fluttering eyelashes.

My rage monster twitched. *Stop flirting with my friend!* But urghhhh, Ryleigh was right. The important thing was that Danny was okay. So I smooshed my twitchy anger down.

"Yeah, I never would have been able to make that jump if it hadn't been for Ry," said Danny.

Ry? They were doing *nicknames* now? And what—like I *wouldn't* have helped him make that jump?

"You okay, Momo?" Danny asked.

"I'm fine." I forced a smile. "I'm uh, just glad you're okay."

Niko jumped right in with a rant. "We are *all* lucky to be okay. I told you this was a terrible idea, but did you listen to the wise words of a well-meaning mentor? No! 'We *must* go to the *Takarabune!*' you said. 'We'll do it without you!' you said. And so, being the kind, conscientious, caring custodian that I am, I agreed to come with you, and then what happened? A dance with death. If I hadn't promised your mother I'd look after you, Momo, I'd let you try your luck alone after this!"

Oof. I couldn't blame Niko for being mad at us for bullying him into letting us risk our lives—he was just worried about us. And maybe, like me, he was worried about Mom. But there was nothing I could do about that. All I could do was keep going on the path we'd chosen.

"We all knew we were taking a risk," Ryleigh pointed out.

"Yeah," Danny agreed. "And we're all okay! So let's just be glad we're all okay and move on."

Ryleigh flipped her ponytail and gave Danny a hug, and I had to work *very* hard to just be glad we were all okay.

The first time I saw the Sea of Heaven, it had been close to sunset, and the water had been pinkish orange under a lavender sky. Today, it was a deep, dark blue with golden specks, and the sky was pale green. Now that we were all safely on the boat and on our way, it was fun to see Jin's and Ryleigh's eyes grow big and round as they took it all in: the colors, the endless expanse of water. Jin pulled out his notebook ("It's dry!" he exclaimed). "Leap of faith . . . all okay . . . green sky . . . float away," he whispered to himself as his pen moved across the page.

"What are you writing?" Danny asked.

Jin looked like he'd been caught doing something he shouldn't. "Nothing," he said. "Just some thoughts." He snapped his notebook shut and changed the subject. "I can't believe I'm going to the *Takarabune*! It's gonna be so cool. I hope my mom will show up. My dad and I used to visit her shrine once every couple of years, but . . ." He trailed off and looked wistfully at the horizon.

I glanced at Danny, who had a look on his face like he understood how Jin felt and was trying to make up his mind about whether to say something. I knew Danny wondered about his birth parents sometimes: who they were, what they were doing now, and why they'd arranged for him to be adopted. But then he seemed to change his mind and kept his mouth clamped firmly shut. I wished he didn't feel like he had to be all tough in front of other people.

"Does anyone else know that Benzaiten's your mom?" I asked.

"Are you kidding me? No way! It's tough enough to manage the press and the fan base already. Can you imagine how it would be if they knew my mom was a goddess? It'd be out of control!"

"Oh, yeah, a hundred percent." I nodded like I *totally* understood, like if I told people about Mom, my millions of adoring fans would also go completely bananas.

"I mean, that's if they didn't all think I was having some

kind of mental breakdown. It would be all over the internet. It'd probably affect sales and I'd probably have to go on hiatus or something." He sighed. "It's weird. Knowing that there's this thing about you and not being able to tell anyone. It's nice to finally meet someone who really gets it."

Jin was smiling down at me and I couldn't tell if he was doing his celestial glitter thing on purpose or if it was happening naturally, or if I was turning into a Jin fangirl. I would *not* become a fangirl! Jin needed real friends who understood him, and who wouldn't go all gaga over him just because he was famous (and handsome and talented) and had a goddess for a mom. *I* would be the real friend he needed, because I "really got it."

What would a real friend say?

"Uh. Yeah, same. Totes same." Argghhh!

"I know exactly what you mean, too," Ryleigh said, because apparently she couldn't live in a world where she wasn't part of the conversation. "I can't tell anybody about being a ninja."

In a world where I didn't lose my nerve around Ryleigh every time I had to talk to her, I would have said, "You could have told *me,* you hypocrite." But that wasn't the world we were in.

It wasn't long before the mast of the *Takarabune* appeared on the horizon, followed bit by bit by the rest of the ship. As if motivated by the prospect of being home again, the dragons began dipping and whirling faster through the water, which churned in gold, white, and pale blue flecks around us as we sped forward. By the time we were close enough to read the giant character on its sail (福, which means "luck") we were going so fast, my eyes teared up. At some point, I realized that the *swish-splish* of the water against the wooden sides of the boat had stopped; when I looked over the gunwale, I knew why.

"We're flying!" Danny shouted. "Woo-hoooo!" He raised his hands like we were on a roller coaster. Ryleigh's and Jin's hands immediately went up, too. With the warm wind on my face and my hair streaming behind me, it was impossible not to catch everyone's enthusiasm. Even Niko was on his feet, with his forepaws on the little platform at the bow and his fur rippling in the wind. I kept one hand on the side of the boat (you couldn't be too careful) and raised the other one, and we all whooped and yipped and hollered our way through the air toward the ship.

The closer we got, the faster we seemed to go, which didn't feel right to me. "Are we going faster?" I shouted above the sound of the air rushing around us. "Niko, is this normal?"

"How should I know? I'm not an authority on aerodynamics." But I noticed that he'd taken his paws off the platform at the front of the boat.

Soon we were all screaming at the dragons to PLEASE SLOW DOWN! but they either didn't hear or didn't care, because our little boat kept zooming toward the ship like a guided missile. Finally, at the last possible second, the dragons put the brakes on and I caught a brief flash of the water churning and whirlpooling underneath us before we were dumped unceremoniously onto the deck of the *Takarabune*.

I Don't Have Time for This Nonsense

"Ooofff." Jin groaned, and I'm pretty sure he spoke for all of us as we struggled to our knees, rubbing our elbows, ribs, shoulders . . . pretty much everything hurt.

"There was no need for that, you miserable monsters!" Niko called over the railing.

In response, both dragons streaked up out of the water and splashed back down, sending a huge spray over the deck and soaking all of us. "Grbhbhbh!" Niko shook himself. "They think they're so funny."

I looked around, half expecting Daikoku or Bishamon to appear and scold us for making a mess. But the ship remained silent and the deck remained empty.

"Why would they leave it unattended?" I wondered out loud.

"And what do we do now?" Jin asked.

But Ryleigh was already peering through the windows of the cabin in the middle of the ship, where Ebisu had taken us when he'd escorted us home after our last adventure. "I don't see anyone in here. Or any*thing,* for that matter." We joined her and put our faces to the glass. There was nothing but swirling darkness, with scattered pinpricks of light that pulsed and glimmered briefly before going out: the Aum.

"Yeah, let's maybe not try in there," said Danny. "I wouldn't want to get lost."

We walked around behind the cabin, but the deck in back was as silent and empty as the front.

"Do you have any message paper with you?" I asked Niko.

"We don't need paper! This ship has its own communication console!" Niko was already all the way at the stern. Behind the tiller stood a simple wooden torii—a sacred gateway made of two posts connected at the top by two crossbeams. Just on the other side of the torii were a little stone basin of water and a bamboo ladle; beyond the basin on its own little deck was a tiny shrine with a tiled roof that flared out on all four sides.

Inside the shrine stood seven statues on a wooden platform. I recognized Bishamon, the warrior god, scowling in his camouflage fatigues, with a spear in his hand and a very unhappy demon under his foot. Daikoku looked businesslike in her pinstriped suit and fedora. Her watch and tiny mallet dangled from a chain on her vest. Hotei, wearing his bathrobe and flip-flops, leaned on his bottomless bag of goodies, while Ebisu held out his fishing pole and smiled under his bucket hat as he waited for that lucky catch. Of the remaining three, I figured the kami with the flowy jacket, boots, and guitar must be Jin's mom, Benzaiten, the goddess of music and poetry. The other two were jolly-looking old men.

"Um, no offense, Niko, but I don't see a communications console," said Ryleigh.

Niko sighed and pointed to the roof that overhung the front of the shrine. A golden jingle bell the size of a bowling ball dangled from the eaves, with a long silken rope attached to it that hung nearly to the deck. A little card was pinned to the rope, and on it someone had scrawled:

Ring bell for service ☺ —H

Beneath that was another card, in crisp, neat lettering:

We do not guarantee a response —D

And beneath that was a third card:

Definitely worth a shot, though! —H

We passed under the torii one by one. After using the ladle to wash our hands with the water from the basin ("to purify yourselves," explained Niko), we lined up in front of the shrine while Niko gripped the rope between his teeth and gave it a good shake. The bell clanked cheerily.

"Now bow twice, deeply and with respect."

We followed his instructions.

"Now clap two times. All together, slowly and loudly so they hear you! Ready, get set, go!" Obediently, we gave two loud claps.

"O mighty gods of luck, we beg you to bless us with your august presence," Niko called out. "We know you told us to wait, but certain disobedient children refused to listen to my goodhearted guidance, so please do not blame me for bothering you."

He bowed once more, and we did the same.

"Do you think that was enough?" Danny wondered aloud

as we walked back toward the bow of the ship. "I wish we could just text them or something." But almost as if she'd been waiting for exactly the right moment to prove that the clapping and bowing and bell-ringing *had* worked, Daikoku emerged from the cabin as we walked around the corner. Thank goodness. I could have cried with relief.

"Daikoku!" I shouted. "You heard us!"

Niko fell into a bow and motioned frantically to us to follow suit while he babbled, "Your Worshipful Wondrousness, Your Gracious Greatness, Your Eminent Elegance—"

"Enough." Daikoku interrupted him briskly. "Stand up straight, now. I don't have time for this nonsense. None of us do."

Niko launched into a long, loud apology, which Daikoku also shut down immediately.

"Listen, all of you. I want to make it clear right off the bat that you shouldn't have called. In case you haven't noticed, despite your defeat of Shuten-dōji and his army, the world is a bit of a mess right now, and the people of the Middle Lands need all the good fortune and joy they can get. Oh. Speaking of which . . ." Daikoku reached into her jacket pocket and produced an impossibly large gift bag, which she handed to me. "Hotei sends his greetings." Inside the bag were a four-pack of Twix bars (Danny's favorite), a box of Auntie Anne's cinnamon sugar pretzel nuggets (my favorite), a bag of sour gummy worms ("Oooh, I love those!" said Jin), and a bag of Takis ("Those have *got* to be for me," Ryleigh said, reaching out her hand). The last thing I found was a giant pepperoni pizza, which made Niko drool appreciatively.

My first bite of those warm, buttery pretzel nuggets was

heaven. I felt better already. "Okay, so what about you? Can you help us?" I asked.

Daikoku's face grew impatient. "I told you. This is a dark time, and we're stretched far too thin as it is. I've been scrambling to rescue every moneymaking enterprise from family food trucks to entire national economies. Bishamon has been pulled into wars and uprisings across the globe. Benzaiten is working herself to the bone trying to inspire musicians and writers to help the world experience a little bit of joy and beauty. Dealing with your problem will take time and energy that we can't spare right now."

For the first time since she'd stridden out of the cabin, I noticed the dark circles under Daikoku's eyes. But my worry and frustration poured out anyway. "But how can you ignore us? People could *die*! Mrs. Meade—or whoever she is—is probably about to commit mass murder! Don't you care at all?"

"We do care. But people are dying everywhere, as we speak. Children are dying. Do the children who've been abducted by your demon deserve to live more than any other children?"

"But—but Jin is Benzaiten's son!"

"Jin is not in immediate danger," Daikoku said.

"His dad is."

Daikoku sighed. "This is not going to be easy to hear, but you need to understand one thing: Benzaiten has more important things to worry about than the health of the father of her child."

Jin looked like she'd slapped him.

"I'm sorry." Daikoku did look genuinely sorry, but it couldn't have made up for the fact that Jin's mom had chosen not to even come and see him when he'd personally asked for her help. It was that whole kami thing, I guessed—live for thousands of years and it's hard to get too attached to any one human being. It made me realize just how special Mom and Dad's relationship had been. I remembered the way Dad had made me feel like the most important person in the world. Maybe that was how Mom had felt with him. Was that why she wasn't here to help me? Because I didn't make her feel that way? Had she forgotten about protecting me from Izanami after all?

The very thought of Izanami sent a chill down my spine, and without warning, a memory washed over me: the suffocating darkness of the cave where we'd met, her skeletal face and burning eyes, and the way her icy fingers had trailed across my cheek when she told me I was bound to her. I remembered how Mom had protected me with her life to prevent that from happening, how worried she'd been for the last few weeks since I'd returned. What could have happened to make her leave me now?

"Hey!" Ryleigh's sharp voice brought me back to the ship. "Are you okay?"

"Huh?"

"I said, are you okay? Because you're all like . . ." Ryleigh made a zombie noise: *"Uunhhhhh, unhhhh."*

I realized that everyone, even Daikoku, was staring at me. Had I really been groaning like that? And was Ryleigh worried, or was she mocking me? "I'm fine," I said, my cheeks burning.

"Are you, though?" She raised a skeptical eyebrow. "Because you don't seem fine." She turned to Danny. "Does she seem fine to you?"

Danny looked at me with concern, but the last thing I wanted to do was add another liability (*has disorienting flashbacks about Izanami the Destroyer*) to Ryleigh's long list, so I snapped, "I said I'm fine, okay? Leave me alone!"

And I didn't even get to have the last word, because Ryleigh did one of those raised-eyebrow faces and went, "Okay, *anyway* . . . ," in that snarky mean-girl way that meant, *Wow, you're weird.*

I could feel my rage monster getting ready to stomp her, so I asked Daikoku, "Isn't there anything you can do? Or anyone else we can ask?" to prove to Ryleigh and everyone else that I was *just fine*.

"As a matter of fact, that is what I am here to tell you. I've just received an offer of help from someone in your family," Daikoku said.

"But my mom is missing!"

"Indeed." Daikoku fixed me with a hard stare. "Rather unreliable, isn't she? An unfortunate family trait."

That made me so angry I couldn't even speak. How could she say something so rude? Couldn't she see how worried I was about Mom?

"Hey! You can't talk about Momo's mom that way. Or Momo. They're both totally reliable," Danny said hotly. "Susano'o's the one you can't trust!" I was so glad and grateful that he'd stuck up for me, I almost cried.

"Indeed," Daikoku said again. "Families are such strange things, aren't they? You'd think you would get along with the people closest to you, but sometimes it doesn't work out that way. I survived eighty brothers who tried to gang up on me and kill me. Twice." Daikoku rolled her eyes. "Sibling rivalry is the worst."

Now it was Ryleigh who, oddly, looked like she wanted to cry.

"Don't fret, child," Daikoku said to her. "I have faith that you and *your* sibling will live to become good friends. Your entire family, in fact." Ryleigh's face softened into an anxious smile. I thought of her phone conversation with Tommy, how strained it had been. Was Ryleigh worried that her own brother didn't want to be friends with her? And what was that about her family?

"Er, I hope I am not being rude or rushing you, but you mentioned something about a family member?" Niko reminded Daikoku. I wondered who it was. I hoped it wasn't Susano'o— I did not trust my grandfather any farther than I could throw him, which was exactly zero of every unit of measurement ever invented. Plus I hated being reminded of how alike we were inside. But he was the only family member I knew of besides Mom.

"Yes. Thank you for keeping us on track, Niko. Time, both linear and layered, is passing quickly, and you must act quickly as well." She clapped her hands and the rowboat rose out of the water and hovered next to the ship's railing. "In you go."

"Now?" I'd been impatient for someone to help us, but this felt so abrupt. It made me nervous.

"I told you. I don't have time to waste, and neither do you. Get in," Daikoku said.

"Where is it taking us?" Danny asked as he climbed up on the railing and into the boat. "Are we going to see Momo's relative?"

"Yes."

67

"Who is it?" I asked. I really hoped she would say it was an auntie or a second cousin or something.

"You'll find out soon enough."

Great.

The rowboat sank toward the water, and as the dragons pulled us away from the *Takarabune,* they began to sing . . . not words, exactly, but images. A full moon in an ink-black sky, the light dancing on ocean waves. A magnificent storm, with rain lashing down on whitecaps that crashed over themselves, and lightning streaking down from dark, heavy clouds. Then, as the storm wore itself out, the moon again, fading as the sun rose over the horizon and turned the ocean gold and orange.

The dragons glided around us in a circle, faster and faster, until we were spiraling inside an enormous whirlpool. "They're sending us through a portal," I told Jin and Ryleigh, happy to offer comfort to Jin and to show off to Ryleigh, who (sorry, not sorry) I was glad to see looking pale and nervous. Walls of water rose around us and we spun down, down, down, until we shot through a tunnel. The music kept cycling through the moonlit sea, the storm, and the sunrise, while underneath, a vague thread of a melody about families and siblings simmered and swirled. Every color I'd ever seen—and some I hadn't—sparked and popped beneath my closed eyelids. My atoms drifted apart from each other, condensed into a point so small I felt like I might blink right out, and then expanded once again.

Ah, that was better.

And *cold.*

This Is Going to Be So Much Fun

"Brrr, I'm *freezing!* Where *are* we? The North Pole?" Danny asked.

A quick look around confirmed that we were *not* at the North Pole, but on a huge platform dominated by a giant building with antennas the size of rocket ships. An icy wind cut through my hoodie as I rushed toward the building, which unfortunately didn't appear to have any doors in it.

"I think we're on the roof of the Willis Tower," Jin said through chattering teeth. He pulled his hoodie tight around him and walked carefully out to the edge of the platform. "Yeah, this is definitely it! It's where we shot 'Love You High as the Sky!'"

"Ooh, I love that video!" Ryleigh began humming the tune, and Jin nodded, smiling.

"That's the one!" He started humming the harmony and waved us over. "You guys should come take a look. The view is amazing!"

"Ooh, I'm a big rock star. I did a music video here!" Danny muttered to me. He wrinkled his nose and stuck out his tongue. Whatever. He was just afraid of heights. And probably jealous of Jin. I joined the others on the edge—though when I thought about how high up we were, and how the giant building and the antennas behind me were just the very teeny-tiny tippy-top of the skyscraper under my feet, I almost turned around and went back to Danny, who hadn't budged.

I was glad I didn't when I saw the view—a grid of orange streetlights extending all the way to the horizon. "That's the west side," Jin told us. It was hard to believe there were nearly three million people down there, living their tiny little lives. I could almost understand how the kami might not be concerned about losing a few hundred of them. Almost.

We crossed to the other side of the roof to see a huge body of water stretching into the darkness. The reflection of the silver moon shimmered on its surface. "Lake Michigan," Jin said. "You can see it in the video."

From his spot in the middle of the roof, Danny called, "Can we please stop talking about music videos and focus on why we're here now?"

He had a point. "Yeah, okay." I went back to him, and Ryleigh, Jin, and Niko followed.

"So what do you think?" I asked Niko, hoping against hope that it wasn't what *I* thought.

He shrugged. "Daikoku is the kami of commerce. This is a business building . . ."

"Why would Daikoku send us here to do business?" Jin asked. "What kami lives at the top of the Willis Tower?"

"Or maybe it's a kami who lives *under* the Willis Tower." Niko looked significantly at me and Danny. "We are in Chicago, after all."

My heart sank. He was talking about Susano'o, who lived in a place called Ne-no-kuni, or the Land of Roots. After being banished from the Sky Kingdom, Susano'o had retreated there and built a fortress for himself, and it was only accessible through a single portal in the city of Chicago.

"But the portal to Ne-no-kuni is in that one subway station," Danny protested. "Why would Daikoku send us up here?"

"Because this is as close as my master will agree to come to Ne-no-kuni," said a quiet voice behind us. We whirled around to see the silhouette of a rabbit. It was the rabbit in the moon, who'd once helped us get to the Ne-no-kuni portal by summoning the oboroguruma of Wayne Steak (aka Steak Knife)—a car that was fueled by its former owner's rage and resentment.

"How did you get here?" Danny gasped.

"I am made of moonlight," the rabbit said. "I go where it goes."

"Cool," breathed Jin. He whipped out his little notebook and started scribbling. "Made . . . of moonlight . . . go . . . where . . . it . . . goes," he murmured. When he saw us watching, he blushed and shoved the notebook into his back pocket.

"Your master is Tsukiyomi, right?" I asked the rabbit. "The Moon Prince?"

The rabbit nodded. My heart lifted. Tsukiyomi was Susano'o's older brother, which meant that he was my great-uncle. Maybe *he* was the relative we'd been sent here to meet.

"Why are we meeting him in Chicago? What does Ne-no-kuni have to do with him?"

The words were barely out of my mouth when a blast of wind howled around the building. We flattened ourselves against the wall in terror. From our vantage point on the rooftop, we could see Fūjin, the god of the wind, standing on the eastern horizon and holding an enormous empty sack above his head—its mouth was wide open and flapping around the wind that streamed out of it, pushing a huge bank of clouds toward us over the darkness of Lake Michigan. The clouds tumbled and rolled over each other almost like they were fighting. Raijin, the god of thunder and lightning, leaped his way through them, kicking up fog in huge puffs and billows each time he took off and landed. He was lit up from below by the streetlights and by the flashes of lightning that tore through the sky in his wake, and his face was split by a broad grin as he swung two clubs at a string of drums that danced around him: *BAM-ba-ba-ba-ba-BOOM-ba-ba-ba-ba-BAM!*

We cowered against the building as it swayed and shuddered with each crash of thunder.

Ba-ba-ba-ba-BOOM! BANG!

Whooooo!

Boom-bam-boom!

Jin had turned pale. "You guys, I really think we should—"

BABABABA-BOOM! BANG! BOOM!

There was a blinding flash and everything shook—the building, the rooftop, the antennas, even the air. Out of the light stepped a giant of a man with wild gray hair, a tangled beard, and eyebrows that looked like troll hair. He wore torn, dirty jeans and combat boots, and his enormous shoulders, barrel chest, and protruding belly strained against a leather biker jacket. When he saw us cowering by the wall, he burst into laughter. The air crackled with electricity as he strode toward us.

"HAHAHA-HAAAA!" Susano'o, Lord of the Seas, Master of Storms, and Ruler of Ne-No-Kuni—that is to say, my grandfather—had arrived.

Niko immediately threw himself flat on the ground.

"Well, well, well, if it isn't my little guppy girl and her funny friends! Stirring up trouble again, are you? I like it!" Susano'o let out another thunderous blast of laughter. "So! Are you taking good care of Kusanagi for me? Having lots of fun with it?"

"I am," I lied. "But I don't *stir up* trouble. I'm *in* trouble."

"That's not what *I* heard," he singsonged.

"What did you hear?"

"My sources tell me that you and Kusanagi were in a fight, little girl. If that's not stirring up trouble, I don't know what is—don't look so upset! A fight's a fight and I love an underdog! That's you, by the way, guppy girl." He pointed a ginormous finger at me and winked. "That is, you and your little crew."

"Wait—so, um, pardon me for interrupting, sir, but does this mean you're helping us? Will you come and fight for us?" Jin asked.

"Fight *for* you?" We were almost knocked over by another roar of laughter. "Whoo, that's good! No, of course not! Where's the fun in that? Much more fun to watch you do it." He squinted at Jin. "And who are you, now?"

Jin cleared his throat. "I'm Jin Takayama."

"Benzaiten is his mom," I said.

Susano'o's bushy eyebrows went up. "Benzaiten's kid, eh? Too bad you didn't inherit her looks. No wonder she took off."

Jin turned bright red—I bet no one had ever implied he was ugly before. Or that anyone had ever joked about his mom leaving.

"Ahh, I'm just kidding, boyo," Susano'o said. "Seeing what

73

you're made of. A little vain, a little hurt, but I like that spark there! We'll see how you do on the team. By the way, Benzi-benz doesn't stick around for anyone, so don't take it personally. All right, bunnykins." He turned to the rabbit, who had been waiting paitently for him to finish. "Where's Moony-baloony?" Susano'o turned back to us and said in a stage whisper, "He's a piece of work. Wait'll you meet him. Whoo-wee!"

I could have sworn the rabbit sighed as he bowed. He reminded me of a fancy English butler who doesn't particularly like the loud, obnoxious guest at the party but will never not do his job properly because of it.

But before he could say anything, Ryleigh cleared her throat and stepped right up to Susano'o. She stuck out her hand, flicked her ponytail, and said, "My name is Ryleigh and I'm part of the team, too."

Niko let out a little scream and threw himself to the floor again. "I beg your magnanimous mercy, Your Mightiness! She's just a human girl, she has no idea what she's doing!" Then he flopped in front of the rabbit and apologized again.

I would have been happy for Susano'o to call up a little storm to scare Ryleigh into not trying to be the center of attention all the time. But Susano'o, who had been staring at Ryleigh's hand with a look of shocked confusion on his face, threw his head back and laughed. "Ah-ha-HAAA! She wants to shake my hand! Now *that's* spirit! You could learn from this one, fox! Stop groveling and get up!"

I felt a stab of jealousy, partly because Susano'o had said that Ryleigh had spirit (*What about me?* I wanted to say. *I have spirit, too!*) and partly because I wished I had her nerve—how did she walk up to one of the most powerful gods in the universe and just introduce herself like it was nothing?

I felt a little better when Susano'o didn't actually shake her hand but smiled at me again.

"You've got a good team here, guppy girl," he said. He gave me what he probably thought was a gentle pat on the back, which sent me flying into Ryleigh, who glared at me like I'd run into her on purpose. "Now let's see what that snooty old lily-livered big brother of mine has to say." He tilted his face to the sky and bellowed, "Hurry up, Tsuki-dooky! You're LATE!" He rubbed his hands together and grinned. "This is going to be so much fun."

Moments later, the rooftop was flooded from above with a cool, silver glow. The wind died down. And even though the lightning still appeared to be having a massive, out-of-control party just a few feet away, the thunder sounded muffled and far-off.

"Good evening." A voice came from the source of the silver light: a pale, slender, handsome man in a white suit who floated gently to the ground. Actually, "pale" isn't quite the right word—it was more that his skin was glowing the same color as the cool brightness that surrounded us. His silver hair was pulled back into a ponytail. The only thing dark about him was the color of his eyes, which were so black, the pupils blended into the irises. "I'm so glad to see you here. Do you know who I am?"

"His Most Luminous Excellence, Tsukiyomi, God of the Moon and Prince of the Night," said Niko, who was flat on the ground again.

Tsukiyomi smiled and crouched down to touch Niko's head. "What lovely manners you have, little fox. I am honored. But do stand up, and let us dispense with formalities, for I would like us to be friends." His voice was quiet and clear and refined, like the finest crystal. It made me think of words like "solitude" and "serenity," of a figure skater gliding gracefully across a sheet of gleaming white ice. It filled me with peace. I could have listened to it all night.

"How 'bout you and me, big brother? Would you like for us to be friends, too? Or don't I count?" Susano'o's thunder-and-lightning voice shattered the glimmery vibe like a rock through a plate glass window.

I barely caught a glimpse of Tsukiyomi's jaw clenching in annoyance before a spike of lightning screamed out of the sky and actually *did* pierce the cool, calm bubble around us. *Ugh, Susano'o,* I thought.

Tsukiyomi stood with his hands folded in front of him, as poised and still as ever, shimmering like—well, like moonlight on a lake. The rabbit stood at attention next to him, his ears swiveling and alert. Behind us, I could hear the deep rumble of Susano'o laughing to himself. It came from much higher above than before, and when I craned my neck and looked up, I saw that he had grown into his true giant form. "HA! Haven't changed one bit, I see—don't want to get that pure white suit dirty with the likes of your grimy Earth-loving baby brother, eh? Oh—hang on, kids, better run for cover! I think I have to . . . ah . . . ah . . . ah . . . ah-*CHOO!*"

Danny, Jin, Ryleigh, Niko, and I dove behind Susano'o's massive legs just in time to avoid the torrent of snot and spit that came shooting out of his nose and mouth—right down at Tsukiyomi and the rabbit. In a flash, Tsukiyomi was as tall as

Susano'o; he raised his hand and a spiral of light sprang out of it like a shield between them. It was made of clouds of sparkling stars swirling around a dark center, like a little galaxy, and all the grossness got sucked into that dark hole in the middle, followed by the clouds of light, and then there was nothing left but a dark sphere that collapsed in on itself and was gone.

"I see you haven't changed, either," Tsukiyomi said mildly. He shrank back down to human size, and I saw that even though his voice was unemotional, his lip was curled just the tiniest bit with disgust. Who could blame him? I caught both Jin and Ryleigh looking back and forth between me and Susano'o, who was using his sleeve to wipe snot off his upper lip. I could tell they were thinking, *She's his granddaughter?*

I wished Tsukiyomi were my grandfather instead of my great-uncle. Then I'd have inherited his gleaming galaxy-conjuring power instead of Susano'o's tsunami-causing rage monster.

"Too bad you need me to get this done, eh? Ah, I bet it was so painful for you to come to me and ask me for help!" Susano'o's guffaws must have sounded like thunder in the rest of the city—I swear I heard it echoing around the streets below us. Then his enormous upside-down face appeared in front of us and winked. "Hey, guppy girl and friends, don't worry. I prom-ise I won't sneeze again." He shrank himself down to human size and walked ahead of us toward Tsukiyomi. "The floor is yours, Tsuki-dooky. Take it away."

What Was That About Stabby McStabbypants?

"My dear Momo. As you might guess, the kami-verse has been keeping a close eye on you ever since you defeated Shuten-dōji during Kami-Con. And as the chief kami of the night, I have been informed of the valiant battle you and your friends have just fought," Tsukiyomi began.

"But we lost," I said timidly. "Mrs. Meade—I mean, the demon—disappeared with everyone."

"Next time, don't hold back!" Susano'o said. "I'm telling you, guppy girl, if you want to defeat ol' Tama, you gotta just go for it! Let 'er rip!"

Tsukiyomi smiled kindly. "No. Had you fully accessed your power, you might have destroyed her, but you also could have killed the very people you were trying to protect. You did the right thing, child," he said.

"Thank you," I said. I glanced at Susano'o, who looked strangely thoughtful. I wondered if he suspected that Izanami had visited me during the battle, and if he'd told Tsukiyomi about my connection to her. "Uh . . . who's ol' Tama?"

Susano'o's eyebrows shot up. "You mean to say you don't know who you're up against? Well, that might explain you trying to fight her at half power, then! Tamamo-no-mae, guppy girl! Don't tell me you don't know who she is!"

Oh, right. How could I have forgotten? "She's an ancient demon—a nine-tailed fox who became a beautiful woman and used her beauty throughout history to fool powerful men into doing terrible things to innocent people. But a thousand years ago, a monk finally caught her and trapped her inside a boulder."

"Bingo! Good for you—you've been doing your homework, I see!" Susano'o grinned.

"She said someone freed her last month," said Danny. "Prince . . . Prince Something."

"The Prince of Darkness," Jin chimed in. "That's what she said."

Susano'o's face turned bright red. "And if I find out who in the blazes that is, I will SMASH that little snake to SMITH-EREENS!" As if in response, Raijin banged extra hard on his drums and the building shook with ear-shattering booms of thunder. When it subsided, Susano'o said more quietly, "Releasing that kind of evil on the world takes a special kind of slime bucket, and while I don't normally like to intervene in your tiny little lives, I will take pleasure in pounding the poop out of that punk, whoever they may be."

That seemed unnecessarily violent. And also peak Susano'o.

"That's so weird and gross," Ryleigh said. "Why does she think she has to be young and pretty to get what she wants? Why does she have to trick men into doing stuff for her? Why can't she use her brains and do things on her own?"

"*That's* what bugs you? That she doesn't do terrible things to innocent people *on her own*?" said Danny.

"I mean, obviously being evil is bad," Ryleigh said. "But why does her power have to be, like, all about her looks?"

"And seventh grade isn't ruled by the pretty girls?" Tsuki-yomi arched one eyebrow at Ryleigh. I wanted to cheer—he'd said exactly what I'd been thinking.

Ryleigh's cheeks flushed pink.

"Ha-ha! Welcome to the patriarchy, kids!" Susano'o guf-fawed. "Men hog all the power and women compete for access by being young, pretty, and sneaky! Impressive how long it's lasted."

I felt like that was exactly how school worked: the most powerful girls were the ones who the boys thought were pretty. Were we *all* supposed to be fighting for attention from the boys? Yuck. That didn't seem fair to anyone.

"But Danny and Jin are boys, and they're popular because of their looks, too," Ryleigh protested. Then she blushed even harder. "I mean, partly."

Oof. Awkward on so many levels. But she did have a point. (Also, who made the rules about who was pretty, anyway? Was that the patriarchy? And why was it always a boy-girl thing? Was *that* the patriarchy?)

"Yeah, I'm also cool!" Danny said, grinning, and then added more seriously, "Anyway, plenty of women have lots of power now. And most of them are old."

"Yeah, but men are still in charge of most of the world. And my makeup artist on my last video said people care way more about women's looks than men's," Jin said. "Even if the women are CEOs and senators and stuff. And they also said that one reason men don't want to wear makeup is because it blurs the lines between genders. 'Cause power only works when it's easy to tell who's supposed to have it and who isn't."

"Ooh, look who's a feminist!" Susano'o chuckled. "Next you'll be telling me to expand the story beyond pretty ladies and powerful men, and using words like 'heteronormative' and 'gender binary'!"

"Well, that, too," said Jin.

Susano'o slapped his knee. "Ha-haa, yes! Progress! I like it!"

"Perhaps the world has changed enough so that Tamamo-no-mae will attempt to rise to power in the Middle Lands on her own," Tsukiyomi said. "But I doubt it. Being trapped in the boulder has aged her, and old habits die hard. I expect that she is capturing children in order to extend her life and to replenish the energy she needs to create the illusion of youth and beauty in her human form."

"How?" Danny asked.

"When you are born, you have countless options ahead of you—like a tree or a river with infinite branches. With every life event and every choice, some of those branches are pruned off. Sometimes others sprout up, but as a rule, the further you go, the fewer options you have left to choose from. Conversely, the younger you are, the more possible lives are available to you. Tamamo-no-mae is collecting children so that she may harvest their youth and their infinite possible lives, thereby extending and expanding her own life possibilities."

"So she's going to kill all those kids and, like, drink their lives?" I asked. "So she can look young and pretty, and then she'll . . ."

"Attach herself to someone powerful, most likely—someone

with the power to kill many people at once," Tsukiyomi said. "Or perhaps she will find a way to become such a person, as Danny has suggested. Think of the greatest human tragedies of the past centuries. If Tamamo-no-mae rises to power there will be even greater ones to come."

"I think she needs chaos and violence. It nourishes her, somehow," Susano'o mused. "Whereas for me, it's more like a delicious snack." He opened his mouth for a mighty yawn, which turned into a mighty belch.

"*Must* you?" said Tsukiyomi with a long-suffering sigh.

"I must," Susano'o replied gleefully. "Just be glad it didn't come out the other end."

Next to me, Danny turned a laugh into a sort of coughing snort. I suppressed the urge to smack him and tell him to grow up, and I wondered if maybe I really *was* Tsukiyomi's grandchild and not Susano'o's. Mom, with her quiet grace, seemed more like Tsukiyomi than Susano'o, for sure.

The moon god cleared his throat and clapped his hands lightly. "Let us get back to the matter at hand. You and your friends are lucky. Tamamo-no-mae has not killed anyone yet. I believe she is building up to eight hundred and eighty-eight—a number laden with luck—and will wait to kill them until New Year's Eve, since the moment that the year renews itself is powerfully magical. Coincidentally, I will be at my brightest that night, making the magic doubly powerful. Tamamo-no-mae has waited a thousand years; she will happily wait a few more days if it means reaping such an enormous benefit."

"What he's saying, kids, is that there will be a full moon on

New Year's Eve," said Susano'o. "I can give you a full moon right now if you want."

He started to turn around, but Tsukiyomi said in a voice that froze even me to my core, *"Don't. You. Dare."*

"All right, all right," Susano'o grumbled good-naturedly. "You don't have to be such a party pooper. I was just kidding, anyway."

Tsukiyomi rolled his eyes before saying to us, "My point is, I know how you can stop Tamamo-no-mae."

"We're listening," said Ryleigh, as if she spoke for all of us—as if she were our leader. On the other hand, if she wasn't the leader, who was? Me? I wasn't sure I was up to it.

"Do you know about the Three Sacred Treasures?" Tsukiyomi asked. "One of them is in Momo's possession."

We nodded. He was talking about Kusanagi. When Amaterasu, Goddess of the Sun (and Susano'o and Tsukiyomi's older sister), sent her great-grandson to the Middle Lands to set up shop as the first earthly ruler, she gave him three gifts as a sign of her blessing: Kusanagi, the Sword of the Wind; Yata-no-kagami, the Eight-Sided Mirror of the Sun—also known as the Mirror of Truth; and Yasaka-no-Magatama, the Jewel of Kindness. All three items were supposedly locked away in sacred shrines in Japan. But it had turned out that the Kusanagi in the shrine was a fake and that Susano'o had been hanging on to the real sword for centuries—the same one that was now in my backpack.

"The fact is, neither the mirror nor the jewel is where its human guardians believe it to be. Yata-no-kagami was Amaterasu's favorite mirror, and—"

"How does someone have a favorite mirror?" Danny interrupted.

"Shhh! Be quiet and listen," Niko said.

"No, it's all right. Danny poses an excellent question, and its answer is the basis of our plan," said Tsukiyomi.

Danny could not have looked more pleased with himself.

"Yata-no-kagami is very special to Amaterasu. It was forged specifically to lure her out when the crimes of my dear brother made her hide herself away from the world in despair." Tsukiyomi glowered at Susano'o, who was whistling to himself and picking dirt out of his fingernails.

"For the millionth time, *she* started it. And I apologized, didn't I?" he grumbled. "*And* I got kicked out of the Sky Kingdom forever as punishment, so I don't know why you're still mad at me."

After another dirty look at his brother (honestly, we were all giving Susano'o dirty looks at this point), Tsukiyomi continued. "As its name—the Eight-Sided Mirror—implies, Yata-no-kagami has many features. One side is a portal from which no one has ever returned. The other sides reveal different aspects of the viewer. One side shows you your greatest strength, one shows your greatest weakness, one shows you how others see you, one shows your true potential, one shows you how you've changed, and one shows you in your best light."

"Wait. That's only seven sides," I said.

"That's because the final side is just a regular old mirror," said Susano'o.

"Amaterasu's favorite side is the one that shows you in your best light. She generates so much light herself that all she ever sees in most mirrors is light. Yata-no-kagami shows her actual face," said the rabbit.

"And it is the most radiantly beautiful face one could ever hope to see." Tsukiyomi's voice was soft and sad. His own marble-white face took on a slightly pinkish tinge, and his light grew a degree or two warmer. And—was that a tear trickling down his cheek like a watery pearl? I remembered that sometimes the kami fell in love with each other, even when they were related to each other—strange (to us), but true.

"Aww, boo-hoo, Moon Man, when are you gonna stop crying?"

"I can't help it if I miss her." Tsukiyomi took a handkerchief out of his suit pocket and wiped his eyes.

"She's a conceited, stuck-up control-freak know-it-all. You just miss living in the Celestial City."

"*You* are a heartless boor."

"Ha! At least *I'm* not in denial about what I did to get booted, Stabby McStabbypants." Susano'o gave Tsukiyomi a sly, slightly sinister grin.

The air grew suddenly frigid as Tsukiyomi drew himself up and glared at Susano'o. "I will not have you, of all kami, casting aspersions on my character just to save your own sorry hide. Isn't it enough that you've gotten me cast out of my beloved home, you murderous, lying brute?"

Another colossal streak of lightning speared through our quiet little bubble with a deafening *CRACK*, and suddenly we were watching what Niko would call a brotherly brawl. But instead of two human figures, it was the elements: icy white fog swirled against thundering black clouds. A blizzard of silver dust tangled with torrents of rain. The howl of the wind and the roar of space were punctuated with shouts of "Take that, you fiend!" and "Ow!" and "Ha! Who's the big brother now?"

"What was that about Stabby McStabbypants?" Jin wanted to know.

Niko explained. "Ukemochi, the goddess of food, invited Tsukiyomi to dinner one time, way back in the early days. He's a bit of a clean freak, and folks say that when he saw that all the food she was serving came out of the holes in her body"— "Gross," said Ryleigh—"he lost control of himself and killed her. When Amaterasu heard what had happened to her little sister, she was so furious with Tsukiyomi that she refused to see him again, ever."

"And that's why we have night and day," I said. "He can only come out after she's left the sky."

"Whoa." Jin nodded. Then he whipped out a little notebook and scribbled in it, muttering, "My world . . . is dark . . . without you."

"Dude, seriously, what are you writing?" Danny said.

Jin blushed and put away the notebook. "I told you, it's nothing important. Just . . . stuff."

"What kind of stuff?"

"I don't know—stuff, okay? Can we get back to Tsukiyomi? Why did he call Susano'o a liar?" Jin said.

"A lot of kami, including Tsukiyomi himself, insist that he was wrongly accused, and that it was really Susano'o who murdered Ukemochi," said Niko.

"*I* believe it," Danny muttered. "N-no offense," he stammered when Susano'o glanced in his direction. The sibling battle had ended in a draw, and the two kami were backing away from each other, brushing moondust and electrical sparks off themselves.

"*Thbbbttt.* If I've heard it once, I've heard it a million times." Susano'o waved Danny's comment away as if it were a pesky fly. "Blame all the murdering on Susano'o. *He's* the worst."

"You attempted to kill your *very own granddaughter!*" Tsukiyomi burst out, pointing at me. "Three times!"

"She didn't die, did she? And when she proved herself, I gave her Kusanagi!" Susano'o protested, like that made the triple-attempted-murdery part okay. "Look, all I'm saying is you gotta embrace your dark side. You'll be happier. And less uptight. And less boring."

Jin and Ryleigh started to inch away from Susano'o—and from me—and toward Tsukiyomi. I didn't blame them. Who wants to stand next to the target of an attempted murder when the murder-attempter is right there?

"Anyway. Forget all of that. Let's get on with the plan," Susano'o said. "Rabbit! Get me a map of the Sky Kingdom, pronto!"

The rabbit scampered in a circle between us and Tsukiyomi, and the powdery remains of Susano'o and Tsukiyomi's fight whipped itself into a sort of holographic map. On the southern edge was a sparkling body of water with the words SEA OF HEAVEN floating above it. The rest of the map showed a stretch of land that appeared to be divided into quarters by season: pale green meadows traced with streams in the eastern quarter;

lush, dark green forests in the south; red-leafed maple trees and golden fields of grain in the west; and a desolate, wintry wasteland in the north. In the center was a perfectly square walled city crisscrossed with glowing lines that must have been streets and avenues. The city was guarded on each side by a different giant animal: a blue dragon at the eastern gate, a bright red bird at the southern gate, a white tiger at the western gate, and a black tortoise at the northern gate.

"You are looking at the Sky Kingdom, our ancestral home." Tsukiyomi's voice sounded wistful. "In the center is the Celestial City, which has grown up around Amaterasu's palace over the millennia."

"And Yata-no-kagami is in there somewhere," said Ryleigh, gesturing at the map.

"Aha! Clever girl," Susano'o said, though it wasn't exactly rocket science. Why else would he have been showing us this map?

"The mirror was brought back to Amaterasu ages ago from the Middle Lands; it is now kept in the Hall of Mirrors in the Palace of the Sun." Susano'o pointed, and a huge section in the center of the city glowed gold. "Your mission, should you choose to accept it—"

"—is to break in there, steal the mirror, bring it back, and trick Tamamo-no-mae into looking into it so she gets trapped inside," Ryleigh said. "I mean, that's kind of obvious, isn't it?"

"Correct." Susano'o looked a little bit annoyed. I could tell he didn't like having his thunder stolen, ha-ha.

"Do you have a more, uh, specific plan for us?" I asked.

"Nope! But I do have crucial information that could help you."

"I still don't see why you couldn't have just given it to me," Tsukiyomi groused.

"Because I wanted an excuse to see you, of course!"

"You mean an excuse to torment me," Tsukiyomi said. "I can't believe you're bragging about your 'crucial information,' seeing as how you only got it because you destroyed the palace."

"Relax! All I did was smash up the furniture, break down some walls, poop on the floor, and throw a skinned horse through the roof," Susano'o protested.

"And you killed Amaterasu's favorite handmaiden," said Tsukiyomi coldly.

"I've told you a million times—that was an *accident*! How was I supposed to know the horse would land on her?"

The others turned nearly as pale as Tsukiyomi. "I think we may want to attempt a slightly subtler approach," Niko said.

Susano'o chuckled. "Fair enough, my foxy friend! My shenanigans got me into a lot of trouble with Little Miss Sunshine." He sighed happily and said, "Who knows what they might do to you? They could send you straight down to Izanami in Yomi! By the way, guppy girl, have you mastered"—he bent down and whispered—"all that you have inside?"

I shook my head, and Susano'o nodded and said in a normal voice, "I thought not. Well, if you can't control your power, I guess you'll just have to be sneaky and two-faced like my brother."

Tsukiyomi gave him a chilly glare.

Susano'o chuckled. "I love how hard this is for you. I love that you need my help. Isn't it just grand, working together?"

Tsukiyomi grimaced and said only, "Let us continue, shall we?"

"By all means." Susano'o twirled a mocking hand at his brother. "Please do!"

Easy-Peasy Lemon Squeezy

"You will be traveling disguised as tourists from the Middle Lands," Tsukiyomi began.

"Tourists?" Jin asked.

"What with the winter solstice and the approach of the new year, Celestial City will be flooded with Middle Lands kami on holiday, so it will be easy for you to blend in," Tsukiyomi explained. "You will each have first-class tickets on a yacht to the Sky Kingdom, and a tourist visa to get you through customs. Once you clear customs, you will board a coach bound for the Vermilion Phoenix Gate, in the southern wall of the city."

"Sweet! This is just like James Bond!" said Danny, because he only ever saw the fun adventure side of things, never the what-if-we-get-caught side.

"I know, right? We're totally gonna crush this," Ryleigh said, and she gave Danny's arm a squeeze. "Ooh, check out those biceps!" Who else but Ryleigh would turn this very serious, very dangerous situation into a fun flirting opportunity?

"Once you're within the city walls, the rest should be easy. With one tragic exception"—here, Tsukiyomi glowered at Susano'o, who leered back at him—"no crime or unlawful violence of any kind has ever occurred in Celestial City. Everything is free, so there is no need for money. Everyone is comfortable, everyone is happy; my sister's presence affects the entire population. She has even found a way to prevent people from getting angry."

Whoa. I wondered how she did it. What would it be like to never be angry?

Susano'o sighed with a faraway look on his face. "It felt so great to shake that place up!"

"I can't believe you're nostalgic about a literal crime against heaven," said Tsukiyomi coldly.

"It was awesome! I don't regret a minute of it."

"Just tell the children about the Hall of Mirrors."

"All right! Zoom in, bunnykins!"

We got a close-up of the Palace of the Sun—a walled city within the city, full of courtyards and buildings. The southern half was a huge empty space labeled PARADE AND CONCERT GROUNDS. At the northern end of the concert grounds, an enormous building labeled THRONE ROOM was backed by a maze of walkways and compounds—groups of little buildings around their own tiny courtyards. The compounds on the east side were labeled SERVANTS' QUARTERS, STABLES, KITCHENS, and the like.

"This is as close as I can get, sir," said the rabbit.

"No worries, no worries! I've got it." Susano'o swept his arm over the map, and the palace blew away like sand. He stared at the empty space it had left and muttered a few unintelligible words. In a flash, we were looking at a brand-new map: a detailed view of one section of the palace.

Susano'o said, "Okay, kids. *This* map is why Tsuki-dooky

needs me—because he's never been in the palace. This building is the Hall of Mirrors." He pointed, and a rectangular building at the center of a network of walkways glowed with a soft yellow light. "It's only accessible through a single entrance in the middle of this walkway." Now the walkway that connected the Hall of Mirrors to a jumble of other buildings lit up. "It's guarded by a warrior kami and by Yatagarasu, the divine three-legged crow." Another light pulsed halfway down the passage, where it connected to the Hall of Mirrors.

"I can totally get us past those guards," Ryleigh said. "I'm an infiltration specialist. I'm great at stealth and deception."

Yeah, you are, I thought.

Susano'o ignored her and pointed at the Hall of Mirrors again. "You'll need to be careful once you get in. The Mirror of the Sun is in there somewhere, but the other mirrors can be distracting. There's one that shows you what you wish to become, one that answers your deepest questions, one that shows you your fondest memories . . . Me, personally, I'd be watching the memory of myself slaying Orochi the Eight-Headed Dragon. What a day that was!" He puffed up proudly. "Anyway, be careful."

"How are we supposed to know which one is Yata-no-kagami?" Danny asked.

Susano'o shrugged. "It has eight sides?"

Tsukiyomi groaned and put his forehead in his hands.

"So all we have to do is fake our way across the border, sneak into the palace, get past the guard and the three-legged crow, find the mirror, steal it without getting sucked into one of the other mirrors, and leave the Sky Kingdom before anyone finds out?" Jin said. His voice shook a little. "No problem."

"Exactly!" Susano'o clapped his baseball-mitt hands and spread his arms wide. "Easy-peasy lemon squeezy!"

"How *do* we get out of the Sky Kingdom? And how do we find Tamamo-no-mae once we're back?" Ryleigh asked.

"Excellent questions, young lady," Tsukiyomi said. "There should be several boats docked at the shore of the Sea of Heaven. As long as you make it to the harbor before word gets out about your theft, your tickets should be good for a return passage. I will know by that time where Tamamo has hidden herself, and I will send my trusty assistant here to help you with the rest." He looked affectionately at the rabbit, who responded with a dignified bow.

"With every possible ounce of due respect, Your Luminosity, it still sounds like a precarious proposition," Niko fretted.

"It is! So what?" Susano'o bellowed. "Courage, fox!"

"This is your only option. You must have heard that the other kami do not have time to save your friends," Tsukiyomi pointed out.

"Um, Tsukiyomi? Sir?" A stubborn question had been rattling around my head for a little while now. "Why are *you* helping us? I thought the kami don't usually like to involve themselves with human problems. I don't mean to say that you're not super kind or that all those kids aren't important," I said. "But even the Seven Lucky Gods aren't helping us, so . . ." I didn't want to come right out and accuse him of having ulterior motives, but . . .

"Why would I want to help you when no one else will?" Tsukiyomi spoke my thoughts out loud, and I nodded, embarrassed.

The Moon Prince glowed even brighter. "You are wise to

ask this question, Momo," he said. "Not all who offer help are trustworthy. But rest assured that I am on your side. My fellow kami may have lost sight of our responsibility to care for the Middle Lands over the millennia, but I have found that I cannot stand idly by as your world edges toward chaos. I have seen great power and great good in you, Momo, and I have a sense that I should aid you in any way that I can."

Relief washed over me. Finally, someone who actually cared!

"Oh, hey! I have a question," Jin said.

"Yes?"

"Why can't we just *ask* Amaterasu for the mirror?" Jin said.

"Oh, come *on*, boy! Don't turn down adventure when it comes knocking on your door!" Susano'o griped. "You and your mother are just the same. Always looking for the peaceful solution. Peaceful, schmeaceful, I say."

But Jin didn't look like he minded being compared to his mom like this at all. And "peaceful, schmeaceful" sounded better than "breaking and entering," so I looked hopefully at Tsuki-yomi. He shook his head. "I told you, it is her prized possession. She trusts no one but herself with it."

"I bet she'll think you're trying to overthrow her, seeing as you've already got Kusanagi and all." Susano'o winked at me. "She'll probably kill you on sight!"

"*What?*" I felt my throat constrict, and the edges of my vision started to go dark and blurry.

"Ah, calm down, guppy girl! I kid! I kid!" Susano'o roared with laughter, then wiped away a tear. "Mostly, anyway."

I felt Danny's hand on my shoulder. "Don't listen to him.

It'll be fine," he assured me. That helped, but only a little, because he always thought everything would be fine.

"I'm down," said Ryleigh. "I'm not afraid."

"You *should* be afraid," Niko said to Ryleigh. "Momo is wise to hesitate."

"I wasn't hesitating," I snapped.

"Well, *I'm* hesitating! The risks and consequences are huge, you grumbling grouse! And what if your mother comes back home and you're dead? What will I tell her?"

"You can tell her she shouldn't have left me alone with a fox for a babysitter! You can tell her she should have made sure we could contact her!" I felt my heart picking up speed and my breath coming faster and faster. Why had Mom left us and where had she gone? What would I do if something happened to her? The thought of a future without Dad *or* Mom loomed like a tidal wave and threatened to engulf me.

"You've got this," Danny whispered in my ear. "I know you do."

I closed my eyes and tried to think clearly. I still didn't know where Mom was or if she needed me. If I stayed home, I'd be no use to anyone. If I went to the Sky Kingdom, I might go to prison, or I might fail, but there was a tiny chance that I could help save all those kids, plus Danny's, Jin's, and Ryleigh's families. The choice was obvious.

I took another breath and opened my eyes. "I'm in. When do we leave?"

"Ha-HAAA! That's my guppy girl!" Susano'o bellowed, and smashed me on the head and messed up my hair. "Susano'o's descendants never back down! Look out, Sky Kingdom, we're storming the gates!" Thunder crashed so loudly outside our bubble that the building shook.

"That is exactly what they will *not* do, you brute," said Tsukiyomi. "Now." He pulled a gleaming white box out of the air and laid it on the ground. "Rabbit, if you please."

The rabbit opened the box, took out a crystal perfume bottle, and gave us each a generous spritz. "Kami Cologne," he said. "It will temporarily disguise the stench of your human mortality." I sniffed my arm—nothing. But Tsukiyomi, Susano'o, Niko, and the rabbit seemed satisfied.

Next, the rabbit pulled out five golden coins. "One each. Whatever you do, don't lose them! Everything you need is loaded onto them: your boat ticket, your ID, and your visa all in one. As long as you have the coin in your pocket, you'll be able to pass safely through any security checkpoint."

Once we were all set, Tsukiyomi beamed down at us. "Good luck, children. Go with my blessing. I have faith in you." With that, he rose higher and higher, taking his light with him. The rabbit gave us a quick bow and scampered after his master. Within seconds, they were gone, and the dark, the cold, and the blustery winds returned.

"And good luck from me, kiddos! And one! And two! And—"

BOOM. Thunder clapped and everything went dark.

What Do You Think You're *Doing?*

We found ourselves standing on a broad, tree-lined boulevard crowded with people bundled up against the cold. It stretched alongside a glimmering harbor and appeared to end somewhere out on the water; about halfway down, a giant Ferris wheel flashed baby blue, flamingo pink, and bright white.

"What is this place?" I wondered out loud. "Are we somewhere in the kami-verse?"

"No, it's Navy Pier!" Jin pointed at a low concrete wall carved with the words NAVY PIER. "That means we're still in Chicago—it's right on the shores of Lake Michigan. I love this place! I came here last summer."

"Lemme guess—you filmed a video?" Danny deadpanned.

Jin gave him a hard stare and said, "Nope. Just came for fun with my dad. I do have a personal life, you know. Just because you only see my public life doesn't mean that's all there is."

"Sorry," Danny mumbled.

"It's fine." Jin sighed. "I just get tired of being that guy. Like I'm nothing but a handsome face and a golden voice."

Danny snorted. "Yeah, it must be so hard to be a star and have people telling you how good-looking and talented you are all the time."

"Danny!" I glared at him. He wasn't usually snarky like this. What was wrong with him?

"Seems you're not as sorry as you said," Niko added.

"I am!" Danny insisted. "But he literally just said—"

"That's not what I meant," Jin said.

"You mean people don't know the real you and you're tired of acting all the time," I suggested. "Is that it? Or maybe you want to do something besides what you're doing?"

"Yeah. Both of those things." Jin gave me that smile that made me feel like I was floating. No wonder he was everyone's favorite member of SttTopp.

"I totally get it. I feel the same way," Ryleigh said, and then she did something shocking: She *didn't* smile at him with her big brown Bambi eyes. She looked sad.

Strange.

"What *do* you want to do?" I asked Jin.

"You'll think it's silly."

"No, we won't," I said.

"We might," Danny said. "Just kidding!" he added defensively when even Ryleigh gave him a reproachful look. "Seriously, I was just joking! What do you want to do?"

Jin cleared his throat a couple of times. "I think it would be cool to be a writer—like a novelist. Or a playwright. Or a poet. Even a songwriter. That's what the notebook's for—just cool stuff I might want to use one day." He took it out of his pocket and flipped through it, then put it back. "Or maybe I'll become an astrophysicist—I dunno. I just want to do something besides touring and making albums all the time."

Ryleigh wrinkled her nose. "Really? *Writing?*" She said it like she couldn't think of a nerdier, more loserly thing to do. "I thought you were gonna say you wanted to have a solo career." She shook her head—she seemed almost angry. "You can't quit making music. You're so good at it!"

"Yeah, I know. That's what everyone says." Jin looked dejected. Why was Ryleigh so angry at him? Why would she want him to keep doing something he didn't like?

"I would read your books," I said.

"Thanks."

"Anyway," Ryleigh cut in. "I thought we were supposed to catch a boat. I bet it's at the end of this thing." She pointed down the long pier. "And"—she nodded toward a group of tourists— "I bet all of those folks are here for the same boat."

I looked in the direction she was pointing and realized that if you looked closely, a lot of the bundled-up tourists were kami.

Tree spirits with woody skin walked alongside lake, river, and waterfall kami with sparkling, translucent hair that had frozen into icicles. Then there were book kami and musical-instrument kami with words and music notes printed across their faces. I even recognized a few former humans: extra-good and extra-powerful people whose spirits were so strong and so beloved that they were allowed to stay in the Middle Lands after their bodies died.

How had I missed this? And why did Ryleigh have to be the one to point it out to me?

There were three tour boats lined up along the pier. Two were decorated with strings of holiday lights and docked next to brightly lit ticket booths with cheery staff members handing out hot cider to the few brave tourists who stood shivering in line. The third boat, docked all the way at the end, didn't even need the enormous neon sign hanging next to it announcing SKY KINGDOM CRUISES for me to know it was ours; its hull gleamed with a golden light all its own that danced and twinkled on the water, and its name was painted in sparkly letters on the bow: *Yume Maru*—or *Ship of Dreams*. The line in front of it was long, and the passengers glowed against the dark night sky as they walked across the gangplank to the deck.

"How is everyone around here ignoring that boat?" Jin wondered.

"It's in the spirit dimension," Niko explained. "Regular humans don't see it because they don't expect to."

As we watched the line of kami shuffling forward, Ryleigh screamed. We whipped around to see something green and scaly about the size and shape of a little kid gripping her ankle. Ryleigh was kicking her attacker in the head, but to no avail. It was dragging her steadily toward the water, making greedy scrabbling, snarfling noises.

"A suiko!" Danny shouted.

"Look who's been studying up on his yōkai!" I said.

"Just get her!" He was right—we didn't have much time. Suiko are small, but they are strong, fast, and vicious.

Jin and Danny got to Ryleigh first. They each grabbed one of her arms, and Niko was doing his best to bite the suiko's ankle, but all three of them were being drawn closer and closer to the water. "Help! Help us!" I shouted, but no one came. The humans around us, who had changed their perception of reality to fit what they could understand, were shouting something about a giant snapping turtle; the kami only hurried on without looking.

If no one was paying attention to three kids and a fox being dragged into the lake, they wouldn't see one kid with a magic sword. I swung my backpack off and grabbed Kusanagi out of it. Instantly I felt a *zing!* of power ripple through me.

The suiko had been joined by two of its buddies, and between the three of them, they were easily winning this deadly tug-of-war. They kept licking their chops and drooling, muttering in their wet, raspy voices. One of them even tried to clamp its jaws around Ryleigh's leg. The only reason it didn't tear out a mouthful of flesh was that one of its companions kicked it in the back and screamed at it. *No fair starting early!* it seemed to be saying.

I rushed at them with Kusanagi upraised. When they saw the sword glowing in my hands, their big, shiny eyes bugged out and they screamed and let go. All three suiko scrambled over the edge of the pier and dropped into the water with a splash.

Danny helped Ryleigh up, and she brushed the mud and slush off her clothes. She looked pale and shaken. "Were those . . . baby kappa?" she asked.

"Worse," said Niko, panting. "Suiko. They would have drowned you and sucked your blood like little aquatic vampires."

"You okay?" Danny asked her, and she nodded.

I waited for her to thank us for saving her life, but instead, I heard Jin shout, "Run!"

He'd been at the edge of the pier, looking into the water to see where the suiko had gone, and he shoved us ahead of him, his face contorted with fear. Behind him was a horde of suiko—twenty, at least. As I stumbled backward away from the water, I saw even more water demons rise up: a red-eyed ushi-oni with the horned head of a bull and the body of a giant spider; a slug-like sazae-oni with a slimy, sinuous body and a face that was less a face than a gnarled, pitted shell; and a shivering, dripping-wet human-looking woman with a crying baby in her arms—a nure-onna.

The actual humans were now running away, shrieking about an attack of killer turtles. Some were taking videos with their phones. An old lady wearing a Chicago Bears hat with a bright orange pompon stepped forward to take the baby from the nure-onna's arms. "You poor dear!" she said. "Let's get you and your baby somewhere warm before you get hypothermia."

"No!" I shouted, but it was too late. The very kind but totally misguided lady staggered and sank to her knees—I knew it was because the baby in her arms suddenly weighed as much as a bag of bricks. The nure-onna pounced. Her legs turned into a serpent's tail, and a long, forked tongue flickered out of a fanged mouth that she opened wide to take her first bite of the woman's neck. I dashed forward and plunged Kusanagi into the nure-onna's tail. She reared back, screaming and hissing at me. I barely had time to withdraw the sword and swing it again before she struck; when the blade met her neck, she turned into a nure-onna-shaped blob of brackish water that began squiggling its way back toward the lake. I took one last swipe, and finally it splatted flat and sank into the pavement. The lady I'd just saved was crab-walking backward and away, sobbing and babbling about a killer octopus.

Before I could catch my breath, more suiko had scrambled out of the lake, and other yōkai were attacking us as well.

"What's going on?" Jin shouted. "Why are we being attacked like this?"

I wished I knew. It felt like an ambush, but who would have known we'd be here?

A nurikabe had now planted itself across the pier, creating an impenetrable, unscalable stone wall between us and our boat. It was hurling chunks of itself at Danny, Niko, Jin, and Ryleigh. Niko was using his telekinetic powers to catch most of them and hurl them back, but the others were still having to dodge hunks of rock as they fought off the yōkai. Jin was singing his heart out, trying to calm a hari-onago who was whipping twisted locks of her long black hair at him—every strand ended in a needle-sharp hook. Danny shot arrow after arrow at the oncoming army of suiko. Ryleigh hurled a variety of glinting shuriken at the ushi-oni and the sazae-oni with seriously impressive speed and accuracy. Knife-tipped stars, little wavy crosses with razor edges, and disks with pointy spikes along their rims spun through the air and lodged themselves in their targets with a wet *thik*. It was strange to see her in action as a ninja warrior, after all these years of thinking her biggest weapons were mean-girl contempt and sarcasm. I made a quick mental note not to get too far on her bad side. But I also silently thanked the kami that Ryleigh was on our team—that felt strange, too.

Black liquid streamed from every place the shuriken had struck the sazae-oni's body, but the ushi-oni seemed unharmed.

In fact, it seemed angry—it was pawing the ground with one of its front legs, snorting and snarling and shaking its big bull head. As skilled as she was, Ryleigh was about to need my help.

This is good, I thought. *We'll be a team.*

With Kusanagi humming for action in my hands, I yelled, "You get the sazae-oni—I'll take the ushi-oni!"

"No! *I'll* take the ushi-oni and *you* get the sazae-oni!"

There was no way Ryleigh's tiny shuriken were going to do anything to that giant bull-slash-spider except make it angrier.

"I'm taking the ushi-oni!" I shouted, and rushed forward. I would chop off one of its giant spider legs and cripple it, then finish by chopping off its head or maybe plunging Kusanagi into its belly.

But just as I got within striking range, something looped around my ankles and yanked my legs out from under me, and I crashed to the ground. I felt myself being jerked sideways and dragged backward on my stomach. I managed to turn myself over so I could see what had attacked me—as soon as I got close enough, I would stab it with Kusanagi.

It was Ryleigh.

We locked eyes for a fraction of a second, and just as I screamed, "What do you think you're *doing?*" she straightened and hurled two shuriken over my head. A roar of pain and anger erupted behind me—the ushi-oni. As I rolled out of its path, I promised myself that if I survived, the first thing on my to-do list would be to murder Ryleigh. If I didn't survive, I'd come back as a ghost and haunt her forever. A grappling hook flew past me, and the roar turned into a strangled gurgle—the hook had been attached to a cord that had wound itself around the ushi-oni's neck, just like the one around my ankles. On its back now, the ushi-oni thrashed and flailed to right itself onto its horrible spider legs. One last shuriken flashed over me and lodged itself deep in the ushi-oni's throat, and I was yanked away just in time to avoid getting splashed by the river of oily yellow goop that flowed out of the wound.

"I told you I had it!" I shouted at Ryleigh, but she was already focused on the sazae-oni that had lumbered closer to us in the meantime. She wasn't fighting it, though. She was just staring. Was she suddenly paralyzed with fear? Was she trying to think it to death? Did she have actual laser vision?

"I said, I told you I had it!" I shouted again. "And if you're not going to do something about that sazae-oni, I will!" I was so angry, I was shaking. Fighting yōkai was *my* specialty, not hers, but she'd just taken over and acted like I was a clumsy amateur. I used Kusanagi to slice through the rope around my ankles; it begged me to attack her, and I was very, very tempted to give in.

"Shut up." Ryleigh's voice was low and commanding and made me even madder.

"Don't you tell me to—"

"I just saved your life. Did you forget that ushi-oni blood is venomous? That stuff on the ground would have been all over you if I hadn't pulled you out of the way." She pointed to a puddle of hissing, bubbling, yellowish liquid that was eating away at the paving stones around it. "And that"—she paused as the sazae-oni made contact with the edge of the puddle and let out an unearthly, rasping shriek as it disintegrated in the venom—"would have been you."

I knew I ought to thank her, but it was just so hard when she was being like this.

On the other hand . . . I sighed.

"Thanks for saving my life," I muttered through my teeth.

Ryleigh shrugged. "It's fine." Then I heard her mumble, "Thanks for saving mine, back there with the suiko. And I saw you fight the nure-onna. You're . . . not bad."

I almost fell over. She didn't have her usual sarcastic smirk plastered on her face. Had she really meant it?

But there were still more yōkai climbing over the edge of the pier, and—I heard their ear-splitting *ka-ka-kaaaa*s before I saw them—a squad of tengu was swooping in from the sky. I recognized the leader as Gara, the tengu who had stolen the legendary sword Dōjikiri right out from under our noses back in the fall. His gigantic booted feet hit the ground and he strode forward, brandishing his staff as he swept the scene with a beady-eyed gaze. The Ryleigh-Momo mutual respect moment would have to wait.

The five of us were now standing back to back, assaulted from all sides by demons and yōkai. It was like they'd been summoned—like they knew we'd be here. The question was, who had summoned them?

The battle went on and on, but no matter how hard we fought, the yōkai kept coming.

"You need to use more power, Momo," said Danny.

"You know I can't risk it!"

"We'll miss the boat unless you do! You don't have to go full rage monster—just, like, seventy percent."

I didn't know what to do. Danny, Jin, Niko, and Ryleigh were fighting with everything they had—I was the only one holding back. If we missed the boat to the Sky Kingdom, it would be my fault. Kusanagi glowed and sent an electric surge up my arms. *Come on, you coward,* it urged me. *We're more powerful than all those monsters put together. Do you want to be the reason this mission fails?*

I didn't. For the second time that night, I took a shaky breath and closed my eyes. *Please let this work.* It was easy—I was already annoyed at Ryleigh for being a stuck-up, super-talented warrior (I know, it wasn't fair of me, but that's how I felt), and angry at myself for not seeing the kami on the pier first—and for forgetting about the ushi-oni venom. Kusanagi sensed the power that was starting to swirl through my body. *Dig deeper,* it urged me. I was angry at Danny, too, for laying our chances for success at my feet and, after all we'd been through, for sometimes acting like we were friends again and sometimes acting like he preferred Ryleigh. Angry at Mom for promising everything would be better and then disappearing and leaving me to deal with this alone—again. Angry at Daikoku, Hotei, and the other Luckies for not helping . . . The effects of my power were already leaking out. My feet were cold and wet from the waves that were sloshing over the pier and flooding the boulevard. I could sense the tengu fighting the wind that had risen up and begun to whirl around them.

Control. Control. I need to take control. But that thought felt small and far away, like a tiny fishing boat on a stormy sea. I poured all my energy into keeping my head above the surface of my anger as wave after wave of rage-fueled power crashed through me. *Open up! Let me out!* my rage monster roared.

No, I told it. *No. Go back where you belong.*

The sound of rushing waves told me a tsunami was building. But through the churn and crash, a clear, strong voice rang out:

Aw, baby, don't be mad
I got your back when things get bad

A tiny golden speck of hope glowed in the whirling darkness.

When you're all in your feelings and you can't get out
Just look me up and gimme a shout

Inside me, the rage monster took a break from trying to drown me so it could roll its eyes. *Are you kidding me with this?* it groaned. In that moment, I saw Jin's warm smile shining like a beacon. He was singing to the hari-onago, but he might as well have been singing to me. Without thinking, I called his name. If I could just get him to look at me, it would help me pull myself back to consciousness.

But when Jin looked my way, he didn't see the hari-onago's next strike coming. He cried out as a lock of hair wrapped itself around his arm, tore through his shirt, and started dragging him forward. But I was afraid to help him—I hadn't regained full control. I was bursting with power and useless at the same time.

"Danny! Help! Niko, Ryleigh! Jin needs help!" I called out.

"Can't!" Danny panted. While I'd been struggling to control Kusanagi and my rage monster, the suiko and tengu had gained the upper hand and were steadily closing in on us. Danny was barely holding off the tengu above us with his arrows, and Ryleigh and Niko were just managing to keep the suiko at bay behind me. I was the only one doing nothing—worse than nothing. I'd taken myself out of the fight *and* I'd put Jin in danger. Jin was pulling desperately at the hair noose around his neck and trying, with his last breaths, to sing.

The tengu's wings beat the air above us; the suikos' eyes gleamed yellow as they snapped their jaws and scrabbled closer and closer.

Then I heard another voice—deeper and older, bright and strong. "Take heart, yo! Help has arrived!"

A tall, muscular man with long hair pulled into a man bun burst out of nowhere and bounded toward us, brandishing a long, shining sword. With him were an enormous yellow dog, a screeching, pink-faced monkey, and a bird with a bright red head, a blue neck, a brilliant green breast, golden wings, and a sweeping white-and-black-striped tail. I didn't need to see the enormous peach embroidered on the front of the guy's hoodie to know that he was Momotarō, the boy who was born from a giant peach and who grew up to defeat an army of oni with the help of his animal friends.

The pheasant attacked the tengu and pecked out their eyes; the monkey leaped onto the back of the hari-onago, pulled out a knife, and began chopping off her needle-hair. She screamed and tore at him, but he was too quick, climbing all around her and swinging on what was left of her long locks. Free of his bonds, Jin grabbed a handful of the hari-onago's writhing hair and began using it to ensnare the suiko and hurl them back into the lake.

Momotarō strode around slashing at suiko and tengu, leaving whirlwinds of black smoke and puddles of oily goo wherever he went. Meanwhile, the yellow dog ran to the wall and started scratching at it as if he were trying to dig his way through to the other side. The nurikabe stopped attacking us and tried to collapse itself onto the dog, but Niko had gotten with the program and started digging in a different spot. I could see the nurikabe giving up—the rain of rocks and hunks of plaster stopped, and the wall began to crumble.

Kusanagi sent a jolt of energy up my arms. *What are you staring at? If you're not going to let me lead, at least let me fight!* it seemed to shout. But now that I finally felt ready to join in, the tengu and the suiko were in full retreat. I hadn't contributed a single thing. I thought of Ryleigh's assets and liabilities chart. I was definitely a liability.

A few minutes later, we stood alone on the pier, catching our breath. "Great fight, young heroes! I'd say I got here just in time, but you weren't doing half bad on your own!" Momotarō went around high-fiving and fist-bumping everyone, and I tried my best to shake off my gloom and look happy. Besides—Momotarō! He's literally the most famous hero in Japan. Everyone looked like they'd forgotten all about the fight for the moment and were trying to get up the courage to ask for a selfie.

"Where did you come from?" Danny asked.

"I was fighting crime somewhere—a bank robbery. And don't ask me where. I just go where they send me." He waved a piece of paper at us. "Anyway, there we were, thwarting the criminals, and the moon rabbit showed up and told me I was needed here. Not the usual protocol, but when Tsukiyomi summons you, you go. But darn it all, I couldn't leave the criminals unthwarted, could I? So we finished up and then popped over to help you. I wish we could've gotten here sooner, but I guess it worked out all right!"

"Is that your job?" Ryleigh wanted to know. "Fighting crime?"

"Well, I am a superhero, after all," said Momotarō with a modest smile. "And that's what we superheroes do. Though I gotta hand it to you young heroes for facing down those monsters without freaking out. Little rabbit told me a coupla you were part kami and a couple were spiritually gifted, but even so, dang. That was a serious attack you were dealing with."

"Thank you, sir," Niko said. "We are eternally grateful for—"

"Uh. You guys?" I'd just noticed something that made my mouth go dry.

"Hush, Momo, don't interrupt. I'm thanking our hero," Niko said crossly before starting over. "We are eternally grateful for your—"

"*Niko.*"

"—altruistic assistance." Niko glared at me. "Please accept our humble and heartfelt—"

"Niko! Stop! This is important!"

Finally, he stopped and sighed. "What is it?"

I pointed because I couldn't even say the words. The *Yume Maru* had hauled anchor and was slowly pulling away from the dock.

"Nooooo!" Danny led us down the pier, waving our arms and shouting. "Wait! Wait! Come back!"

But the crew and passengers of the *Yume Maru* either didn't hear us or didn't care, because they only waved and smiled as the boat turned slowly but steadily away from us and toward the middle of the lake. We kept running, hoping against hope, until the moment when we were about halfway down the pier and the *Yume Maru* rose gracefully out of the water and sailed into the sky.

You're Not Dead, Are You?

We stood there panting until the golden glow of the boat faded away and there was nothing left to stare at but sky. We'd failed before we'd even gotten started. A painful lump formed in my throat and I had to wipe away a couple of tears of frustration. *Stop,* I told myself. *Pull yourself together.* I was *not* going to cry in front of Jin Takayama. Or Ryleigh Guo, for that matter.

"Maybe there's another boat," said Danny hopefully. "That couldn't have been the only one."

"Our tickets were for that boat, and that boat alone," Niko replied gloomily. "Check your pockets."

I plunged my hand into my pocket. Nothing. My other pocket—nothing. All four of us spent the next few seconds frantically checking every pocket in our clothes and searching through our backpacks and bags: nothing.

"Do you think Susano'o and Tsukiyomi would replace them for us?" Jin quavered. "If we asked them nicely?"

But I knew even before Niko shook his head that the answer was no. "It's a miracle that either of them agreed to help us in the first place. Momotarō said Tsukiyomi sent the rabbit to request a rescue—he's already done more than strictly necessary." He looked suspiciously around the pier, which was slowly starting to fill back up with people. "Frankly, I can't help wondering if malicious malcontents are trying to undermine our mission."

"Who, though? We only just *got* our mission," Ryleigh said.

Niko shrugged. "You never know with the kami."

Great, just what we needed: a secret enemy. I had to agree with Ryleigh that it was unlikely, but this attack did seem suspiciously well-timed. Had Tamamo-no-mae planted a bug on us? Or worse, had Izanami set this up to remind me of her claim? The very thought made my stomach do its tied-up-in-knots thing, and I wished that the kami—Susano'o, especially—would try a little harder not to accidentally toss me into the jaws of death.

"What if we tried to get to the Sky Kingdom on our own?" Danny suggested. "Is there a portal like the one at the Golden Gate Bridge that we can use to get to the Sea of Heaven? Maybe the rowboat will meet us and we can ask the dragons to take us to the Sky Kingdom."

"Without orders from one of the Luckies, the dragons' only destination is the *Takarabune*. The *Takarabune* itself only takes orders from the Luckies. And they've already said they won't help us," said Niko.

"Maybe . . . maybe Momotarō can help us?" Jin asked.

We turned around to ask him for advice just in time to see his silhouette, surrounded by the shadowy shapes of his companions, waving from the middle of a shimmery peach-shaped cloud a few feet away. His voice called out faintly, "Gotta go . . . another crime in progress . . . good luck, young heroes . . . ," and he was gone.

I sank to my knees and buried my face in my hands. Despair

didn't even begin to describe what I was feeling. I felt like my soul had been tossed into a garbage truck, mashed up into smelly, slimy mush, and dumped back onto the street to be ground into the pavement by even more garbage trucks.

Why hadn't I done better? If only I could have accessed the full power of Kusanagi without losing control of myself, I could have saved us in time to catch the boat. If only I didn't have to deal with that rage monster—if only I had power that wasn't destructive—like Jin's voice and his charm, or Danny's optimism, or Ryleigh's spycraft skills.

Someone was poking me. "Momo. Momo, look."

"Stop it, Danny," I said, and swatted his hand away. "Leave me alone."

"No, seriously. Look. It's—I think it's Dustin Limbershake! And Wayne 'the Boulder' Thompson. For real! And—and it looks like a boy band. It's not SttTop but—oh, it's TBS. It's a whole big group of stars!"

"Ha-ha."

"Look." Danny physically unfolded my arms and lifted my head up so I could see what he was talking about. Not twenty feet away from us was a crowd of absurdly good-looking people that did, in fact, include Dustin Limbershake, the Boulder, and TBS, the most popular boy band of the decade.

My first thought was that maybe there was some kind of awards show going on, or maybe a huge movie premiere. The Boulder was Dad's favorite movie star, and I suddenly felt myself wanting to ask for his autograph, even though I knew Dad would never see it. It was strange how the most random things

(I mean, *the Boulder*? Really?) could make my heart ache with longing for Dad.

I was still mulling this over when Ryleigh said, "Something's weird."

We watched the stars stroll past us, all dressed up in fancy clothes and sunglasses.

"They don't have coats on?" said Danny.

"There's no fans or paparazzi," Jin said. "No one's even looking at them."

"Omigosh, you're right! I don't think anyone can see them but us!" Danny said.

"But how can that be? They're real people. Unless—" I gulped. Could the unthinkable have happened to all of these stars all at once?

"No, they're all still alive. There's nothing on social media about them," said Ryleigh, scrolling through her phone.

"Are they impersonators?" I asked. We'd started following them without even thinking about it. We were now headed up a broad set of steps to the second level of the pier, which was home to a mini–amusement park with a Ferris wheel, a carousel, and a mini-golf course.

"No, I know the TBS guys. That's definitely Ashwin and Fabian, and that's Malcolm and Lex . . . and Zeke's bleached his hair and grown a mustache, but I'd know him anywhere," said Jin. "Zeke and I did this awesome event together in New York City last year with Beyonc—"

Danny groaned loudly. "Seriously? Like, you tell us you just want an average life, but then you're always talking about all the famous-person stuff you do. You're acting like the exact oppo-site of the person you said you wanted to be."

Jin turned red. "But—"

"I'm right, though. Am I right?" Danny turned to the rest of us.

"Kinda?" I said. Danny's words were harsh, but he was being fair, for once.

Niko nodded, too, and Ryleigh smiled apologetically at Jin. "He has a point," she said.

"Hm." Jin pressed his lips together and didn't say anything for a few seconds. Then he said, "Fine. Point taken." He let out a breath. "But I can still ask them for help, right?"

"I didn't say don't ask them for help. I just said don't pre-tend you hate being famous," said Danny.

"But I—"

"Whatever. Fine. Some of it stinks. But you gotta admit that some of it's great and that you kinda show off about it sometimes."

Jin grimaced. "I don't mean to show off. It's literally my life." Danny rolled his eyes and Jin added hastily, "But I get it. I'll be more . . . low-key about it. Okay?"

"Fine," Danny said. He glanced at the stars, who still hadn't noticed us. "So are you gonna ask for help, or what?"

Jin grinned, waved at the group, and called out, "Hey! Zeke!"

Zeke looked over and smiled when he saw Jin. "Jin! Wass-uuup! Look, guys, it's Jin Takayama! Bro, how you been! I haven't seen you since the Beyoncé thing!"

Jin rushed over and did a bunch of those combination handshake-snaps with the TBS guys, and then shook hands with Dustin Limbershake and the Boulder.

"What are you guys doing here?" he asked.

"We're on our way to the Sky Kingdom!" said Zeke. "We're performing at the New Year's Eve Festival."

"The Sky Kingdom . . . New Year's Eve Festival?" Jin looked back at us. "But how . . ."

"We've got stars—that's how you qualify."

"Stars?" Jin repeated.

"Yeah. You know—a Hollywood star. Like on the Walk of Fame," said Ashwin, pointing to a golden star on the back of his hand before running that hand through the dark ringlets that made his fans swoon.

Now that he'd pointed it out, I saw that all the famous spirits gathered around us had little golden stars on their hands, like stickers.

"Wait—where's your star?" Fabian asked. "You're—you're not dead, are you?" He reached out his finger and gave Jin a cautious poke, and Jin stumbled backward. "Oops. I guess not. Sorry, bro."

"Anyway, we qualified. And then last week, we got an invitation and a visa. Show 'em the visa, bro," Zeke said.

Lex, the quiet, serious one, stepped forward and brandished an official-looking piece of paper that said:

GROUP TOURIST VISA

NAME: TBS
OCCUPATION: BOY BAND
NUMBER IN GROUP: 5
STATUS: QUASI-KAMI

"Quasi-kami," Niko gasped. "Manifestations of people who are worshipped as gods on earth, but who haven't passed into the spirit realm yet. I've heard of them but I've never seen one before."

"So you're not . . . real?" Jin asked.

"Our human selves are out there in the human world," Zeke said. "But just because we aren't attached to human bodies doesn't mean we're not real."

"But what about you? If you're not dead and you don't have a star . . ." Fabian's forehead wrinkled as he tried to puzzle it out.

Zeke let out a whoop. "You're human! Bro! You are! How are you able to see us? Are you going to the Sky Kingdom, too? Can you? I thought humans couldn't get in."

"I'm . . . basically human," Jin said. "But I'm going to the Sky Kingdom, too. It's complicated."

"Hey, I don't mean to be rude, but how are *you* guys getting to the Sky Kingdom? The yacht already left." Ryleigh butted in. Rudely. Though I'd been wondering the same thing. "And omigosh I'm, like, such a huge fan! Like, I'm *literally* dying right now."

"The yacht's for fancy kami," Ashwin explained. "It's total first class—free food, private cabins, the works. But us quasi-kami have to go that way, on the Ferry wheel." He pointed ahead of us at the giant Ferris wheel.

"Uh, don't you mean 'Ferris wheel'?" Danny said.

"Uh, no." Ashwin looked at Danny like he felt sorry for someone who knew so little about the world. He spoke slowly, as if explaining something to a toddler. "I mean *Ferry* wheel.

There's a special compartment that's actually a ferry between here and the Sky Kingdom."

"Oh. Okay, got it. Cool, cool, cool," said Danny, giving Ashwin a double thumbs-up and not looking cool at all.

Ashwin went on. "Anyway, you go through security at TSA, and then sit in this crowded cabin without any free food, and *then* you get dropped off way outside the freezing-cold Tortoise Gate on the north side of the city, instead of at the nice warm Vermilion Phoenix Gate on the south side. And you enter the city with the quasi-kami performer's visa."

"TSA?" Jin asked.

"Transitional Spirit Authority," said Fabian. "Kinda like at airports, but you don't have to take your shoes off."

I looked at the dark waters of Lake Michigan and felt the loss of our golden coins all over again.

"Hey, bro, are you okay?" Jin's voice brought me back. I turned to see Zeke flickering, like an old fluorescent lightbulb or a bad phone signal. Panic and confusion were written across his face as he looked down at himself.

"Wha—hap—ing?" he sputtered. "Why—dis—pear—?"

"Zeke! What's going on? What're you doing?" Fabian tried to grab Zeke by the arms but his fists closed on air.

"Oh no." Ryleigh stared at her phone. "TBS management has just announced that due to a shoplifting accusation that surfaced earlier today, they're cutting ties with Zeke Su. They say they wish him the best of luck and they hope he finds help. Auditions for his replacement will begin in the new year."

"His star is already fading," Niko said, pointing to Zeke's

sputtering hand. He was right—even in the moments when Zeke was fully visible, the glowing star on his hand was almost gone.

"But—nev—shoplift—! I've—framed! Someone—out—get me!" Zeke wailed.

Ashwin, Malcolm, Lex, and Fabian looked at each other and back at Zeke, their eyes wide with terror. "Am I still here?" Fabian asked.

The others nodded. "Uh-huh. Am I?" they asked him.

Fabian nodded back.

"What a bummer," said Dustin Limbershake. "Same thing happened to my bandmates when I was a kid—they faded into obscurity. I'm the only one left."

"Nooooo . . ." Zeke's voice seemed to come from far away— I could only catch the occasional glimmer of an outline now. The other four band members looked like they might be sick.

"Hey, don't look so sad. It's not like he's dead," Dustin said. "Real-life Zeke is alive and well. And you never know—he might shake this scandal and come back to TBS and be famous again. And the rest of you are still here, which means you still have a famous future ahead of you, as long as your luck holds. And that's all that matters!"

We were silent for a moment, wondering about luck. And whether fame and fortune were really all that mattered. At least, that's what I was wondering. Then Ashwin moaned, "What are we gonna do for our performance? We can't go on without Zeke."

The others looked stunned.

"We're gonna have to rechoreograph every piece! We're

gonna have to reassign the solos! The biggest event of my entire spirit life could be *ruined* because Zeke decided he didn't want to pay for a pair of pants! What're we supposed to do now?"

"First of all, we don't know that's what happened. And second, I don't know! I don't know!" Malcolm shouted back. The entire band started arguing and moaning and waving their hands around until suddenly, Ryleigh broke in.

"Hey—what if Jin joined you? I'm sure he can do all of Zeke's parts."

Everyone turned to stare at Ryleigh, and then at Jin, who looked startled, and then reluctant. "I can't take Zeke's place," he said. "That would be disrespectful."

"It would be easier than adjusting the choreography," said Lex uncertainly.

"It could be like a special guest appearance," added Fabian.

"But . . . isn't he, you know. Mortal?" Malcolm asked.

"No, he's not. The thing is—"

"Wait." I cut Ryleigh off. She looked just as surprised as I felt. But I felt a little ambushed by this sudden change in plans—okay, okay, we didn't *have* a plan to start with. So let's say I felt a little ambushed by this . . . plan. If it even was a plan. "Can you excuse us a moment, please?" I said to TBS-minus-Zeke. I motioned to Danny, Niko, Jin, and Ryleigh to step aside with me. "We just need to discuss something really quick."

Do I Get My Way, or What?

"Thank you, Momo!" Niko said once we'd huddled up. Then he turned on Ryleigh. "What is *wrong* with you? Have you crossed your crayons? Have you gone out of your gourd? Broken your brain? Misplaced your marbles?"

Thank goodness Niko was already on my side.

Ryleigh held up her hand. "Just listen for a sec, okay? If Jin joins those guys, it could be really good for us. He'll be around the palace for rehearsals, and he'll have access to areas and people that we won't. And maybe he could get us free tickets, or maybe even backstage passes."

"But, um, shouldn't we be focused on stealing the Mirror of the Sun? Because I—I think that, um, saving those kids should be more important than, um, front-row seats at a TBS concert." I hated how I sounded—way to be assertive, Momo!

Ryleigh rolled her eyes. "We can trade those tickets for favors, duh. Or information."

"Ooh, like real spies! Sick!" Danny said, his eyes sparkling.

"Right?" Ryleigh sparkled back at him.

Even Jin was nodding slowly now, like he might be climbing on board this runaway train.

"But how do we even make it into the Sky Kingdom? We don't have visas! And isn't Jin supposed to have a star on his hand?" I asked.

Ryleigh reached into her little black handbag and pulled out her gold gel pen. "Gimme your hand," she commanded, and Jin obediently stretched out his hand. She drew and colored in a gold star on it. Like that was going to fool anyone. "Done. Anyway, TBS has a group visa, remember? And they can just say we're part of the crew or whatever. Bands like TBS and SttTop have tons of people who go with them everywhere on tour, right, Jin? I bet you all skip security at the airport, right?"

Jin nodded again, slowly. "Yeah, but that's only if—"

"And I bet you've gotten your friends into all kinds of parties and clubs without invitations," said Danny.

"Well, yeah, but—"

"But this is a preposterous plan!" Niko cut in.

"No, it's not. Jin is *friends* with people who've been *invited to perform at the palace*. He's our best shot at getting in!" Ryleigh said.

"I don't think getting into parties is quite the same thing as getting into the Sky Kingdom," I said.

"Yeah, I'm with you," said Jin.

"Oh, okay," Ryleigh said, crossing her arms and giving me her meanest Mean Girl Death Glare. "If you're so smart, do you have a better idea?"

Of course she'd get mad at me, and not Jin or Niko. Of course she thought she could push me around, just like she always did. She and Danny were acting like the Sky Kingdom was going to be just like seventh grade, where if you're popular, you do whatever you want. My head started to buzz and my hands started to tingle. I felt Danny grab my arm and pull me aside.

"What?" I yanked my arm back.

"Hey. Calm down. Now's not a great time to go full rage monster." He chuckled nervously.

"Why should I calm down?" I burst out. "Ryleigh's idea is terrible and you know it. You're only going along with it because . . . I don't know why. Because she's pretty." I was struck with a sudden realization. "She's just like Tamamo-no-mae," I said.

Danny's mouth fell open. "That's not even true!"

"Oh, puh-leeze." I did a Ryleigh-level eye roll.

"You *really* don't like her, huh," he said sadly.

"Would *you* like someone who spent the last three years treating you like a total loser?" I demanded. "And she's always putting me down in front of you."

He grimaced. "I don't like that stuff, either, you know. I've told her to stop."

"Well, she hasn't. And ever since you and I started being friends again, she's been trying to get between us."

"No, she hasn't!" Danny seemed relieved to be able to deny something, but I was not about to let him or Ryleigh off the hook.

I glared at him. "She's always getting you to take her side. Like just now. All she wants is to go to a free TBS concert."

But Danny glared back. "It's her friends who are being held hostage. And her parents. And my friends and my parents. Do you think we don't want to save them as much as you do? Do you actually think we care more about getting in with a bunch of famous singers and scoring free concert tickets than we do about our own *families?*"

I couldn't argue with that. I crossed my arms and looked away.

"I just don't see why you're friends with a girl like her."

"She's not as bad as you think. She's pretty cool when you get to know her."

"I think the problem is that *she* doesn't want to get to know *me.*"

Danny groaned. "It's not that. It's just . . . it's complicated."

I rolled my eyes.

"Look, I'll talk to her about . . . about how she treats you. Okay?"

"Whatever," I said. I was pretty sure "talking to her" wasn't going to make a difference, and anyway, I was getting tired of this argument.

"But, um, I really do think we should listen to Ryleigh. She's good at plans and strategies stuff. I mean, she's a ninja!"

"You literally just found that out tonight."

"All I'm saying is that she's not messing around."

I heaved a sigh. "Fine. But I don't like making it up as we go. It just doesn't seem safe."

"Making it up as we go is my brand, bruh," Danny said with a grin.

"It's not mine," I said.

"I know. But look, at least we'll get to the Sky Kingdom, right? If we don't make it in on the TBS visa, we'll figure something else out."

"That's what I'm trying to say, Danny! Jin might be

believable as part of TBS, but we *definitely* won't make it on their visa. We need to have our own papers! It's not like we can just pull them out of thin air . . ."

Danny and I looked at each other. We checked our backpacks.

"I hate these things," I said when we came up with nothing.

Danny nodded and looked back at the others. Then he smiled and said, "I've got another idea. What if . . ."

Once he'd explained it to me, I couldn't believe I hadn't thought of it myself.

"Just call me Dan, the man with the plan," Danny said smugly.

We went back, and Ryleigh looked at us with an expectant smile that said, *So? Do I get my way, or what?*

"Operation Jin Joins TBS for the win!" Danny declared, and Ryleigh's smile turned into a triumphant little grin.

It didn't take long for Jin to convince the TBS guys to let him join them. And when he came back, I turned to Ryleigh and said, "Do you have any notebook paper we could use?"

Ryleigh narrowed her eyes at me and put a protective hand on her bag. "Why?" But when she heard that this was Danny's idea, she happily dug out a piece of paper.

I gave the paper to Niko. "Do you have enough magic to make that into a visa?"

His face lit up. "Of course! Our own personal papers! Why didn't I think of that? Jin, fetch me that visa so I can render a reasonable replica."

Jin went back to TBS and returned with their visa. Soon we

were the proud owners of a fake Sky Kingdom visa for a band called Niko and the Noisemakers—Niko's idea, of course.

"How long will the illusion last?" Ryleigh asked.

"Long enough," Niko said. Then he cleared his throat and added, "Most likely." I found that a little worrisome, but I didn't want to make Niko feel bad.

"Just watch. It's gonna be fine," said Danny as we rejoined the quasi-kami.

I wasn't so sure. But once we got in line, things went surprisingly well. A bored-looking turtle in a uniform and a badge barely looked at us as he waved us through to the TSA scanning station.

"Next!" A white cat put its paw up and beckoned to Dustin Limbershake, who sauntered through with no problem. Then the Boulder passed through, then Lex, Malcolm, Ashwin, and Fabian, and finally Jin. "Here goes nothing," he breathed, and strutted through the archway like he was walking onstage.

No alarms went off, no guards came running. The mortality-hiding perfume had worked. I let out a sigh of relief.

Being an actual magical fox, Niko did not need perfume, and pranced through the arch with the tip of his tail bobbing jauntily to and fro. Ryleigh, Danny, and I passed through without a problem. Thank goodness *something* had finally gone right.

The giant wheel in front of us turned. A carriage the size of a train car came to rest at ground level, and its doors slid open to reveal probably the most beautiful Ferris wheel compartment in the kami-verse. The interior was made of polished dark wood, with richly upholstered benches along the sides and plush red carpet on the floor. Chandeliers swung gently from the ceiling, and a few framed posters advertised hotels and upcoming events in Celestial City. "There's us!" Fabian said, pointing to one of them. At the far end of the car was a television monitor showing a news program. The anchor kami was announcing in bland, neutral tones that the weather in Celestial City would be sunny and warm and that Amabie had predicted that this year's New Year's Eve celebration would be a blast.

A few more quasi-kami crowded in after us: I recognized a couple of movie stars and a rock star or two. Danny poked me. "Look, it's Wayne Steak!" He was the rock star whose wrecked car had come out of the lake and driven us to the portal to the Land of Roots in the fall. Steak swaggered into the cabin, fist-bumping some folks and glaring at others. Then he sat down and pulled out a battered paperback book. I snuck a peek at the cover. It said *Pride and Prejudice*.

"What a boring title," said Danny.

I had to agree.

The last to enter was a group of little old ladies who chattered and giggled and clucked together like chickens. A few of them wore glowing star deely-bopper headbands, a few had on those little fairy-light necklaces, and they all carried strings of jingle bells, like they were about to go Christmas caroling.

"Who's that?" I whispered to Niko.

"They're stars," he whispered back. "Real ones. From the Gemini constellation."

The door slammed shut, and the car gave a lurch and a shudder. A satiny-smooth voice announced, "We are now departing for the Sky Kingdom. Please keep your hands inside the car at all times. Estimated time of arrival: dawn." Everyone cheered. I knelt on a bench and looked out the window as the pier fell away and the people on the ground faded into the shadows. The skyscrapers transformed into skinny building blocks speckled with light, then melted into the bright orange grid of the city. The grid became a glowing orange blob surrounded by the darkness of farmland to the west and the lake to the east.

I had slipped into a pleasant, dozy little nap when Niko jabbed me awake.

"What?" I said, a little crossly.

In response, he pointed at the monitor. Underneath the news anchor was a chyron that read BREAKING NEWS: DEMON TAMAMO-NO-MAE CONFIRMED TO BE AT LARGE IN MIDDLE LANDS. The anchor kami was saying in her detached, news-anchorly voice, "The nine-tailed fox demon has been abducting mortal children by the hundreds; authorities on terrestrial demon behavior suspect she is planning a major comeback on New Year's Eve. Earthly kami connected with human communities have been overwhelmed by requests for protection and have, in turn, asked the Celestial Peacekeeping Forces for divine intervention." Behind her, the screen flashed a series of clips of crying human families praying at shrines, temples, and churches. "Of course, the CPF have a noninterventionist policy regarding earthly demons, so the Middle Lands will probably suffer heavily at the hands of Tamamo-no-mae in the near future. We will keep you updated on the situation as it unfolds. Such a shame. So sad for those poor Middle Lands folks." The anchor kami sighed and shook her head, and her face took on a sorrowful expression, which she held for about a second

131

before putting on a pleasant smile and saying, "On a lighter note, we take you now to our weekly segment, 'Meet a Municipal Kami,' where we talk to one of the many wonderful kami who keep Celestial City running. This week, our featured guest is Mizumaki-no-kami, who is part of the crew that keeps our sewer system flowing."

"Celestial City has sewers?" Danny wrinkled his nose and then his eyes glinted in a way that told me he was about to say something gross. "What do you think kami poop smells like?"

"Why do you insist on being disgusting?" Niko complained.

"I was just curious," Danny grumbled. "Jeez."

"You should be curious about why Tamamo-no-mae has made it onto the nightly news. The Kami News Network rarely covers Middle Lands events unless they are extremely . . . extreme."

"But it doesn't sound like they *think* it's important," I said. "It doesn't sound like they're going to do anything about it."

"No, I don't suppose they will. Doesn't your country cover news of extreme events in other places without any intention of intervening?"

It was true. How depressing. And terrifying. In spite of myself, I'd gotten a bit caught up in the excitement of battles and secret identities. The reminder that real people were at stake—real kids and real families whose lives depended on us—made me want to run away and hide. On top of that, thinking about families made me think about Mom, and my heart tightened with worry.

I looked at the others: Jin was busy scribbling in his notebook again, mumbling, "extremely extreme . . . don't intend . . . to intervene." Ryleigh had wandered off toward the star aunties. Danny smiled at me.

"We got this," he said. "We're Team DaMoNik, remember?" He put one arm around my shoulder and put his other fist out for me to bump. That made me feel a little less alone and a little more hopeful.

"Team DaMoNik," I repeated gratefully.

"Actually . . ." Danny looked thoughtful. "Now it's RyJin DaMoNik. Like, Raging Demonic, get it? We're even better than we were before."

"Even with Jin?" I asked, just to bug him.

"I mean, he can be annoying, like he thinks he's so *mature* and *sophisticated* and he's all, 'Let's discuss this,' and 'Let's discuss that.'" Danny deepened his voice to mimic Jin's. "But I guess he's cool underneath it all. And his powers are kinda cool. I dunno. The more, the merrier, right?"

"Yeah." I couldn't quite say the same for Ryleigh, but at least Danny seemed to be making his peace with Jin.

Meanwhile, Ryleigh was chatting up the star aunties. I heard her say in a voice as sweet and light as cotton candy, "Are you really stars from Gemini?"

"Yes, that's right, dear!" A star auntie in a lavender jacket bobbed her head, and her silver deely-boppers snapped and sparkled. "We always visit the Middle Lands in December, and then we stop in Celestial City for the New Year's celebrations on our way back home."

"Ooh, how exciting! I've always wanted to meet a real star.

This is my first time visiting Celestial City. What's it like? Have you ever been to the palace?" Ryleigh clasped her hands and made gigantic Disney princess eyes.

Lavender Jacket Auntie leaned forward and said, "My great-grandniece is a sunset spirit, and *she* has served at court for the last two hundred years."

"As a kitchen maid," snorted a pink-haired auntie. "Don't give yourself airs."

"But that's so exciting! I'd give anything to work in the palace." Ryleigh let loose a sigh so full of longing that she seemed to be channeling Cinderella, Ariel, Mulan, and Moana all at once. "Just for a day, even as a kitchen maid. It would be a dream come true." I half expected her to break into song.

"Well, it's certainly better than being a stablehand," said Lavender Jacket Auntie with a sideways look at Pink-Haired Auntie, whose face turned the same color as her hair.

"Working with the horses is an honorable vocation!" she sputtered.

"Ooh, I *love* horses!" Ryleigh simpered. "They're my favorite."

"It's such a shame, though. My poor niece lives on the palace grounds but she has to miss the New Year's Eve concert. They ought to give the palace staff the night off on such a special occasion," Lavender Jacket Auntie said.

By the time the melodious voice announced our approach to the Sky Kingdom, Ryleigh was the Gemini aunties' favorite little girl in the kami-verse. "You must get in touch with my niece!" Lavender Jacket Auntie gushed, handing her a slip of paper. "Her name is Kabo. Here's her information."

"And my nephew! Ask for Nobu," interjected Pink-Haired Auntie, passing over another slip of paper.

"You'll get along wonderfully, my dear, I just know it!"

Lavender Jacket Auntie held out a handful of star-shaped candies wrapped in cellophane. "One for you and each of your darling little friends," she said. "Just pop it in your mouth when you want to get somewhere quickly, and name your destination. Mind you, they're just little candies, so their portals don't go very far."

Ryleigh called Jin over from the far end of the cabin, where he'd been boy-band-bonding with TBS, and we took one candy each. I examined mine. It was bright red, and a tiny light pulsed at its center. I wondered what it would taste like. If I ate it right now, where would I go?

"Don't look at it too long, or you'll eat it and open a portal right on the spot." A tiny wrinkled hand appeared on top of my own. I realized that I'd already unwrapped the candy and was about to pop it into my mouth.

Aaand I'd proven myself unworthy *again*. I put it in my pocket, hoping no one else had witnessed my humiliation. "I'm sorry," I said.

Pink-Haired Auntie gave me a wink. "Don't be. I know who you are."

"I—I don't know what you're talking about." I looked around, panicked. Had anyone heard her? Did she mean what I thought she meant?

"I'm sure you have your reasons for going undercover. But you would do well to accept that you are who you are, and let that *be* who you are. Because the path before you will only lead you

135

where you need to go if you are who you are. If you catch my meaning."

I most definitely did not catch her meaning. Her meaning whizzed right over my head and circled it like a fly before buzzing away for good. But I nodded anyway, and she gave me another wink before tottering off to join her friends and leaving me to hope she was just an eccentric old auntie who enjoyed giving unsolicited, unintelligible advice to unsuspecting tweens.

"Now entering the Sky Kingdom," said the announcer voice, and everyone flocked to the windows. At first all I could see was the deep blue nothingness of the night sky. But then I looked up and saw light filtering down through a glimmering, rippling surface—we were underwater! Soon, we had broken through and were skimming along the surface of the Sea of Heaven. Everyone flocked to the windows to ooh and aah at the sparkling water and the rosy, dawn-pink sky all around us.

We flew up onto the shore and across a lush summer landscape of deep green leaves and bright tropical flowers, and then over miles and miles of sunlit rice fields lined with maple leaves in full autumn color. The carriage swerved, and we entered a snowy-white world dotted here and there with frozen ponds and bare trees hung with icicles.

Not long afterward, the northern wall of Celestial City came into view. It was tall and gray, with enormous brambly bushes running along its base. It looked like it was miles long. I could see intricate designs carved around what must have been a doorway in the center, but my view of the door itself was blocked by a geodesic dome of some kind. It was smooth, solid, and black, like it was made of a bunch of giant sheets of obsidian.

Everyone around us began taking their visas out. Niko waved our enchanted visa at us and smiled. *Please let this work,* I prayed.

Then we were all trudging through the snow toward the city's forbidding northern wall and the big round dome in front of it. As we got closer, the giant dome rose out of the snow. That is, it sprouted a head the size of an SUV at the end of a neck the length of a school bus, and rose up on four legs so thick you could have driven the SUV and the school bus right through each one, side by side. It wasn't a dome at all. It was Genbu, the Black Tortoise of the North.

Interesssting

"WHO . . . APPROACHES . . . THE SACRED . . . NORTHERN . . . GATE?"

Genbu's voice reverberated like a gong in a deep, dark cavern. As he spoke, a huge black snake slithered out of a hole in the ground and wrapped herself around his body a couple of times before sweeping her hog-nosed head down to our level and fixing all of us with a glittering, beady-eyed stare.

"Ssstate your name and purpossse," she hissed. Her voice wound around us and between us like a deadly strand of silk. "No falsssehoodsss, or I'll ssstrangle you."

I froze on the spot, but my heart took off like a jackrabbit.

"I forgot about the serpent! We're crushed as cracker crumbs," Niko moaned. "Sunk as sea snails."

"Shh!" Ryleigh glared at him. "How are they going to believe us if you act like that? You have to act like we *deserve* to get in."

"Exactly." Danny nodded emphatically at Ryleigh, like they were On the Same Page. *You and me, we get it,* he seemed to be saying. *Fake it till you make it.*

I have *to learn how to do that,* I thought.

The Gemini aunties fluttered their papers and were waved through with hardly a glance. The Hollywood stars took longer to process; Genbu and the snake examined them one by one. We inched forward. How much longer would Niko's fake visa last? My breath was coming faster, and as I struggled to slow it down, it occurred to me that if I were really a spirit—even a quasi-kami—I probably wouldn't have to breathe. I probably wouldn't even have a heartbeat. Could the snake tell? Every time she glanced my way, I felt sure it was because she'd heard my heart thundering, a dead giveaway of our impostor status—*dead* being the key word.

"Hey." Ryleigh jabbed me with a sharp elbow. "Calm down!"

"I'm *trying* to."

She let out an exasperated huff. "Do, like, box breathing. Breathe in while you count to four. Then hold your breath for four. Then breathe out for four, and then rest for four. Keep doing it until you calm down."

I really didn't want to do anything Ryleigh told me to do, but I noticed she was doing it, too. Maybe she needed to calm down as much as I did. So I tried.

In, two, three, four.

Hold, two, three, four.

Out, two, three, four.

Hold, two, three, four.

It took a few rounds, and I don't know if it was a physical thing or a mental thing, but Ryleigh's box breathing technique worked. By the time we were second in line, my heart and my lungs were back under control—though just barely, and only as long as I concentrated fully on breathing. Of course, this made me anxious in a new way because if I was focused on breathing it meant I wasn't figuring out whether to fight, run, or grovel when our identities were inevitably exposed.

It was TBS and Jin's turn before ours. They stood in front of Genbu, who peered at them for approximately five days (well, that's what it felt like, anyway) before he said, "YOUR . . . IDENTIFICATION?"

"We're TBS," Lex said in a shaky voice. "We're performing at the New Year's Eve party."

He thrust his visa out for Genbu to see. Genbu squinted at it, and the snake swooped down to examine it as well. Lex's hand trembled and the paper shook. "Hold sssstilll!" she snapped. "You're giving me a headache!" Lex squirmed and turned pale but managed to keep his hand steady.

The tortoise looked at the visa, humming and muttering to himself; the air seemed to pulse with the low thrum of his voice. Meanwhile, the snake stared at each member of the band in turn. When she got to Jin, she drew herself right up to his face and her tongue flicked, as if she were tasting the air around him.

"Sssusspiciousss," she hissed.

Genbu tilted his great head and stared at Jin, still humming.

I held my breath. Forget box breathing—I felt like if I didn't beam my entire attention on the current situation, it would all fall apart.

But Jin didn't flinch. He didn't even blink. And an eternity later, Genbu droned, "ALL . . . IS . . . IN ORDER." I let out a sigh of relief. I felt like I might crumple to the ground like a pile of dirty laundry.

"But sssir," the snake protested.

"YOU . . . MAY . . . PASS."

The snake withdrew, looking sulky.

"Okay, then! Let's go, fellas! Before anyone changes their mind, heh, heh!" Ashwin chuckled, with a sideways glance at the snake.

But Jin didn't move. "I think we should wait for our friends."

"Bruh!" Ashwin had already walked several steps along the path. "Come *on*!"

"No, guys, I really think—"

"Don't delay, you dithering donkey." Niko's voice was low and urgent. "Go. We'll catch up." And even though I knew he was right, I wished he hadn't said it.

Jin gave us a wild, desperate look. "But—"

Malcolm clapped Jin on the back and said, "Great idea! Let's do what the fox says, huh?" He and Lex each took one of Jin's arms, and finally, Jin seemed to give in.

"I'll see you in there, okay? Right? Look for me! I'll talk to you soon!" He gave us one last agonized smile before allowing himself to be half dragged, half pushed toward the city.

And then it was our turn. Genbu hummed and muttered over the paper in Niko's outstretched paw, and the snake lowered her head so she could look into our eyes.

"Box breathing," Ryleigh murmured from the other side of Danny, who was next to me.

Danny repeated under his breath, "Box breathing."

I closed my eyes and began breathing boxes like my life depended on it—who knew, maybe it did.

"I think I'll ssstart with thisss one," the snake's voice hissed in my ear. My heart and lungs burst right out of the boxes I'd been building with my breath and galloped away from me, practically screaming bloody murder. As I struggled to get back under control, I felt the snake's thoughts slide into my head, and everything around me seemed to stop moving.

Who are you? she whispered—the question slithered around my brain, poking its nose into corners, making loops and lassos like it was hoping to snag something it could use against me. *I am part of Niko and the Noisemakers,* I tried to answer, but the thought slipped away from me like a fish, as if it knew it didn't really belong in my head. I tried breathing again: *In, two, three, four*—but the snake flicked her tongue and the numbers scattered like leaves in the wind. Why was this so hard?

I'd been able to survive looking Susano'o in the eye— something regular humans couldn't do. I *had* to be able to do this.

Snap.

The snake caught the memory in her jaws and coiled herself around it: me looking into Susano'o's eyes and feeling like I'd been tossed into a hurricane, and how he'd praised me afterward for not losing my mind.

Sssusssano'o . . . Interesssting. I heard the surprise in her voice.

How had she seen that? What else could she see? Desperately, I tried to close my mind, but now that this crucial memory had leaked, it was as if a dam had burst; images and memories came flooding out, and I was helpless to stop them. The snake snapped them up at random as they surged by.

Mom telling me she had to leave.

Snap.

Arguing with Danny about Ryleigh's party. Ryleigh shoving me off the stage.

Snap. Snap.

All those kids trapped in Tamamo-no-mae's spirit bubble. The blue fire, the whips, the way the onibi had attacked us near the Golden Gate Bridge.

Snap. Snap. Snap.

The more I fought, the more my thoughts and memories spun out of control, until I felt myself being sucked into the vortex of my worst memory of all:

The cave on the Island of Mysteries . . . Izanami telling me she was the source of my power . . .

"WHAT . . . IS . . . THIS?" Genbu's voice boomed into the memory, and everything seemed to happen at once. The snake withdrew from my brain and I heard myself gasp. The fog lifted and I was back on the snowy field with Danny, Ryleigh, and Niko.

"Imposssstersss! Evildoersss!" the snake screamed from above.

The air in front of us began to shimmer and sputter, like a mirage, or a glitch in a video game.

"Follow me!" Ryleigh shouted, and disappeared into the glitch—only to be spat back out almost instantly, looking dazed.

"Sssilly girl!" The snake hissed with laughter as Ryleigh

staggered to her feet. "You cannot open a portal through the gatessss of Celessstial City with a mere wishing ssstar!"

Someone far in the distance was shouting, "This way! This way!" but I couldn't move. I looked up to see the snake's pink mouth wide open and her gleaming fangs rushing toward me. *I'm dead,* I thought. A hand grabbed me around the wrist, and I was yanked into darkness.

Ill-Advised, Imprudent, and Irresponsible

When I opened my eyes, we were standing in front of a golden field of rice. The sun shone warm on my shoulders, a mild autumn breeze ruffled my hair, and the horrible snake was nowhere to be seen. A procession of carts loaded down with rice trundled past us toward Celestial City, which lay in the distance behind the same forbidding wall that we'd seen from the North Gate. Each cart was pulled by a black-and-white-spotted horse and driven by a short, cheery-looking farmer. But in spite of the pleasant surroundings, I felt a dull ache in my chest. If it hadn't been for me, we'd be on our way inside the North Gate instead of . . . wherever we were.

"Where are we?" Danny asked.

In response, Niko held up an empty portal candy wrapper. "I asked it to take us to an alternative access point." He looked around. "I assume from the autumnal atmosphere that we are on the western side of the city. But as Ryleigh has proven, our portal candies aren't powerful enough to get us inside, so we'll have to rely on our wits rather than our wishes."

So that was what had happened with Ryleigh and the

glitch—she must have tried to open a portal through the city wall and been rejected.

"I didn't know! How was I supposed to know?" Ryleigh said angrily.

Danny tried to soothe her. "Hey, it's okay. It could have happened to any of us."

"No. It's not okay. It shouldn't have happened to *me*." Ryleigh began pacing furiously up and down. "You know what? It doesn't matter that I didn't know. I should have been prepared. I should have thought it through. I should have asked for something more general, like Niko did."

"But we're okay now," Danny said. "And you meant well."

"Meaning well isn't enough," she snapped. "Not when there's hundreds of kids and maybe even our parents' lives on the line." She looked away, breathing heavily, and I saw the slightest glint of a tear in the corner of her right eye.

I was shocked to realize that I kind of wanted to give her a hug. She was being so hard on herself, and for a mistake that any of us could have made, like Danny had said. But hugging the girl I'd hated/envied/feared for years felt a little (a lot) awkward, so instead I took a deep breath and said, "Hey—you're only human."

But she took it all wrong. "Oh, that's right, I forgot. Thanks for rubbing it in, Miss Demi-kami. I'm sorry I'm *only human*. Maybe if I were as awesome and powerful as you are, I wouldn't have failed so hard."

I could only blink at her in astonishment. "What? That's not—I didn't—I wasn't—" Where was my rage monster, and *why* couldn't I stand up to Ryleigh without it? Finally, I mumbled, "I only meant that everyone makes mistakes."

"Not you, apparently," Ryleigh sniffed.

"Huh?" Hadn't the snake called me out in front of everyone? The dull ache that had been sitting in my chest for the past few minutes intensified. It was my fault that we'd been discovered. My failure that had forced Ryleigh to try to open a portal through the wall. I'd let us down every time it mattered—not to mention those kids back home, and Ryleigh's, Jin's, and Danny's parents.

"I'm to blame!" Niko wailed. "Genbu saw through my illusion and revealed the fakery!" He held up a slightly crumpled piece of notebook paper. "Ryleigh saw it happen, and she opened that first portal—that's the only reason I knew to ask for alternative access. I'm not clever at all; I'm a dim-witted disaster." He flopped to the ground and covered his eyes with his paws.

So . . . it wasn't just me who'd failed. The ache in my chest eased a little bit. For a moment, I considered letting Ryleigh keep thinking that I was perfect—it might be nice, for a change. But when I saw how miserable she and Niko were, I knew I couldn't.

"I let her in," I said quietly. "The snake, I mean. She figured out I was a fake. She saw . . . all kinds of things." I decided not to say what those things were. I had to draw the line somewhere.

There was a pause. Then Danny said, "See, Ry? You're not alone. It's okay to mess up every once in a while."

"Yeah, well." Ryleigh sniffed again. "I told you. It's not okay for me."

"Oh, come on. Says who?" Danny demanded.

"Says me. Says my parents."

"They do not."

"Maybe not exactly. But Tommy's the only one who ever gets any attention, because he's a *genius* and a nationally ranked *gymnast* and he's just *so great*. And even though he's rejected the whole family tradition and he acts like we don't even *exist, I'm* the disappointm—" She stopped abruptly, as if she'd just remembered where she was. "Whatever," she said. "Anyway."

I could hardly believe it. Ryleigh—with her perfect face and her perfect hair and her perfect clothes, with her supreme confidence and her superior attitude—felt like she was a disappointment? If you'd taken a video of me right then, you'd have seen a girl with rainbow pinwheels for eyes, and a sign on her forehead that said, ERROR. DOES NOT COMPUTE.

I tried to imagine Ryleigh growing up in her brother's shadow, always overlooked and ignored. I thought about her brother rejecting the ninja tradition and her parents still not seeing how talented she was. For the first time in my life, I felt like I might have gotten the better deal—in some ways, at least. Sure, it could be hard living with Mom, but Mom had never made me feel like I was a disappointment. I'd never worried that our family would fall apart because we were mad at each other.

It gave me just enough courage to say, "I'm sorry. I think you're a great . . . a great fighter." (I mean, I wasn't ready to go all in and say I thought she was a great *person*.) "And I bet your parents think you're awesome."

Ryleigh blinked at me, like she was shocked. *I* was kind of shocked, to be honest. "I'm not sure about that second part," she said. "But thanks."

"And I hope your brother—"

But Ryleigh shut that down right away. "Anyway. Does the snake know where we are?"

I shuddered, remembering the way the snake had infiltrated my mind. Could she reach us here, the way Izanami had reached me from the depths of Yomi? Speaking of which, could Izanami reach me here?

"She will certainly notify the other sentries soon. We need to move swiftly," said Niko.

"Okay, so let's see," Ryleigh said. She looked around, and I could see her doing her ninja spycraft thing: assessing the environment, listing resources, assets, liabilities, blah, blah, blah. "Those must be farmers going into the city with rice, right?" She pointed at one of the carts rolling past. "It's probably the same farmers going in and out all the time, which means that whoever's guarding the gate probably knows them and trusts them. So all we have to do is pose as one of them, or maybe hitch a ride on one of those carts, and we should be able to make it through, no problem." She looked at us triumphantly, as if to say, *I'm BACK, baby!*

"As a shape-shifter, *I* could pull it off. But the rest of you? No. No more false-identity fiascos," Niko said. "The snake was bad enough. I would rather not toy with the White Tiger of the West. And hiding won't work, either," he said when Ryleigh started to protest. "He'll sniff you right out."

Ryleigh crossed her arms. "You got a better idea?"

"No. So use your brains and come up with something brilliant, or we're as mashed as marshmallows. And those children back in the Middle Lands are as doomed as dust."

What else did we have to work with? I reached into my

backpack, but once again, it provided me with a big fat bunch of nothing. Ugh! What was the use of a backpack that was supposed to give you everything you needed if ninety-nine percent of the time you needed something, all you got was infinite empty space?

Wait a sec.

"Danny," I said. "What if we used one of our backpacks?"

He looked at his own backpack, and then at me. "You mean . . ."

"There's supposed to be infinite space in there, right? What if we all get into one of the backpacks, and Niko shape-shifts into a farmer and wears it?" I nodded at Ryleigh. "Like you said, they're probably not checking the farmers that carefully." Maybe by giving her credit, I could get her to go along with my idea.

"Bruh, that's genius!" Danny said.

Ryleigh mumbled something that sounded a little bit like "It's pretty good, I guess."

Only Niko looked unhappy. "Do you have any idea what could happen if you should lose your hold on each other in there?"

Oh. We would probably float off into the infinite space. And then . . . "What would happen?" I croaked.

"I don't know! Because no one has ever tried such a pea-brained plan!"

"It'll be fine," Danny said.

Niko shook his head. "No, it won't. It's ill-advised, imprudent, and irresponsible."

"What if we tie ourselves to the outside of the backpack?" I said. "Danny, do you have your magic thread?"

"Bruh! I know I already said this, but you're a genius!" Danny beamed at me. I hoped Ryleigh was watching. Danny reached into his pocket and produced the tiny spool of invisible thread that Hotei had given him as a gift. It had come in handy when we'd needed to find our way out of Susano'o's fortress in Ne-no-kuni.

Over Niko's fretful protests, we tied the end of the thread to one of the plastic buckles on the outside of my backpack. Then we tied the thread to each of our wrists, leaving a few feet of slack between us: first me, then Ryleigh, then Danny at the end, holding the spool.

We entered the backpack in the opposite order: first Danny, then Ryleigh, then me. Danny's and Ryleigh's faces were pale and their jaws were tight, but otherwise they made it look easy—just put one leg in, then the other, then lower yourself down, like you're scooching into a swimming pool, and then let go.

When I stuck my feet downward into thin air, I realized why Danny and Ryleigh had looked so nervous. It might have *looked* like inching your way down into a pool, but what it *felt* like was inching your way through a hole in the ceiling of one of those domed football stadiums. At least you know you're going to float in the water; all I could feel holding me up now was nothing.

It's okay, I told myself. *Danny did it. Ryleigh did it.* I could hear them chatting quietly, like floating in the all-encompassing

Aum was no big deal. *Come on, Momo.* I tried to let go of the clump of grass I'd been hanging on to, but when I thought about the vast emptiness below me, my stomach lurched and my fist clenched even tighter.

"You got this! You'll be fine!" Danny called.

This was my idea. Hundreds of kids were depending on me to trust myself. Danny said I'd be fine.

I took one last breath and let go.

I sank gently downward, and then I was floating in the Aum, staring up at a narrow strip of light. The round, backlit shape of Niko's farmer head appeared and said anxiously, "All okay down there?"

"Yes!" we chorused, though I wasn't *totally* okay, not yet.

Niko's head withdrew, and the light disappeared as he closed the backpack flap. At first the darkness was so complete that I found myself gasping for air, like I might suffocate. But as my eyes adjusted, my breath came back. Tiny stars glimmered in the distance. Ghostly forms and figures filled the space around me. Some barely moved at all; others bobbed and somersaulted like tumbleweeds; still others whizzed past like little rockets. Next to me, I could make out the shadowy shapes of Danny and Ryleigh. And all around us was a deep, echoey hum that sounded like the meditation audio track that my sixth-grade English teacher, Mrs. Rasul, used to play for us sometimes: *aum . . . aum . . . aum . . .*

It calmed me until I had another thought: without the light from the backpack opening, I couldn't tell what we were anchored to. What if the thread snapped and we floated away? What if I got sucked through a portal to another world and never came back? Once again, my lungs began to cry out for air. But as I panted and curled into a ball, I felt the tug of the thread on my wrist—my link back to the world. Then I felt Danny's hand on my arm and heard his voice in my ear. "Hey. I'm here and Ryleigh's here, and we're still attached to the backpack. Okay?"

"Box breathing, remember?" said Ryleigh's voice. "Do that."

Oh. Right. Okay.

So I did a few rounds, tugging every now and then on the thread to remind myself that I was connected to a place and time—and to Ryleigh and Danny.

"What if we get right up next to the opening?" Danny suggested. "Maybe we can hear what's going on." I agreed gratefully. Having Danny next to me always made me feel safer.

"But we have to be quiet," Ryleigh said. "Like, totally silent. Got it?"

Duh. "Got it."

"Because I can kind of hear you breathing," she explained.

Sigh. I mean, *sigh.*

We crowded around the closed flap of the backpack and listened. Almost immediately I heard a deep, rumbling, slightly muffled voice say, "You're early—it's the first time in a thousand years that I've seen you arrive before sunset!"

"Er, yes, sir, Mr. Byakko, sir," said Niko's voice. "I was hoping to catch a show in the city before I go home."

"Speaking of catching, I have been informed that there are dangerous criminals roaming the area. Two human children, a fox, and some kind of half-kami tried to sneak past Genbu at the north gate, but they jumped through a portal before they were captured. Have you seen anything suspicious?"

"Oh, no, sir. Never. Not me. Nothing suspicious at all."

"Some of the other farmers have reported seeing characters matching that description out in the rice fields. You're sure you didn't see anyone?"

"Alas, I pulled off the road to take a nap. Perhaps they passed me while I was asleep."

Byakko laughed—a deep, throaty chuckle. "Yes, perhaps they did. Well, get on with you, then."

"Yes, sir!" There was a short silence, after which Niko could be heard saying as if to himself—but loudly enough for us to hear, "Goodness gracious, what a magnificent beast that Byakko is. I'm certainly happy that I had nothing to hide from him! Ah, here we are, past the gate and properly in Celestial City! How very, very glad I am to be here!"

I breathed a long sigh of relief.

We were in.

Expand Your Expectations

Eventually, a line of bright light split the darkness, and Niko whispered, "Now! Get out now! And quickly!"

As I scrambled out, I wondered what Niko would look like as a human. Had he kept the form of the red-haired, mischievous boy I'd first seen when he'd visited Mom in human form? Or would he be suntanned and rugged, the way I imagined a farmer would be? When I looked up, I gasped.

"Ah! Safe and secure, I see," Niko said. "Please save your questions until everyone has exited. I hate repeating myself." So I waited while Ryleigh climbed out and gasped and Danny did the same.

"Uh, Niko? Why are you a girl?" Danny asked.

"Why not?" Niko asked back. She flipped her ponytail just the way Ryleigh did.

"Because . . . I mean . . ." Danny trailed off, and then shrugged. "I guess it doesn't matter."

"It does matter, but only because I am feeling feminine. Beyond that, you are correct. It doesn't matter."

"Should we say 'she' instead of 'he' now?" Ryleigh asked. "Or . . ."

" 'She' and 'her' will do fine, thank you."

"Are you ever, uh, feminine when you're a fox?" I asked.

"In my fox form, you may think of me as 'he' and 'him.' Goodness, I'm glad you children have *some* manners."

"Speaking of manners, are you going to return the cart?" I asked.

"I unloaded the rice at a sake factory and sent the horse back home." Niko sighed heavily and rubbed her temples. "It's about time *something* went according to plan."

That was exactly how I felt. Hopefully, things would get easier from here on out—though I didn't see how breaking into the Hall of Mirrors would be easier than sneaking into the city.

"Do you hear music?" Ryleigh asked next.

"Yeah, but I can't tell where it's coming from. Can you?" Danny said.

The music didn't seem to be coming from anywhere in particular—not from the flowerpots, not from the walls, not from the trees that lined the street. It was in the *air*, somehow. It was catchy and upbeat, and I found myself wanting to hum along even though I didn't know the tune. But I couldn't allow myself to be distracted. We still had to find Jin and make a plan to steal the mirror.

Just as I had this thought, Danny said, "Hey, let's go get something to eat and chill out for a while. I think we deserve a break."

"No. We have to find Jin," I pointed out.

"But I'm hungry and I want to relax. We can worry about Jin later," Danny said.

"But Jin waited for us—well, he wanted to wait for us. We owe it to him to start looking for him now!" I argued.

Danny waved his hand dismissively. "Those guys are international superstars. They're probably hanging out in a hot tub or something," he said.

"I'm with Danny," Ryleigh drawled. "I mean, no offense, Momo, but you're being a drag. Loosen up!"

What? My rage monster lifted its head. *You tried so hard to be kind to her when she messed up with the portal, and this is how she treats you?* And what a hypocrite! *Loosen up?* What happened to "I should have been prepared?" What happened to "Meaning well isn't enough?"

A jolt of heat seared through me. The pain faded quickly but I felt hot and prickly all over—especially at my hairline, just above each eyebrow. I reached up with both hands to see what was going on, and almost screamed. Those itchy spots above my eyebrows? Two hard lumps as big around as quarters.

I thought I heard someone laughing in the distance—and not in a nice way. It was a voice I didn't recognize—a woman's voice, wild and barely in control. It made my hair stand on end.

"Momo, you're a monster!" Ryleigh said.

"*You're* a monster!" I blurted out. My forehead was throbbing now, and my skin felt like it was on fire. A faint red haze descended like a veil in front of me.

"No, you're literally a monster," she insisted. "Here, lemme show you." She took out her phone and started holding it up like a little mirror.

I lifted my hand to push the phone away, and gasped.

Instead of fingernails, I had a full set of claws, and my skin was turning bright red.

"Calm down! Get out of sight! Danny, Ryleigh, help me!" Niko whispered urgently, and the three of them practically shoved me into an alley.

"Niko!" I shrieked. "What's going on? What's happening to me? Someone give me a phone!" Danny held his out and I snatched it out of his hands. What I saw made me scream again.

"Shhh! Shhh! Quiet! Quiet!" Niko hissed.

"Calm down, Momo," Ryleigh muttered between her teeth. "Breathe."

"Shut! UP!" I barked. I had every right to scream: I was the color of a tomato. I had bulging yellow eyes. There were antlers growing out of my forehead.

"Momo, please!" Niko begged. "You must calm yourself."

"I can't calm down—look at me! What's happening?"

"It's the way of this place—of Celestial City. I've heard stories, but I didn't know . . ."

"Stories about what? What didn't you know?" I shouted. "And why didn't you warn us?"

"I didn't know the stories were true! Do you remember how Tsukiyomi said that anger isn't allowed here? It seems that if you feel or show too much, you begin turning into an oni," Niko said.

Ohh. Oh no. No no no no—

"But it's temporary! You will revert back to your old self once the anger abates," Niko added hastily. She put her hands on my shoulders. "Now. Concentrate on calming yourself, and your symptoms will subside."

"Are you sure? Do you promise?"

"I'm sure. I promise."

Niko didn't sound sure at all, but I closed my eyes and tried Ryleigh's breathing exercise anyway. Almost instantly, my anger faded. My skin stopped prickling and my forehead stopped itching. I opened my eyes a minute later and checked myself: skin color back to normal. No claws, no antlers. Whew.

"Okay. So. If we don't want to get in trouble, we have to stay calm and not get mad at each other," Danny said. "We can do that, right?"

"The music!" Ryleigh said suddenly. "I bet that's what it's for—to help us stay calm and happy!"

Now that I thought about it, it made sense that Amaterasu—who was all about light, love, peace, and order—would do everything she could to keep her city free from anger. Maybe this would be good for me. I could become a new person. I would be calm, cool, and—

Hee-hee-hee-heeee! Ohh-ho-ho-ho! Mo—mo—!

It was that laughter again. I looked at the others. "Did you hear that?"

Danny, Ryleigh, and Niko looked at each other.

"Hear what?" Ryleigh asked.

"Someone laughing? Like . . . demonically?"

"Uh. No?" Danny said.

"Maybe it's an aftereffect of your anger," Niko suggested.

Oh. Right. That was probably all it was. An aftereffect. I just needed to breathe. Think happy thoughts. I was fine. Everything was fine.

At Niko's suggestion, we made our way to Suzaku Boulevard,

which ran through the center of the city from the southern gate to the Palace of the Sun. The closer we got, the busier and more festive the atmosphere became, and when we turned onto the boulevard itself, it was like being in the opening scene of a musical where everyone sings about how great their hometown is. The street was broad and bright and lined with shops and restaurants. People tapped their feet and nodded their heads to the music. Birds harmonized with each other. Jewel-toned butterflies filled the air with color.

Almost immediately, Niko shoved us behind a kiosk while she picked out three baseball hats and three pairs of sunglasses.

"Your disguises," she said, handing them to us.

"That's not much of a disguise," I said. "Especially compared to yours."

"*This* is not so much a disguise as a state of being," said Niko airily as she checked her reflection in a shop window. "Anyway, I watched all the Marvel superhero movies last month on a laptop that Hotei lent me. Baseball hats and sunglasses work for *those* heroes every time."

Dad and I had always laughed about those Marvel hero disguises, and I found myself swallowing an unexpected lump in my throat.

But the city's magic—and all the free food—did its job, and when Niko declared that we would look for Jin tomorrow ("He's at the palace with the proper paperwork," she reasoned. "He's safer than we are.") I was able to smush my negative feelings down with only a little difficulty.

"What we really need to do is find a place to stay," she said.

"Are hotels free here, too?" Danny asked.

Niko nodded.

"Sweet! Can we stay at one with a pool? Do you think they have cable?"

"I suspect that cable is not an option here," she said dryly.

Finding a place to stay turned out to be quite difficult. At all the shiniest, sparkliest hotels that we tried, the people at the desk smiled apologetically and said, "Sorry, we're full! Have a lovely day!" It was the same at hotel after hotel, farther and farther away from the center of town, until finally a white-haired granny at a tiny little inn nodded her head and told us she had space for us. Obaa-chan, the sweet little innkeeper, gave us a strange look when we followed her to our room without taking our hats and sunglasses off.

But Ryleigh put on a cute little smile and said, "We're trying to start a new trend. What do you think?"

Obaa-chan chuckled. "Oh, is that what it is? Well, I think you look very nice."

There was no television, she told us when Ryleigh asked if we could watch the news. "We do have a newspaper, though!" she said brightly, and handed us a copy. "I hope you find it entertaining!"

We gathered around the table in the middle of the room and opened the paper. There was no news of suspects trying to break into the city, so we were safe for the time being. But there was other news. "Tamamo-no-mae abducts eight hundred twenty-three children," Ryleigh read out loud. She bit her lip. "That means she only needs sixty-five more to get to eight hundred eighty-eight."

Danny groaned. "I can't think about that right now. Read something else."

Ryleigh turned the page. "Ooh! The quasi-kami acts for the New Year's Eve party are rehearsing all day tomorrow in the outer courtyard of the Palace of the Sun."

"Excellent!" said Niko. "And now that we've determined our destination for tomorrow, I suggest we all go to sleep immediately." And she curled up on her futon and did just that.

That night, I dreamed I was in the throne room of the Palace of the Sun, kneeling before Amaterasu as her royal court sat behind me and watched. I was having a hard time sitting still— I was full of that same restless, buzzing feeling I always got when I held Kusanagi, or when I was around Susano'o. I felt a sudden surge of fury—why was I even here on this mission in the first place? Amaterasu was Queen of the Sky Kindom, for crying out loud. She was supposed to want peace and prosperity for the people of the Middle Lands. They were suffering and scared— and she was up here throwing a party. My anger burned through me, and I was sure I was bright red again, with horns, fangs, and claws to rival any oni. I could hear the horrified gasps and whispers of the crowd. Humiliation leaked into my anger, and just when I thought I might explode, I heard someone calling me. *Momo! Momo, come outside! I can help you.*

It was the voice that had laughed at me when I'd nearly turned into an oni earlier in the day. Without a second thought, I got up and rushed out of the throne room. But I tripped over the threshold—and woke up.

I wasn't in bed, where I should have been. I'd ended up

outside, somehow, next to the wall that ran around the garden behind the inn. The night air was cool and soothing, and even at this hour, there was faint music playing: the plinkety-plunk of a koto—a Japanese harp—and the whispery sighs of the shakuhachi, the bamboo flute. I watched the stars twinkling. They seemed to be chattering softly to each other, in voices like tiny little bells.

But I was still hot and jittery with the anger from my dream, and my head was pounding. I leaned against the wall and tried to focus on the cool air and the music. But the voice called to me again: *Momooo. Down heeere. I want to seee youuu*, it sang. It was jagged and rough, but also wheedling and persuasive; dark and wild, but also exciting, like a promise to satisfy a craving that I knew was dangerous.

My head filled with fog, even as my physical senses seemed to grow sharp and alive. *Underneath you*, said the voice. I crouched down and found a large pile of leaves and twigs at my feet. I began brushing it aside, and my fingers caught on narrow iron bars—a grate. A sharp, choking odor like a cross between cigarette smoke and burning rubber filled my nostrils. Like the voice, it filled me with fear and revulsion—but it also felt like scratching an itch. I listened again. Something down there was burbling and bubbling. *Yes, Momo, that's right. Now lift up the grate. . . .* I had just closed my hands around the bars when I heard another voice.

"Momo! What in the holy handbags of heaven are you doing over there?"

I glanced back and saw Niko in his masculine fox form,

peeking out of the back door of the inn. Annoyance prickled my scalp. Why was Niko awake in the middle of the night, and why did he always have to be nosy? It was none of his business what I was doing. I gripped the bars tighter and steadied myself on the ground.

A sliding door clattered behind me, and in a second, Niko had knocked me off my feet and out of my trance.

"Momo!" he said again. He sat on my chest and stared into my face. "Wake up!"

"Ugh." He had the worst pepperoni breath. "I *am* awake. I *was* awake." I shook my head as the fog slowly cleared. "Wasn't I?"

"You seemed to be under some sort of spell."

That voice. "Something down there was calling to me," I said. My body went cold and clammy with fear—but under the fear was a thread of curiosity. "What do you think it is?"

Niko cast a nervous glance at the grate, from which smoke twisted and curled like grasping fingers. "I don't know and I don't care to find out. Whatever it is, it's not your friend, my gullible little girl. I'm going to complain to management and make them cover that grate properly. It's a health hazard." He bustled about, sweeping the garden debris back over it until the odor faded away.

He herded me back inside, and as I walked, I took in deep, calming breaths of night air and listened to the music, and to the stars. I was suddenly very sleepy. I crawled under my covers, and this time I didn't wake up until I felt Niko's cold, wet nose snuffling my cheek in the morning.

I Know You Can Hear Me

We left the inn the next morning in good spirits, but they evaporated half a block later when Niko spotted a poster with sketches that looked a *lot* like me, Danny, Ryleigh, and Niko in fox form. Underneath our picture was a caption: WANTED! *If you have seen one of these very nice people, please notify Celestial City Security! We would love to chat with them about their stay here. Have a nice day!*

"What the . . . ," Danny murmured.

"Everything in Celestial City is supposed to be perfect, so the authorities have a hard time admitting it when things go wrong," Niko explained.

It was clear what Celestial City Security *really* wanted. We pulled the brims of our hats as low as we could over our faces.

By the time we reached the wall that surrounded the palace grounds, the plaza in front of the central gate was humming with activity. The gate itself was easily five stories tall, with gleaming white walls and heavy vermilion-painted pillars that rose up like trees to meet the swooping double-decker roof. Three sets of massive red double doors were dotted with gold studs as big as bowling balls.

We stepped through the doors, over a threshold as high as my knee, into a courtyard as big as I don't know how many football fields. (It would help if I knew how big a football field actually was, I guess.) Like the plaza outside, it was already crowded and busy. Official-looking robed kami bustled back and forth with official-looking papers in their hands; tourist kami of all shapes and sizes strolled around checking their guidebooks. Worker kami were busy putting up huge bleachers on both sides of the courtyard. Balloons and butterflies bobbed and dipped above us, and brightly colored silk banners fluttered in the breeze.

"These are the official parade grounds," said Niko, reading a brochure and gesturing broadly with one arm. "The New Year's Eve celebrations will take place here, with the concert stage at the other end."

From where we stood, the stage seemed to be empty. "Looks like we haven't missed anything yet. Come on," said Ryleigh, and she plunged into the crowd.

The stage was still empty when we reached it, so we wandered along yet another wall that separated the parade grounds from the inner courtyard and the palace itself, where only palace personnel were allowed. We peeked through a gate that was being held open for a procession of horses and their riders.

"Ooh, you can see the stables just over there. Look!" said Ryleigh. She took Danny's arm and pointed beyond the line of horses. I tried not to care. About the arm thing, I mean. The stables might be important.

This was when the opening a cappella harmonies of TBS's international megahit, "Ur My Angel," drifted toward us from the stage: *From the moment I saw those stars in your eyes / I knew that my heart was no longer mine.*

The singing only lasted a few seconds—just long enough for a sound check—but we were gathered at the bamboo barriers around the stage before the last notes faded into silence.

"Jin! Jin!" I jumped up and down and waved my hands wildly in the air.

"Shush!" Ryleigh hissed.

Oops. I would make a terrible spy.

But I felt better when Jin saw me and his face broke into a wide, relieved smile. He rushed to the edge of the stage and dropped to the ground, waving away the uniformed security kami who hurried over. "Don't worry, I'm just gonna say hi to my friends over here. It'll only take a minute."

Then he threw his arms around me. I had a moment of dizzy disbelief: Jin Takayama was hugging me—and for real, this time! He hugged Ryleigh next, and after a moment's hesitation, bro-hugged Danny with a combination handshake/shoulder bump/backslap.

"Where's Niko?" he asked, looking around.

"Ahem." Niko cleared her throat loudly.

We explained, and Jin laughed and gave Niko a hug. "Sorry!" Then he said, "I've been so worried about you! I would have stayed—I *tried* to stay, but—" He looked back over at Malcolm, Lex, Fabian, and Ashwin. His shoulders slumped a little. "They kept telling me I was our best chance and I had to stick with them to stay undercover, but I still felt terrible."

After reassuring Jin that he had done the right thing, we told him what had happened to us, starting with our escape from the snake, all the way up to the TBS rehearsal.

"Speaking of which," Ryleigh said, "can you get us some backstage passes? Or front-row tickets?"

Jin could. But first the band had to finish their sound check and rehearsal, and then Jin had to learn all the choreography. We agreed to meet for dinner in the plaza just outside the palace gates to make a proper plan.

We spent the rest of the day wandering around the city, lounging in cafés and taking down WANTED posters when no one was looking. Now that we weren't battling yōkai or sneaking into the Sky Kingdom, Ryleigh was flirting with Danny harder than ever—ugh. I tried to remind myself of how hard she'd been on herself about the portal candy, and how she thought she was a disappointment. But she kept talking about her ninja training this, and her trip to New York City that, and whispering with Danny and flicking her ponytail and saying things like "Doesn't this totally remind you of the time when . . ." I felt like we were back on Earth, in a whole other world—a whole other life. I had to take a lot of deep, calming breaths.

By the time night rolled its way across the sky, I was exhausted from squashing my feelings down all afternoon. Even worse, that awful, unsettling voice had returned.

Momo . . . Momo . . .

No one else seemed to hear it, and I was too afraid to say anything about it after Niko's reaction the night before.

I know you can hear me.

It was fuzzy under the constant upbeat music playing on the street, but it scratched and grated in my ears like the beginning of a bad cold. And like a cold, it made me tired and irritable. If I couldn't find a way to be less angry about Ryleigh, I'd explode and give us all away.

Finally, Ryleigh was distracted by a shop window that show-cased a dress made of weather. As she watched the swirling white snowflakes on the skirt give way to rainbows and then to a sparkling night sky, I pulled Danny aside.

"What?" he asked, eyeing me warily.

Keep breathing. "You haven't talked to me once this whole afternoon. Because *someone's* been freezing me out." I glanced significantly at Ryleigh. "I thought you said you were going to talk to her."

Danny let out a long, slow breath. "I did talk to her. I think she's trying."

I almost laughed. "Well, she's not doing a very good job."

"Yeah, maybe not," he admitted glumly.

"So? Why don't you say something? Why don't you at least stick up for me?"

"I—because—but, like—" Danny babbled, and I felt my skin start to prickle. But then he stopped and groaned. "You're right."

"I know."

"I should be a better friend. I *will* be a better friend."

The prickles on my skin floated away.

"Annyway, you don't need to worry about me and you," he continued. "We're, like, bonded. Nothing could make me stop being friends with you. Okay? I mean it."

I felt a warm little glow inside my chest in spite of myself. "Really?"

"Duh."

I sat there enjoying the glow until Danny said thoughtfully, "You know, if you have a problem with Ryleigh, maybe you should tell her, not me."

"*Pffft.*" I could not imagine Ryleigh ever talking it out with me, much less apologizing and trying to be friends with me. Not in this life, anyway.

Ryleigh and Niko rejoined us, and soon we reached the plaza outside the outer palace gates, where we sat on a bench to wait for Jin. As we waited, I realized that we were still wearing our sunglasses and hats. Would we look suspicious, now that it was nighttime? Would someone demand that we take them off, and then recognize us? I scanned the plaza for Jin. Where was he? I wished he would hurry.

"Jumping juniper berries, will you stop that swiveling!" Niko whined. "It's driving me to distraction!"

I stopped swiveling, but I couldn't stop feeling nervous. "Where is he? He should be here by now. Maybe he couldn't make it. Do you think anyone has recognized us? What if this is an ambush?"

"Omigosh, can you please chill? We're trying to look cool, here," Ryleigh said. "I know you're not, like, great at it—no offense. But you could at least try."

Something inside me cracked. Danny wanted me to tell Ryleigh I had a problem with her, did he? Fine. I took a deep breath. "Why do you have to be so mean to me all the time?"

I could hardly believe I was saying this right to her face. But I was so tired of her attitude—too tired to even be angry, I noticed.

Ryleigh's chin jutted out defensively for just a moment

before she recovered and gave me an appraising stare. "Are you serious? Like, is that a serious question?"

"Yes."

She looked at Danny, who shrugged, then back at me. Then she looked back again at Danny and Niko. "Danny. Niko. Am I mean?" She tilted her head and tossed her ponytail and used the best Disney eyes I'd seen yet. I held my breath.

The two of them looked at each other, and then at Ryleigh.

"Well . . . yeah. You can be," said Danny.

"Yes, quite," said Niko.

Ryleigh clucked her tongue once and frowned and looked away. I wanted to pump my fist in the air and shout, *Ha! In your face!* in Ryleigh's face because even though she wasn't apologizing or even admitting that she'd done anything wrong, my friends had come through for me, and that felt like a huge win. Instead, I gave Danny and Niko each a little smile and mouthed *Thank you.*

Ryleigh continued to sit facing slightly away from us with her arms crossed, and no one else seemed to have anything to say, and the longer we sat, the more awkward it got, so when Danny jumped up and shouted, "There he is!" we all breathed a sigh of relief, and not just because we were glad to see Jin heading toward us from across the square with a big smile on his face.

What's the Secret Recipe for Heinz Ketchup?

"**I brought some VIP passes** like you asked." Jin reached into his pocket and pulled out three gleaming silver cards. "They should be a pretty hot item."

Ryleigh and I both reached out our hands. I felt my shoulders rise and tighten, but Ryleigh waved her hand at me and said, "Oh—sorry. You take them, Momo."

Probably she was trying to prove she wasn't as mean as we all said she was. Who knew how long this new Ryleigh would last—best to just enjoy it. So I smiled and took the tickets. "Thanks."

"I don't have a lot of time," Jin said. "So let's get planning! Do you have any good ideas?"

As it turned out, Ryleigh had an entire plan already—surprise! (Not.)

"First, we'll get in touch with the Gemini aunties' niece and nephew, and we'll give them two of those VIP tickets in exchange for trading places with us," she said briskly. "Then Danny and I will infiltrate the palace and do reconnaissance. On New Year's Eve, while Jin and TBS are onstage, I'll be in the palace stealing the Mirror of the Sun. Danny and Jin will create a diversion during the show, and while the palace is in chaos, the three of us will escape. We'll use Jin's portal candy to get us to the city gate, and once we're outside the city, we can use Momo's portal candy to travel to the Sea of Heaven. Then we catch a ride home on the boat and trap Tamamo-no-mae in the mirror. And that's it." Ryleigh nodded in agreement with herself about the brilliance of her plan.

"Okay. Cool, cool, cool." Jin nodded slowly. "So, um, how are you going to steal the mirror? And how do we create a diversion?"

"That's what the reconnaissance is for," Ryleigh said. She smiled sweetly at him. "Don't worry. Danny and I will figure it out and make sure you get the information. We're gonna be a great team."

I had another question. "Uh. What about me? Why don't I get a job? Why am I stuck out here with Niko?" It wasn't like I *wanted* the stress that would come with infiltrating the palace, but Ryleigh's plan left me feeling like it was her birthday party all over again—cool kids on the inside, me on the outside.

Niko was upset, too—at me. "Oh, I'm not good enough for you? You'd rather hang with your *human* friends?" She tossed her ponytail indignantly at me.

"No, it's not that!" I protested. "It's just that—"

"Okay, so first of all, like, no offense?" Ryleigh said. "But I'm trained in reconnaissance, and you're not."

"Neither is Danny," I argued.

"Well, I need *someone* on the inside with me," said Ryleigh. "And the stablehand is a boy, and Danny is a boy."

"But—" Honestly. Of all the silly excuses.

173

"You and Niko have to figure out the boat ride home, since we don't have our tickets anymore. You can use the third VIP concert ticket as a bribe or something. *That's* your job."

"Oh," I said. I couldn't argue with that—the boat was a crucial part of the plan. There was no point in stealing the mirror if we couldn't bring it back. On the other hand, Ryleigh had just organized it so I would be out of the way while she got to hang out in the palace with Danny for three days. "Okay, but—"

"Cool." Ryleigh gave me a smile that seemed genuine. Maybe I was being unreasonable; maybe she really was just being a good, professional spy. I looked at Niko, who was still pouting about not being appreciated. Did I think Niko wasn't cool enough to hang out with? Was *I* the one with the problem?

There are thousands of lives at stake, I reminded myself. *Stop obsessing over who's hanging out with who. Focus on the mission.*

We sat quietly for a little while, watching the fireflies and listening to the splash of the fountain in the middle of the plaza. Jin took out his notebook and wrote something in it before saying, "This place is so cool. I wish we could hang out and enjoy ourselves instead of worrying about everything we have to do."

"Haven't you been to tons of cool places?" Danny asked.

"Yeah. But it's kinda like now. You're there, but you've got the show and whatever, so you never get to see anything."

"Okay, so I know you're not showing off, right?" Danny put his hands up. "But I still don't get it. Are you seriously complaining about being a world-famous star?"

"I told you, it's not like I'm not grateful. I know I'm super lucky, and I love my fans. But yeah. I don't like it."

"It looks like so much fun, though," Ryleigh said.

"I know it probably looks that way from the outside. But it's not real. We're *supposed* to act like we're having fun all the time," said Jin. "And there's all those people, all that pressure, everyone following your every move, asking about your clothes and your hair and your freaking skin care routine, even. It's exhausting. I just want to be alone. I like things to be quiet. But I can't complain about it because it's, like, everyone's dream to do what I do."

"But you're *good* at singing. You can't just give it up and walk away because you don't like being famous," Ryleigh protested.

"That's what my dad says. He says I have a gift and I shouldn't waste it. And what if I'm never this successful again? What if I'm a failure at everything I do after this?"

"That's why you should keep doing what you're doing," Ryleigh said. "Anyway, it's not fair to the people who sacrificed for you and who want you to succeed. You *owe* them!"

"Great grasshoppers, you've got some strong sentiments about someone else's future!" Niko observed mildly.

Ryleigh rolled her eyes. "I just don't think it's fair for him to be all, 'I don't like this anymore,' and walk away like—" She snapped her fingers.

"You sure you're talking about Jin and not about Tom—" Danny started, but Ryleigh cut him off.

"Yes."

"No, I get it," Jin said, looking miserable. He shook his head and let out a sigh. "I wish I could see the mirror that answers every question. I'd ask it what I should do."

"Wouldn't we all," said Niko.

Jin jogged off to join TBS for an after-dinner rehearsal, and Ryleigh, Danny, Niko, and I strolled back down Suzaku Boulevard. We picked up a few items at the shops and sent a message to Kabo and Nobu, the niece and nephew of the Gemini aunties from the Ferry wheel.

I couldn't stop thinking about the question-answering mirror—I had so many questions. There were the I-need-answers-now kind: *Will Ryleigh's plan work? Will Niko and I be able to find a boat home? How exactly are we going to trap Tamamo-no-mae and save the kids?* And the maybe-I-don't-need-answers-*now*-but-I-still-really-need-to-know kind: *Where is Mom and why did she leave me again? What ever happened to Dad, anyway? Is there any way I can escape Izanami's hold on me? Will I ever learn to access my power without destroying everything I love? Whose voice keeps calling to me up here?*

"What would your questions be?" I asked the others. "If you could look into that question mirror."

Danny jumped right in. "What's the secret recipe for Heinz ketchup?"

Tsk. "Come on, I mean for real. Be serious," I said, though I doubted he would be.

But Danny shoved his hands in his pockets and shocked me by sighing, looking around nervously, and saying, "I dunno, I guess . . . I guess maybe I'd want to know who my birth parents are. What they're like. Why they . . . you know . . ."

Niko, seeming to forget that she was in human form, nudged her forehead against Danny's shoulder. "Do you think you're ready for that?"

Danny answered without looking up. "I don't know. It's just a question I have, that's all."

Danny rarely showed this side of himself, and it made my heart go all warm and melty—I felt like I was watching a sweet, furry little puppy wobbling around on his sweet, furry little paws.

That is, until Ryleigh said, "Oh, Danny," put an arm around his shoulder, and gave him a squeeze. Then I felt like I was watching an eagle swoop down and carry my sweet little puppy away in her strong, glistening talons. I wanted to swoop after her and shout, *Give him back!* and maybe I would have, if it hadn't been for the sudden searing pain that shot through me.

Ow. Ow. Ow. I closed my eyes and mushed down my feelings and tried to believe: *He will always be my friend. He will always be my friend.*

I bet you can't wait to get out of here so you can get as angry as you want. Hee hee!

That voice.

Maybe I should *tell the others,* I thought. But what good would it do? They'd just tell me to ignore it, like Niko had. Maybe they'd even decide they didn't want me around, in case whatever was talking to me was dangerous and could compromise the mission.

So when Niko asked me what was wrong, I put on a smile and said, "Nothing!"

"I don't believe you," she said. "In fact, I think you're feeling left out and lonely because you don't get to sneak around the palace with the others." Then she leaned toward me and whispered in my ear, "Don't worry. You and I will play our part with such panache that we will be the heroes of the heist."

I couldn't tell if she really thought that was what I was worried about, or if she knew I was worried about something else. Either way, I was grateful to have Niko as a friend.

We found Obaa-chan waiting for us at the inn with sweet bean soup and a thousand questions about our day: "Where did you go? What did you do? Goodness me, are you still wearing those sunglasses?" We slurped down the soup and gave Obaa-chan a series of vague answers before hurrying upstairs to fine-tune our plan for the next afternoon.

According to the newspaper we found in the hall, four not-at-all-dangerous criminals were on the loose in the city, and Tamamo-no-mae had now abducted a total of 859 children. I scoured the paper from front to back but found nothing that even hinted at the whereabouts or activities of the goddess Takiri-bime—Mom's real name.

I mushed some melted candle wax into earplugs so I wouldn't hear that strange voice if it called to me while I slept.

I'm, Uh, Edamame

The next morning, we donned our sunglasses and hats and were walking out the door when Obaa-chan shuffled up and thrust a handful of pink paper tickets at me. "Tickets for the midwinter cherry blossom ceremony," she said. "I've been so many times, I don't need to see it. But you should go!"

"Midwinter cherry blossom ceremony?" I repeated, puzzled.

"Oh, yes, dear, it's beautiful. All the cherry trees in the royal park spring into bloom, all at once, in honor of the new year. It's one of the highlights of the week!"

I took them and thanked her, even though we'd probably be too busy to go. It was a bummer; she seemed so eager for us to have a good time.

Half an hour later, we reached a little tai-yaki shop tucked away on a side street near the palace. We picked a table, ordered a pile of the hot, fragrant pastries in the shape of fish, and sat down to wait for Kabo and Nobu, who had agreed to trade identities with Danny and Ryleigh for two days in exchange for the VIP concert tickets.

"Man, I hope these kids like Middle Lands music." Danny

179

jiggled his knee and crammed an entire chocolate-filled tai-yaki into his mouth.

"What if they don't? Do you think they'll show up?" I couldn't help worrying, as usual.

"Even if they don't like Middle Lands music, who wouldn't want to trade two days of work for two days of freedom on a holiday?" said Ryleigh. "We've made them an offer they can't refuse. They'll show up."

We waited for hours, and I was about to suggest that we give up when two kids wearing traditional servants' kimonos wandered into the shop . . . followed by a third kid we hadn't invited.

Kabo, Nobu, and the third kid sat down. "This is Jun," said Nobu. "She's my little sister."

When I put two tickets on the table, Nobu shook his head. "We were promised three tickets," he insisted.

"You're lying. We offered you and Kabo one ticket each to trade places with me and Danny. That's two tickets," said Ryleigh.

"Well, now we want three." Nobu crossed his arms, and Kabo and Jun did the same.

"Two." Ryleigh crossed *her* arms. "That's all we have," she lied.

"We're not doing this unless we get three, so I guess it's off, then," said Nobu. He and the two girls turned to go.

"Ryleigh!" I said between gritted teeth, but she refused to budge.

"They'll come back," she muttered. "Watch."

But they kept going, going, going, and finally Ryleigh shouted, "All right, all right, three!"

Nobu turned around with a broad grin splashed across his face. We left the café and ducked into an alley to make the exchange.

Nobu, Kabo, and Jun took their servant passes—little golden tablets on silk lanyards—from around their necks. Instantly, their palace staff uniforms disappeared and two girls and a boy dressed in street clothes—jeans, T-shirts, and in Nobu's case, a super-emo black button-down shirt—stood before us. We gave them our VIP tickets, and seconds later, Danny and Ryleigh were dressed as a kitchen servant and a stablehand from the Palace of the Sun. I stuffed the third servant's pass into my pocket for safekeeping. Danny and Ryleigh headed to the palace, and Niko and I went back to Suzaku Boulevard to find a ride home.

By late afternoon, I was ready to cry. Every seat on every boat back to the Middle Lands was booked, and we had nothing that anyone wanted to trade for. We couldn't even trade our tickets to the cherry blossom ceremony—everyone already seemed to have their own already.

"Can we go to the cherry blossom ceremony?" I asked Niko finally. "We might as well use the tickets."

She agreed, so we got in line to see the bare cherry tree branches burst into clouds of creamy pink-and-white blossoms at a park just across the plaza from the central palace gate. An enormous guard kami stood at the front of the line, dressed in a black kimono emblazoned with bright golden suns on either side of his chest. Next to him on a wooden perch was a cute little baby crow. Tourists held up their tickets, and the crow pecked at them and went, "KAA! Go ahead!" He looked very proud of himself. I wondered if this was the kind of thing that Yatagarasu, the three-legged crow, did outside the Hall of Mirrors.

When it was our turn, Niko and I held our tickets up and the little crow pecked at them and went "KAA!" just like it had with everyone else. But after that first "KAA," instead of telling us to go ahead, it started flapping and hopping around on its perch and making horrible coughing noises. The guard looked at it with some concern. "What's wrong, little guy?" he said, and then looked suspiciously at us. "Did you poison your tickets or something?"

"No, sir! Never!" Niko held up her hands and looked at me with alarm.

I shook my head. "I haven't done anything to them!"

The crow coughed twice more and then shook itself and stood still. I held my breath. Maybe this was just a fluke. Maybe it'd pecked off more than it could chew.

The guard peered at his assistant and stroked its back with one tentative finger. "You okay, little guy?" he asked tenderly.

The darling little crow fluffed its feathers, opened its mouth, and blared out in a voice like a siren, "INTRUDER ALERT! INTRUDER ALERT!"

"*Run!*" Niko shouted, and she twisted away from the guard's outstretched arms.

I didn't need to be told twice. We left the line and sprinted across the plaza.

"Stop them! Stop those children!" the guard shouted from behind us.

We dodged our way around food carts and T-shirt vendors

and souvenir kiosks. We'd gone about a block when a kami at a cart selling toys pointed a bamboo tube at us. A stream of red ropes shot out of it with a *bang!* The net just missed me, but Niko was caught.

"Niko!" I froze and watched in horror as the magic of the net did its work: the human girl faded away and Niko's true fox form emerged.

"Go!" he yelped. "Save yourself!"

I hesitated for one anguished moment, then turned and ran. But where could I go? Where would I hide? All the guards in the city would have been alerted by now. It was just a matter of time before one of them caught me.

"Your pocket!" I heard Niko bark in the distance.

My pocket?

My pocket.

I stuck my hand in, and my fingers closed around the servant's pass. Another guard was rounding the corner on the next block. No time to lose. I ducked down a side street and into the first shop I saw—a bookshop clogged with a maze of shelves and tables.

When the guard burst in just a few seconds later, the only customers he could see from the door were an old boulder kami, a frog kami, and a waterfall kami who the owner kept chastising for dripping all over the merchandise. Oh, and a servant girl from the Palace of the Sun with neat braids down her back. Her face was buried in a manga about a girl whose father made magic puzzles, and she was so absorbed that she nearly bumped into the guard as she passed him on her way out the door.

"Oh! I'm so sorry," she squeaked, and bowed deeply.

"Yeah, yeah," he grunted before plunging deeper into the shop in search of his quarry.

I left the manga on the sidewalk and walked quickly down the street, trying to look casual, which was tough because I was on the verge of hyperventilating. The guard came out of the bookshop and entered the shop next door. I turned the corner and walked faster, turning more corners here and there at random until I felt certain the guard wouldn't track me down. I sat down in a dingy little tea shop to collect myself and figure out what had happened.

The tickets had triggered an alarm, but how? And why? I thought about the way Obaa-chan had pushed us into taking them . . . all of her questions about our plans . . . how ridiculous we'd been in our sunglasses and hats. It wouldn't have been difficult for her to figure out who we were. The tickets must have been a trap all along.

So now what? I couldn't go back to the inn. But I couldn't go to the palace, either, or there'd be no one left to arrange our escape from the Sky Kingdom, because Niko had been captured. What was happening to him? Miserably, I finished my tea and went back to the street. Maybe I could find another inn to stay at—if I could avoid being caught myself.

I was blinking my eyes against the daylight when a shadow fell over me; I looked up to see a massive palace guard. My heart jumped and I nearly bolted again, but the guard's giant hand had already grabbed me by the shoulder. I looked down at my feet, praying he hadn't gotten a good look at my face.

"What are you doing out here playing hooky, young lady? What's your name?"

Playing hooky? They had school here? Then I saw my palace uniform and understood. "Uh." Shoot. A name. Something innocent. Something small and inconsequential. "Edamame?" I quavered. *Say it like you mean it!* I heard Ryleigh's voice say in my head. And Danny's voice: *Fake it till you make it.* "Edamame," I said more firmly.

"Well, Edamame, I'm shocked that a palace servant would be shirking her duties like this. I thought they only took on the very best workers."

Fake it till you make it. Say it like you mean it. Be a faker. No—be a spy. Like Ryleigh. What would Ryleigh do? I tossed my braids, still taking care not to look directly at the guard. "They had a contest to see who could work the hardest, and the prize was an entire afternoon off," I said in the sweetest, most innocent voice I could muster.

"They did, did they?"

"Uh-huh." I nodded. Was he buying it?

"That sounds highly irregular to me. I'm taking you back to the palace."

"Oh! Uh, no, that's really okay. I can—I can go there on my own. I wouldn't want to take up any of your time. Aren't there criminals on the loose or something?" I babbled.

"We've caught one of them, and it's only a matter of time until the other one is caught, so don't you worry about that, little lady. We've got everything under control, and everyone is safe. But I can't have you lolling about drinking tea when your friends are all working hard in the palace. If you cooperate, I won't tell anyone that I caught you here, and you can get right back inside the palace walls, where you belong."

Whew. He hadn't recognized me. But I still didn't have any choice but to walk with him back to the palace. On the way, we passed a large monitor on which the anchor kami said blithely against a background of gorgeous pink cherry trees in full bloom, "Two criminals attempted to attend the midwinter cherry blossom ceremony, behind me. One of them remains at large, though security personnel are confident that they will find her. The other was this fox, whom you may recognize from the public notices posted around the city. We take you live now to the action." The screen flashed to a scene of Niko being dragged by two warrior kami to the gate in the south wall of the city. My body went cold as he was passed roughly over the threshold and presented to Suzaku, the Vermilion Phoenix of the South. The majestic bird cocked her head and eyed him for a long moment, as if she didn't know quite what to make of him. Then she took a big breath, lowered her head, and obliterated Niko in a river of flame.

Whoa. That Was Weird.

I felt like someone had taken a spade and scraped everything out of my chest. I'd only avoided capture because Niko had reminded me how to protect myself, even as he himself was being captured—and then I'd run away. I hadn't even tried to look for him to help *him* escape. I'd been a terrible friend. And now he was gone. I thought I would burst with the tears I was holding back. I felt like I was made of them.

"See?" the guard said jovially. "Told you we got 'im. Sent him right back where he came from."

Wait. "Where he came from?"

"Somewhere in the Middle Lands. The fire blasts you through a portal," the guard said. "Though it's anyone's guess where you end up. Could be back at home, could be at the bottom of a well. Who knows?"

Relief swept through me and a pinprick of hope sparked to life in my chest. Maybe Niko was okay after all!

"Of course, that's assuming he survived the blast—that fire can be a doozy, I've heard." The guard chuckled as if foxes drowning in a well or burning up in a fire portal was a funny little joke. The hope flickered out, and my chest felt dark and empty again.

A few minutes later, my guard presented me to another guard at a service entrance in the palace wall. He gave me a broad wink and said, "Now then. Off you go and be a good girl," before sauntering away, whistling merrily to himself.

I was shoved inside, where I paused for a moment, disoriented. What should I do? Where should I go? What was I going to tell the others? And how could I continue now that Niko was gone?

"Oi! Hurry up and get back to the kitchens!" the guard shouted at me from the gate.

Right. Kitchens. Sure. Where were they?

I was standing in a long, open, sandy yard between the outer wall and a cluster of thatch-roofed outbuildings. To my left, I saw an equestrian shooting range where elegantly dressed kami galloped around on horseback, shooting arrows at targets. The stables had to be near here. Maybe Danny was, too.

"Hey, you! You in the indoor uniform! Get indoors! Shoo! Scat! Begone!" said a voice. It came from a trio of monkeys carved into the top of a torii. One monkey had his hands over his eyes, one had his hands over his ears, and one had his hands over his mouth: Mizaru, Kikazaru, and Iwazaru. Or in English, See Not, Hear Not, and Speak Not. Mizaru did not see, but could sniff out danger; Kikazaru blocked out sounds, but saw everything; Iwazaru didn't speak, but listened to everyone's business. It was Kikazaru—Hear Not—who was speaking to me now.

I wanted so badly to ask them where the stables were so I could talk to Danny, but I didn't dare. "Y-yes sirs," I stammered, and passed under the torii toward the palace proper. I glanced back over my shoulder, and my heart lurched. The monkeys were on *this* side now. Kikazaru and Iwazaru were staring fiercely at me. Mizaru was frowning and sniffing the air.

I wandered aimlessly for a long time and eventually arrived in what appeared to be the female servants' dining hall, just in time for dinner. It was a large, brightly lit room full of long, low tables. Kami of all ages sat on the floor and chatted with each other over bowls of noodles and broth. In the far left corner was a large group of girls my age.

Not surprisingly, Ryleigh was sitting in the middle of a table of the girls with the sleekest hair and the cutest noses. I watched her flip her ponytail, look around as if to check for eavesdroppers, and lean forward, like she had a big, juicy secret to share. Like flowers stretching toward the sun, the other girls instinctively leaned toward her. Instantly, they changed from a group of individual flowers to one tightly closed, impenetrable bud of the coolest servant girls in the palace. How did she *do* that? And what would she do when she spotted me? She'd be furious, probably. But Niko was gone. We were in trouble. I had to tell her.

I swallowed the painful knot that formed in my throat at the thought of Niko, and threaded my way across the room toward Ryleigh. As I got close, we locked eyes; I saw a flash of surprise, which she covered with a laugh before she shook her head just a fraction of an inch and smiled again at her new friends.

Great. Just like back at home, I thought. Only I *had* to talk to her. I stood there and considered barging in anyway, but she caught my eye once again. This time she held my gaze a little longer and full-on shook her head and said out loud in her syrupy mean-girl voice, "Sorry, this table is full." All the other girls at her table turned and stared at me, and while they were staring, she mouthed, *We'll talk later.*

I sat down at the empty end of a table at the edge of the kids' area, feeling confused. *We'll talk later.* Whatever. Why couldn't I sit with her now and also talk later? Why had I listened to her? What had happened to standing up for myself? Most confusing of all: Why wasn't I angry about it? Instead of anger, or even pain, I felt . . . nothing.

"Sometimes I wish I could be like them," said a girl who had just sat down next to me.

"What?"

The girl was short and had brown-black hair, a tiny, sweet mouth, and bright, friendly brown eyes with impossibly long eyelashes. She was watching me watch Ryleigh, and smiling. I wondered if she was smiling because she meant it, or if she was just trying not to turn into an oni. "I mean, look how beautiful they are," she said.

I stared at her. "First of all, you do not want to be like them. And second of all, *you're* beautiful!"

"Not as beautiful as Kiku."

"Who's that?"

"The one with the red ribbon around her ponytail. Sitting next to the new girl." Which is to say, the one who was already giggling with Ryleigh like they were best friends.

"Somebody needs to get over her crush on Kiku." A tall, athletic-looking girl with gold-colored eyes leaned over from the table behind me. "You must be new, too. My name's Taka.

190

This is Suzume." Hawk and Sparrow. They fit their names perfectly. "Suzume has a thing for toxic kids. Her last crush was a messenger from the scribes' offices, and he was the worst."

"I'm, uh, Edamame. I just got switched from the, um, diplomats' quarters."

"Ooh, a soybean spirit!" Suzume clapped her hands. "We'll call you Eda for short."

By now, Ryleigh had pulled out her phone and was playing a TBS song and teaching her new friends the dance moves that went with it. Pretty soon, the room was full of girls learning the steps to TBS's latest hit, "Let's Go."

"What's wrong?" Taka, true to her name, had been watching everyone—including me. I realized I'd been staring.

I shrugged. "I dunno. It's all so silly and shallow. I mean, who cares about learning the latest dance moves? There's so much more important stuff in the kami-verse."

Taka raised an eyebrow and cocked her head. "Isn't it important to have fun? And if you think it's so silly, why do you know the moves and all the lyrics?"

I blushed. In addition to staring, I *might* have been mouthing the lyrics and kinda-sorta low-key doing the dance steps by myself. "I mean, I—"

"I think maybe you wish you were part of their group. So you're telling yourself that they're shallow and silly so you can feel better about being alone."

"That—that's not true!" I stammered. Why would I ever want to be part of that backstabbing . . . hateful . . . um . . . empty-headed . . . um . . . How odd. It was like my anger

191

couldn't sustain itself. Like my rage monster had been shut in a closet full of cotton. Which was a relief, because I'd come to dread that flash of pain and the prickling skin, but also? I felt . . . empty. And unsatisfied. I kind of *liked* being angry, I realized. Huh. That was weird. And kind of troubling.

Ryleigh was making a big show of not wanting to leave her group, and then leaving it. She strode over to me and said nonchalantly, "Oh, hey, so, like, I totally didn't mean to be mean or anything earlier, okay? It's just that we needed some space, that's all. Okay, bye." As she turned to go, she wrinkled her nose at me and said, "By the way, you should really get some new socks."

I checked my socks and saw something next to my foot: a neatly folded triangle of paper.

Taka was rolling her eyes and saying, "Wow, *she's* not very nice, is she," but I barely heard her because the unfolded piece of paper said, *Meet me in the vegetable garden in five minutes.*

Weird and Different?
Same Thing.

Even with Taka's careful directions, I made four wrong turns, but I finally found Ryleigh hiding behind a row of tomato plants. "You're late," she said without even looking at me.

I braced for the stabbing sensation of anger—which didn't come—and said nothing.

She pulled an orange Sungold tomato off a vine and popped it in her mouth. "What are you doing in the palace? You're supposed to be out getting the boat tickets."

"Okay," I said carefully. "I have to tell you something."

After I told her what had happened to me and Niko, Ryleigh let out a huge breath and didn't say anything for a long time. Finally, she said very quietly, "I'm sure he's fine."

"Yeah." I didn't want to think about the alternative. I wiped away one tear, and then another.

She was still for another moment before she said, "I mean. I hope he's fine. He'll be fine. Right?"

I just nodded because now my throat felt like one big, painful rock.

"We'll have to tell Danny and Jin at some point," Ryleigh said.

I nodded again. "Where are they? Are they okay?"

"Jin's in the entertainers' quarters and I'm guessing Danny's in the boys' dorm. We're going to meet during lunch break tomorrow and share our intel."

I nodded a third time.

Ryleigh plucked another tomato off the vine and said, "So, guess what. I told that girl Kiku that you would take her shift scrubbing the floor outside the Hall of Mirrors. Follow me and I'll show you where the supplies are." She got up and started walking.

"What?" I said, confused by her sudden change of gears.

"You're welcome. Are you coming or not?"

I hurried after her. "But—"

"It's a good place to eavesdrop and maybe pick up some information about the guards' shifts, and that three-legged-crow, Yata-something."

"Yatagarasu," I said to her back.

"Right," she replied.

"What about you?" I asked.

"I'd do it, but I'm busy." She crossed a covered walkway that connected our compound to another one.

"Doing what?"

"Hanging out with people."

"Oh." Where was my rage monster? Why wasn't I upset?

Maybe Ryleigh heard something in my voice, because she turned and put her hands on her hips. "Now what?"

What I wanted to say was, *We're supposed to be a team, but here we are again, just like at school, and you're literally making me do the dirty work while you hang out with your new friends, like you don't even care about my feelings.* But I could barely summon the energy to even *think* it.

Ryleigh must have figured it out on her own, because she said, "A lot of those girls serve Amaterasu's ladies-in-waiting, so they could give us crucial intelligence. *Someone* has to get in with them."

"I could do it," I said—unconvincingly, I guess, because Ryleigh snorted.

We went down a short flight of steps and passed through a courtyard; on one side was the wall that separated the palace grounds from the rest of the city. Was that why the air felt a little different here? I caught a whiff of something vaguely familiar that intensified as we passed a pair of pine trees growing near the wall. It smelled vaguely piney, but the pine seemed to be disguising something else—something darker and sharper. It made me feel strong. Reckless, even.

I took another deep breath and followed Ryleigh reluctantly across that courtyard, onto a veranda, and around a building to another courtyard, with a well and several wooden buckets in the center. Ryleigh went down the steps and over to the buckets. She picked one up, and as she lowered it into the well, she said, "Okay, you know what I think? I think you're jealous of me because I'm popular and you're not. Because I know how not to act weird, and you don't."

I felt like I'd been punched. How could she be so cruel and so clueless at the same time? "I'm not weird," I said, surprised at the energy in my voice. "I'm . . . different."

Ryleigh hauled the bucket out and poured the water into

another, empty bucket. She gave me a pitying look. "No offense, Momo, but weird and different? Same thing. And if you want to be popular, you can't be weird."

"Are you kidding me? That's not even the point! I don't *care* about being popular. I just don't want people to treat me like garbage. You could have warned me not to talk about the spirit dimension in front of other kids. But you let people make fun of me. *You* made fun of me!"

Ow. There was that flash of pain and the prickly feeling in my forehead.

Ryleigh glanced around nervously. "Look," she said soothingly, "I'm not trying to be mean, okay? But—"

"And another thing. I hate it when you say 'I'm not trying to be mean, but . . .' and 'No offense, but . . .' It means you know that what you're about to say *is* mean and offensive, and you're just trying to weasel out of taking responsibility for it. So if I *do* push back, it seems like it's *my* fault for taking things the wrong way."

Then, just as suddenly as it had flared up, the prickling began to fade, all on its own, and so did my desire to keep arguing. Maybe it was because I'd told her to stop picking on me, and here I was, still alive. Had I won her respect somehow? Or was she just biding her time? Or maybe I'd stopped giving her the power to scare me. I sighed and picked up the bucket. "I guess we should go clean that hallway."

Ryleigh bit her lip, picked up her bucket, and led me back down the veranda the way we'd come. We crossed wooden footbridges and went around corners until I lost all sense of where I was. By the time we entered the long corridor that led past the Hall of Mirrors, the prickling in my skin had drained away.

Halfway down the corridor stood a magnificent guard kami. She was all decked out in a golden robe that hung loosely over a white blouse tucked into wide scarlet hakama pants. The handle of a sword peeked out from her sash. I forgot my beef with Ryleigh and began worrying about the mission again. How were we ever going to make it past that guard?

Ryleigh handed me a rag, and I was shocked when she knelt beside me and dipped her own rag into the water. We worked our way silently down the hall together until she said without looking at me, "I was trying to be popular, okay? I had to. It's part of being a ninja."

She must have taken my silence for disbelief (she was right) because she kept going. "Ninja have to infiltrate the most powerful groups and learn their secrets. So I had to become one of the popular kids. And popular kids think it's weird when you talk about seeing monsters."

She'd made my life miserable for three years because of her *ninja training*? That wasn't a valid explanation—it was a bad excuse. But once again, I didn't feel like arguing—I knew I should feel angry, but the spark just wasn't there.

We inched down the corridor, scrubbing, scrubbing, scrubbing until we reached the guard, who stepped aside to let us wash the spot she'd been standing on. I took a peek down the short passage behind her that led to the Hall of Mirrors. There was Yatagarasu at the other end—snoring, with his head tucked under a wing.

Interesting.

Once we'd moved past the guard, Ryleigh said quietly, "Being popular isn't as great as you think it is. It's super stressful, actually. I'm always worried about if people like me. I feel like I can never let my guard down." She sighed, and I almost felt sorry for her.

Almost.

It wasn't her fault that popularity was such a messed-up game. And it sounded like she didn't really like playing it. But she didn't *have* to play. She didn't have to be mean to people.

I remembered what Susano'o had said about Tamamo-no-mae—about girls having to fight each other for power and attention, especially from boys: "Welcome to the patriarchy!" Even Danny had once said that being "normal" was a game—except for him it was about acting tough and playing the right sports. Was *that* the patriarchy? Or was it just the way people were? Whatever it was, I decided I hated it.

"If it's that bad, then stop trying to be popular," I said.

It took a moment before she said, "I can't."

"Why not?" I demanded.

She didn't reply.

We moved our buckets to the shorter corridor where Yatagarasu was asleep. Three ladies-in-waiting turned the corner and wafted past without even looking at us. When they reached the door to the Hall of Mirrors, one of them simply opened it and they drifted through. Then the door closed and we were alone again. Yatagarasu never even stirred.

"Weird," Ryleigh mused, standing. Then she pulled a classic Ryleigh gear-shift: "Okay. I'm out of here."

"You're leaving?"

"Well, yeah. I have to get back to Kiku and the others, remember? We're playing cards in the dorm."

I *wanted* to be angry now—I didn't care if it hurt. I closed my eyes and tried to summon my rage monster. *Come on,* I called to it. *Wake up!*

"I'm not doing it to be mean, I promise," Ryleigh said. "I told you—Kiku's popular, and she's in charge of job assignments, so one of us needs to be friends with her. And no offense, but—"

Ow. Finally! It was just a sputter of irritation, but it was better than nothing. "Could you please stop saying that?" I wrung the rag out and started wiping the floor again. "Whatever. Just go do your thing."

Ryleigh didn't move for a while, and as my anger drained away, I wondered if she was going to apologize for real this time. I dipped my rag back in the water, and when I turned to look at her, she was gone.

A few more ladies passed in and out of the Hall of Mirrors over the next hour—what did they do in there, I wondered. Did they take turns checking out their reflections in their best light? Did they ask the question-answering mirror about their futures?

I watched and listened as hard as I could, but not a single one of them said or did anything interesting or useful. No codes, no passwords, no secret buttons or levers. The guard never left her post at the other end of the corridor, and Yatagarasu never untucked his head from under his wing. Maybe Susano'o's information had been wrong and the door wasn't locked after all.

Wouldn't it be funny if, after all of Ryleigh's talk about spy tactics and social skills, I just walked right into the Hall of Mirrors and took the Mirror of the Sun myself? That would show her.

I peered up and down the corridor. It was empty. Now was my chance.

Okay. Be casual. I stood up and wandered—casually—toward the door. Probably best if I backed up to it so I didn't look like I was trying to get in. I turned and s-t-r-e-t-c-h-e-d my arms uuup and baaack and dowwwn and reeeached behind me for the handle.

My fingers felt only air. Hmm. Maybe if I took another step back.

And that's how I tripped over the water bucket. I flailed and windmilled, trying to keep my balance, and my hand knocked into something soft.

Whap.

And feathery.

"KAAAAA!!"

And very, very loud.

Yatagarasu launched himself into the air and I threw my arms over my face just in time to avoid having my eyes pecked out.

"KAAA! Intruder! Attacker! Thief! KAAA! Guards! Guards!"

The golden guard rushed over and twisted my arms behind my back.

"No, please!" I begged. "It was an accident!"

"She was trying to break into the Hall of Mirrors!" Yatagarasu said to the guard.

"I wasn't. I just tripped and fell, I swear to you!"

The guard turned me around and looked deep into my eyes,

and I felt a little woozy. Was she searching for a lie? I *had* just tripped and fallen, after all. I hadn't been trying to get in—I'd only been testing the door.

Did she believe me? I couldn't tell. She let me go without a word and returned to her post. But not before I saw a key on a cord around her neck.

Yatagarasu returned to his perch and fixed his black button eyes on me. "Just you wait. I have sounded the alarm, and—KAAA—Niwataka will be here in a moment. You can—KAAA—tell *him* that you tripped."

Moments later, a middle-aged kami in a silver-gray kimono bustled around the corner, looking decidedly grumpy.

"What is it this time? Who have you apprehended?"

Yatagarasu presented me with a flourish of his big black wings. "KAAA! I apprehended this dastardly criminal in the act of attempting to—KAAA—break into the sacred Hall of Mirrors of Her—KAAA—Holy Incandescence."

Niwataka closed his eyes and sighed deeply before looking at me and asking, "What were you doing here, girl?"

"I was just washing the floors, sir. I tripped." Best to keep it simple.

"She lies! She's a thief! She is a threat to the safety of our beloved queen!"

I could have sworn Niwataka rolled his eyes. "Do you intend to do any harm to Amaterasu, Celestial City, or the Sky Kingdom?" he asked me. "Or to our honorable three-legged friend here? Tell the truth, child." This time I definitely saw a little twinkle in his eye.

"No, sir."

"Of course she says no!" Yatagarasu squawked. "What a question to ask!"

"You weren't trying to steal anything?"

I shook my head. *Not this time, anyway.*

"Test the door!" Yatagarasu insisted.

Niwataka pulled a stick out of his sleeve and passed it over the door. "No sign of anyone even *touching* this door who isn't authorized to enter."

I suppressed a sigh of relief. Thank goodness I'd tripped.

Yatagarasu gave me such a fierce, fiery stare that I had to look away. "Do not believe her, Niwataka. KAAA! Mark my words, she is not to be trusted! I recommend you clap her in irons and throw her into the sludge, where she may drown in her lies and her evil intentions! KAAA! KAAA!"

"I will do no such thing," Niwataka said. "She is a child, and she tripped, and you are far too quick to see danger where there is none. Loosen up, you ridiculous old bird."

"I will take this to Amaterasu herself! I will not rest until I am heard!"

Yatagarasu began cawing and squawking and jumping up and down until Niwataka finally waved his arms and said, "All right, all right! I will report the child to her supervisor and arrange for the door to be locked at all times. Does that satisfy you? Will it make you stop your infernal racket?"

Yatagarasu agreed, although reluctantly. We left him preening his feathers and grumbling to himself about lax security standards and incompetent management. I decided not to point out that he'd been asleep on the job, so technically *he* was the incompetent one.

Niwataka escorted me back through the palace and apologized for Yatagarasu's behavior. "He served as a lookout for Her Brightness's army long ago, and he sees everyone as a potential traitor."

I smiled as innocently as I could and thanked him for being so understanding.

"Now, off to bed with you and get some rest!" he said when we reached the walkway outside the girls' sleeping quarters. "Only two days left until New Year's Eve, and we've all got lots of work to do!"

He was more right than he knew. I thought of all those kids being held hostage by Tamamo-no-mae. They would become empty shells of themselves if Danny, Ryleigh, Jin, and I didn't rescue them. Two days left. How in the kami-verse were we going to make this work?

I Smell a Lie

Everyone in the dorm room had already laid out their futon and gone to bed for the night. It looked like a giant slumber party. I picked my way around until I found Ryleigh toward the center of the room (of course), and brought her outside to tell her what had happened.

"I told you to be *careful!*" she whispered.

"Well, I'm sorry for not being a professionally trained burglar."

"*Tsk.* Whatever. I'll figure out how to deal with this tomorrow." Ryleigh heaved an enormous sigh, like I'd tried to pour her a glass of milk and spilled it all over the table. Without another word, she turned to go back to bed.

I thought about pointing out that I hadn't *asked* to have after-dinner floor-scrubbing duty, but I was tired and stressed out and couldn't be bothered. I stumbled around the edges of the room until I found an empty futon, and crawled under the covers and fell asleep immediately.

In my dream, I was kneeling before Amaterasu as she pulled her mirror out of a rosewood chest. I knew somehow that we were in the Hall of Mirrors, though I couldn't tell what it looked like—the light that emanated from her reflected off every surface so that I felt like I was standing in a space made of nothing but sunlight.

Amaterasu was facing slightly away from me, but even at that angle, she was so bright and beautiful it almost hurt to look at her. She was dressed in an old-fashioned twelve-layered kimono; each layer was a slightly different shade of gold. Her hair streamed down her back like a river of onyx through a sunlit field.

She is here, a voice whispered. All around me, it echoed: *She is here, she is here, she is here.*

Who was talking? And who were they talking to? *Who* was here? I looked around me, pointlessly.

Look in the mirror.

Helpless to resist, I leaned forward and peered into the polished bronze surface of Amaterasu's mirror. Amaterasu's warm, bright light shone all around me, but the mirror itself was as dark as the night sky, and my face in it was a pale, featureless oval. I watched in horror as my features emerged, slowly, slowly, until I was looking not at myself, but at someone with broad cheekbones and a proud mouth, his nostrils flared and his stormy black eyes flashing with wild, uncontained fury: it was the elemental face of my grandfather, Susano'o. Then that face began shifting, blurring, and then sharpening into something even more horrible: the pale, cold, skeletal beauty of Izanami, wearing her crown of finger bones. She smiled, revealing a mouthful of blackened teeth.

Come to me, Momo.

Izanami stretched a bony hand out of the mirror. From behind her, Susano'o reached out with his own massive paw.

Come, now. Don't be afraid.

I tried to scramble up and away from both of them, but it was like I was moving underwater. My limbs felt heavy and awkward, and they refused to do what I wanted them to do. I felt thin, cold fingers closing around one wrist, and thick, rough fingers clamping around the other. I tried to scream, but my tongue swelled up and filled my mouth, and no sound came out.

Momo!

I sat bolt upright, sweating. My heart pounded and my head throbbed.

Momo. Come to me. I can help you.

That voice—that call—it hadn't been Izanami or Susano'o. I'd forgotten my earplugs and been woken up by the voice from the inn, and from the city, the one that was part promise and part threat, that had led me outside in the middle of the night and almost made me climb into a hole in the ground. I lay back down. *Ignore it,* I told myself. No good could possibly come of listening to a voice that wanted you to climb through a grate in the ground.

But it wouldn't let up. *Momo. You need me. Come out here.*

I squeezed my eyes shut and pulled my covers over my head. *No. This is one hundred percent a trap. I'm not going out there.*

It wheedled and whined; it coaxed and cajoled; it asked questions that squicked around in my brain like an awful itch. *Don't you want to know who I am? Don't you want to know how I can help you? Aren't you even a little bit curious? Momo. Come and find out.*

I *was* curious. And I *did* need help.

Maybe if I just took a peek. I would be very careful and I would not let the voice talk me into doing anything dangerous. Going outside was safe, right? I was inside the palace walls, after all. I pulled back the covers and crept out of the room, down the veranda, following . . . a feeling. It was that same buzzing jittery sensation I associated with Susano'o and my rage monster—and as much as I hated and feared it, I couldn't help feeling a little relieved that it was still there. Which made me wonder: What kind of person was I if I was glad that the worst part of me was still alive and kicking and ready to rumble?

Over here, Momo.

I was in a courtyard next to the wall that separated the palace grounds from the rest of the city—the same one that Ryleigh and I had passed through earlier; I recognized the twin pine trees growing on the far side. Torches flickered at every corner, making the shadows dance. I climbed off the veranda and crossed the yard. I was practically vibrating with pent-up angry energy now—I found myself wishing someone would come and insult me so I could yell at them. Why?

I found the answer at the base of the wall, under the two pine trees. A flat wooden well cover had been moved to expose an iron grate. Just like at the inn. That same sharp, smoky odor rose up, so thick I could practically taste it—like resentment, rage, and irritation.

That's right. Down here. I can help you get what you need.

"How do you know what I need?" I whispered. Every cell in my body begged me to lift the grate and jump in.

I know every naughty thought and feeling that anyone has in

207

this town, said the voice. *Most of them are borrrrinnng. In fact, most of yours are boring. But stealing the mirror—that's fun. And I can help you. All you have to do is climb down here.*

I had to sit down so my legs wouldn't take me the last few steps. "No."

No! The voice cackled, and I heard it echo underground. *I like that! I like "no." But if you want the mirror, you need my help.*

Maybe. Something inside me quivered with excitement. Maybe I could stick just my head in? Maybe just for a moment. I saw my hands on the ground, pushing me onto my feet. I saw one foot out in front, then another, and then my hands reached toward the grate, closed around the iron bars . . .

"Who goes there?" A sharp voice snapped me back into consciousness, and I whipped around to see who was talking.

"Uh. Me?" I croaked. "I'm just a, uh, lowly servant girl!"

Three shapes detached themselves from the shadows—it was Mizaru, Kikazaru, and Iwazaru, the guard monkeys from the equestrian shooting range. What were they doing here?

"I smell a lie," Mizaru said with his hands over his eyes.

"I saw you bending over the grate," Kikazaru added, his hands clamped firmly over his ears.

I looked down at the grate, which was—thank goodness—silent. "I was just, ah, taking a walk. I couldn't sleep."

"Iwazaru heard you talking to someone," Mizaru said accusingly, and Iwazaru grunted and nodded his head, his hands still covering his mouth. "He says he heard them say you needed help."

"Oh! No, that was me. Talking to myself. About how . . ." I looked at the grate and the wooden cover next to it. "About how I needed help with the grate cover."

208

Iwazaru grunted again, and Mizaru said, "He says you were definitely talking to someone else."

"Do you see anyone here besides me?" I asked. "Or hear anyone?"

Mizaru sniffed the air and Iwazaru cocked his head to listen. He nudged Kikazaru, who looked around, frowning with his hand still covering his ears. Finally, Kikazaru admitted, "No one."

"So I guess I'll just fix this by myself, then," I said, and dragged the cover back over the grate. Once it was in place, it was like I'd unplugged myself from my power source. Suddenly I was exhausted.

"We will take you back to your quarters," Mizaru declared. "We do not trust you."

But that was fine with me. I didn't trust me, either.

When I woke up the next morning, my first thought wasn't about the voice, or about Yatagarasu, or the Hall of Mirrors. It was about Niko, who would have woken me by shoving his wet nose in my face. The thought lay like a rock in my stomach. *Please be okay. I'll come and find you as soon as we rescue those kids,* I promised him silently as I dragged myself out of bed.

The morning got worse when Kiku caught me by the sleeve on my way to breakfast.

"Did you try to get into the Hall of Mirrors last night?" she asked with a smile that wasn't quite a smile.

My mouth fell open. Had Ryleigh told her? Why? "It was an acci—"

"Whatever. The point is, the manager is taking it out on me

because even though *you* woke up Yatagarasu, it was technically *my* shift. So we've both been assigned to dishwashing duty for the rest of eternity. And I had a ticket to go to the New Year's Eve concert tomorrow night, but they took that away from me, too." Her voice was lilting and sweet, but her eyes were like daggers.

"Oh." I swallowed. "I'm sorry."

Then Ryleigh was there—as usual, she'd appeared as if out of thin air. "I'll take your shift, Kiku," she said. "It was my fault for telling Edamame to sub for you."

"No, it wasn't. How would you know that she'd go and make a mess of everything?"

"No, seriously, it's fine." Ryleigh's face was sweet and sincere. "It's totally unfair for you to get punished."

"Are you sure you don't mind?" Kiku said.

"I don't mind at all. It would be my pleasure," said Ryleigh with a sideways glance at me that made me feel queasy.

"You're a good friend," said Kiku, and gave Ryleigh a hug. Then she turned to me and sang, "Have funnn!"

"Uh . . . what just happened?" I asked Ryleigh once Kiku was out of earshot.

"She thinks I'm going to spend my day ignoring you so she doesn't have to. I'm just doing her a favor."

"*What?* But that's . . . How do you know?"

Ryleigh shrugged. "It's like a code, I guess."

I was *very* sure now that I wanted nothing to do with the popular mean-girl clique, whether it was in the Palace of the Sun or back at Oak Valley.

"Is that how you survive at home?" I asked Ryleigh.

Ryleigh nodded grimly.

"You really need to leave your friend group. I don't think it's good for your soul."

"Yeah." She nodded again. "Maybe after we save their lives."

"Ha-ha, yeah." I was too scared and anxious to laugh for real at that joke.

"Also," she continued, "now we have all day to plan together. See? Access to power has its upsides."

It *was* pretty impressive how she'd managed to outsmart Kiku and turn my mistake last night into an asset. So was Ryleigh sneaky, or was she just a great strategist? I guessed it depended on your perspective.

"You did fix it all up," I admitted.

"Yep." Ryleigh cleared her throat. "Um. By the way. Some of the stuff I said last night, about being popular? I know it's messed up. So, you know. I'm . . . I'm sorry. About everything. And I'm sorry I was rude to you when you came back from your stakeout. I know you did your best." She looked everywhere but at me, like she was trying to pretend I wasn't the one she was talking to. And *then* she said, "And I know you're worried about me and Danny being, uh. Friends. But you shouldn't be. He talks about you, like, all the time. He thinks you're 'dope.'" She did air quotes for "dope" and rolled her eyes and grinned at me.

Then she stopped grinning and said, "What?"

I realized I was staring at her like she'd sprouted a pair of antennae. Or wings. Or both. I thought about saying, *Who are you, and what have you done with Ryleigh?* Instead I just said, "Thanks."

Ryleigh and I spent the entire morning washing an endless stream of plates, cups, bowls, chopsticks, pots, and pans. In the meantime, we listed our assets (not many) and our liabilities (tons). We gossiped about Suzume and Kiku. I told Ryleigh about the monkey guards—but not about the voice from the grate, which scared me too much to talk about.

At lunchtime, we met with Danny and Jin as planned.

"Hey, what are you doing here? Aren't you supposed to be out in the city with Niko?" Danny asked.

"Yeah, about that. The thing is . . . ," I started. I'd prepared myself for this, but I still had to stop for a moment to keep my voice from trembling. I turned to Ryleigh for help. "Can you . . . ?"

She shook her head. "You were there. Niko was—I mean, he *is*—your friend."

"Wait, what? Did you say *was?*" Danny said. His eyes grew big. "Momo, what happened to Niko? Where is he?"

I told the story as quickly as possible. When I was finished, Jin looked grim. And sad. But Danny looked like someone had hit him in the head with a baseball bat. He started babbling, "I'm sure he's fine. He's a spirit fox, right? He'll survive the fire. He's . . . he's probably hanging out on the Island of Mysteries right now. Or waiting for you at home. Or . . . or . . . Anyway. I'm sure he's fine. He's fine. He has to be fine."

Ryleigh moved to hug him, and I felt a wave of despair because I hadn't thought to do it, and now Ryleigh was going to be the good friend, and I wasn't. And then I was worried that I wasn't angry about it. *Then* I was *worried* that I was worried that I wasn't angry. Who knows how long I would have spent on this mental merry-go-round if Ryleigh hadn't let Danny go and whispered to me, "I think he needs a hug from *you.*"

I blinked at her in confusion. "Huh?"

She rolled her eyes. "Go give him a hug. Team DaMoNik or whatever, right?"

Wow. First an awkward apology and now this? It seemed like telling her off last night really *had* made a difference.

I gave Danny a hug. "He's fine, right?" Danny kept saying. "He'll be fine."

I almost said, *I don't know.* Because how would I know if Niko was fine? What if he wasn't? What if he was dead?

Instead, I said, "I'm sure he's fine. You know him. He'll be fine."

This seemed to calm Danny down a little. "You think so?" he said.

No. Not a hundred percent. Maybe not even fifty percent. Because the fire that had come out of the phoenix's mouth had looked *very* deadly. But I knew Danny needed to believe that everything would be okay, so I said, "A hundred percent."

Danny nodded and let me go with a little grin. "Well, I mean, if *you* think he's okay, then that's a good sign. Because you never think anything's gonna be okay."

"Ha-ha." I rolled my eyes. And even though I'd been lying just now, I felt a little better. Maybe Niko *would* be okay.

"We're all gonna be okay," Jin said. He wiped away a tear and sniffled a couple of times. "Can I have a hug, too?"

"Group hug!" Ryleigh shouted. "Right now!" And for once, I didn't mind her taking over.

Ryleigh and I went over the details of our new plan with the boys, and Danny gave us a tour of the stables; I'd been right—they were just around the corner from where I'd first met

Mizaru, Kikazaru, and Iwazaru. We double-checked TBS's set list. The guard monkeys showed up, and Ryleigh and Jin turned their charm on full blast and we all had a nice chat. Then lunch hour was over.

For the first time since we'd started off on this mission, I felt a sliver of real optimism. I never would have predicted that I'd be truly, honestly grateful to have Ryleigh on the team, but she really was good at this. And she wasn't as scary or as evil as I'd always thought. And we had a proper plan.

On our way back to the kitchen, we overheard the guards talking about the latest news from the Middle Lands: 888 children had gone missing now, and so had Tamamo-no-mae. The guards wondered where she was hiding, and how much power she would gain from drinking these children's lives, and if she would grow strong enough to consider attacking the Sky Kingdom. They doubted it.

Ryleigh and I exchanged worried looks.

"It'll work," said Ryleigh. She set her jaw and tossed her ponytail. "Trust me."

"I trust you," I said. And I did.

Above and Beyond
the Call of Duty

I've never been as busy as I was the day of the New Year's Eve concert. The palace was full of guests who were hungry and thirsty all day long, and I scrubbed dishes in the kitchen until I thought my waterlogged fingers might fall off like soggy pretzel sticks. Luckily, the kitchen was so busy and the cooks were so distracted that no one noticed when one of the hot-pots I washed didn't make it back to the pantry. No one saw me tucking mochi cakes filled with sweet bean paste into my sash, or sneaking bottles of sake into my sleeves on my lunch break.

Little Suzume had been happy to take Ryleigh's place next to me at the sink. When I asked her about my missing anger, she blithely informed me that out of respect for the high rank of the kami inside the palace, anger wasn't punished—it was muffled. "Didn't you know? Only true, roaring rage can break through the filter," she said. When I suggested we take a walk around the stables during the afternoon break, the cute new stablehand came over and flirted with her so hard that afterward she confided to me that maybe she had a new crush. More importantly, she never saw me hide the hot-pot, sake, and mochi cakes under the straw in an empty stall that the flirtatious stablehand had made sure to leave open.

Ryleigh spent the day doing Suzume's job, running to and from the kitchens to rooms all over the palace, carrying trays and delivering packages. If anyone saw her stealing—a couple of flints here, a candlestick there—no one said anything. No one saw her carrying a hot-pot out of the stables, and no one thought twice when, on one of her errands, she brought a silk-wrapped package to the performers' dormitory, with a note addressed to Jin Takayama.

No one cared when Jin lit a tiny hibachi stove to make some candy in a hot-pot—he needed it to soothe his throat for the concert, he said. It smelled terrible—like gunpowder, in fact—but didn't all singers have their quirks and their silly magic potions? There could certainly be no harm in it. No one paid attention when Ryleigh dropped off another package for Jin as evening approached, and as a thank-you, he gave her a few pieces of the "candy" he'd made.

Later that evening, the new stablehand—the same one who'd flirted with Suzume during her lunch break—offered Mizaru, Kikazaru, and Iwazaru a gift of three bottles of sake and a plate of mochi. They were more than happy to accept. No one had ever done anything like this for them in the many thousands of years they'd faithfully guarded the palace grounds every New Year's Eve.

"It's about time someone appreciated our hard work, for once. Even if it's only a stablehand." Mizaru took his hands off his eyes, because how else was he supposed to find the sake bottle and bring it to his lips?

"Indeed," agreed Kikazaru. He'd been able to hear Mizaru because he'd taken his hands off his ears to reach for a sweet mochi cake.

Iwazaru was silent. But that was only because he was busy washing down a mouthful of mochi with a swig of sake.

None of them paused to wonder why a lowly stablehand would be the one assigned to bring them a gift of food and drink meant only for the kami of the highest orders.

Even later in the evening, the serving girls crowded around a special holographic screen that broadcast live video of the concert so that everyone could enjoy the festivities even if they couldn't attend in person. The concert opened with a series of quasi-kami acts. Dustin Limbershake and Sailor Twist performed a duet to delighted applause from the crowd. Then there was a wrestling match: the Boulder versus Akebono, one of the greatest living sumo wrestlers. TBS, the most recent recipient of a star on the Hollywood Walk of Fame, was the final quasi-kami act in the lineup.

Nearly everyone in the dorm had worked themselves into a frenzy of excitement over the Middle Lands' most popular boy band. They swooned over holographic portraits; speculated about Jin Takayama, a guest member from rival boy band Straight 2 tha Topp; and practiced the dances. When I put on my backpack and slipped out the door, the only person who noticed was Ryleigh.

． ． ．

Jin Takayama, boy band superstar and international teen heart-
throb, checked his reflection in the mirror and smoothed an
eyebrow. He was almost ready to go. Artfully torn jeans, check.
Flowy white shirt with the top three buttons undone, check.

"Ten minutes!" someone called, and the official members of
TBS jumped up and followed the stagehand out of the dress-
ing room. Jin lagged behind the others, rummaging through his
rumpled pile of street clothes.

Fabian stuck his head in the door and called to him impatiently. "Jin! What are you doing? We're up!"

"Yeah, I know. I forgot my watch—it'll just take a sec. Go
on, I'll catch up."

Once Fabian was gone, Jin pulled out the rest of the "candy"
he'd made in the hot-pot earlier that day—two shapeless black
lumps—and tucked them carefully into his pocket along with
a flint that had gone missing from someone's room earlier that
day. Each lump of candy had a piece of string sticking out the
top of it, like a wick.

Or a fuse.

I had just turned the corner into the passageway that led to the
Hall of Mirrors. I heard footsteps behind me, and then came
Ryleigh's voice:

"Hey, Edamame, I saw you sneak out! Where are you going?
Stop! Get back here!"

I picked up my pace, my heart pounding.

The guard in the middle of the corridor turned toward me,
her eyebrow lifted. She was magnificent, as before, in her gold

robe and scarlet pants. Around her neck I could see the cord that held the key to the Hall of Mirrors.

"Hey! I said stop!" Ryleigh had turned the corner and was closing in. I hitched up the bottom of my kimono and ran.

"Excuse me! Pardon me!" I panted as I slid to a stop in front of the guard. She crossed her arms and stared down at me imperiously. "I have a message from Lady Kono-hana. She says—"

"She's lying! She's lying!" Ryleigh came pelting down the hallway. "She's been confined to the kitchens all day! Don't trust her!"

I scurried behind the guard, clutching her robe and using her as a shield. "Please, just let me finish! I have a message to deliver!"

"Hey!" The guard twisted around to grab me and shove me forward, but I hung on tight.

Meanwhile, Ryleigh had caught up. "Liar!" she shouted, and threw herself at me. I staggered and dragged the guard and her robe to the floor with me, and we ended up in a tangled heap of arms, legs, and luxurious golden fabric.

With Ryleigh's help, the guard shrugged off her outer robe and sprang to her feet, her hand instinctively gripping the hilt of her sword, her eyes flashing.

"Both of you go back to your quarters. Now." She'd let go of the sword, but her voice was low and deadly.

"I'm so sorry, I'm so sorry. It was my job to make sure this girl didn't get out—she's such a troublemaker." Ryleigh glared at me, and then hung her head. "I have failed. Please don't report me."

The guard sighed. "You caught her before she caused any real trouble, little sister. Next time be more careful."

"I will! I will!" Ryleigh rose and grabbed my arm to yank me to my feet. "Get up, you." Then she bent to pick up the golden robe. "Please, may I help—"

But she was interrupted by a *BANG*. Then two more: *BANG*. *BANG*.

The guard whipped her head in the direction of the sound, which had come from the hallway that Ryleigh and I had just left. When a thread of black smoke curled around the corner, she pointed at both of us. "Don't. Move." Then she sprinted away, calling over her shoulder, "Yatagarasu! Watch over these two!"

Ryleigh and I smiled at each other. One guard down, one to go.

TBS was halfway through their set list when the stablehand who'd flirted with Suzume and brought the monkeys their sake and mochi—that is to say, Danny—came running out of the darkness. "One of the archers wants a different horse, and I can't find the stablemaster. I don't suppose you could come and unlock . . ."

But Mizaru was curled in a little ball, fast asleep, using Kikazaru as a pillow.

"That stablemasher—*hic*—is an irreshponsh—*hic*—irreshponsible shlacker." Iwazaru, who usually kept his hands over his mouth to prevent himself from saying anything evil, waved one of them loosely for emphasis as he steadied himself against the wall of his hut with the other. He hiccuped again and took a swig from the sake bottle by his side.

"Right." Danny glanced over his shoulder. He could hear the screams and shouts of the audience in the courtyard as TBS launched into a new song. "So, the thing is, the archers are in kind of a hurry—"

"Here." Iwazaru fumbled with a ring of keys that hung from his belt, and took one off. "You do it."

Danny took the key with a bow. "I'll bring it right back," he said, and sprinted toward the stables.

I should give that boy a promotion, thought Iwazaru as he drifted off to sleep. *He has truly gone above and beyond the call of duty.*

"Got it?" I whispered to Ryleigh.

She grinned, and I had a split second to see the key on the severed silk cord in her palm before it disappeared into her sleeve and Yatagarasu was flapping over us. He perched on Ryleigh's shoulder and aimed a beady-eyed glare at me. "KAAA! I knew it! I knew you weren't to be trusted! Should have—KAAA—insisted you be thrown to the phoenix immediately! I ought to peck your eyes out!"

"But I haven't done anything!" I protested.

"You want to, though, little beetle, I can tell. I don't know what it is—KAAA—but you're not going to do it, not while Yatagarasu is here! Worm! Slug!" He clacked his beak at me and probably would have spent the next ten minutes going down a long list of insults if a high-pitched whine and a series of loud *pop*s near the door to the Hall of Mirrors hadn't caught his attention. Yatagarasu shrieked and lifted off Ryleigh's shoulder, and we followed him down the short passage. White smoke was pouring out of the corner nearest the door, where Ryleigh had tossed a lit smoke bomb while Yatagarasu had been scolding me.

"KAAA!" Yatagarasu zoomed down the hall and out of sight, calling, "Fire! Fire! Help! Water!"—apparently happy to leave us to turn into two strips of crispy girl bacon.

Ryleigh slipped on the guard's robe and we rushed through the choking smoke to the door, where Ryleigh fitted the key in the lock.

Ryleigh and I looked at each other and grinned. Feeling exhilarated and generous, I pulled open the door and made a sweeping motion with my arm: "After you."

TBS launched into their hit single, "Never Gonna Stop," to roars and wild applause from the audience. Jin Takayama twisted and dipped and punched the air. He was easily the most charismatic quasi-kami on the stage.

A mysterious benefactor had given free tickets to the evening's concert to the stablehands, and they only felt a little bit bad about leaving Danny, the youngest, newest boy, to mind the horses. That meant that no one was there to stop him when he led a string of horses out of the stables, through the yard, and toward the courtyard where TBS was whipping the crowd into a singing, dancing frenzy.

"Ow! Why did you stop?" I rubbed my nose, which I had banged into the back of Ryleigh's very hard head. "What're you waiting for? Come on, we need to hurry!"

I gave her a little push forward, but she didn't budge. "*Move!* What are you—"

"I'm stuck!" Ryleigh turned to me, frustrated. "It's like there's an invisible wall!"

222

Oh no. I shoved her aside, thinking, *No, no, no, no, no, not after all this*—and walked right into an invisible wall.

"Maybe only part of it's open?" Ryleigh said.

She tried squeezing through the side of the doorway. Nope.

"Maybe it depends what foot you start with?" I suggested.

We tried switching feet. We tried holding our breath. Ryleigh tried ditching the stolen robe.

Wall, wall, and wall. Precious seconds were ticking away. I could see panic rising in Ryleigh's face, and I could feel my own heart drumming faster and faster. I glanced over her shoulder. The guard would be back any minute now—if Yatagarasu didn't beat her—demanding to know if it was us who'd set off the fire-crackers and smoke bombs outside the dormitory, and by that time, the ones that Ryleigh had tossed in the corner by the door would have sputtered out as well. It would all be over.

"Maybe the door can tell you're human," I said.

"Maybe it can tell *you're* human!"

"I'm half kami," I pointed out.

"The perfume is supposed to disguise my human-ness," Ryleigh countered.

"Maybe it's wearing off."

"Maybe we should figure out another way to get in."

"Maybe you two should stop arguing and come with me."

I See Fireworks, Yes I Do

This was not part of the plan.

The guard looked down at us with fire in her eyes as she snatched the key out of Ryleigh's hand and looped the cord around her wrist. Then she grabbed each of us by the shoulder and marched us back down the hallway. "Yatagarasu!" she shouted. "Where are you, you good-for-nothing birdbrain!" Her grip tightened painfully, and she stopped walking abruptly. I looked up to see her wincing, a look of surprise mixed with the pain on her face. Ryleigh and I glanced at each other as she closed her eyes and breathed in slowly, and then exhaled. In . . . out. In . . . out. Suzume's words came back to me: *Only true, roaring rage can break through the filter.* The guard must have been really furious. One more breath, and she readjusted her grip on our shoulders and we were walking again.

TBS had just begun their final number, "I See Fireworks," and Jin was taking his turn on the mic, singing lead. Concert security guards, long since distracted and enchanted by his voice, had moved forward so they could watch the show properly, and they didn't notice Danny leading the horses out of the stables, through the bamboo concert gates, and around the edge of the parade grounds behind the crowd.

The guard's grip tightened on my shoulder again as we walked onto a veranda, with one end open to a small courtyard. Strains of "I See Fireworks" floated on the air, and my heart and lungs seemed to freeze—we were supposed to be inside the Hall of Mirrors, stealing Yata-no-kagami, right this very second. The next step of the plan was moments away. What were we supposed to do?

"Are you gonna get in trouble for leaving your post?" Ryleigh said in a fake-innocent voice.

"I left you with Yatagarasu," the guard replied grimly. "It's his fault."

"Is it, though?" Ryleigh asked. "I mean, you were in charge of the key."

The guard didn't reply this time.

"I can't believe you let me steal it," Ryleigh continued. She raised her eyebrows at me.

I raised my eyebrows back—the universal sign for *What?*

Help me, she mouthed. *Make her mad.*

It seemed like a terrible idea to make the guard even more upset with us. I gave her a look that said, *Are you serious?*

She nodded. *Just go with it.*

So I went with it. "You really should have been more careful," I said, hoping my voice wasn't shaking too much.

Ryleigh added brightly, "Gee whiz. How embarrassing to get conned by a couple of servant girls!" She smiled and nodded at me: *Your turn.*

225

"I know *I'd* be embarrassed," I said. I still didn't know where we were going with this, and I was still scared, but a tiny part of me was thinking, *We're a real team! This is actually kind of fun!*

"Right? Me too! So, ma'am, are you, like, super embarrassed, or—"

"Enough!" the guard barked at us. She stopped abruptly and spun us around to face her. "Shut your mouths right now, or I'll—"

Ryleigh shot me a brief glance before she stomped hard on the guard's foot. The guard's face twisted with fury, then with pain, and she let go of us to clutch her head. We ran.

We jumped off the walkway, ran across the courtyard, scrambled onto the veranda on the other side, and skidded around its outer corner. There, we slid off again and ducked underneath it. Huddled in the shadows, we heard the guard leap onto the veranda and pause, looking down first one walkway, and then another. I held my breath.

"Where are you, you little gnats?" the guard said quietly. "Surrender and come peacefully, and it will be much better for you. Resist arrest and you will be very, very sorry."

A plan. I needed a new plan. But my mind was a blur of panic. Could I breathe to calm myself down? Would the guard hear me? Should I use Kusanagi? Could I even access its power here? Or maybe it would attract too much attention. I wondered if Ryleigh was calm. I wondered if she had a plan.

Above us and just to the left, the boards squeaked—*uguisu-bari*, I remembered—lots of wealthy homes had a "nightingale floor," built to squeak on purpose so that people inside would know if an intruder was walking outside.

The guard cursed under her breath and leaped silently to the ground.

I saw her land in a crouch and stay there, perfectly still as she peered under the far end of the veranda to our right. She had grown a full set of fangs, antlers, and dangerously sharp-looking claws. She pivoted slowly, still in her crouch, examining every inch of the shadows. I didn't dare move; I could tell she was listening for the faintest rustle of fabric, the tiniest crunch of gravel. Just a few more seconds and she'd see us, for sure.

I realized that I'd been holding my breath; slowly, carefully, I let it out. When I breathed in again, the air was laced with the scent of cigarette smoke and burning rubber.

I see fireworks, yes I do
Whenever I loooook at . . . youuuuu!

Jin's silvery voice held the last note of the song as actual fire-works shot into the sky and exploded into eight giant sparkling red-and-gold flowers. The crowd looked up, oohing and aahing, united in wonder. No one was prepared for the mayhem that was about to erupt around them.

On the ground, another set of fireworks exploded. They weren't nearly as fancy or impressive as the beauties in the sky—just a *BANG!* And a series of pops from the edge of the parade grounds: *Pop-pop-pop-pop-pop! Pop-pop-pop-pop-pop! Pop-pop-pop-pop-pop!* At the same time, two more explosions onstage produced a thick, choking smoke.

Shouts of delight turned to cries of dismay as six terrified riderless horses galloped into the crowd, spooked by the sound of the firecrackers going off practically under their feet. Kami scrambled and pushed and shoved each other to get out of the way. Meanwhile, on the stage, band members and stagehands stumbled over cords and called out to each other as they groped their way toward the exits.

In the chaos, no one noticed Jin slide off the stage. He pushed through the crowd to join Danny in the shadow of the palace wall and scurry back toward the inner courtyard.

From her raised pavilion across from center stage, Amaterasu, Great Goddess of the Sun and Queen of the Sky Kingdom, was flooded with visions of Susano'o's violent attack on the palace in the early days of her reign. She shrieked in terror as she gathered her ladies-in-waiting around her. "Guards!" she screamed. "Archers! To arms! Find the attackers! Protect the palace!"

The night sky turned red and gold with the glow of the fireworks, briefly lighting up the yard in front of us and the wall on the far side, and I realized where we were. This was the courtyard at the outer edge of the palace compound, where the monkeys had caught me trying to climb into that strange well the other night. I could see the twin pine trees and smell the sharp, bitter odor—threatening and invigorating at the same time.

From the front of the palace came a series of muffled bangs and pops, followed by screams and shouts. The guard looked up, confused and momentarily distracted.

RUN, said a voice—*that* voice. *NOW*.

I grabbed Ryleigh's hand and ran.

The guard spun around and shouted at us to stop. Next to me, Ryleigh shrieked, "What are you *doing?*"

I didn't have an answer. I didn't have a plan. I didn't have a goal. I was going on pure instinct—or maybe, looking back, I was following orders. And those orders had been to run.

Over here. The voice came from the well. Beside me, Ryleigh stumbled—the guard had lunged at her and just missed.

"Hey, Momo! Ryleigh!" Danny and Jin were standing in an open portal; behind them I could see the stables. "Get over here!"

"No! You guys come with us!" I heard myself yelling.

"No!" Ryleigh veered toward Danny and Jin and tried to tug me along.

But the voice kept calling to me: *Here. Down here. Trust me,* and I couldn't resist. I yanked on Ryleigh's hand and dragged her with me.

"Momo, come *on!*" Danny shouted.

Ignore him, said the voice.

Just a few more feet. The iron grate over the opening melted away as Ryleigh and I approached, and the opening itself widened, like a mouth. I could smell the tunnel underneath—sharp and wild and electric. My rage monster took in the scent and propelled me forward. Out of the corner of my eye, I saw the guard stumbling backward, coughing and wiping her eyes.

"MOVE!" I shouted at Jin and Danny.

"Momo, what the—" Ryleigh started.

I tightened my grip on Ryleigh's hand and jumped.

229

Ticky-Tocky Goes the Clocky

At first, I thought I was back in that cave on the Island of Mysteries. We'd fallen through some kind of portal, it seemed—the mouth had closed over the night sky above us and made the darkness even darker. But the wind that swirled around me didn't carry that same bone-chilling menace that had made my skin crawl and my heart turn cold. It was something else—nervous, chaotic, angry energy. It reminded me of Susano'o—except I knew he wasn't here. He wasn't allowed. What was going on?

"Ryleigh?" I said.

"I'm right here," came the answer, not too far away from me. Thank goodness. If you'd told me a week ago I'd be glad to hear Ryleigh's voice in the dark, I would have laughed and walked away. But here we were.

"You okay?" I asked her.

"Yeah. Are you?"

"I'm fine."

"Momo?"

"Danny!" They'd come through with us after all! "Is Jin with you?"

230

"Yeah, I'm right here."

I reached out with my arms and inched forward. In a few seconds we'd found each other's hands and huddled together.

"Where are we?" Jin asked.

"I don't know."

"Then why'd you make us jump?" Ryleigh's voice was tense, and I couldn't blame her. "I mean, the guard didn't follow us, but are we any safer than we were before?"

"I don't know. Something was calling me. Or someone."

"I don't love this," Jin whispered. "What if it's a trap?"

"Shh!" I hissed. I could have sworn I'd heard something—like someone laughing softly to themselves.

There was a long, awful silence as we listened, broken only by unsettling gurgles and blurps that echoed around us. Was that what I'd heard?

"Hellooo, little Middlings!" We all jumped. It was the voice that had called me down here. It was high and nasal now, like a fairy-tale witch, and hollow and echoey, as if it were coming from every direction. "Welcome! I'm so glad you finally accepted my invitation."

There was a scraping sound, and a tiny flame appeared next to me: Ryleigh. I had just enough time to see her gaze darting around—up, left, right—before the flame was snuffed out, as if invisible fingers had pinched it. "Ah-ah-aahh," the voice cautioned. "Little Middlings mustn't play with fire if they don't want to go . . ."

BOOM!

The air shook with an explosion and the voice shrieked with laughter when all four of us jumped again.

"Wh-where are we?" I quavered. "Who are you? What do you want?"

"I want to help you, silly-billies." The voice giggled. "Don't you remember, Momo? I've been wanting to help you for days now—I know you've heard me. And then an opportunity presented itself, and here you are! Look—ta-daaa!"

Whoosh. The space was suddenly lit by the faint glow of torches burning in garish colors: ice blue, neon green, hot pink, bright orange. We were in a large tunnel, on the banks of a canal or a river of some kind that ran through the middle of it. The walls and ceiling were black and oily, and glinted in the light of the torches.

"Well? Aren't you going to thank me, little Middlings? Aren't you going to ask me what to do next? Don't you want to find the mirror?"

I bit my lip. That old buzzing, thrumming, electric sensation was blooming inside me. It was clearly responding to something down here. That couldn't be a good sign.

Danny whispered, "Do you know . . . whoever that is?"

"No!"

"Then why did she just say she's been offering to help you?"

"Because . . . okay, I mean, she *has* been, kind of, but I've been trying not to listen."

Danny, Jin, and Ryleigh looked at me as if I'd just revealed a deep, dark, terrible, horrible secret—which I guess wasn't far from the truth. "Since when?" Jin demanded.

"And why didn't you tell us about this?" said Danny.

"Since the first night. I don't know why I didn't tell you," I said helplessly. "I was scared."

I glanced at Ryleigh, waiting for her to say something, too, but she had stopped paying attention. Instead, she was looking up, down, and all around the tunnel, her eyes wide and unblinking.

"Ticky-tocky goes the clocky! Better hurry up and decide, Middlings!" screeched the voice.

"No. We don't need your help. We've got this."

I gaped at Ryleigh. "What do you mean, *we've got this?*" I hissed. "We do *not* got this!"

Ryleigh clicked her tongue impatiently. "Look around you, Momo. Where are we?"

"In a tunnel?"

"Wrong. We're in the sewers."

"Fine. Sewers. Whatever. So?"

"What do you mean, *so?* They were on the map that Susano'o showed us."

I could only stare at her. Danny and Jin looked confused, too.

She groaned. "Seriously? Fine, I'll spell it out for you. There were lines across that map that clearly showed a sewer system, and I bet it runs under the palace."

When I said nothing, Ryleigh said, "Hello, like, under the Hall of Mirrors? We follow the tunnels until we're under the Hall of Mirrors, and then we break in that way, through the floor. Come on, people, keep up. It's not that complicated."

"You don't have to talk to us like we don't know anything," I growled through clenched teeth. Wait, no—I didn't want to be angry. I took a deep breath and pushed the anger back down.

"Well, you obviously *don't* know anything," Ryleigh said. "I'm basically carrying this entire mission."

"Ninja girl is right! You *don't* know anything, chickadee! Not a single thing! Your brain is as empty as a big balloon! Ha, ha! Balloon brain! Balloon brain!" the voice sang gleefully. "And the same goes for you, ninja girl! I promise you Middlings won't get anywhere without my help!"

"Leave us alone! I know where I'm going!" Ryleigh shouted. To us, she said, "Are you coming with me, or not?"

"I'm not sitting here waiting around for some monster to tell me what to do," said Danny. "Let's go."

"What is *wrong* with you, bruh?" Jin said. He sounded irritated. Which was odd. Jin never got mad. "Why do you always have to go bombing off like you're in some kind of superhero movie?"

"Oh, excuse me, rock star. Have you already done your own superhero movie? Is that why you think you know better than me?"

"Danny!" I said. "What the heck?"

"You're taking his side? Some friend you are," Danny said. "Well, guess what. I don't need bad friends like you. Come on, Ry, we can do this without them." He and Ryleigh stalked off down the tunnel and disappeared into the darkness.

"Who are you calling a bad friend? Get back here! I said, GET BACK HERE!" I shouted after him. My entire body was buzzing now, and my hands itched to pull Kusanagi out of my backpack. "I *knew* you'd ditch me! I *knew* you weren't really my friend!"

"Wait, Momo. Hang on," said Jin. He shook his head and blinked hard a couple of times. "Something's not right."

"Oh, you think so?" I said. But even as I said it, I knew it was

234

true. I had a funny feeling that I shouldn't be *this* angry. I was even angry at Jin, who hadn't done anything wrong.

"Hey!" It was Ryleigh and Danny, coming up on me and Jin from behind us.

I gawked at them. Hadn't they just walked off *ahead* of us?

"How did you get in front of us?" Danny demanded, as if we'd played a mean trick on him.

"Uh, we haven't moved. You literally walked away from us like ten seconds ago," I said, pointing in the direction they'd gone.

"Oh, and we walked in a circle? I think we'd know if we'd walked in a circle that small," said Ryleigh.

"Oh, because of your perfect ninja sense of direction?" I sneered.

"Well, it's better than—"

"Stop!" Jin shouted. "Everyone stop for a second. Why are we fighting like this? We should be working together. We need to cooperate!"

"I tollld you," the voice crooned. "I told you that you couldn't do it without me and I was riiighht."

I looked around, startled. I'd forgotten all about the voice. "Who *are* you?" I asked.

"Why, I'm your auntie, little Middling! Susano'o is my daddy! That's why I want to help you and that's why you could hear me up in Prissy Perfect Land. They keep me down here with all the anger that gets drained out of the kami who live up there."

The others stared at me, but only for a second, because in the next second we were *all* staring at the sludgy liquid in the canal, which had begun burbling and blurping ominously. Soon, we were cowering against the wall as a sludge geyser roared up and cascaded over itself.

It died down to reveal a giant of a woman with green skin and greasy black hair. Her eyes glowed pale orange under thick, bushy eyebrows, and the nostrils of her long, beaky nose sprouted a forest of spiky hair. Her narrow lips parted in a croco-dilian smile, complete with a set of very sharp, very yellow, very dangerous-looking fangs. She flung her arms out. "TA-DAA!" she screeched. "I am the Noblewoman of No! The Duchess of Defiance! The Doyenne of Disobedience, the Countess of Contrariness, the Princess of Provocation! I am the reason why you're feeling so feisty! I am . . . LADY . . . AMANOZAKOHHH!"

Amanozako took a theatrical bow and the sludge boiled around her as the torches flashed and the sound of canned applause echoed through the tunnel. I had a sudden memory of seeing a toddler have a massive temper tantrum at the grocery store and Mom joking that Amanozako had taken over his body—because Amanozako was born when Susano'o vomited up the most contrary, unreasonable, oppositional part of his spirit. Though it was hard to imagine someone more unreasonable than Susano'o.

When the applause died down, she stood and glared at us. "Hey! Why aren't you clapping? Clap! Clap, if you know what's good for you!"

We hurriedly clapped our hands and Danny even managed a wolf whistle. But our hearts weren't really in it. It reminded me of when we first met Susano'o and he kept making us cheer for his terrible performance as the lead singer of his band, Susano'o and the Scorpions.

"Stop! Stop!" Amanozako shrieked. "Stop clapping, for crying out loud, you're going to make my ears fall off!"

We stopped and looked at each other, confused.

"WELL?" she bellowed now, growing so big that she loomed over us, dripping sludge that sizzled as it hit the ground. "Do you want my help, or don't you?"

"We—I—y-yes, please," I stammered in a small voice. It seemed like we didn't have much of a choice at this point. "We're looking for Yata-no-kagami, the—"

"Eight-sided Mirror of the Sun, I know. What, do you think I was born yesterday?"

"No! Not at all, I just—"

"And why should I tell you where it is? Maybe I don't want to!"

Ryleigh frowned. "But you just said—"

"NO! You snively little Middlings have been ignoring me for days and now your time is up! Too bad, so sad, thanks for playing, goodbye!"

Amanozako dove back into the sludge with a *SPLOOSH* that sent the smelly stuff splattering everywhere.

"Ugh, whatever. Who needs her anyway?" Ryleigh muttered. "Mean old hag." The sludge burbled as if Amanozako had heard her through it, and Ryleigh took a hasty step back.

But Danny disagreed. "Uh, *we* need her."

"We do not!" Ryleigh said.

"We do, too!" I felt my anger boiling up again.

"Hey, stop!" Jin said. "We'll never get anywhere if we keep getting mad at each other."

He was right. "Maybe . . . maybe you could sing to us?" I said. I know. Cringe. But Jin nodded and started humming quietly. And it worked. Ryleigh and Danny each took deep breaths.

But Amanozako was right, too. I *had* been ignoring her. And now that we were here, I felt pretty sure she did want to help us. Why was she acting like this? I stared at the sludge while I racked my brain. How could we get her to cooperate if her favorite thing to do was to defy others?

Oh.

I cleared my throat and said loudly, "Ryleigh's right. We don't need Amanozako. I mean, I know she's super powerful and all that, but I'm not taking her advice, that's for sure." I eyed the sludge, which had suddenly started sloshing around again. I lowered my voice. "Hey, listen." I whispered my theory to the others.

Danny was the first to speak. "Yeah, I agree. I don't trust Amanozako one bit," he said. He grinned and nodded at Jin: *Your turn.*

"She probably has no idea where the mirror is," Jin said.

"Even if she does, she's probably lying," Ryleigh announced.

"She's a lying liar who lies, you can just tell," I said. "We're much better off—"

"I *DO* KNOW WHERE THE MIRROR IS, I AM *NOT* A LIAR, AND YOU *WILL* ACCEPT MY HELP, WHETHER YOU WANT IT OR NOT!" The sludge went everywhere as Amanozako exploded out of it.

"No, thanks, we're good," I said. "Come on, gang, let's go." I picked a direction and started walking. The others followed.

"NO!" There was a flash of light and a gust of hot wind. Suddenly the four of us were hurtling through the tunnel on a little rubber raft, and the canal had turned into a raging river of sludge.

"Stop! Let us off! We don't want your *hellllp!*" Danny's grin turned into a mask of terror as the tunnel curved and fell into a sickening drop. We bounced and bobbed, gripping the handles on the sides of the raft like our lives depended on it (which—let's be real—they did), until finally the raft spun itself onto a narrow strip of black sand and dumped us out like *it* was sick of the ride, too.

"Ha! Too bad, Middlings, you didn't want my help, but I helped you anyway!" Amanozako called from the sludge behind us. "That door in the wall leads to the back entrance to the Hall of Mirrors, and Yata-no-kagami is behind it. You know how I know? Because I'm the guardian! Because I am the Ruler of the Reverse! The Overseer of Opposition! Ha-haaa! I win, you lose, goodbye!" She blew a big raspberry and dove back into the river, which had slowed back down to its original lava-flow pace.

Yes! I'd gotten it right. On a whim, I called out, "Boy, am I glad that Amanozako didn't give us anything to drink! I'd hate to have four bottles of fresh, cold water!" Because the sludge was like lava, and it was freaking *hot* down here.

Four hydroflasks shot up from the sludge and landed at our feet. Ryleigh picked them up and handed them out. "Nice work!" she said, and I knew she meant it.

But even better? As we guzzled down our water, Danny sidled up to me and said in a low voice, "Hey, uh. I know it was Amanozako who made us say all that stuff we didn't mean. But just so we're clear. I don't think you're a bad friend. You're my best friend, actually." Then he ruined the moment by draining his hydroflask and belching.

"Gross. But same," I said.

Jin pulled on the iron handle of the door, and it slid open easily. A cool breeze wafted out, carrying the low murmur of voices that were both clear and indistinguishable at the same time, like a thousand faraway wind chimes.

It's Too Early to Panic

The space inside was cool and dimly lit from above; a spiral staircase twisted up the middle toward the light and the murmuring voices.

"So now all we have to do is go up there and get the mirror," said Danny. "It should be easy, now that we're going in the back, right? We should have done this in the first place!"

I didn't think I would ever understand how Danny could always be so wildly optimistic. "Danny. We still have to get out of here," I reminded him. "How are we supposed to do that? They probably have extra guards posted there now, since they know we tried to break in."

"Great attitude, Momo," said Danny. He gave me two sarcastic thumbs up.

"She's not wrong, though," said Ryleigh. "We have to figure out what we're gonna do once we have the mirror. We need a plan."

We need a plan. Music to my ears.

"Why don't we just go back out the sewer? It has to lead out of the city, right?" Jin said.

Of course! "We'll just go back out there and tell Amanozako

241

that we really don't want to leave the city, and she'll guide us right out!" I turned to Danny. "Okay, *now* we can get excited."

"Finally!" He grinned. "Look at us working together. Team RyJin DaMoNik for the win!" When Ryleigh and Jin gave him puzzled looks, he explained. "First two letters of each of our names. Well, the first *three* letters of Jin's and Niko's names." And then he seemed to remember that Niko wasn't with us. He stopped grinning and said, "As soon as we've taken care of Tamamo-no-mae . . ."

"We're going to look for Niko," Ryleigh finished.

"Definitely," said Jin. "We're all in this together."

I smiled at Danny, and he smiled back. "Team RyJin DaMoNik," he said again. "Let's do this!"

As we climbed the staircase to the Hall of Mirrors, the voices grew clearer and the light grew brighter. At the top, a doorway had been carved into the stone, covered only by a curtain of glass beads that clicked against each other as I pushed it aside.

What we stepped into—the Hall of Mirrors—was literally a hall of floor-to-ceiling mirrors, all at different angles to each other. How many? It was impossible to tell, the way they all reflected each other, one after another after another. I felt like we were standing in a crowd of hundreds of kids who looked just like us. And there was the hum of a thousand murmuring voices—one from each reflection.

Look at me and I will show you all your possible futures, whispered one. *Look at me and I will show you your best memories,* offered another. And on and on from all directions: *Look at me and I will show you your greatest enemy. Look at me and I will lead you to your beloved. Look at me, look at me, look at me.*

CLACK.

We spun around. The glass curtain was gone, and in its place was yet another mirror.

"No!" Jin ran back to the mirror and pushed. But it didn't open. "We're trapped!" I heard a note of panic in his voice.

Don't panic. Don't panic. It's too early to panic. "There's got to be a mirror in here that reverses spells," I said in a voice that was much, much calmer than I felt. "That seems like something a magic mirror would do, right? We just have to find it and bring it here and ask it to open the door."

"Great idea. Which one of these hundreds of mirrors do you think it is?" Danny grumbled.

"Okay, then. Let's make a plan," I said.

"We don't have time for a plan!" Danny said. "We have to move! We have to do something!"

"What if we just listen for the mirror that answers questions? It's gotta be in here somewhere. We can ask it to tell us where the Mirror of the Sun is. And then we can ask it how to get out of here," Jin suggested.

Danny whooped. "Yes! I like it!"

So we listened.

Look at me and I will show you your deepest desires. Look at me and I will show you your past mistakes. Look at me and I will show you the best hairstyle for your face shape.

Jin heard it first. "It's over there!" he said, and started walking past the hundreds of Jins, Dannys, Ryleighs, and Momos that surrounded us. I tried to follow him, but the mirror-walls kept fooling me into thinking I was following Jin when I was only following a reflection, and I kept bumping into mirrors instead of walking past them. So I closed my eyes and strained to hear the mirror instead. Eventually, one voice separated itself from the others. *Look at me and I will answer your questions.* Keeping my eyes closed and my mind focused on the voice, I went forward.

When the voice was right in front of me, I opened my eyes. "Okay, I'm here, finally. Who's gonna ask the question?"

But Ryleigh was already staring at the question-answering mirror. Her face was pale, and she was breathing hard. "How do I make Mom and Dad and Tommy stop being mad at each other?" she asked.

Meanwhile, Jin seemed to have gotten distracted by another mirror. He stood in front of it totally transfixed, his eyes shining with tears. "Please, Dad. I just want to try something else."

Danny was the only one who wasn't spellbound. "I think Jin's looking at the future or something," he told me. "Ryleigh's got the right mirror, though. Hey, Ryleigh!" He shook her shoulder. "Ryleigh, turn around!"

Ryleigh turned to us, blinking, like she was surprised to see us. "What?"

"Ask it where the Mirror of the Sun is!" I said.

She furrowed her brow. "Why?"

"Because that's what we need to know!"

"Oh." She glanced back at the mirror, like it was playing her favorite show and she couldn't wait for us to leave her alone so she could go back to it. "Um . . ."

"Ryleigh!" I said.

"What?" she said again, absently, and then, "Hey! Stop

shoving!" because Danny had been slowly nudging her out of the way.

"I wanna try. Give me a turn." Danny was already staring at his reflection.

"But I wasn't done!" Ryleigh pushed him.

"Yeah, well, it's my turn now! You can go after I get my question." Danny pushed her back.

"Um, I think maybe we should all stop looking at the mirrors," I said.

"I know we need the money," said Jin from across the room. "Maybe we could move into a smaller house."

This was starting to feel really dangerous. "Stop. Looking. At. The. Mirrors!" Fear and anxiety made my voice high and shrill. I shook Jin by the shoulders. "I said stop looking!"

Jin shook me off impatiently and Ryleigh and Danny continued to scuffle. I felt a wave of panic rising.

I closed my eyes and tried to calm myself, to shut out the murmuring mirrors, as well as Danny and Ryleigh, who were now yelling their questions at the mirror so that it would listen to them:

"Who are my birth parents? What are they like? Why did they put me up for adoption? Do they ever think about me?" Danny shouted.

"Why are Mom and Dad so obsessed with Tommy when he's the one who hurt them?" Ryleigh demanded. "Why can't they see *me*?"

Breathe, I told myself. *Get calm and come up with a plan.* If the others were stuck, I'd have to figure this out on my own.

People's lives depended on us. We didn't have time to mess around, and we couldn't fail.

I closed my eyes and did Ryleigh's box breathing method to calm myself down. Gradually, Ryleigh and Danny's questions fell away, and the thousand mirror voices became a low shushing, like ocean waves.

Okay. I wasn't strong enough to tackle any of my friends to break their connections with the mirrors that had caught them. I'd have to try something else. Maybe if I listened for the Mirror of the Sun, I could follow its voice until I found it. I'd keep my eyes closed to avoid being trapped. Then I'd grab it and listen my way back to Ryleigh, Danny, and Jin. If I told them I had the Mirror of the Sun, they'd hear me for sure. And then we'd leave. That was a good plan, right?

I kept my eyes closed. What would the Mirror of the Sun say? What should I listen for?

Here. The mirror you seek is over here.

I was so surprised, I almost opened my eyes. I followed the sound of the voice for what felt like a long time, walking slowly, turning corners until I knew I would never find my way back. But I had to keep going. Finally, I heard it say, *You have found me. Open your eyes.* So I did, being careful not to look straight ahead.

But instead of a hundred reflections of myself, I found myself in a room full of light. In front of me was a woman with jet-black hair cascading down her back, over the twelfth of twelve golden robes. She was facing away from me, looking into a mirror that reflected her light onto every other surface in the room.

Amaterasu. Just like in my dream.

Resist! Refuse! Defy! Deny!

"I know why you are here," she said in a rich, warm-honey voice that made me think of a field of wildflowers bathed in sunlight under a bright blue sky.

"You do?" Maybe Yatagarasu had found her and told her. Or had she known all along that I would sneak in through the back? Was I in trouble? I remembered that in my dream, Izanami and Susano'o had sprung out of the mirror and tried to drag me with them. Had my nightmare been a prophecy? I edged backward, away from Amaterasu.

"This mirror is my greatest treasure, and I will not risk any harm coming to it simply because you are afraid to fight Tamano-no-mae."

"But—"

"No. I know who you are, and I am not interested in your excuses. The palace is in chaos because of you, and your very presence here is an offense to me. Now, go. I am working to restore my inner peace." Her voice wasn't warm and sweet anymore—it scorched and burned, like the hood of a car on a hot sunny day.

My Susano'o nature bristled and buzzed in response, but it was like I was hearing it through a thick, cottony filter, just like in the palace. In fact, I *was* in the palace, I suddenly remembered. I could feel the anger struggling to get a message through. What was it? Oh, yes. "People are about to lose their lives," I said. "Kids. The mirror is the only way I can help them." But I sounded unsure of myself. I *felt* unsure of myself.

Amaterasu turned to me—I shut my eyes just in time, but I could feel the power of a white-hot sun searing my eyelids. In a harsh, metallic voice that rang in my ears, Amaterasu said, "You have brought evil and darkness into my kingdom, child of Izanami. You have come to steal my precious mirror, the only thing that brings me joy. You have come to claim by force a power that does not belong to you, just like Susano'o, your grandfather. I cannot allow you to stay and continue to upset the peace that I work so hard to maintain."

Amaterasu extended a fiery arm and gripped my shoulder. My uniform started smoking, and I instinctively jerked away, but her grip was iron. *I am going to die here,* I thought. My friends were trapped in the Hall of Mirrors and Niko was missing or maybe dead (*No, not dead. Not dead.*), and Tamamo-no-mae would drink all the potential and possibility of those kids' lives. And I would go down to Yomi and end up with Izanami after all.

No.

What? Was that me? My rage monster?

The voice was shrill and angry and in my ear . . . No, wait. It was a tiny little blob of sludge on my shoulder. And it was *talking.* Or more accurately, shrieking. "Amanozako?"

No! No! No-no-no-no-no! Don't do what she says, you ninny!

What happened to your spine? She's not the boss of you! Do you know who you are? The granddaughter of the god who destroyyyyyed her! Resist! Refuse! Defy! Deny!

Her voice was as piercing and screechy and annoying as a fire alarm. And it woke up my rage monster, which had been shoved down and put to sleep by Amaterasu's anti-anger magic. I felt it stretch and sniff the air. It raised its hackles and growled.

You are the granddaughter of Susano'o! The spirit daughter to Izanami! it said. It was the strangest thing. I'd always dreaded hearing my rage monster's voice, but now I felt like I was hearing the voice of an old friend—though I have to admit I flinched at the Izanami part.

We're just trying to help people, for crying out loud! the monster continued. *Get out that sword!*

The sword . . . the sword! How could I have forgotten?

Kusanagi buzzed to life in my backpack. *Here I am!* it called to me. *Let's do this!*

And then it was in my hands.

"How *dare* you draw that weapon in my presence?" Amaterasu let go of me, and I felt more than saw the ball of fire she hurled at me. I swung wildly and felt it burst into a million stars.

Come on. We've got this, said Kusanagi. *Let loose. She can take it.*

But Amaterasu wasn't fighting me anymore. She was just talking to me.

"Come here, child. Look at my mirror. It will show you how beautiful you could be without your anger." Her voice was warm and soft and sweet again, like daffodils in the spring.

No! my rage monster howled.

No-no-no-no-no! screeched the tiny Amanozako blob.

"Anger is destructive and ugly. It is a terrible, violent monster, and it will turn you into a monster as well. Don't you want to be beautiful? Don't you want people to love you as they love me?" Amaterasu said in her spring sunshine voice. I felt myself being pulled as if by a magnet toward the mirror until I could feel Amaterasu's warmth reflected on its surface in front of me. Should I look?

Amaterasu's voice came from behind me now, and her hands lay gently on my shoulders. "I know that you are curious. Open your eyes, and you will understand. Look in the mirror and see how beautiful you are. Put your sword down and rid yourself of that monster inside forever."

My rage monster roared in my ears. *No! No! Anger is power! Anger is fuel! Anger is strength! Fight! Resist! Or we'll be trapped in the mirror and die!* I felt its energy surge into my arms. Without knowing what I was aiming for or why, I swung Kusanagi one more time, as hard as I could.

CLANG!

The sound of the steel blade smashing against the bronze of Yata-no-kagami nearly shattered my eardrums. It was followed by the sound of bits and pieces of the Mirror of the Sun pinging and clanging to the floor all around me.

No! No, no, no, no, no! I'd done it again. I'd let the rage monster take over. And now the Mirror of the Sun was broken, and there was no hope left for anyone, and—

"Thank you, my dear Momo. Ah, how good it feels to be free!"

250

What was she talking about? How had I freed her? Hadn't I just smashed her prized possession into a thousand pieces?

"The mirror is intact. What you have broken is the spell that it had over me," Amaterasu said, as if she'd read my mind. "You may open your eyes safely now. I will not look upon you directly."

I wasn't quite sure if I could trust her yet, but I opened one eye just a crack. True to her word, Amaterasu was facing mostly away, and looking down at the floor.

"You know that I sent the mirror down to the Middle Lands with my great-grandson long ago, do you not?"

I nodded.

"It was returned to me one day, after having been lost under the sea for hundreds of years. I was glad to have it back; I'd missed it quite a lot. Perhaps it is vain of me, but I do love looking at my own face." She blushed a little, and the light in the room turned a warm sunset pink.

"But the mirror had been cursed—I don't know by whom. Once I looked into it, I became obsessed. It was all I could think about. I sat in court all day, overseeing the business of the Sky Kingdom, shedding my light on the Middle Lands, and longing to return here at night to sit with my beloved mirror and take comfort in the reflection of my own beauty. It helped me to forget the ugliness I saw growing everywhere, and the anger and evil that kept sprouting up in the Middle Lands despite my best efforts to stop them. As time passed, I found I could not live fully during the day, and I was less and less soothed by my mirror at night—yet I could not stop myself from looking into it.

This mirror was a refuge at first, but increasingly it has become a prison. And you and Kusanagi have freed me from it."

Amaterasu looked at me expectantly, but in my shock, all I could say was "Oh."

"A curse on one of the Three Sacred Treasures can only be broken by another one of those treasures," she continued, probably realizing that I wasn't going to add anything intelligent to the conversation. "Because I had banned Susano'o and Kusanagi from entering the Sky Kingdom, and the Jewel of Kindness has been lost for centuries, the curse on my mirror could not be broken. You sneaking into the Hall of Mirrors with Kusanagi turns out to have been the best thing that could have happened to me. It's very strange the way things work out, is it not?"

"Uh-huh. I mean, yes, ma'am. I mean yes, Your Highness. I mean, Your Majesty."

"I owe you my deepest gratitude," she said. "Thank you." On my shoulders, I felt the light of the sun when you walk outside on the last day of school.

"You're welcome," I said automatically—and finally, it sank in. Kusanagi and I had *freed her from the curse of the mirror.* That was huge! So huge that maybe she'd be willing to give me more than her gratitude. Maybe . . . There was an awkward silence while I tried to scrounge up the courage I needed to ask my question.

"You have a request," said Amaterasu. "You wish to take my mirror back to the Middle Lands to defeat Tamamo-no-mae."

Oh, right—Amaterasu already knew why I was here. I nodded. "She's holding all these kids hostage, and she's going to drink their lives so that she can live for thousands of years, and I can't beat her by myself, and—"

"I'd really rather you didn't."

"What?" I know you're not supposed to say "What?" to someone as powerful as the Queen of the Sky Kingdom. But I was taken off guard, okay?

"It is an extremely powerful magical item," Amaterasu said. "And it is still mine. I cannot trust a child to use it responsibly." Which was a little hypocritical, I thought, given that I had just freed her from literally hundreds of years of using it irresponsibly. But I knew it would be useless to point this out, because that's just how grown-ups are sometimes. I hate that.

But then Amaterasu said, "However, despite my doubts, I will consider allowing you to have it as a token of my gratitude— *if* you can prove yourself worthy."

Tsukiyomi had said she'd do this. And it sounded suspiciously like a trap. No magical being ever gives you a chance to "prove yourself worthy" of a magical item if they really think you'll succeed. On the other hand, I didn't feel like I had much choice. "How?" I asked.

"I will activate one side of the mirror, and you must look into it. If you can resist its power, you will have earned the right to use it yourself."

This was *definitely* a trap. "Uh, I beg your pardon." (At least I remembered my manners this time!) "But it's not still cursed, is it?"

"No, Momo, it is not. Are you ready to test yourself against Yata-no-kagami?"

No. Of course I wasn't. But Tamamo-no-mae was somewhere

253

in the Middle Lands with 888 kids. And Danny, Ryleigh, and Jin were still trapped in front of their own mirrors. And— I swallowed down a lump of grief—Niko had sacrificed himself so I could do this. I nodded. "Yes, I am."

"Good. Look up. Look into the mirror."

Amaterasu held Yata-no-kagami out in front of her, facing me. It was octagonal, just like its official name: the Eight-Sided Mirror. Each of its eight edges emitted a bright light: one edge glowed white, and the other seven edges shone with each color of the rainbow. My reflection gazed back at me from the center. The purple edge began to shimmer and flash as my reflection lifted her hand toward me. I found my own hand rising, and our fingers met on the surface. For one long second, I felt smooth, cold metal. Then my reflection reached out, clasped my hand in hers, and pulled me through to the other side.

I was alone in another mirrored room—nothing but mirrors, nothing but reflections of me. Eight of them, to be exact. Eight mirrors, eight Momos. Each Momo reflected a different angle of me, and each one tilted their head and raised their hand when I did, and behind them, infinite Momos disappeared into a swirling white mist.

There was a ninth Momo standing next to me—the one who had pulled me into this eight-mirrored room. She was three-dimensional. But she wasn't quite the same as me, either. I took one small step away from her.

"Welcome!" she said. I took another nervous step away. "It's okay, I won't hurt you." Mirror Me laughed. "You're not in any danger."

"Where am I? Who are you?" All around me, the eight other Momos mouthed the same questions.

"You're in the mirror dimension. And I'm the spirit of Yata-no-kagami."

Whoa, hang on a sec. I stared at her. "But—but you look like *me.*"

"I'm a reflection of you. I look different to each person who comes in here."

"And I'm . . . inside the Mirror of the Sun?"

"Inside the eighth side, to be exact. It's a portal hub with doors to other realities."

Other realities? Alarm bells started ringing in my head, but it was too late. "The portal that no one has ever returned from?" I croaked.

"Portals, plural. To other dimensions. To other versions of reality." Yata-no-kagami gestured at the eight mirrors. "Those are the portals."

I felt like my brain might explode. This was the side that we were supposed to use to trap Tamamo-no-mae. And if a demon as powerful as Tamamo-no-mae could reliably be trapped in here and get pulled into another dimension . . . and I was in here now . . .

It felt like the air had been sucked out of the room. My throat closed up, and my heart and lungs went into overdrive. I gasped and panted, but I just couldn't get enough oxygen to keep up— I was trapped and I was going to die here. And if anyone came looking for me, they'd find me here dead, and then *they'd* be trapped. And then—

"Hey! Hey, get it together!" Someone was patting me on the cheek. "Breathe. Slowly. Slowly. There you go."

The room swam back into focus, and I was staring at myself—I mean, Yata-no-kagami—again. I screamed and shut my eyes.

"Oh, for crying out loud, Momo, just stop. Why does everyone always freak out like this? I'm not a demon, after all. I'm *trying* to *help* you, so just listen, okay? If you want to go back to the life you came from, all you have to do is choose it."

I opened one eye. "Choose what?"

Yata-no-kagami smiled. "All of these reflections lead to different versions of your life, and one of them is the life you just came from. The others are the lives you'd be living if events in your past had ended differently."

"Huh?"

"Like, there's a version of you that tripped at the mall a couple of months ago when the shikome chased you, and she caught you and, er, ate you." Yata-no-kagami waved her hand at one of the mirrors and motioned for me to touch it. "Just take a look."

"Um, no thanks. The last time I touched a mirror, I got stuck inside."

"You won't this time. With these reflections, you have to choose to go all the way in."

I gave her some very heavy side-eye.

"I promise. It's the rules."

Curiosity got the better of me. I poked the mirror with just the very tippy-tip of my fingernail and moved the curtain of mist to the side. The mist cleared enough to reveal a pale, empty-eyed version of me stumbling around in a desolate wasteland. I was dressed all in black rags, my hair was falling out, and my breath came in loud, raspy death rattles. Horrified, I jumped back.

"Is that . . . ?"

"Yomi. You're turning into a death hag."

Just the thought chilled me all the way through, and I had to do a full-body shake to get rid of the feeling.

"I take it you don't want that one," Yata-no-kagami said with a twitch of her brow.

"No." I shuddered again. "I want my old life. My real life."

"They're all real. They're all happening. I think you should look at all of them before you go back to the life you came from, though, because you might find a life you like better."

Yata-no-kagami pointed at a different mirror. "Like that one? That version of you also fought Shuten-dōji all those weeks ago, but you didn't call for help, and you let your power take over. It's pretty dramatic."

I knew without even checking that I didn't want that one—Danny and Niko would have died in that version of my life. I just wanted to go back. I looked around me, but of course all the mirrors were the same, and I couldn't remember which one was mine—that is, the one I'd come from.

"Can you tell me which one I need to choose?"

"Nope. It's against the rules."

"What do you mean, against the rules? You just told me what happens in two of them!"

Yata-no-kagami sighed. "Well, you obviously weren't going to choose those two. I'm not allowed to help you choose, is what I mean."

"What happens if you do?"

"I don't know. Maybe nothing. Maybe it would set you free. Or maybe all the realities would bleed into each other and there would be chaos. Or maybe everything would cease to exist."

I turned to look at the reflections behind me. I only had six left. I should get going. I pushed the mist aside on the one closest to me and peeked in.

I Love You from
My Head To-matoes

In this life, I was tied up with ropes made of light; the Tortoise of the North poked at me sadly while the snake hissed and announced that it wasss time for me to faccce my consssequencesss. Yikes. I backed out right away.

In the next mirror, I was wearing makeup. I was in the quad at school, giggling and whispering with Ryleigh over a phone . . . what was on it? Somehow I knew it was a text from Danny. Another girl asked to see, and I turned slightly so that she could only see my shoulder. Ryleigh and I smirked and rolled our eyes at each other, and an expression of surprise and hurt crossed the other girl's face. I let the mist fall and stepped back. Yuck. I'd never wanted to be friends with Ryleigh that way. I liked the way our friendship was now.

In the third mirror, I was dressed in a long white robe, standing beside a tall woman in a robe that matched mine. She had pale skin and eyes that burned like fire; she was beautiful and terrifying and she wore a crown made of bones on her head: Izanami. She was looking down at a black stone basin filled with water and murmuring something to the version of me in the white robe. Then Izanami looked up at me—the real me, the one inside Yata-no-kagami. She could see through the mist, I realized. Her eyes lit up as she leaned closer, and her mouth split into a smile that made my skin grow cold. I tried to back away, but it was like everything about me was frozen: my legs, my hand on the mirror . . . Even my lungs wouldn't fill up with the air I needed to scream. But before she could touch me, I fell backward, and the image went dark.

Five down, three to go. I almost didn't want to keep going. What if Izanami was in another one of my lives? I didn't think I could face her again. It was bad enough worrying that she'd decided to come for me in my old life. Did I really want to risk having her capture me in here?

But I had to get back. People's lives depended on it. So I swallowed my fear and pushed the mist aside in the next mirror.

I found myself somewhere dark and cold and quiet. I was underground—no. I was underwater. Two whales glided into view, one big and one little—a parent and a child. I stared, mesmerized. There was something familiar about them. What was it? I looked at the older whale. He had a kind, sad, fathomless expression in his eye that I knew I'd seen somewhere before . . .

Thunder crashed around me. I was on a boat, in a storm, clutching the arm of a man—Dad. A wave broke over the bow and we tumbled into the sea.

Then I was with the whales again. They breached over and over off a coastline of bluffs and rocky beaches. They were intensely connected to each other, you could feel it. They loved each other, even. But they were also indescribably sad.

What the . . . ? I felt myself drifting back out of the mirror.

"What was that?" I asked Yata-no-kagami.

"One of your lives."

"I was a *whale*?" How was that even possible?

Yata-no-kagami tilted her head and gave me a searching look. "You went with your dad on a research trip. There was a storm."

"And . . . we turned into whales?"

Yata-no-kagami shrugged. "Apparently."

The whales were me and Dad—that was why they'd felt so familiar. That was why I'd felt all that love between them. Without warning, I was flooded with a longing so sharp and deep, it took my breath away. I missed Dad. So much. I missed his kind face and his rough black hair. I missed his laugh and his morning coffee breath. I missed how he always came in to kiss me good night and the way he used to write punny dad jokes on sticky notes and put them in my lunch: *Orange you glad it's Friday? We make a great pear! I love you from my head to-matoes.* Every day, I'd thrown those jokes in the trash with the rest of my lunch waste without a second thought. I hadn't even saved a single one.

Yata-no-kagami cleared her throat. "Do you want to go back in there?"

From the mirror came the low hum of a whale song, and I ached to be with Dad again, even if he was a whale and I was a whale. I thought of the two of us breaching at the surface along that rocky coast, connected and together. But also sad. Because they—we—missed Mom. I knew it without having to ask.

"Where's my mom?" I asked.

"In that life? Ah. Well, when *your* life turns out differently, it can affect other people's lives. Shuten-dōji still sent his minions to destroy the Island of Mysteries. But you were a whale, so you couldn't defeat him and seal the portal, and he succeeded."

And if he'd succeeded in destroying the Island of Mysteries, that meant Mom had died.

It was so hard to turn away from my whale life and face the next mirror. I missed Dad so much, and I wanted to have him back more than almost anything else in the world. But this wasn't the way.

I parted the mist in the seventh mirror and recognized the beach on the Island of Mysteries—the island where Mom was from, and where I'd been born. Where I'd defeated Shuten-dōji and closed the portal to Yomi. I was wading through clear blue water. In front of me was a tall, dark-haired man. He turned to wave at me, and I gasped, my heart squeezing tight. Dad again! Alive. And human. The mirror version of me followed, laughing. This must have been a life where Susano'o hadn't discovered me and Dad hiding on the island, where he hadn't caused the storm that had swept me into Izanami's arms. This was a life where Mom was still guarding the portal to Yomi.

Dad dove into the waves and surfaced, smiling at me. "Come on, Momo! Swim!" I swam. Just as I reached him, there was a flash of light, and there were three of us sitting around a low table: Dad, me, and Mom in her shining kami form. Mom was strong, healthy, laughing, and totally *there*, the way she'd been before Dad died—but even better. There was no rage monster. No anxiety, no fear, no grief. I was *happy*, all the way down to my bones. This was the real, true me. This was the life I was meant to live: here on this island with Mom and Dad, alive and well.

I took a step forward and found myself on the beach again.

A gentle breeze carried the sound of energetic yips over the sound of the ocean. Niko! He was playing on the shore, leaping in and out of the waves as they broke on the sand. All three of us—Mom, Dad, and me—ran with him on the beach and laughed at his antics.

All I had to do was choose this life, and it would be mine. I could leave all the awful stuff from my other life behind—Dad's death, Mom's constant absence, my horrible classmates. Niko getting burned up by the vermilion phoenix. I wouldn't have to worry about being taken over by my rage monster, I wouldn't have to fight demons, and I wouldn't have to be afraid of Izanami taking me down to Yomi.

Another step. I could feel the breeze on my face now. The sun was warm. The water was cool. I could be happy. I could forget about . . . that other life. I tried, lazily, to remember what had been so important: something to do with a mirror. Something to do with friends . . .

The ocean shushed and whooshed and beckoned me forward. But now, all of a sudden, I heard something else, like bells ringing far, far away. It was that word, "friends," that had done it. What was it about my friends?

A face shimmered to the surface: *Jin*, the bells said.

Ryleigh.

Danny.

They didn't exist in this life—at least, not to me. I could leave them behind in my former life and never miss them in this one because I wasn't friends with them here; I hadn't even met them.

But they are *your friends in the life you came from*, said a tiny voice in my head—not Amanozako, not Izanami, not my

263

rage monster or Kusanagi but *me*. And I was right. How could I leave Danny behind? And Jin was my friend now, too. Even Ryleigh. If I went to live happily ever after on the Island of Mysteries, they could be trapped in the Hall of Mirrors forever. And if we didn't get home with the Mirror of the Sun, Tamamo-no-mae would drink the lives of those 888 kids. And then what? Tamamo-no-mae would rise to become Izanami's second-in-command, probably. And then what?

My heart felt like a knot in a giant rope, tight and heavy. It took all my strength to step back—the island pulled hard on the rope, and I worried I might have to leave my heart behind. But there was a tug on the other end that I knew I had to follow.

"Goodbye," I whispered through a throat closing up over rising tears. I didn't want to go. It wasn't fair that I should have to give this up. But I couldn't leave everyone in my old life—it wasn't right. I squeezed my eyes shut and wrenched myself out of the reflection. When I landed on the floor inside the Mirror of the Sun, I felt hollow inside; I felt like I'd lost Dad not once but twice in this awful place, and my worries about Mom's absence settled back on my shoulders like a heavy black cloak.

"You made it out!" Yata-no-kagami sounded surprised.

"I couldn't stay."

"Really?"

"Really."

"But wasn't it . . . I mean, it seems like a very nice life. *Everyone* who comes in here finds a life they like better than the one they came from."

"I didn't say it wasn't better. I just said I couldn't stay." I wished Yata-no-kagami would stop asking questions. I was afraid I might change my mind.

"Are you *sure?*"

"Yes, I'm sure!" I snapped. "Why do you keep bugging me about it? I said I want to go back to my first life and I meant it!"

Yata-no-kagami waved her hands in surrender. "All right, all right, I get it, I get it! It's just that no one's ever made that choice before." She cocked her head and looked me up and down before saying to herself, "Huh. Who knew?" Then she gestured grandly toward the eighth and final mirror. "Ta-da! Off you go!"

Deep breath. I squared my shoulders, stepped through the fog, and gasped. This couldn't be right. Instead of meeting Amaterasu in the Hall of Mirrors, I saw myself fighting Tamamo-no-mae. I had Kusanagi in my hands and was shouting and swinging it viciously at her. That wasn't supposed to happen! Hadn't I just proven myself worthy of wielding the Mirror of the Sun? The entire purpose of coming here was to *avoid* having to fight Tamamo-no-mae.

Had I walked into the wrong mirror somehow?

What frightened me most was the *thing* that stood right behind me as I fought. It was a menacing, shadowy mass that buzzed and flashed on its surface with electrical sparks, like a monster made of thunderclouds: my rage monster. Our movements were simultaneous and nearly identical: the monster swiped its arms, and I swung Kusanagi; it lunged forward, and I stabbed at Tamamo-no-mae. I was nothing but a puppet of my anger. And then I saw the other figure who stood off to the side, whispering instructions and encouragement. She was pale and translucent, and her night-black hair flew around her face like it was alive. Izanami. Or her spirit, anyway—her physical form would still be trapped in Yomi. And I couldn't see them, but I could feel the limp forms of Danny, Ryleigh, Jin, and Niko lying on the ground somewhere.

I had to get out of here. This was not the life I'd come from! This wasn't the life I wanted!

The rage monster made me raise my sword high. Rain stung my cheeks. The wind howled. I knew what would happen next—the rage monster was going to make me call a hurricane and a deadly tsunami. Everything I'd fought and planned for—everyone I loved—would be swept away. The blade flashed, thunder boomed, someone screamed, *"No!"* and everything went black.

The screaming continued in the darkness until finally I realized that I was the one screaming, and opened my eyes. I was back inside the eight-mirrored room.

"What are you doing here? I thought you were on your way out," Yata-no-kagami said. "Not that I'm not glad to see you."

"Something's wrong with the mirror. That isn't me. I mean, that's not the me I want to be. It's not the life I want."

"Ohhh." Yata-no-kagami nodded knowingly. "You saw the future, didn't you. And you didn't like it. Sometimes that happens."

"That can't be my future."

"But it's the life you came from."

"But I don't want that thing to control me. It's a monster!

I don't want to use Kusanagi to destroy things! And *she* was there."

Yata-no-kagami gave me a questioning look.

"Izanami," I whispered. Even saying her name frightened me. It took everything I had not to check over my shoulder to see if I'd called her.

I thought about Izanami whispering next to me, about my rage monster swiping and slicing the air with its arms, and about the deadly storm that had been about to break. "There has to be another way," I said. "Are you sure there aren't any other choices? Is there another future in there?"

Yata-no-kagami gave a doubtful frown. "I suppose you could try for one. But I doubt it. Like, the odds are probably a gazillion to one. It might make more sense just to embrace it."

"But who I am in there—what's inside me, it's bad. It's destructive. I mean, it's literally a monster! I'm not embracing any of that!"

Yata-no-kagami raised her hands defensively. "Hey, don't yell at me! I didn't say you had to choose that life. You can go live on your island for all I care."

I looked back at the mirror that led to my life on the Island of Mysteries. I wanted so badly to go. Every molecule in my body missed the sand and the water and that sense of safety I'd felt, that feeling of being whole and happy. I ached to be back there together with Mom and Dad so much and so deeply, there was hardly room for anything else.

As for my original life . . . why? Why had I fought yōkai, snuck into Celestial City, lost Niko, outwitted Amanozako,

267

faced down Amaterasu, and found the Mirror of the Sun? Why had I done all of that if I was just going to have to go back and do the exact thing that I'd set out *not* to do? I was still going to have to fight Tamamo-no-mae one-on-one and succumb to my rage monster. I was still going to risk putting myself under the control of Izanami the Destroyer. What had Yata-no-kagami said were the odds that I'd avoid that fate? A gazillion to one. It wasn't fair. It wasn't right.

And yet.

If I chose to go back to the Island of Mysteries, I would become someone who abandoned her friends and took the easy way out when things got bad. I would become someone who chose a life of comfort and beauty with her parents while hundreds of kids lost all the possible lives they had in store for them. I would become someone who allowed a greedy, power-hungry demon to devour all those lives and keep them for herself.

I couldn't be that person.

A gazillion to one that I could change my future—but not impossible. Maybe I could shake off my rage monster in time to save everyone.

So I took one last deep breath, closed my eyes so I wouldn't see my fight with Tamamo-no-mae, and walked through the eighth mirror.

Piles of Icky Gunk

This time, Amaterasu was waiting for me, still facing slightly away.

"You made it out." I could hear the surprise in her voice, but I could also tell that she was smiling, even though I couldn't see her face. "I suppose I should have expected as much, given who you are."

"Huh—I mean, I beg your pardon?"

"You have Susano'o's strong will and stubbornness, and his connection to the elements of the Middle Lands. It makes sense that you'd withstand the temptations of the mirror so you could come back to defend the people of the Middle Lands. Your mother is the same way. She got her warmth and her healing powers from me, though."

Wait, what? "I'm sorry, I didn't quite understand the last thing you said."

Amaterasu smiled and repeated herself. "She got her warmth and her healing powers from me. I am your mother's mother."

"*WHAAAT?*" (Oh, come on. Give me a break—there's no way anyone could be expected to be polite after hearing news like that.)

Amaterasu sighed. "It's complicated. Let me show you what happened." She was still facing away from me, so all I could see of her was her long black hair and her extra-long outermost robe, which lay spread around her like a little golden lake. The fabric was embroidered with clouds that began to drift and swirl like real clouds as I watched. I spotted two figures moving through the scene: the beautiful, shining Amaterasu, and a swaggering Susano'o—he was dressed in fancy silks, but his hair and beard were as wild and shaggy as ever. They seemed to be arguing about something.

Amaterasu took off all of her beaded jewelry—a necklace, hair ornaments, bracelets—and traded them with Susano'o for his sword. Then she broke the sword into three pieces and began . . . *eating* one of them. At the same time, Susano'o crammed as many beads into his mouth as he could fit. Each kami chewed and chewed, scowling at the other one the whole time, until Susano'o puffed his chest out and spat two gobs of chewed-up jade on the ground.

Ptuh! Ptuh! He looked up at Amaterasu triumphantly.

I rolled my eyes. So gross. I hate being related to—

Ptuh! Amaterasu spat the contents of *her* mouth on the ground: a single glob of chewed-up steel.

This is disgusting! I wanted to yell at them. *You're kami, for crying out loud—stop acting like a couple of babies!*

But they kept chewing up and spitting out bits of each other's things, until all that was left of the sword and the beads were five lumps of ground-up jade and three piles of shredded steel, all gooey and goopy with spit. Nice. *Way to work out your differences,* I thought.

But then the piles of icky gunk began to glow and twitch, until one by one, they burst open, and in their place stood five male kami and three female kami.

Ohhh. Amaterasu and Susano'o had each contributed to the creation of the kami, so they were those kami's mother and father.

"The middle one is your mother," said Amaterasu. I stared. It *was* Mom. She stood there, all brand-new and shining, smiling next to her sisters.

"But she never told me." I'd asked her so many times who her mother was, and she'd always changed the topic. Why? It wasn't the same as not telling me that Susano'o had tried to kill me, or that Izanami the Destroyer had forged a spiritual connection with me—I could see why she might want to protect me from that information. What could be bad about knowing that my grandmother was the Great Goddess of the Sun and Queen of the Sky Kingdom?

"I sent your mother and her siblings to the Middle Lands and took away their memory of their birth so they would never return or claim me as their mother," Amaterasu said sadly. "I am sorry for that. But I was still recovering from what Susano'o had done to me."

"You *what?*" I asked. Mom had been banished by her father *and* her mother?

"I was not myself."

I didn't say anything. I could understand why a big angry jerk like Susano'o might banish his daughter in a fit of rage, but Amaterasu was supposed to be kind, generous, warmhearted. . . . Though now that I knew her better, maybe I shouldn't have been *quite* so surprised. I thought about her perfect city: the music in the air, the butterflies and fireflies, the happy faces, even the cheerful WANTED signs—and how all that beauty and pleasantness covered up a literal river of toxic rage. It felt a little bit like Ryleigh's fake niceness—or, come to think of it, the way I went around all meek and quiet while I swallowed my anger. It might seem nice on the surface, but it wasn't honest. It wasn't the same as being truly good, or truly happy. Why would anyone choose to build an entire city like that?

"Susano'o claimed that he'd won the kami-making contest, since he had produced more kami. But it was my jewels that yielded those kami, so really I won," said Amaterasu. "Susano'o was furious. He ruined my rice fields, skinned my horses, and attacked my home. And he killed my best friend."

The room grew darker around me as Amaterasu remembered the tragedy and the scene played out against the golden background of her robe. After Susano'o had destroyed everything she loved, Amaterasu had been so grief-stricken that she'd run away from the Sky Kingdom and hidden herself deep inside a cave, and the world was plunged into darkness. For weeks, Amaterasu refused to come out or even speak to anyone. Demons and other evil spirits started taking over, and everything began to die. Finally, Omopikane, the god of wisdom, and Uzume, the goddess of laughter, made a plan to bring Amaterasu back: They called all eight hundred thousand kami together outside the cave, and Uzume performed a wild, booty-shaking dance on top of a rice barrel (thereby inventing drums and dancing at the same time). Eight hundred thousand kami cheered and clapped and roared with laughter. The sound of all that joy reached Amaterasu in the darkness, and finally she got curious and asked what the heck was going on. "We're cheering for the new goddess of the sun," they told her. When she peeked her head out of the cave to see who this upstart was, she was met with the face of the most beautiful woman she'd ever seen. Enchanted, she crept out of the darkness toward the woman—who turned out to be herself. That is, the beautiful woman was actually Amaterasu's own reflection in Yata-no-kagami, which Omopikane had hung on a tree directly facing the cave. The other gods quickly pulled Amaterasu back into the world and used a shimenawa to seal the cave.

"So you can see why I have banned anger from my city. It destroyed everything. It nearly destroyed me—and, by extension, your precious Middle Lands. And because I was terrified that your mother and her siblings might one day become like their father, I banned them as well."

"Oh." It all made sense now. Of course she'd be afraid of another disaster like the one Susano'o and his out-of-control temper had caused. Just like I was afraid.

"What about Amanozako, then? Why is she here? Isn't she one of his children?"

"She is a necessary evil." Amaterasu released a long breath. "In order to drain my city of anger, I need somewhere for it to go. So I allow Amanozako to live in the sewers and attract all the anger and defiance that the city generates. She lives on it. She lives *in* it."

"She helped me find you, actually."

"I am not surprised," Amaterasu said. She looked thoughtful. "It is remarkable that you, Kusanagi, and Amanozako are the ones who freed me. Perhaps the kami-verse is trying to teach me a lesson; perhaps anger is not such a bad thing after all."

"Maybe." I mean, sure, my anger had helped me break the curse on the mirror. And hadn't I just been thinking it was dishonest to keep swallowing it down? But Susano'o's violent temper had nearly ended the world by sending Amaterasu into hiding. Izanami seemed to be fueled by a cold, vengeful fury. And the vision I'd seen inside the mirror of my rage monster and me . . . What was I missing? Could there be a different way to think about my anger?

"In any case, dear child, it is time for you to go. You've more than earned the right to my mirror, and I am happy to give it to you. Cast your eyes downward, please."

I did what she said, and as Amaterasu turned to face me, I was hit by a wave of light and heat so powerful I felt like it might blast me into a million pieces and carry me out into the endless Aum forever. A velvet-covered octagon appeared in my line of vision, and I took it.

"Thank you."

"You're welcome."

I looked at Yata-no-kagami—how cool was it that I'd proven myself worthy of it? But now I had to try to ask for more from Amaterasu, even though I was pretty sure I knew what the answer would be. "Why does it have to be me? You could send your warriors to stop Tamamo-no-mae. You could come down yourself if you wanted."

Amaterasu shook her head slowly, and her hair shimmered in the light from the mirrors around her. "I do not descend to the Middle Lands, nor can I ask my people to risk contamination or death by battling the vile creatures that call it home."

"But you're supposed to take care of people in the Middle Lands!"

"And I do," she said. "I provide warmth, light, and beauty. I am the source of life, energy, and good. There is a reason why evil thrives in the hours when I turn my face away."

"So—"

"I must also protect the citizens of the Sky Kingdom. There is only so much I can do for you, Momo. I am sorry."

I sighed. It had been worth a shot.

"And now, let us collect your friends. I have a few gifts for them as well, since you could not have made it to me without them. And once you are fully armed, I will send you on your way."

I Didn't Want to Say Anything, but . . .

We found Danny squirming facedown on the ground; Ryleigh knelt on top of him, gripping his wrists behind him and digging an elbow into his back.

"Ow! Let go! Lemme *go!*" Danny bellowed. He thrashed and kicked, but Ryleigh didn't budge.

"Not . . . until . . . I ask . . . my . . . question," she grunted through clenched teeth.

Meanwhile, Jin stood in front of another mirror, swaying back and forth and humming softly to himself. His eyes were glazed and his lips curved in a private, dreamy smile. "It's such an honor to receive the Nobel Prize for literature. I'd like to thank my dad, who's always supported my dream to become a great writer."

How much time had passed? Seconds? Hours? Days? It was impossible to tell. All I knew was that even if we hadn't run out, we didn't have much of it left.

"Hey!" I shouted. "Jin, wake up! Danny! Ryleigh! Stop fighting! We need to get out of here!"

No one listened. No one even seemed to hear me.

"Let me try." Out of the corner of my eye, I saw Amaterasu

lift her hand. "Close your eyes," she said. There was a burst of light, like a camera flash but about a billion times brighter, and a blast of hot wind just like the one that had nearly bowled me over a few minutes ago. It was a split second, but it was enough. Jin, Ryleigh, and Danny turned toward me and Amaterasu.

"Hey," I said. "Um, this is Amaterasu." She had considerately turned her back on us so we wouldn't burn our retinas out by accident.

"Yeah," Ryleigh said, who was shading her eyes with her hand anyway. "I figured."

"She's going to give us some gifts. To help us fight Tamamo-no-mae."

Jin's face fell. "Oh. So does that mean you didn't get the—"

"No, I did." I held up the mirror, covered in velvet.

Danny looked at it doubtfully. "That's it? How are we supposed to trap Tamamo-no-mae in there?"

"The same way you were trapped by the mirrors around you," Amaterasu said. "But facing her will still be dangerous. That is why I wish to make sure you are well armed."

Danny, Ryleigh, and Jin looked at each other in confusion for a moment. Danny recovered first and said, grinning, "Gifts! Lay 'em on me, Your Majesty!"

Niko would be so upset with you, I thought, and then I remembered once again why Niko wasn't here. It was strange how quickly I could go from wanting to laugh to wanting to cry. But I couldn't think about Niko now. And that made me sad, too. Swallowing hard, I turned my attention back to Amaterasu.

"For you, my young archer," she was saying, "some new

arrows. Perhaps you will need them in your impending battle, perhaps not. But I hope they will be useful to you at some point."

Three arrows appeared and hovered in the air in front of Danny. One was dark wood with white feathers, another looked like it was made of diamonds, the third was silver. The dark arrow drifted forward. Danny reached out and grasped it.

"The Hundredfold Arrow will split into a hundred arrows when it is released. Each one will hit its target, and the original will return immediately to your hand."

Danny's face glowed. "Aw, this is dope! We're gonna kick butt with arrows like this one!"

Amaterasu went on. "The arrow made of diamonds is the Summoning Arrow. Shoot it into the air as you speak the name of your target. It will find that target and serve as an automatic portal back to you."

"Sweet!" Danny plucked the glittering diamond arrow out of the air.

"But I should warn you," Amaterasu said. "This arrow is one of a kind, and it's too dangerous for you to keep once the world knows you have it. Therefore, after you have used it, it will return to me. You tend to be a little impulsive, do you not? If you choose the wrong target, or if you choose the wrong moment, you will have wasted your shot."

"Oh." Danny's smile faded a little bit.

Finally, the silver arrow floated into his hands.

"This is the Rescue Arrow. Anyone touching the bow when you shoot this arrow will be instantly transported to safety. It too can be used only once, so save it for a time when you have no other options."

Danny had turned pale and was looking at his arrows like he wasn't sure he wanted the responsibility.

Amaterasu said, "I do not give these to you lightly, my child. You're holding these arrows because I trust you to use them well. Being nervous is a good sign. It shows that you care."

"Okay." Danny swallowed. Then he remembered his manners and said, "Thank you," and put his arrows away.

Meanwhile, Amaterasu had moved on. "Next! The ninja." A flattish, dome-shaped straw monk's hat spun out of nowhere and landed at Ryleigh's feet.

Ryleigh picked it up and put it on her head. "How do I look?" she said to Danny. She was probably batting her eyelashes at him, but I couldn't tell because she looked like she was surrounded by a curtain of water that fell from the brim of the hat.

"I mean . . . ," Jin said.

"Blurry," Danny said.

"The hat makes you invisible to your enemies," Amaterasu said. "Though your allies will still be able to see you, as they have just proven."

Ryleigh could not have looked more excited, but before she could say anything, a bulging black pouch clanked onto the floor. "And these are the shuriken you threw during the fight at Navy Pier, when you defeated the ushi-oni."

I remembered how Ryleigh had hurled them with deadly accuracy at the giant bull-headed spider—and how she'd saved me from its gushing venom. Ryleigh loosened the drawstring, peeped into the pouch, and smiled. "Thank you."

"You will notice some new ones," Amaterasu said. "The red shuriken will cause its target to become disoriented and confused for a short time, if you need to escape or to pass unnoticed without engaging in a fight. The silver shuriken will split into a hundred once you've thrown it, just like Danny's arrow. And all of the shuriken have been enchanted to return to you once they have hit their mark, so you will never have to leave them behind again."

Ryleigh looked like she might cry from happiness. "I promise to use them well."

"See that you do."

Next, a white feather drifted out of the sky, landed on Jin's shoulder, and transformed into a cloak made of feathers of all different colors. He twisted around to look at it cascading down his back: shining golds and yellows, iridescent greens and blues, brilliant scarlet, rich purple, pure white.

"Hold the edges in your hands and spread your arms," Amaterasu instructed, and when he did, Jin rose into the air and started glowing. His jaw fell open and his eyebrows shot up. He looked like a very surprised angel.

"I'm floating! I'm flying! Can I fly? How do I stop?" he babbled.

"Simply decide to stop, and you will stop," said Amaterasu.

Jin stopped. He floated to the left, then to the right, and after a couple of awkward false starts, he got the hang of it and started zipping around the Hall of Mirrors like a very tall, very colorful bird. When he landed, Danny, Ryleigh, and I burst into applause.

"Does he get anything else?" Danny asked. "Like a bomb or a net or something? Or like a pair of magic binoculars so he can scout out where Tamamo-no-mae is?"

"Power is more than just the abiility to destroy things," said Amaterasu. "Hold out your hand, Jin."

Jin did as he was told, and a little glowing green bottle appeared in his palm.

"What's in there?" Danny asked, leaning toward it.

"It is a bottle of concentrated sunlight infused with healing powers. It will heal any illness and repair any wound it touches. You will need to wait until exactly the right moment. Once you open the bottle, all the light will pour out at once, and you will be unable to control it or to put any of it back."

Jin closed his fingers around the bottle and bowed awkwardly. "I'll do my best to choose well."

"And now, children, you really should get going. Gather in front of that mirror over there." A mirror across the room began to glow orange.

"Wait!" Ryleigh said. "You forgot about Momo. Doesn't she get a gift?"

Amaterasu shook her head and said, "Momo has everything she needs to defeat Tamamo-no-mae."

I stared at her. "What do you mean? Like, the mirror itself?"

"Well, yes. But you'll need more than that. And you have it," she said cryptically.

"What do you mean?" I asked again.

"You must figure that out for yourself."

"Um . . ." Why did the kami always have to be so mysterious and vague? "Could you maybe be a little bit more . . . clear?"

I felt the warmth of Amaterasu's smile. "Remember who you are," she said. "That is the secret to defeating the forces of darkness."

Typical. Oh well. I tried to focus on who I was and how that made me powerful. *I am the daughter of Takiri-bime, guardian of the Island of Mysteries. I am the granddaughter of Susano'o, Lord of the Sea and Master of Storms, and Amaterasu, Queen of the Sky Kingdom. I have friends: Danny, Ryleigh, Jin, and . . . yes, and Niko. Who's in the Middle Lands, waiting for us to come home.*

I was pleased to find that I *did* feel braver and more powerful. But then I heard a low growl: *I am a rage monster. I am the vessel of Izanami the Destroyer, Queen of Death.*

I gasped. Had the others heard it, too? What would they think?

Danny gave me a puzzled look. "Are you okay?"

"Uh-huh." I nodded hard. "Fine. I'm fine."

You are not me, I told my rage monster. *I don't have to become what I saw in the mirror. I will choose a different path.*

Amaterasu said, more firmly this time, "Children. If you wish to save your friends in the Middle Lands, you have no time to waste. Go through that portal, and I will send you to Tamamo-no-mae."

We went to the glowing orange mirror. I reached out and grabbed Ryleigh's hand on one side and Danny's on the other. Jin stood on Ryleigh's other side and took her hand.

"Ready?" I said.

"Ready," said the other three, and we stepped through the portal together.

Well, Well, Well!
Look Who's Back!

We landed in the center of a wide, barren plain ringed by craggy mountains. The ground was uneven and the entire area was littered with jagged boulders and sharp rocks. Not too far away was a perfectly conical hill; behind it was that familiar blue glow. Spirals of foul-smelling steam puffed up from cracks in the ground all around us and drifted across the landscape like lost ghosts. The full moon cast a silver-white glow from above that should have been comforting but just made the spooky things even more spooky, casting ragged shadows and lighting up the ghostly spirals all around us.

It's okay, I told myself. *That's Tsukiyomi up there. He's got to be watching over us.*

"What is this place? I feel like we're standing in a giant bowl of evil," Jin said.

"I think we're in a volcano," said Ryleigh.

"You've got to be kidding. Please tell me you're kidding," Jin said.

"I mean the crater of a volcano. That's why it looks like a bowl. And that's a cinder cone over there. Like the remains of a mini-volcano, basically. I bet Tamamo-no-mae came here because it's isolated and no one will bother her," Ryleigh explained.

"Cool, cool, cool. Sounds totally safe." Danny said. "So, um, who's got a plan?"

"How would we have a plan already? It's not like we've had a whole lot of time to think of one," I snapped—and realized there was no stab of pain. *Ahhh.*

"Hey, calm down," said Danny. "I would've thought you'd be happy I even asked."

"*I* have a plan," said Ryleigh.

Thank the kami-verse. "Let's hear it," I said. And I wasn't even a little bit jealous.

She tossed her ponytail. "Okay, so here's what I think. Tamamo-no-mae probably has a bunch of onibi with her again as a first line of defense, right?"

"Oni-what?" asked Danny.

"Onibi," Ryleigh said. "Those little blue lights, remember? You can see the glow over there behind the cinder cone."

"Oh. Right."

Ryleigh looked at me for a second like, *This guy,* and I couldn't help smiling. She went on. "That has to be where she's got everyone. That's why Amaterasu put us here. So Danny and I will go first, and Momo will go right behind us. Jin, you don't have any weapons or defenses against the onibi, so you stay under cover."

Jin nodded.

"When we see Tamamo-no-mae or her onibi, Danny and I will throw everything we have at them. That'll make her look at us, and then Momo will jump out with the mirror, and

Tamamo-no-mae will get sucked in. Once she's trapped, we can finish off the rest of the onibi. Meanwhile, Jin, you fly around and find all the prisoners and open the bottle of sunlight over them. And that will be that!"

"I like it. Great plan, Ryleigh," I said. And I meant it.

We got our equipment ready and started walking. A couple of minutes into the long walk across the basin toward the hill, a fox trotted out from the shadow of one of the boulders. I stopped in my tracks, hoping against hope as the fox passed in and out of the shadows and the steam. Could it be?

It was. Niko was alive! He'd survived the fire blast!

Relief flooded through me. I forgot about everything except how glad I was to see him—all I could think was *He's alive! He's okay!* "Niko!" I pelted toward him with my arms outstretched, ready to wrap him in the world's biggest hug.

But he laid his ears back and snarled, baring his sharp white teeth.

"Niko?" I faltered. I was sure it was him. He looked a little skinnier and scruffier than before, but otherwise he was just the same as ever.

Why was he acting like this? Was he angry with me? "Niko, it's me! I'm so glad you're okay!"

But now that I was closer, I could see that his pupils had dilated to the point where his eyes were now entirely black instead of gold. They were rimmed with a pale, glowing blue. "*Are* you okay?" I asked.

He sprang at me with his lips pulled back in a snarl. I tried to push him away, but he twisted and snapped with such ferocity that I couldn't grab him anywhere. "Niko, stop!" I shouted.

"What are you doing?" But he only fought harder. I tripped and fell backward, and he was on my chest with his sharp teeth about to close on my throat when he yelped and slumped to the ground.

I scrambled to my feet as the others rushed forward. One of Ryleigh's shuriken was lodged in Niko's shoulder. With a cry, I knelt to take it out. Blood welled up from the wound and trickled down his leg, and he looked up at me, panting. He shook his head as if to clear it of something unpleasant. His eyes had lost their laser focus, but they were still all black emptiness. No gold, no white.

"It's okay, Niko, I'm here. It's Momo!" My voice sounded shaky and scared. Niko twitched, and just for a moment, I caught a glimpse of my friend behind those demon-possessed eyes before they clouded over again.

"I'm so sorry," said Ryleigh, who had knelt beside me. She looked anguished. "I didn't want to hurt him, but I couldn't let him attack you like that. I used one of my new shuriken to confuse him." She reached into her bag and pulled out a little wet wipe, which she used to dab at the wound. "I'm sorry, Niko." Niko flinched but didn't protest.

Jin and Danny knelt on Niko's other side and stroked his fur. "What's wrong with him?" Jin asked.

"I think he's possessed," I said. "Look at his eyes."

"You sure that's not the shuriken's magic?" Ryleigh asked.

"They were like that before you hit him," I told her. Ryleigh flinched, and I added, "I'm not mad at you. I know you had to do it."

"Maybe Tamamo-no-mae possessed him," Danny said.

At the mention of Tamamo-no-mae's name, Niko's ears perked up a bit and he snarled softly, but then went limp.

Ryleigh said, "I hate to say this, but we need to tie him up or something. Amaterasu said the confusion is only temporary, right?"

I reached into my backpack, praying for a shimenawa or even a regular rope, but all it gave me was three large pepperoni pizzas. I laid them down in front of Niko.

"Your favorite, remember?" I said. He sniffed at the first one suspiciously, and then tore into it as if he hadn't eaten in days.

"Do you think that'll hold him?" asked Jin doubtfully.

"It's only a few minutes to midnight," Danny said, looking at his phone. "If we don't defeat Tamamo before he finishes that pizza, it'll be too late, anyway."

Jin nodded. "Fair enough."

"Okay." I wanted to be brave, but my heart was racing again and my stomach clenched painfully. "Let's do this."

Following Ryleigh's plan, Ryleigh, Danny, and I approached with our weapons drawn while Jin hung back in the shadows. Tamamo-no-mae was over there in the blue glow on the other side of the cinder cone at this very moment, waiting for midnight so she could start draining her victims of their lives. I hoped everyone she'd trapped was all right. I hoped there'd be someone left to save after we dealt with her.

Kusanagi hummed with energy, and I could feel my entire body buzzing in response. I wished I had the power to make a full connection and defeat Tamamo-no-mae without wiping us all off the map. But if all went according to plan, I wouldn't have to worry about that. I looked at Danny with his bow drawn and his first arrow nocked, and at Ryleigh with a razor-sharp shuriken in her hand. All we had to do was stay alive until we could get Tamamo-no-mae to look at the Mirror of the Sun, which was a solid, comforting weight in my pocket.

Where is she? Danny mouthed at me and Ryleigh.

I shook my head and shrugged, but Ryleigh held her finger up to her mouth and cocked her head: *Shhh! Listen!*

Nothing. Just Niko's little whines and lip-smackings in the distance, and the wind whistling down the mountains that surrounded us on all sides.

The sky erupted into an avalanche of fiery blue orbs. "WELL, WELL, WELL! LOOK WHO'S BACK!" Tamamo-no-mae's voice ripped the air around us like the whine of a fighter jet engine. "Are you here to save your little friends? You can see them if you want—they're just over there, on the other side of that cinder cone. But you'll have to get past me first!"

Hundreds of silver-blue orbs hurtled toward us. I raised Kusanagi, and onibi glanced off its blade, smashing into boulders and plowing into the ground. Danny's arrows and Ryleigh's shuriken hissed and whirred through the air, which crackled with hundreds of explosions and showers of light as the sharp points met their targets. Tamamo-no-mae had come at us with way more force than we'd expected. *It's okay. All we have to do is defend ourselves until she looks at us,* I thought.

As if she'd read my mind, Tamamo-no-mae shrieked with laughter. She was still nowhere to be seen, but her voice filled the crater. "What's the matter, children? Too scared to go on the offensive?"

In response, Kusanagi lurched in my hands; I felt like I'd been struck by lightning. *She's asking for a fight—fight her! We can take her!*

No. No fighting! Giving in to Kusanagi's bloodlust would ruin everything. I pulled back with all my might and shoved Kusanagi into my backpack.

"Ohh, wait—you're missing someone!" Tamamo-no-mae called to us from a cloud of onibi. "Could it be . . . this guy?" Jin fell out of the cloud and landed with a thud about ten yards away, eyes closed, still wrapped in his feather cloak. I gasped and felt my chest grow cold. "Silly, silly me! I meant to tell you right away that I'd grabbed him, but I guess I forgot. I was having so much fun doing *this!*" A torrent of onibi streamed toward us, and Danny and Ryleigh just barely managed to deflect them.

"What do we do?" I panted. Without Kusanagi, I felt paralyzed and exposed. I didn't dare take out the Mirror of the Sun—if Tamamo-no-mae saw it and realized what it was, our plan would fail.

"Get the sunlight," Ryleigh whispered. She put her hat on, went all shimmery, and dashed across the rocky field. Tamamo-no-mae was so busy raining fire that she must not have noticed Ryleigh suddenly disappearing. Ryleigh crouched next to Jin, took the bottle out of his hand, and darted away.

She hurled her shuriken at the onibi as she ran back to us. A few of them diverted their paths, but because she was running and invisible, they always missed by a couple of feet—until they didn't. She stumbled and fell, still shimmering. The glowing jade bottle flew from her hand.

I froze, because apparently that was what I did now when people I cared about got hurt. But Danny lunged forward and caught the bottle just before it hit the ground. He rolled over his shoulder and popped to his feet like the hero of an action movie.

Abruptly, the shower of onibi stopped, and Tamamo-no-mae's voice said, "What is that thing in your hand?"

Danny picked up his bow and drew an arrow from his backpack.

"No, no, not that." Danny lowered the bow; his gritted teeth and trembling arms told me it was happening against his will. "It was smaller. It was glowing. Come here and show me what it is."

Tamamo-no-mae swirled out of the darkness and landed in front of Danny. His face was pale, and he was sweating with the effort of resisting her.

Meanwhile, I was still frozen to the spot.

"I see you're not carrying your fancy sword," Tamamo-no-mae said to me with a sharp-toothed smile. "I've heard you're afraid to use it. Is that true? What a shame."

But I didn't need Kusanagi. Casually, I put my hand in my pocket.

Tamamo-no-mae stretched and yawned. "You know what? It's nearly midnight, but I am feeling a bit peckish." She licked her lips and leered at Danny. "So I think I'll have you as an appetizer. And then I'll take a look at whatever it is that you've got in your grubby little paw." Tamamo-no-mae put a hand on each of Danny's arms. He strained away from her with his eyes shut tight. Good. As she leaned down and opened her mouth, I shouted, "Hey! Look over here!"

I tapped the purple edge of the mirror just as Danny opened his eyes. He faded into an outline of himself, like a drawing or a paper doll, and fluttered, twisting and spinning, into Yata-no-kagami's depths.

I Am Here to Help

Tamamo-no-mae's brow furrowed in confusion as she watched Danny's outline flap away from her—but just before she looked into Yata-no-kagami herself, she turned away and threw a barrage of onibi at it. They knocked it out of my hand, and it went spinning into the dirt.

Tamamo-no-mae turned her glittering eyes on me. "My goodness," she said. "Aren't you a tricky one. I am disappointed to have lost that delicious little morsel, but I suppose I can't complain, since he seems to have suffered the fate that you intended for me."

Her words barely registered—I was still reeling from what had just happened. I stared at the spot where the mirror had buried itself. Danny was trapped in there, and it was my fault.

I also had a hazy sense of Ryleigh sprawled on the ground just outside my field of vision, eyes closed, still shimmering slightly under her hat. And Jin just beyond her, pale and unmoving. Then there was Niko, probably still possessed somewhere out there.

I don't know how long I would have stood there frozen like that if Tamano-no-mae hadn't decided to finish me off. She

292

sprang at me; I had just enough time to see a mouthful of sharp fox teeth before I came back to my senses and rolled away. Her jaws snapped on air, and she stood up, back in her human form again. I staggered to my feet and drew Kusanagi out of the backpack, trembling.

"Ah, there's the sword! Unfortunately, I can't have you messing around with it." Tamamo-no-mae flung her hands forward, and a swarm of onibi came at me so thick and fast that even with Kusanagi I couldn't fight them off. They lengthened into ropes and wrapped themselves around me.

"You don't have the skill to use it properly," said Tamamo-no-mae. "If you try to defeat me, if you try to call up a storm powerful enough to kill me, you will also kill all those poor innocent children. This little volcano is sitting in the middle of the Pacific Ocean. Your storm will fill it right up with seawater, and they'll drown, sure as I'm a fox. I don't want my hard-earned dinner to get soggy and drown, and I *know* you don't want their deaths on your hands. Your mother would never forgive you." She made a sorrowful face and clucked her tongue.

Something in her tone caught my attention. "You know where my mother is?"

She smiled coyly. "I might."

"Where? Where is she?"

Tamamo-no-mae examined her fingernails. "I can't tell you. That's between me and the moon, as they say." When I didn't say anything, she smiled wickedly at me and said, "I'd start my feast with you because I'm sure you're full of potential. But you'll taste so much sweeter after you witness my triumph. Pain and suffering have such a delightful flavor." Tamamo-no-mae let out a giggle that would have put Ryleigh's best mean-girl giggle to shame. "So I'll save you for dessert instead. Come along now!" She crooked her finger, and we swept across the landscape to the top of the cinder cone, where she set me down and gestured to her victims, who were lined up in neat rows and surrounded by the blue glow of her magic.

"Ahh," she sighed. "Time to restore my girlish good looks!"

I struggled against the ropes that bound me, but it was no good. "Wait! No!" I shouted, desperate to stop her. "You don't have to do this!"

She snorted. "Excuse me, but yes, I do."

"No, you don't! You don't have to buy into that whole youth-and-beauty thing! You don't have to trick men into doing what you want! You've been fooled by the patriarchy! You can just . . . I mean you can, um . . ."

What was I saying? Was I really about to tell her that she didn't need men to mass-murder for her, that she could do it all on her own?

"Fool! I have lived for millennia, and you, who are barely older than a decade, presume to tell me about the world? The impudence!"

Ulp. "I'm . . . sorry?" I offered.

"You think you can bend the world to your will, but you are wrong—it will never change. There is tremendous power in beauty, and there always will be; beautiful women always get more attention, more money, and more power than plain women. But if a beautiful woman gets too powerful, people don't trust her." She paused, and when she spoke again, she sounded disgusted. "It's all those stories of beautiful women who fool powerful men into doing terrible things. Or beautiful women who are secretly evil witches."

"But that's literally what you do! It's who you are!"

"I have merely chosen the shortest path to the greatest power."

"But you—you could change! You could change yourself, you could change the story—"

"I am who I am. Even if I wanted to change, I'm not sure that I could." Her smile was weary. "I have accepted the world as it is, and I work within it to get what I want." Her features shifted into something menacing and cruel. "And you, little mouse, have stopped me for long enough."

Reach, Momo. It was Kusanagi, still trembling in my hand. *Give me your power. We could prevent the deaths of all those children. We could stop Tamamo-no-mae from terrorizing the world for thousands of years.*

My rage monster howled in response, and I had to fight it down. If I gave Kusanagi enough power for us to defeat Tamamo-no-mae, I would kill those kids in the process. I wished, just for a moment, that I *could* become the monster that Kusanagi wanted me to be—that I could become one with the Sword of the Wind and rid the world of Tamamo-no-mae and not care what it took.

If that's what you want, Momo darling, then do it.

My breath caught and my blood ran cold at the sound of Izanami's voice. The vision I'd seen inside Yata-no-kagami came back to me—the rage monster controlling my actions, the storm, Izanami by my side. I felt a sudden, terrible certainty: the thing I'd feared most was about to happen.

"Go away," I whispered. "I didn't call you. Go away, go away, go away."

My dear, sweet child. An icy breeze caressed my cheek. It was as if she were right by my side, murmuring in my ear. I could almost feel the grip of her cold, bony fingers on my shoulders. *Listen to me. I do not care one way or the other whether your friends or any of those children come to live in Yomi. But you care, and you wished to use your power. So I am here to help.*

My mind whirled. Why would Izanami want to help me? What if, by accepting her help, I became as evil as she was? I couldn't bear it.

I am offering you power greater than any human has ever known, and you are considering turning me down because you disagree with my PRINCIPLES? The breeze suddenly became a howling gale, and the mist that had been gathering around my feet swirled into the shape of Izanami the Destroyer. She loomed over me, her coal-black eyes shining in a beautiful, skeletal face contorted with rage.

I shrank away. Then, just as suddenly, the wind died down, the vision disappeared, and Izanami's voice was whispering in my ear again, as icy calm as if nothing had happened. I suppressed a whimper.

You have moments left before she begins gorging herself on those children. If you reject my help in this moment, you are a coward. Timid where you could be bold. Craven where you should be loyal. Decide now! Accept your birthright, or accept the consequences.

Izanami's voice sliced through me like a dagger. She was right. Maybe it took a monster to fight a monster.

The blue light flared, and Tamamo-no-mae's voice floated

on the wind from the bottom of the hill. "Hello, my pretties! Don't you look delicious!"

They might die if you claim your power, Momo. But they'll definitely die if you don't.

It always came down to this: a choice that didn't feel like a choice. "Tell me what to do."

The Meanest Mean Girl
in History

Stop thinking of your anger as your enemy! Izanami commanded me. *It is your ally. It is your defense against fear and pain. It is the source of your power. Use it.*

I took a fortifying breath and opened myself up. My ears filled with the roar of my rage monster shouting, *YES! FINALLY!* And the world around me fell away, except for the ground under my feet and the pale blue light at the bottom of the hill. The ropes around me turned to ash. Waves of fury rolled through me: at Tamamo-no-mae for her bloodthirsty, bottomless hunger for power, for ripping away the lives of all those kids and taking Niko, Jin, Ryleigh, and Danny away from me; at a world that valued beauty and power over kindness and compassion; at Mom, who'd left me alone even though she *knew* there was a powerful demon on the loose; at all the time I'd wasted chasing down that useless, useless mirror; at the Lucky Gods, and at Amaterasu and Susano'o and Tsukiyomi for once again leaving the fate of the world on my shoulders when they could easily have defeated Tamamo-no-mae themselves if they wanted to. It was their fault that I had to turn myself into this horrible monster.

It felt *great*. Finally, after trying so hard to be a quiet little fish in a little fishbowl, swallowing all my anger, I was a shark, I was a tidal wave, I was a typhoon. Wind roared around me as I crashed down the hill with Kusanagi. Lightning blasted from the sky and tore up the ground with each step I took. It was glorious. It was awesome.

But then, just like every time I did this, I felt myself losing control. A tsunami of rage-fueled power reared up and thundered over me, and I struggled to swim to the surface, to stay human and not be blotted out by my rage monster. *I can't do this,* I thought. *Izanami tricked me.* Another wave crashed and pushed me under.

But just before I lost consciousness entirely, she whispered, *Concentrate!*

How? I thought fuzzily. *On what?*

Who hurt you? Who must you defeat?

It took a moment. I was angry at everyone. Everything.

Who must you defeat? Izanami said sharply. *What is her name?*

A name floated to the surface: *Tamamo-no-mae.*

Say it.

"Tamamo-no-mae."

Louder.

"Tamamo-no-mae!"

Louder! Like you mean it!

"TAMAMO-NO-MAE!" I screamed her name and the ground shook. All the power inside me froze for an instant, then gathered itself behind me, searching for the target I had named. I broke through the surface, gasping. I was back!

Amaterasu's words came back to me: *Remember who you are. That is the secret to defeating the forces of darkness.* And the words of the Gemini auntie: *The path before you will only lead you where you go if you are who you are.* And Yata-no-kagami herself: *It might make more sense just to embrace it.* Finally, I understood. I would never escape my rage monster—and squashing it down and ignoring it had never worked. But with its help, I'd faced up to Ryleigh. I'd freed Amaterasu from Yata-no-kagami and its curse. And now I could defeat Tamamo-no-mae. As I swung Kusanagi in front of me, I realized that what I had seen in the mirror had been wrong. My rage monster hadn't been *controlling* my movements. It had been *following* them.

"TAMAMO-NO-MAE!" I screamed again. "Come out and fight me! If you want to rise to power, you're going to have to kill me first!"

I stopped short. Eight hundred eighty-eight kids were laid out in neat rows on the ground in front of me. Tamamo-no-mae crouched next to the first one—a boy who couldn't have been more than five or six years old. She held one of his limp little hands in one of hers; in her other hand, she held his elbow, and her head was bent over his forearm. When she turned to look at me, his blood streamed down her chin. Her eyes widened, then narrowed, and her lips drew back to reveal her reddened fangs. She dropped the boy's arm and let out a low, animal growl.

"Try and stop me. I dare you."

I was gripped with fear. What if it was too late? What if there was nothing I could do? And then I heard Izanami's voice: *Anger hears the call of the weak, the frightened, and the injured, and rushes to defend them.* That was what those kids were right now: weak, frightened, hurt—victims of the meanest mean girl in history. And Kusanagi, my rage monster, and I were their protectors.

I gathered myself and leaped; I was on the edge of control again, but as I flew through the air, Izanami whispered, *SHE took that boy's life. SHE took your friends. SHE forced you into this.* And instead of stabbing Kusanagi into the ground and destroying everything around me, I slashed at Tamamo-no-mae. She spun away just in time and rolled onto her feet. With a shriek, she burst into a stream of onibi that blazed up into the sky and formed themselves into the shape of a giant nine-tailed fox. In her true form, Tamamo-no-mae hung in the air above the clearing and laid back her ears, snarling, before she sprang for my throat.

I swung Kusanagi once, and a bolt of lightning streaked to meet her. She tumbled to the ground as her side exploded in sparks. Instantly, she was back on her feet and growling, the evil in her eyes burning brighter than ever. But she was bleeding—that is, smoke even blacker than the night sky was drifting out of a dark gash on her shoulder—and I felt a little spark of triumph shoot from Kusanagi through my arms and into my body.

"*That* was for those kids," I said through gritted teeth.

We circled each other, and this time I charged first, calling down more lightning, as well as wind and driving rain and sleet to keep her off balance. Another hit, this time on her flank.

"*That* was for my friends," I said.

She snarled again. "Arrogant, delusional little pup. You think you're so powerful, playing the avenging angel with your sword and your self-righteous ideals. You have no idea. You are nothing but a pawn being moved about by those with *real* power."

The image from the mirror flashed in my mind again: me, my rage monster, and Izanami whispering in my ear. She'd claimed she only wanted to help me, but was that true? I knew in an instant that Tamamo-no-mae was right—I'd known it all along, of course, but I'd pushed it to the back of my mind because I needed to defeat her.

Tamamo-no-mae sprang again—and this time, distracted by the thought of unwittingly doing what Izanami had planned all along, I reacted too late. I managed to deflect those murderous fangs with an elbow, but her weight sent me stumbling backward, and Kusanagi flew out of my grasp as a sharp pain shot through my ankle. I willed Kusanagi back to me and got in one wild swipe as Tamamo-no-mae attacked again; this time, lightning struck her other shoulder.

Get up. I felt Kusanagi urging me. *Get up!* I staggered to my feet, wincing at the stab of pain in my ankle, which refused to support my weight. My rage monster responded with a roar that expressed itself as thunder that shook the ground. *Finish her off!*

I could feel the lightning coursing through me, begging to be unleashed. But I had to be careful. Focus. One false step and all that power could go into the earth and cause all kinds of destruction. I steadied myself and raised Kusanagi.

"Weakling," Tamamo-no-mae sneered. "I see you favoring that ankle. You may have the power of the gods in that sword, but your body is still mortal." Meanwhile, smoke was pouring out of her wounds, but she seemed no worse for wear, somehow. If anything, she seemed more powerful than ever.

"That's right, you worthless puddle of vomit. I thrive on pain and suffering—even my own. What doesn't kill me only makes me stronger." Her lips curled back and her eyes glowed, and she was in the air again, flying at me.

I stepped forward to meet her, and my ankle crumpled beneath me. I gasped, tightening my fingers around Kusanagi's hilt as I hit the ground. Pushing myself to my knees, I felt more than saw her sail over me, gather herself, and spring again. Then she was hurtling toward me—her coal-black eyes glowing, her knife-sharp fangs and claws ready to rip me to shreds, and her nine tails flying behind her.

Now, said Izanami.

I dropped to the ground again, rolled, and channeled every last drop of my rage-monster power into Kusanagi as I held it up to meet Tamamo-no-mae just before she landed.

A hiss, like water on red-hot iron, followed by a scream of rage that made my hair stand on end.

BOOM.

Tamamo-no-mae exploded into thousands of streaks of blue light, which whirled around me before spinning away and fading into the darkness in all directions. Her voice shrieked, "Nooo! Nooo! You cannot win! I won't allow it!"

BOOM . . . BOOM . . . BOOM . . .

Nine earth-shaking, light-filled explosions altogether, one for each of her tails. The scent of smoke filled my nostrils as the last remaining blue streaks streamed away from me and fizzled out.

"Too bad!" I shouted into the air. "I think I just did!"

And then I fainted.

Pepperoni Pizza Is a Powerful Panacea

Well done, Momo.

I opened my eyes and sat up—and lay right back down because the world had become a Tilt-A-Whirl and my stomach threatened to turn itself inside out. Okay, then. Maybe I could figure out what was going on without sitting up or opening my eyes.

I breathed in and smelled the lingering odor of smoke. My right hand closed around the hilt of Kusanagi; pebbles and gritty ash crunched in my left hand, and sharp little rocks poked uncomfortably into my back. I hadn't ended the world or destroyed the island, then. My ankle throbbed as the details of the fight with Tamamo-no-mae came back to me.

Was she dead? I'd watched her explode into all those lights and fade into nothing.

That's right. Do you understand now what your anger can do for you?

I raised myself slowly up on my elbows. The ground seemed pretty non-tilty, so I risked opening my eyes. I was lying in the gravel at the base of the cinder cone. To my left, I could see the bodies of all the kids I'd come to rescue, still lined up on

304

the ground—still staring blankly at the night sky and blanketed by a dim blue light. There was Kiki, her strawberry-blond hair spread around her face; there was the little boy whose blood Tamamo-no-mae had been drinking. My throat tightened and my stomach lurched.

Carefully, I made my way to Kiki's side. Her pulse was weak, her breath was icy, and her skin was pale and cold.

"Kiki?" I said. "Kiki, wake up! She's gone now. You're safe!"

But Kiki didn't even blink.

I limped from kid to kid in a panic, shaking and calling to them. None of them woke up.

Tamamo-no-mae was dead, so her magic should have died with her—wasn't that the rule? Then her last words rang in my ears: *You cannot win! I won't allow it!* Had she done something in her final moments to make sure everyone stayed cursed?

Eight hundred eighty-eight kids were still unconscious, and everyone I'd ever loved—everyone I'd ever known—was either dead or as good as dead. Was this the trap Izanami had laid for me? Was this her way of convincing me to give up on my earthly life and join her in Yomi?

My train of thought was interrupted by a low whine. I peered into the semidarkness and listened as hard as I could. I could just make out a Niko-shaped figure creeping toward me in the shadow of a nearby boulder. Right—I'd left him alive, snarfing down pepperoni pizzas on the other side of the hill. He'd finished and was coming back to get me.

Kusanagi lit up, and I hated the feeling it gave me—that electric surge of power in my veins. I shouldn't feel like this just before I was about to kill my only living friend.

"Niko?" I raised Kusanagi.

"Stop standing there like a statue and help me, you dithering demigod!"

"Niko!" I dropped the sword. "You're okay! You're you!"

"Mmmmf!" He struggled free of my very tight hug. "Indeed I am."

"I'm so glad to see you. Everyone else . . ." He let me give him another hug and waited till I was done crying into his fur.

"Where's Danny?" he asked.

"I sent him into the mirror." Through more tears, I explained what had happened.

"And you defeated Tamamo-no-mae all by yourself? With Kusanagi?"

"Yeah. But I lost Danny. And Ryleigh and Jin. And the rest of the kids are still practically dead."

Niko nodded. "But you learned how to channel your power without losing control."

That *was* a pretty huge deal. But it felt meaningless compared to having lost everything else. I was still sad. I sniffled and wiped my eyes.

"Would you like to see Ryleigh and Jin?" Niko asked, and I was suddenly overcome by the need to sit with them and hold their hands one last time.

"Yes."

We walked slowly around the hill. Well, he walked. I limped. It took forever, but finally, there they were.

"Nothing I could do would wake them," Niko said sadly.

I stared down at him. "Wake them? You mean they're alive?"

"Of course they're alive, you anxiety-ridden alarmist! What else would they be?"

"I was afraid they were dead!" I came very close to choking Niko with another huge hug. Maybe there was hope left after all.

What about Danny? said a tiny voice in a corner of my mind.

Don't think about Danny. Focus on Jin and Ryleigh.

I knelt and checked them both. They were pale and cold like the others, but still breathing. Fueled by this new hope, my mind began to race.

"Niko. How did you get better? What happened?" Maybe the curse was temporary. Maybe all we had to do was wait. Or maybe there was some kind of medicine in the confusion-inducing shuriken that Ryleigh had thrown at Niko.

"Pepperoni pizza is a powerful panacea."

"Pana-what?"

"Panacea. Cure-all. Antidote to anything."

"Really?"

"For me, anyway." I must not have looked convinced, because he added, "Or perhaps those pizzas were special. I felt much more myself after I was finished."

I felt my spirits lift, and I silently thanked Hotei and his miraculous backpack. If the pizza had cured Niko . . . "Do you have any left?"

Niko looked embarrassed. "I, er, ate it all."

"*All* of it? Three entire pizzas?"

"I *may* have left a bit of crust behind."

I tore off my backpack and plunged my hand inside, praying for more. But of course, my backpack gave me nothing but nothing. UGHHH! I threw it as far away from me as I could—which turned out not to be very far at all because the strap caught on my wrist. So I threw it on the ground. "This backpack never gives me what I need!" I might have stomped on it, but my ankle hurt too much. I kicked a spray of gravel at it instead.

Something glinted at me from the ground: Yata-no-kagami. I remembered—it had gotten knocked out of my hand just after I'd trapped Danny inside. It lay at my feet reflecting the moon, which had reemerged from behind the storm clouds.

Momo.

I stared at it. I had to be imagining things.

Momo. In the mirror, my mouth made the shape of my name.

"Yata-no-kagami?" I whispered.

Mirror Me/Yata-no-kagami lifted her hand and waved. *Guess what?*

"What?"

Your friend is still in here.

"You mean . . ."

He hasn't made up his mind yet.

My heart began thumping and my head began to swim. What if . . . "Can I—I mean, I know I can't choose another life anymore, but can I . . . maybe go back in there? To see Danny?"

Yata-no-kagami nodded. *Sure! You just have to state your wish to enter.*

State your wish to enter. So simple. So easy. Please let this work.

I took a deep breath and said to my reflection, "I wish to enter Yata-no-kagami again."

Why Are We Whispering?

I was back in the eight-sided chamber of mirrors. Two Dannys stood in the middle of the room. One was completely still and unblinking. Clutched in his hand was the glowing green bottle of sunlight. Next to him was a whole other identical Danny, who turned and smiled at me.

I looked at Yata-no-kagami—that is to say, Mirror Me. "What's going on?"

Yata-no-kagami smiled. "I told you he hasn't made his choice yet. His spirit is in one of the mirrors. And until he chooses, his body remains here"—she pointed at the frozen Danny—"with Yata-no-kagami." She pointed at the smiling version of Danny, who waved at me and said, "Hi, Momo!"

"But I thought *you* were Yata-no-kagami," I said to my mirror self.

Yata-no-kagami said to the, um, *other* Yata-no-kagami, "Explain."

Danny's mirror version said, "I am—that is to say, *we are*—both Yata-no-kagami. Yata-no-kagami is a reflection of everyone who enters, and I can split myself into infinite pieces. So it *looks* like there are four of us, but really there's only three:

309

you, Danny, and me—but I am reflecting each of you. Though technically each reflection is also individual, since each of me—or each of us, if you prefer—reflects an individual. So I guess you *could* say there are two of me and two of you."

I thought my head might explode. I said, "Um, I'm just going to say there are four of us. But could we maybe figure out nicknames or something so we don't get each other confused with . . . each other?"

Mirror Danny looked thoughtful. "How about Yata-no-Danny and Yata-no-Momo for us, and just Momo and Danny for you and Danny?" he asked.

That was fine with me.

With that settled, I was desperate to get back to the reason I was here. "So, when Danny's spirit comes back from the life he's in now, will he be able to see me? Will I be able to talk to him? Like you're talking to me?"

"Probably not," said Yata-no-Danny. "He can only see me. Unless he chooses to return to the life you both came from. Then his spirit will reenter his body so he can go back, and *then* he'll see you."

I turned to Yata-no-Momo. "If he can't see me, why did you tell me he was in here? Why would you get my hopes up like that?" I heard my voice rising in frustration. *Calm down.* The inside of a mirror would be a terrible place to lose my temper.

Yata-no-Momo looked confused. "I didn't mean to get your hopes up—I just thought you'd like to know. I thought you might like to see which life he chooses."

"Why would I—" I started with my teeth clenched, but then stopped. It was pointless to argue; I needed to try another way. "Are you absolutely sure there's no way I can contact him in here?" I pleaded.

"It's never been done before," said Yata-no-Momo. "On the other hand, no one ever chose to return to their original life before you. So who knows? Maybe you can do it."

"Okay," I said. "Which mirror is he in?"

"That one." Yata-no-Danny pointed.

"He's been in there for quite a while," Yata-no-Momo added cheerfully. She said it like we were waiting around for Danny to come back from the bathroom.

I tried not to panic. *Breathe, Momo. Breathe.*

"Would you like to take a peek?" Yata-no-Danny asked.

"Yes, please."

So Yata-no-Momo and I joined Yata-no-Danny in front of the mirror that Danny had entered last.

"After you," Yata-no-Danny said graciously. I pushed aside the mist and stepped into the mirror.

We were at a diner, standing in front of a booth by the window. Danny was sitting with a man and a little girl. They were Asian, and they both looked just like Danny. They were all laughing and talking together—through the sound was muffled and wavy, as if they were underwater. I could see Danny's spirit superimposed on his mirror self, sort of floating inside and around the body.

"That's his birth father and his half sister," Yata-no-Danny whispered. "This is the life where his birth parents stayed to-gether at first, but then got divorced. His dad remarried, and Danny mostly lives with him, since his birth mom travels a lot for work."

The dad said something to the little girl, who giggled and whispered conspiratorially in Danny's ear. Danny's eyes were shining.

"Danny!" I called, leaning over the table and getting right in his face. "Danny, can you hear me? It's Momo!"

"He doesn't know you in this life," said Yata-no-Danny. "He's never been to California."

But the *real* Danny knew me. He hadn't made his choice yet, so he had to remember me. "Danny!" I called again.

Danny's spirit—my Danny—lifted itself from Mirror Danny's body. He wrinkled his forehead and blinked a couple of times, as if he'd heard something important but wasn't quite sure what it was. Even the Danny who belonged to this life looked a little confused. Then his birth dad spoke, and he seemed to snap out of it. My Danny sank back into the other Danny's body.

"There's no use trying to reach him," Yata-no-Momo said softly. "You're invisible, inaudible, and imperceptible."

Panic began snaking through me. I pushed it down. I couldn't give up—I was so close. He *had* heard me, I was sure of it. "Danny, listen to me! It's your friend, Momo!"

Spirit Danny floated out of his mirror body. I held my breath as he looked back at his mirror self with his birth family, and then out toward me again, and then back again at his mirror self.

Come back, I willed him. *Come back. Come back to your old, original life. I need you.*

"I don't think I want you in here anymore. You're supposed

to let him choose. If you keep screaming like that, and he listens to you, you'll take him away from a life that makes him happy," said Yata-no-Danny. His face was dark with disapproval. "That's very selfish of you."

But I need him, I started to say—and then realized that maybe it *was* selfish and unfair of me to take him away from this life just because I needed a friend. He looked so happy here.

Spirit Danny sat back down, and Yata-no-Momo said, "Let's go." I felt the panic rise again. This couldn't be it. But it wasn't fair to make Danny choose me over this whole other life.

Then I remembered—how could I have forgotten? I hadn't come in here for me.

"Those kids need you, Danny! They need you to rescue them! And your parents! Think of your parents!" Impulsively, I smacked my hands on the table in front of him. Spirit Danny jumped in his seat and looked curiously at the spot where my hands had landed. That was it! I just needed to make more noise. How could I make more noise?

I felt a hand on my elbow. I shook it off impatiently. The world needed Danny, and I wasn't going to let Yata-no-kagami stop me from bringing him back. I shouted everything I could think of that might do it. "WE NEED TO RESCUE THE KIDS! AND YOUR PARENTS! RYLEIGH! JIN! NIKO! FOOTBALL! THE GOLDEN STATE WARRIORS! IN-N-OUT BURGER!"

"STOP." This time, four hands grabbed me and yanked me backward and spun me around. I stumbled and nearly dropped Kusanagi to the floor—and realized I was gripping the hilt with both hands. How had that happened?

"Now you've done it," Yata-no-Danny whisper-screamed at me.

"I've done what?"

"Shhh! You were smashing that blasted sword around like a wild thing! See these cracks?" Yata-no-Danny waved his hands in huge circles. I looked around me. The air seemed to be split with tiny lines, like I was inside a diamond.

"You've compromised the magical molecular integrity of the mirror! One more good hit and the entire portal could collapse! Or worse, it could open up!" Yata-no-Momo whispered.

"Why are we whispering?"

"Because what if the people out there can hear us through the cracks? It was bad enough with all your banging around, and now—"

I opened my mouth to yell, but Yata-no-Momo pointed a finger at me and nothing came out. "Should've done that the moment you started shouting. Why did you have to choose today to stop following rules?" she muttered. "And don't even think about trying to break through and pull him back," she added, eyeing Kusanagi. "I've already told you what could happen." Then she sighed and said, "I know it's hard. But you have to let him choose. That's just the way this place is designed."

I didn't know what else to do. I couldn't risk collapsing the portal and trapping Danny here, or tearing it open and sucking other people into the mirror. I put Kusanagi away and whispered to Danny through a closed-up throat, "Have a nice life." Yata-no-Danny held the mist back, and I walked away from the boy who had promised to be my friend forever.

· · ·

I went straight to Danny's spirit-less body at the center of the eight-sided mirror room. The mirror spirits came over and sat with me.

"I don't suppose I could take this with me," I said, tapping the jade bottle of sunlight.

Yata-no-Momo shook her head. "He brought it in. He has to carry it out."

"Yeah, I figured there was probably a rule like that," I said. I pressed the heels of my hands against my eyes to keep from crying. I was totally out of options. My chest felt cold and dark and empty.

"Lucky for you, though, you don't have to break it," said Yata-no-Danny. "Look!"

I took my hands away from my eyes to see Danny's spirit emerging from the mirror and sliding back into his body, which popped and snapped with hundreds of sparks. The cold, dark hole in my chest slowly filled with golden light.

"He's made a choice! He's rejoining his body!" Yata-no-Momo shouted, and she and Yata-no-Danny stood and began dancing around the room together.

Danny—the real Danny—my Danny—opened his eyes and went, "AAAHH!" He reached out and poked my shoulder. "Momo?"

"You're back!" I flung my arms around him. "You chose to come back!"

"Yeah. I almost didn't, though." Danny looked thoughtful.

"What happened?" I asked, glancing nervously at Yata-no-kagami.

"I was in a life where I never left my birth family. It wasn't exactly the way I used to picture it in my head, but we were happy. And I didn't have any questions about where I was from, and no one made me feel like I wasn't *really* my parents' kid, or like I wasn't, like, truly Asian or whatever because my parents are white. It was just simpler, you know?"

I nodded.

"But then, I dunno. It was like this voice in my head kept saying stuff like 'The kids need you! Your parents need you!' and stuff."

Both Yata-no-kagamis scowled at me. But I decided not to care. Danny hadn't said he'd heard anything breaking or shattering, or that it was *my* voice, right? Maybe he'd only heard his own thoughts, like I had. The important thing was that he was here, and when we went back to our old life, the portal to his other life would reseal.

"So, what are you doing here?" he said. "Are you still alive? What happened? Is everything okay? Are Jin and Ryleigh—"

"Everything's great," I said. I couldn't stop smiling. "I'll explain it all later, but yeah, I'm alive. Everyone's alive—except for Tamamo-no-mae. Everything's going to be fine."

Was it really? I didn't know. I didn't want to think about it too much. Or maybe I didn't want Danny to regret his decision. Or maybe just having him back was enough to make me hopeful again.

Danny grinned. "Sweet." Then he said, "Hey, I know it sounds kinda mushy and all, but—"

I couldn't help it. I threw my arms around him again. "Thanks for coming back."

"Don't thank me. This was definitely the right choice."

．　．　．

We came out right where I'd walked in, at the spot where Jin, Ryleigh, Danny, and I had battled with Tamamo-no-mae. I'd just tucked the Mirror of the Sun in my jacket pocket when Niko came bounding over, his whiskers and ears twitching with—could it be?—joy. Of course, what he said was "It's about time you, lazy laggards! Do you have any idea how worried I've been, waiting here for you? Your lack of concern for my feelings is absolutely astonishing."

"Good to see you too, Niko," Danny said with a grin, and he bent down and wrapped his arms around Niko and dug his fingers into Niko's raggedy red coat.

Niko grumbled something about humans being silly sentimental sops, but I noticed that he gave Danny an affectionate nuzzle and a big lick on the cheek.

"All right, enough with the hugs and histrionics," he said eventually. "I have news!" Niko trotted in an excited circle. "In your interminable absence, I found some crumbs of crust," he explained, "and I fed them to—" He looked at Jin and let out an excited bark. "He's waking up!"

Jin's eyes fluttered open and he took in a big gulp of air, as if he'd been swimming underwater and suddenly popped to the surface. He sat up, rubbed his eyes, and looked dazedly at us as we cheered and pumped our fists (or our paws, in Niko's case).

I hugged him with everything I had. "Jin!" I buried my face in his shoulder and murmured, "I'm so glad you're okay."

"Me too," he said, and hugged me back.

All of a sudden, I realized what I was doing—clutching Jin

Takayama to me and *murmuring into his shoulder* like the heroine of some sappy romance novel. Oh, the shame! The awkwardness! What must he think of me? I dropped him and stepped away, my cheeks burning.

"So . . . we defeated Tamamo-no-mae," I said.

"That's amazing! Oof, I feel sore all over." He groaned. Then he saw Ryleigh lying a few feet away, and his face fell. "What happened?"

We spent the next few minutes filling him in and allowing Niko to explain his plan.

Yep. Niko had a plan.

Danny handed Amaterasu's bottle to Jin. "It's all you, bro," he said with a grin. "Total rock star stuff! I'm gonna record it and we're gonna go so viral."

Jin looked unsure. "Could you maybe not record it, though?"

"Bro, what? Why not? You're going to look like an angel—like, literally! You'll totally blow up online and get even more famous . . . maybe you could even have a solo career, like Harry Smyles. Everyone's gonna love you. And then you can do whatever you want!"

"What happened to him being a stuck-up rock star?" I said, giving Danny a little nudge with my elbow.

"I mean. I might have been a little bit jealous," Danny said with a sheepish grin. "Maybe. But now we're friends, so I'm happy for him!"

"Do as Jin asks," Niko said sharply. "Perhaps he wants some privacy. Anyway, you know the rest of the human world won't see what you see. Most likely all they'll see on your viral video is a helicopter full of perfectly pedestrian paramedics."

Danny looked surprised, and then a little bit ashamed. "Yeah, okay," he said. "You're right. Sorry, Jin."

"Of course I'm right," Niko huffed. "When have I ever been wrong?"

"I can think of a few times, actually," I said. Niko turned his nose up at me and grumbled something about being underestimated and unappreciated.

After some debate about whether the light from the bottle would spread everywhere like actual sunshine, or whether it would come out in a single beam that needed to be pointed in a specific direction like a spotlight, we decided to use my portal candy to take us all—including Ryleigh, who was still asleep—to the other side of the hill where everyone else lay.

There, Jin spread his iridescent, rainbow-colored wings and rose over the sleeping crowd. He pulled the stopper out of the bottle, and the entire basin was instantly flooded with light. I felt like a crocus bathing in the light of the first warm spring day after a long, cold winter . . . like a bird soaring through an endless summer sky . . . like scarlet leaves glowing in the autumn sun . . . like a field of pure, untouched snow glistening like diamonds on a dazzlingly bright December morning. I felt the torn, swollen ligaments around my twisted ankle knit themselves back together. My spirits lifted and every dark thought I'd ever had was chased away, and I felt like I could do *anything.* All in all, it was the most glorious, beautiful, fantabulously amazing feeling I'd ever experienced.

When the feeling faded—it was a small bottle, after all—and Jin flew back down to join us, Ryleigh was hugging me, Danny was cheering, and Niko was zooming around in celebratory circles like a little puppy. And 888 kids were waking up, stretching their arms and legs, and looking very confused. The blue glow that had covered them was gone.

"What do we do now?" I said.

"What if I shoot my summoning arrow? Isn't tonight the night when the Luckies go around spreading good fortune? I can summon the *Takarabune,* and maybe they can come here, get everyone, and drop us all off while they go around the world!"

"Great idea," said Jin.

"Perfect! Let's do it," said Ryleigh. "I mean. Momo, what do you think?"

"Go for it," I said.

Danny shot his diamond arrow into the sky and shouted, "*Takarabune!* The Seven Lucky Gods!" We watched it until it disappeared with a tiny flash into the dark night sky.

Man, I Love a Reunion!

A sharp animal cry—part hawk and part lion, if you can imagine it—split the air, and I saw the dragons of the *Takarabune* streaming toward us. Right behind them was the ship itself, coming in so hot and fast, I closed my eyes so I wouldn't have to see it explode when it hit the ground.

But there was no explosion, no spray of dirt and rocks. I opened my eyes to find the ship bobbing silently in the air as if it had simply floated down like a balloon. A thick chain had been lowered and was anchoring the ship to the ground.

"WELL?" Bishamon roared from the deck. "Step lively, rodents, and don't stand around gaping like a bunch of sick snakes! Hup, hup! We haven't got all night!"

A rope ladder tumbled over the rail, and we climbed up as quickly as we could while Bishamon looked over and yelled at us to "hurry up, rodents!"—which I thought was a little unfair, because have you ever climbed a free-hanging rope ladder? It's not easy!

On deck, we faced seven gods standing in a semicircle. Bishamon in his army fatigues and giant flaming halo was scowling at us, but that was normal for him. More worryingly,

Daikoku—dressed in her business suit and fedora, and holding Danny's diamond arrow in her hand—looked every bit the goddess of darkness that she had been before she became the kami of merchants and farmers.

Luckily the other kami looked a lot more welcoming. Ebisu, Danny's spirit dad, tipped his bucket hat at us, and Hotei, the laid-back god of contentment, was absolutely beaming. Next to them were Jurōjin and Fukurokujū, who looked like they were a hundred years old. Their identical wispy white beards and eyebrows sprouted from identical faces as wrinkled as peach pits. The two gods leaned on identical staffs, wore identical robes, and carried identical scrolls. If it weren't for Fukurokujū's ginormous forehead, which was easily as tall as the rest of him, I wouldn't have been able to tell them apart. (That was how Mom taught me to remember which one he was: longer name, longer forehead.) Together, they were the gods of wisdom and long life—I guess the point was that one went with the other.

Finally, there was a tall, graceful kami with dark, soulful eyes just like Jin's, and straight black hair that flowed over her shoulders like water. She wore a long, drapey, rose-colored jacket and a sky-blue silk scarf, and black jeans and boots, and she carried a guitar.

"My son," she said, looking at Jin. "How I have longed to meet you again these many years." She walked to him, and Jin didn't even try to pretend he wasn't crying as he stepped into her arms.

Daikoku cleared her throat impatiently, but Hotei drew huge hankie out of his sack and dabbed his eyes. "You gotta give 'em a *little* time, Daikoku." He sniffled and blew his nose into the hankie before stuffing it into the pocket of his bathrobe. "Man, I love a reunion!"

Daikoku sighed and looked at her pocket watch, but said nothing.

Ebisu limped over to Danny and wrapped him in a hug as well. "You dear, dear boy! It seems you've prevailed!" Then he reached an arm toward me and Niko, and then beckoned to Ryleigh, who hung back shyly. "Come here, new girl. You're part of our family now."

Hotei was openly bawling at this point, tossing used handkerchiefs left and right. Once we'd had our hugs and been introduced to each other, Daikoku stepped forward and held out Danny's arrow, which evaporated.

"As heartwarming as this little reunion has been, we are only here because we received a summons from an arrow of Amaterasu," she said. "And despite our *very* busy schedule"— she paused for a moment, to let it sink in how busy she was, I suppose—"we have responded. Now then. To what do we owe the—ahem—*honor* of being called away from our sacred duty to spread good luck and good fortune throughout the world on the eve of the new year?"

"Aw, come on, Daikoku, you know why!" Hotei drawled. "They killed Tamamo-no-mae and rescued the kids! Way to go, little buddies! Candy and glitter for everyone!" He reached into his sack and began flinging fistfuls of fun-sized candy bars and glitter into the air—at us, and at the kids on the ground.

"Stop that at once!" Bishamon and Daikoku roared together.

Hotei jumped in surprise, then rolled his eyes and stuck out his lower lip. "Way to kill the vibe," he grumbled. "Just when things were getting fun." He pulled out a bag of kettle chips and began chewing very loudly.

Bishamon brushed a shower of glitter out of his beard and watched with distaste as it sparkled to the deck. Then he raised his head and shouted, "Attennn-*shun!*"

Niko, Danny, Ryleigh, Jin, and I snapped to attention, and Bishamon nodded his approval. "Finally, a little order around here." He glared at Hotei, who stuffed an enormous chip into his mouth and flashed the peace sign, crunching happily.

Daikoku spoke again. "As Hotei has noted, it seems that you have not only destroyed the demon Tamamo-no-mae, but prevented her victims from losing their lives. So I suppose that before we proceed with your request, we should first congratulate you on a job well done. To be honest, we weren't sure you'd be able to pull it off; the last we heard, you were at the center of quite a bit of chaos in the Celestial City."

Here, even Bishamon's face softened. "A clever bit of strategy there," he said gruffly. "What with the distractions to draw security away from the target. Good work, troops." He nodded at Ryleigh as if he knew she'd been the mastermind behind the heist. Ryleigh blushed and stood a little straighter, and I felt a little glow of pride for her, too.

"The problem is, we don't know what to do with all these kids," said Danny. "That's why we summoned you." He shifted nervously. "We thought maybe you could help everyone get home. Since you're going around the world anyway."

Daikoku and Bishamon looked at each other, as if to say, *Yep, that's what we thought.* Daikoku took another look at her watch and expelled a long breath. "If we work quickly, we can drop them off in groups. Ebisu, hammocks and a net, please. Benzaiten, call the children to the ship and calm them down—they're milling around like ants down there. Yes, yes, Hotei, a favorite snack for each one. Grandfathers, will you talk to the dragons and tell them that we will need more speed than usual?"

To us, Daikoku said, "Sit. You must be exhausted, and the night is far from over."

"I'll bet you're hungry, too," said Hotei. He looked hopefully at Daikoku, who nodded.

"It wouldn't do to return them to their families without having fed them," she said.

"Wait—our families are okay?" Ryleigh asked eagerly.

"They are safe in their homes," said Daikoku, and Danny, Ryleigh, and Jin seemed to melt with relief.

"What about Mom?" I asked.

"I'm sure she's fine," Daikoku said, and strode off before I could ask what she meant.

Hotei smiled kindly as he handed me my favorite comfort meal: an omelet stuffed with rice stir-fried with chopped onions and ketchup (hey—don't knock it till you've tried it). Danny got an In-N-Out hamburger and fries, and Niko got his pepperoni pizza. Ryleigh had a big plate of lasagna ("Is it vegetarian?" she asked, and Hotei nodded), and Jin got a bowl of chicken soup.

Danny sat next to me and nudged me with his shoulder. "Hey. It's okay. If something happened to your mom, Daikoku would have said."

"Danny told me how awesome your mom is. She's definitely fine," Ryleigh added.

Niko gave an indignant sniff. "Of course she's fine. She's a kami! Doubting her would be downright disrespectful."

"Anyway, we're here for you," said Jin. "And we're your family, too."

Hotei must have added some magic to the dishes, because by the time I was finished, I did feel a little better.

While we ate, the Luckies sprang into action. Benzaiten sang a song that the kids on the ground must have found irresistible, because they all stopped whatever they were doing and walked calmly toward the ship. Ebisu, with a bunch of intricate hand motions, began weaving a giant golden net that unfurled itself over the railing. Daikoku and Bishamon leaped into the crowd and organized the kids into groups with an efficiency that no one but they could have managed. Meanwhile, Hotei wandered around and distributed snacks: pao de queijo, tamales, apple strudel, fragrant pakora, bowls of instant ramen, and bags of chips made of everything from potatoes to corn to plantains to shrimp.

When all 888 kids had been fed, given a hammock and a spot in the ginormous protective golden net that Ebisu had woven around them, and sung to sleep by Benzaiten, the Luckies gathered in front of us again.

"I'll bet the children would like to tell us about how they managed to accomplish their mission," said Jurōjin. He began unfurling his scroll. "Shall we begin recording it for posterity?"

"With all due respect, Grandfather, we'll have to put that off for a while." Daikoku glanced at her watch and at Bishamon, who was muttering to himself and pacing the deck like a caged animal. "We're running behind." She pulled on the chain attached to her watch, and the tiny little mallet at the end suddenly transformed into a full-sized tool. She swung it once, twice, three times. Five fluffy blankets fell out of the air.

"Whoa." Danny's eyes grew wide.

Daikoku clapped her hands. "Now. We have a lot to do and we can't be bothered taking care of you until we're finished. So go to sleep, and we'll speak with you again in the morning."

Jin looked at Benzaiten. "Will we have time to talk a little bit?"

Benzaiten looked pleadingly at Daikoku, who shook her head. "Not now. Perhaps after we finish." She laid a hand on Jin's shoulder and added, "I am sorry to keep her from you. But her first duty is to the world."

She really did look sorry, and Jin swallowed hard and nodded.

Benzaiten kissed him on the forehead and stepped away, and Daikoku went back into boss mode. "Bishamon, the ship is yours."

Bishamon's halo of fire flared up, and he banged his staff on the deck. "Step lively, everyone!" he bellowed. "Not a moment to spare! Anchors aweigh! Good fortune and good luck to all, and good children back to their homes!"

Ropes coiled and uncoiled, chains clanked, the sails filled with wind that sprang up from out of nowhere, and we were off. I leaned over the railing and admired the moonlight sparkling on the sea. Below us swayed the net that Ebisu had woven— a protective golden cocoon around the kids we'd rescued. I felt a pang of jealousy—every kid on this ship but me was going home to someone who missed them. But then the warmth of the blanket that I'd wrapped around me seeped into my bones, and my eyelids grew heavy. Daikoku strode by and saw me. "Go to sleep," she said, so I joined Niko, Danny, Ryleigh, and Jin, who were already asleep on the deck, and curled up next to them. The last thought I remember having was, *I'm glad I have such great friends.*

I Have Something to Tell You

When I woke up, it was still nighttime and we were still flying, and the moon was still bright in the sky. My friends were still asleep, and when I tiptoed around the deck, I saw the Luckies dozing in seven easy chairs at the stern.

"We are crossing an uninhabited stretch of ocean," said a voice behind me. "They are taking a moment of hard-earned rest." I turned to see Tsukiyomi standing in a column of cool silver light. He smiled at me. "Welcome back to the Middle Lands, my child. I am so glad to see you."

"I defeated Tamamo-no-mae! And we saved all the kids! And we stole the Mirror of the Sun, but I didn't even need it in the end!" I told him.

"So I've been told," Tsukiyomi said. "Did you finally learn how to use your power without losing control of it?"

"Uh-huh." I swallowed and suppressed a shiver at the memory of exactly how I'd learned, and who I'd learned it from. To prevent him from asking, I kept talking. "And it turned out that there was a curse on the mirror, and Amaterasu has been under its spell for a long time."

"Indeed?" He raised an eyebrow and steepled his fingers together. "Well, if anyone could have broken the curse, it was you."

"That's what Amaterasu said—the only thing that can break a curse one of the Three Sacred Treasures is another one of the treasures."

Tsukiyomi smiled. "Yes. That is true. I am so very proud of you, Momo. I knew that you would prevail."

I smiled back. I wished once again that Tsukiyomi were my grandfather, and not Susano'o.

"Do you have the mirror with you now?"

I started to pull it out of my pocket, but Tsukiyomi stopped me. "No, no. Don't show me," he said. "You are safe here on the *Takarabune*, but one never knows who might be watching."

That sounded ominous. "What do you mean?" I asked.

Even though there was no one around to hear except the Seven, who were still fast asleep in their chairs, Tsukiyomi bent down and lowered his voice. "As you know, each of the Sacred Treasures is a vessel of extraordinary power; together—if the bearer knows how to wield it—their power is practically immeasurable. In the wrong hands, the Treasures constitute a terrible danger to the kami-verse. Until recently, they were so widely scattered and inaccessible—the Sword of the Wind with Susano'o, the Mirror of the Sun with Amaterasu, and the Jewel of Kindness lost for centuries—that it seemed they would never be reunited. But you now have two of them in your possession."

I stared at him, goggle-eyed. Where, exactly, was he going with this?

He lowered his voice even further. "After your first encounter with Tamamo-no-mae, I believed that the mirror was the only way you could defeat her, and I judged it to be worth the risk for you to bring it back to the Middle Lands. But I have just learned that we were set up by Izanami the Destroyer; she is trying to collect the Sacred Treasures so that she can use them to break out of Yomi and attack the Middle Lands and the Sky Kingdom. She knew you had Kusanagi, and that therefore, you were the only one who could successfully break the curse of the Mirror of the Sun. Izanami arranged Tamamo-no-mae's escape and counted on you to bring the mirror back and defeat her. The moment you are alone and unprotected, Izanami will arrange to have you brought to Yomi, so that she can take Kusanagi and Yata-no-kagami for herself. I imagine she has minions searching for the Jewel of Kindness already."

The hair on the back of my neck went up. "What should I do?" I said. "Should I ask the Luckies to bring the mirror back to the Sky Kingdom after they're done tonight?"

Tsukiyomi nodded thoughtfully. "That is a good idea. But remember, they will be busy listening to prayers and wishes as worshippers visit their shrines for the next three days."

My stomach fell. I would be alone with both treasures for three whole days. Izanami couldn't reach me physically in the Middle Lands, but what if she could reach into the Aum to take the mirror and the sword? That meant that I couldn't keep them in the backpack. She'd said that she wanted me alive, but what if she decided to kill me? She could send a disease demon to get me, or cause a bus to hit me. I was going to go to Yomi and become her puppet after all.

I was just about to start hyperventilating when Tsukiyomi stroked his chin and said slowly, "Perhaps . . ."

"What?" I asked. "Perhaps what?"

He shook his head. "No, no, that won't work. I'm sorry."

"What won't work? Are you sure?"

"I was going to say that the mirror would be safe in my care," Tsukiyomi began. "No one would dare attack the Prince of the Night. But keeping it safe in my palace would cause Amaterasu to believe I was doing it only to spite her. And I could not bear for her to despise me more than she already does."

"Okay, but . . . but what if you brought the mirror back to her?" I suggested. "I know you're not allowed to enter the kingdom, but you could meet one of her guards at the border, and they could take it to her."

"I don't know if I could bear the pain of seeing my old home and being forbidden to enter," Tsukiyomi said. A tear made its way down his cheek.

"Please," I said. I could *not* be responsible for both treasures. "Maybe you could even take Kusanagi. That would make her happy."

Tsukiyomi recoiled. "Oh, dear, no. I try to have as little to do with my brother as possible."

Before I could stop myself, I sighed with relief, and I was surprised when I realized that I didn't want to give Kusanagi away. But Tsukiyomi must have taken it for a sigh of disappointment, because he said, "You're right, child. It's selfish of me not to help you after all the danger I put you in, and after you've been so brave and good." He sighed, too. "Give me the mirror. I will do as you suggest and take it to the border of my sister's lands."

He held out his hand, and I gave him the Mirror of the Sun,

still wrapped in its velvet cover. He gazed at it reverently for a moment before tucking it somewhere inside his suit jacket. "Thank you, Momo, for holding me to my duty as a kami of the sky. Go back to sleep now. Your own duties have been fulfilled, and you can rest easy." He bowed low, gave me one last gentle smile, and rose toward the full moon. I felt a burden being lifted from my shoulders as he disappeared. *Thank goodness for Tsukiyomi,* I thought as I curled back up in my blankets. At least one of the kami put my safety first.

No one could have been more surprised or excited than me when the *Takarabune* had dropped me off at home and I saw Mom waiting for me just inside the torii. I almost fell over the railing in my haste to get down. Mom wrapped me and Niko in a huge, tearful hug, and when I looked up to say goodbye, the ship was already gone.

We spent the rest of that night telling each other all about where we'd been and what we'd done. "You go first," I said to Mom. After all, she'd had Niko's mirror to see where we'd been, but I had no idea where she'd been.

"All right," she said. She paused for a long moment and then said, "I've always told you that Dad's spirit never stopped calling to me after his accident."

I felt like someone had just hit pause on the movie of my life—what happened after this moment could change everything. Was she about to tell me that she'd been right all along? That Dad really was alive? It seemed impossible—Dad was just a regular human. He couldn't have survived the storm that had swept him off the deck of his boat.

Mom said that after our first escape from Susano'o, she had begged Ebisu for a charm that would protect Dad when he went out to sea. "Ebisu told me that it would protect Dad's life, but that was all that he could guarantee," she said. And Dad had been wearing that charm on his last research trip.

I remembered with sudden guilt that she'd told me this once, a long time ago. It was back when I'd convinced myself that she'd lied to me about the kami being real. Her belief in Dad's survival was too painful to watch back then, and I'd shoved the story about Ebisu's charm down so deep that I'd forgotten all about it.

"On the night that you went to Ryleigh's party," Mom continued, "the rabbit in the moon came to me with rumors of a strange sea creature visiting all the places you went to in the fall: the undersea palace of the Taira clan; the Western Pacific Transportation Terminal, where you got on the turtle taxi; and the waters around my island. No one had seen the creature, although Takamori, the injured crab who your father rescued years ago, did say that a strange, sad energy had passed through the region several times. I searched everywhere—the deepest trenches, every bay and inlet—but to no avail. Finally, I decided to try the waters around my island."

That's when it hit me:

Oh. My. Gosh.

Dad was a whale.

He had to be. It made perfect sense: Hadn't Dad and I turned into whales when we'd fallen overboard in the storm in Yata-no-kagami? Hadn't we wandered sadly around the ocean? And, I realized with a start, he wasn't just *a* whale—he was *the* whale. And I'd *met* him in the waters around Mom's island, just after I'd fought Shuten-dōji. That whale had looked so sad, and he'd looked at me like he'd *known* me. It *had* to be Dad. Dad was alive! He was out there in the ocean and I'd met him!

I squirmed in my seat and tried to be patient. Probably Mom was about to tell me that she'd found him there, near the island. If she did, should I pretend to be surprised, or should I tell her the truth right away?

"Did you see him?" I asked. "Was he there?"

Mom shook her head. "I underestimated my father. I thought that the worst that could happen would be that I'd stray too close to the island and be pushed out to sea. But instead I was swept into the Aum."

What? No. This wasn't how it was supposed to go at all. I remembered how vast and dark and terrifying the Aum had been. I couldn't imagine floating around in that infinite nothingness without a tether. How had she found her way home? Niko covered his eyes and whined, "Oh, my gracious goddess!"

"Hush," Mom said, and stroked Niko's head and scratched behind his ears—she was the only person he allowed to do that. "You know that I am perfectly capable of navigating the Aum. The important thing is that I'm back." She smiled, but her eyes were so sad that I knew she was heartbroken about not having found Dad. I had a brief vision of the old days, when she would stare at the sea for hours with those same sad eyes. And suddenly I began to wonder if my "Dad Is a Whale!" reveal was such a great idea after all. Because I knew what would happen: she'd get all excited and determined and rush off to find him again. And I'd be left alone again. Even worse, what if I was wrong? Yes, Dad had been a whale in my other life. But what if the whale in *this* life was, in fact, just a whale? What if Mom left me, and then came back and transformed into the same sad, lonely mother she'd been when Dad had disappeared?

"And now I want to hear what happened to you," Mom said, with another attempt at a smile.

The story that had been quivering and alive and ready to stream out of me just a moment ago was now stuck like a burr in my throat. I couldn't tell her the truth about my whale life. She'd make the same leap that I had, and then she'd be off and searching. What could I tell her instead? I looked at Niko, whose face was still bunched up with worry, and had an idea.

I told my story, and when I got to the mirror with my whale life, I lied. I skipped the shipwreck and told her I'd walked into a forest and found that I'd turned into a fox. And with me was Dad, who was also a fox. Niko said nothing, and Mom smiled sadly. "How hard it must have been to leave the forest," she said. "How you must have longed to stay with Dad."

That part was true, and I nodded and swallowed a real lump in my throat before I went on. I told the story all the way up to what Tsukiyomi had told me about Izanami's plans, and how he had taken the Mirror of the Sun back to the Sky Kingdom.

Mom smiled again—a happy smile this time. "That was kind of him to do. I must remember to thank him for protecting you."

"He is the kindest of kami," Niko agreed.

"Right? I bet Susano'o wouldn't have done that for me."

"No, I suppose not." Mom yawned and said, "I think it's time for you to go to bed. I know it's time for me to go to bed. We can talk more in the morning."

Mom came into my room to say good night. As she leaned over to kiss me, I said, "Don't worry, Mom. We'll find him. He has to be out there somewhere."

She nodded, but said, "Not now. Not for a long time. I should never have allowed myself to become distracted, even for a minute. My most important job is to protect you, and that is what I promise to do, no matter what, until I know that you are safe." Then she kissed me and turned to go.

But I knew what it was costing her to make that promise. And I knew she would be sad until she found Dad and saved him somehow. So I made my own promise: I will find Dad. Whether he's a whale or a tuna fish or an octopus or a sea slug, I will find him and I will bring him back and we will all be together again. No matter what.

Chillin' with My BFFs

A few weeks after we got home, Jin performed the encore at SttTop's sold-out show at Oracle Arena. The audience and the internet went wild. It was his first solo song and before he sang it, he announced that after this world tour, he was going to "take a much-needed break so I can rest and reflect and reevaluate where I want my life to go."

Thousands of SttToppies screamed and sobbed as he sat alone on the stage and sang the bridge and the final chorus:

> *I love you forever and ever, I do*
> *But I looked in the mirror and knew . . .*
> *It's time for me to go*
> *And darlin', I think that we both know*
> *I have to be who I'm meant to be*
> *And you'll be all right, all right without me.*

Ryleigh, Danny, Niko, and I watched the entire concert from the front row, and it was magical—Jin always turned his star power up to eleven for his shows. Just after he took his last bow, he smiled at me, and I felt that familiar heart-fluttering rush in my veins.

Danny poked me and shouted, "You look like a frog with your eyes bugging out like that!" which ruined the moment a little.

After the concert, we got a special VIP limo ride to the hotel, where we met Jin in his room. His eyes lit up when we came in, but he still looked drained—pale and exhausted.

"Is this always what it's like after a show?" I asked.

"Pretty much." Jin smiled weakly.

"I can see why you'd want to quit if it makes you that tired," said Danny, who was playing with the remote-control drapes that covered the window. "Aren't you gonna miss staying at fancy hotels, though? This place is so dope! Your bathroom is bigger than my bedroom!"

"Did you like my last song?" Jin said.

"It's a musical masterpiece," said Niko.

Jin blushed. "It's just a start."

"Do you have more? Are you going to do a solo album?" Ryleigh asked eagerly.

He shook his head. "No. I meant it when I said I was going to take some time off. Like, I'll keep writing because I really like it. But I'm also really into astronomy lately. Did you know that the sun makes up ninety-nine-point-nine percent of the mass of the solar system? And that the moon is actually moving away from the earth?"

"You should do whatever you want," I said. Danny and Niko seemed to agree. Only Ryleigh looked unhappy.

"That's cool, I guess," she said.

"Come on, Ry. Be more supportive," said Danny. "Jin's not Tommy. And Tommy can do what he wants."

"Huh?" Jin's nose and forehead were wrinkled in confusion—I'm sure mine were, too.

Ryleigh scowled at Danny, but Danny rolled his eyes and said, "Just tell them."

She sighed. Then she sighed again. "So the thing is, Tommy—my big brother—has always been the one with all the talent, right? Like he's a world-class gymnast, and he can already speak four languages fluently, and he's figured out how to be super popular without, you know . . ." She hesitated.

"Without being mean to people," I said.

She nodded and took a big breath. "He's my parents' favorite. He's always gotten all the attention from everyone. And he decided not to stay in the family profession, and my parents and him had this huge fight, and they said they wouldn't pay for college, so he moved out and he never comes home anymore. And now I'm the only one left, and I'll never be as good as Tommy. And my parents will always wish it was him instead of me."

"Wow," said Jin after a while. "That's a lot."

"It's a little better now."

Apparently the Guo family had had a long talk after Ryleigh had returned home. "But," she added, "it's still hard, knowing that Tommy could be so good at being a ninja and he's just walking away from it. It really hurt my parents' feelings. And I feel like I have to make up for it."

"So that's why you don't want me to quit my career," said Jin. "Because you don't want me to let people down."

Ryleigh nodded. "But Danny's right. Tommy's Tommy, and you're you, and you should do what you want."

"And *you* could consider being you, too," Niko added. "Instead of trying to be what Tommy could have been."

Ryleigh nodded again. "Yeah . . ." And then she bounced back. "Anyway. Let's take a selfie!"

All five of us crowded into the frame, and Ryleigh took a bunch of two-shots with each of us and uploaded them to her Pixtagram account. She had typed the caption, *Chillin' with my BFFs after the SttTop concert,* and was just about to hit Post when I stopped her.

"Won't Kiki be mad?" I asked. "About the BFF part?"

Ryleigh shrugged. "She knows I'm friends with you now. I can have more than one BFF."

Ryleigh's popularity numbers had taken a hit since we'd gotten back from the Sky Kingdom and she'd started eating lunch with me. It probably would have been catastrophic, but Danny was eating with us, too, so that made it more okay for her. Without one of its twin suns, the seventh-grade solar system was thrown into chaos, and weeks later everyone was still figuring out how to realign themselves. I could tell that the whole situation was sometimes hard for Ryleigh, and there were days when I wondered if it would have been better if she'd stayed away from me and tried to change the entire system from the center, where she had a lot of power.

It made me think about Tamamo-no-mae, and how she'd started off in a time when women didn't have any power at all, and how she'd *had* to use powerful men to get what she wanted. But once she'd figured out how to game the system, that was all she did. She never tried to change the system itself—or even to work outside it, on her own, when she finally got the chance. Why? Maybe she was afraid of failing, or of losing her power. Maybe she thought it would be harder to change than to keep using her old tricks, which had been working for thousands of years. Maybe she didn't have any friends to support her.

But Ryleigh had the courage to try something new. And Ryleigh had me and Danny and Jin and Niko. Maybe together, we could change things.

The day after the concert, Mom and I went to the coast and sat on the cliffs overlooking the ocean, like we'd done ever since Dad died. Only this time, we were both looking for Dad. We stayed there until just after sunset, when darkness had begun pulling itself over the world like a blanket but the moon was still a barely visible crescent in the sky.

"Pssst! Momo! Lady Takiri-bime!"

It was the rabbit, standing behind us in the gray light of dusk. He looked faint and ghostly—due to the lack of moonlight, I supposed. He also looked frightened.

"Rabbit! What's wrong?" I had visions of Amaterasu sending her warriors after Tsukiyomi for daring to appear at the borders of the Sky Kingdom. Or worse, Izanami somehow attacking him and stealing Yata-no-kagami.

The rabbit bowed to Mom and murmured, "I have done great harm, O guardian of the Island of Mysteries. It was unwitting, but the consequences are dire. I have come to warn you, and to apologize for the part I played. I wish I could have come earlier, but I had to wait until I could get away without being noticed."

Mom's eyebrows lowered. "Tell me, rabbit. What have you done?"

Without looking up, the rabbit said, "Tsukiyomi did not return the mirror to Amaterasu. He has brought it to Izanami the Destroyer instead."

My mouth went dry. I looked at Mom, who had turned white.

"Why?" she asked. "How?"

"He is working with her, my lady. It was Tsukiyomi who freed Tamamo-no-mae from the boulder. It was he who sent me to you with the message about your husband, so that you would be away when Tamamo-no-mae attacked Momo's classmates."

Mom looked stricken. "Do you mean to tell me that was a lie? That I was chasing nothing? But I *know* he's alive! I can feel his spirit!" Her voice pitched higher and higher until it was almost a shriek.

The rabbit raised his paws and said, "No, my lady, you are correct! The rumors were real! But Tsukiyomi waited to tell you until it served his purpose. He sent Tamamo-no-mae to attack Ryleigh's party, and that gave Momo a reason to retrieve the Mirror of the Sun for him."

"But Tamamo-no-mae said that the Prince of Darkness helped her escape!" I said.

"Yes. And who do you suppose that really was?" said the rabbit.

Oh no. Why hadn't I seen it before: Tsukiyomi called himself the Prince of the Night. It wasn't a big leap to the Prince of Darkness. A chill started creeping through my chest. Mom must have sensed it, because she pulled me close to her. "But why would he help Izanami?" she asked the rabbit. "He's a sky god! He's the son of Izanagi the Creator!"

"You know he has a dark side, my lady. And he professes to love Amaterasu, but he also hates her for having banned him from his ancestral home. Izanami has promised him that if he helps her escape Yomi, she will give him dominion over the sky. He will return to Celestial City and take over as ruler of the heavens, with Amaterasu as his handmaiden."

Mom wrapped her arms all the way around me and I curled into her in despair. What had I done?

The rabbit continued talking to Mom. "I did not understand my part in my master's plans until just before he met Momo and her friends at the top of the Willis Tower. Until then, I, too, believed that he meant only to help Momo defeat Tamamo-no-mae. But I overheard him speaking with Izanami and realized what he planned to do with the mirror if Momo succeeded in stealing it. I did what I could to prevent the children from boarding the boat to the Sky Kingdom, but it was not enough."

The answer to a question that had been bothering me for days suddenly clicked into place. "*You* called the yōkai to attack us!"

The rabbit nodded. "Once I was sure you wouldn't make it to the boat, I summoned Momotarō to rescue you. But I hadn't counted on Jin being friendly with the Hollywood stars, and you made it into Celestial City after all."

"And now Izanami has one of the Sacred Treasures," Mom said.

"And if she finds the Jewel of Kindness, she will, in essence, have all three."

344

"Because I have Kusanagi, and I'm connected to her," I whispered.

The rabbit nodded.

"You have to give it back to Susano'o," Mom said. "Immediately."

That much was obvious.

The rabbit bowed and said, "The moon is growing brighter. I must not be discovered talking to you." And with that, he disappeared.

Mom drove us home to pick up a few things before we traveled to Ne-no-kuni. On the way, I fell asleep, and Izanami slipped into my dreams.

"Hello, my dear sweet Momo," she said in that voice that made my blood feel like ice water. "I understand that you've heard the good news about the Mirror of the Sun! I *am* grateful to you for your help. But I'm afraid I must ask you for yet another favor. And this time, if you do as I ask, I'll give you a prize. Would you like to see what it is?" My jaws were frozen shut with fear, and Izanami smiled—a beautiful, terrible smile. "I'll take your silence as a yes. Look!"

She waved her hand, and I saw a whale with sad, gentle eyes. He was wrapped in yards and yards of rope made of something black, shiny, and razor-sharp. He was bleeding from long slashes where it must have cut him, maybe when he had struggled to escape.

Dad. It was him. I was sure of it.

Momo. His voice called to me in my head—the same voice I remembered from when I was little. Was this real? My heart began racing. I felt dizzy.

"You recognize each other!" said Izanami. "How very sweet. He's only the cherry on top of the sundae, of course. The *real* prize is a place at my side—but you seem to be curiously unmotivated by power, so love will have to do. So be a dear and get that jewel for me, won't you? I do appreciate it. And I'm sure your father will appreciate his freedom."

Acknowledgments

Writing a book is a lot like pulling off a heist in the Sky Kingdom: you need to ignore the odds, you need to have a plan, and
you need a great team who will pull you through when your
plans go awry. My team has been so, so great.

Leigh Feldman, my agent, plays many roles in my life: cham-
pion, advocate, strategist, cheerleader, friend. I could never have
done this without her.

Liesa Abrams saw where my early drafts could go, trusted
me to get there, and patiently held up the light for me through
draft after draft (after draft . . . after draft) of this book. Emily
Harburg offered suggestions that helped me shape Momo's relationship with Ryleigh and provided all kinds of behind-the-
scenes support. Lowri Ribbons kept my plot on track and
hole-free and made sure I gave Danny the attention he deserved.

The entire Random House Children's Books team—
marketing, school and library, publicity, design, production,
sales, the publishing office, and more—inspired me with their
talent at every turn. Managing editor Rebecca Vitkus kept
everything running smoothly. Designer Michelle Cunningham

and artist Vivienne To created a masterpiece of a cover. In addition to catching my many other errors, copyeditor Barbara Bakowski taught me that it's *grown-up*, not *grownup;* my authenticity reader helped me refine and deepen my characters (any remaining blunders are mine alone); Catherina O'Mara ran the marketing end and was responsible for a bunch of delightful Momo-related goodies; Cynthia Lliguichuzhca arranged and kept track of all things publicity; Katie Halata and her amazing team made sure that teachers and librarians knew all about Momo; Stephania Villar and Elizabeth Ward made the coolest graphics and videos; and Shelley Warnaby and Lily Orgill spread the word about Momo across the pond. Seriously, how lucky am I?

A huge thank-you to the teachers, librarians, and booksellers everywhere (with a special shout-out to my stellar local indies: Linden Tree Books, Hicklebee's, Kepler's Books, and Books Inc.) who advocate for diversity and inclusivity in their classrooms and communities, who foster kids' love for reading, and who direct kids to just the books they need. (And hello to the kids in the St. Francis Book Club in Bradford, England, whose love for Momo crossed the Atlantic and warmed my heart!)

And then there's my writing community. Sonya Mukherjee, J.C. Welker, and Kim Culbertson held my hand and guided me through the "Help, I've forgotten how to write" phase of drafting. Katherine Rothschild organized the most relaxing writing retreat, and Lisa Moore Ramée listened to me blather on and on about my writing insecurities at said retreat. Additionally, Angela Mann, Abigail Hing Wen, Randy Ribay, Stacey Lee, Evelyn Skye, Kelly Loy Gilbert, Joanna Ho, Michael Chen, Kristi

Wright, Keely Parrack, Parker Peevyhouse, Darcey Rosenblatt, Gordon Jack, Traci Chee, Sandra Feder, Louise Hendricksen, Alicia Grunow, Rebecca Siler, Debbi Michiko Florence, Christina Soontornvat, Sayantani DasGupta, Samira Ahmed, and many, many others lifted me up with wise counsel and moral support throughout the entire process of writing this book.

Loving thanks to my families, both found and genetic. My Joan-siblings—Carrie Holmberg, Dani Salzer, Kristin Traudt, Meredith Dodd, Beth Lincoln, Ophny-Ony Escalante, Jeff Muralt, and Anand Marri—make me laugh and let me cry. My blood siblings, Yuka Sugiura and Ken Sugiura, are models of empathy and thoughtful care. Tad, Tai, and Kenzo Hofmeister live with me and continue, miraculously, to love me. My father, Go Sugiura, is one of the most hardworking, resilient, principled men I know. He inspires me daily to strive for excellence and to never give up. Finally, Kaoru Sugiura gave me the strength to keep being weird and different as a kid, even when it was lonely. She believed from the beginning that I could be an author, and she was quietly my biggest fan. Thank you, Mom. I love you.

Glossary

Warning: If you're looking for 100 percent accuracy, you won't find it here—or anywhere, because it doesn't exist! Shintō is a very old religion without a lot of "official" texts about its deities, and folklore (from which many of the yōkai come) is notoriously slippery, with details that change from region to region. In any case, I'm so psyched you've made it here! If you want to learn more, hyakumonogatari.com, yokai.com, and onmarkproductions.com are good places to start.

Amanozako (ah-mah-noh-zah-koh) She was born out of Susano'o's vomit. Uh-huh. And *he* was born out of Izanagi the Creator's snot, so you can imagine just how bad *she* is. Amanozako is ornery, contrary, selfish, violent, and unpredictable—except that you can always bet she'll do the exact opposite of what she thinks you want, because of the contrariness. In spite of being so awful, she's still a kami, and she hasn't done anything quite bad enough to get kicked out of the Sky Kingdom.

Amaterasu (ah-mah-teh-rah-soo) She is technically the queen of the sky, but she is best known as the kami of the sun. She is the older sister of Susano'o and Tsukiyomi (the kami of the moon), and has fought terribly with both of them. To be fair, they were both awful to her. Everybody loves her because she's warm and benevolent, and life can't exist without her, but personally, I think she *might* have a few emotional issues she needs to resolve.

Benzaiten (ben-zai-ten) One of the Seven Lucky Gods, she is the kami of music, water, and literature (or words)—basically, anything that flows. She once married a five-headed dragon who was terrorizing a village every year; luckily, the dragon fell in love with her and promised never to terrorize the village again.

Bishamon (bee-shah-mon) The god of warriors, punisher of evildoers, healer (he battles germs, I guess), guardian of the North, and one of the Seven Lucky Gods. He's a good guy but looks really scary. He's usually portrayed with his foot on the neck of a very unhappy demon or two (or three).

Byakko (byak-koh) Byakko is one of the Four Guardians from Chinese Buddhist tradition. The guardians live in the sky, and each is associated with an animal, a color, a cardinal direction, and a season. Byakko is the White Tiger of the West and is linked to autumn. He takes up the Greek constellations of Andromeda, Pisces, Aries, Taurus, and Orion.

Celestial City My own invention, because Amaterasu's palace has to be *somewhere*. The layout and look of Celestial City are inspired by the ancient Japanese capital of Heijō-kyō (now part of the city of Nara), which is where the Shinto stories were first written down. Heijō-kyō's enormous main gate was located in the middle of the southern wall and called Suzaku Gate, and the central boulevard that extended directly from the gate to the palace was called Suzaku Boulevard.

Daikoku (dai-koh-koo) Daikoku is the kami of farmers, merchants, wealth, and kitchens. Almost always portrayed as a cheerful mustachioed man, Daikoku has spiritual roots in the Hindu goddess Kali, the goddess of death and time, so I chose to portray her as an awesome, butt-kicking female. You can translate his/her/their name as either "great nation" or "great darkness," which I kind of love.

Ebisu (eh-bee-soo) Ebisu is the kami of fisherfolk, merchants, and luck, and he's the only one of the Seven Lucky Gods with a completely Japanese origin story. He was Izanagi and Izanami's first living child—and he was born without bones. They placed him in a basket and put the basket in the ocean. It wasn't the greatest parenting move, but luckily he ended up being rescued and raised by the Ainu people of northern Japan. Possibly because of his boneless babyhood, he walks with a limp.

Fukurokujū (foo-koo-roh-koo-juu) Wow, there sure are a lot of Lucky Gods in the beginning of the alphabet! Fukurokujū is one of the two old grandfathers on the *Takarabune* who represent long life and wisdom. You can identify him by his forehead, which is as tall as the rest of him (I guess because his brain is so big). Some say he used to be the Taoist god Xuanwu. He carries a staff and a scroll, and he has one super-special secret power that no other god has—and I'm not telling you what it is.

Gemini aunties A meteor shower happens every year in mid-December around Castor, a bright star in the Gemini constellation.

There's nothing in Japanese folklore about it, but I thought it would be cool if those meteors were a group of aunties who took a yearly vacation in December to visit Earth and Celestial City.

Genbu (gen-boo) Also known as the Black Tortoise of the North. One of the Four Guardians, he is nearly always portrayed with a black snake companion—don't ask me why cold-blooded creatures spend their time exclusively in a winter climate. Genbu's constellations are (ironically) mostly not visible from the Northern Hemisphere: Sagittarius, Capricorn, Aquarius, and Pegasus. Not only do the Guardians keep watch over the sky, they were also said to guard the gates of the old Japanese capital cities of Nara (Heijō-kyō) and Kyōto (Heian-kyō).

hari-onago (hah-ree-oh-nah-goh) The literal translation is "needle girl." Hari-onago wear their hair long and loose so that they can wrap it around their victims and use the needle-sharp hook on the end of each strand to dig into the victims' flesh. *shudders*

Hotei (ho-tay) I'm just now realizing that his name sounds a little bit like "hottie," which he would love. Hotei is the god of contentment, and he's kind of like a bald Santa Claus. Portrayed in a half-open kimono (he's too content to wear it properly, I guess), he is always smiling and carries a giant, bottomless sack full of goodies.

Izanagi (ee-zah-nah-gee) He and his wife, Izanami, created the islands of Japan out of swirling mucky chaos and then came down to the islands and made everything else.

Izanami (ee-zah-nah-mee) She is the original mother of everything and everyone in the Middle Lands. When she gave birth to the kami of fire, her body was burned so badly that she had to go to Yomi, the land of the dead. Izanagi went down to rescue her but ended up leaving her there. In revenge, she vowed to devote herself to killing as many people as she could, which is how she became *eeevilll.*

Jurōjin (ju-roh-jin) The second of the two wise grandpas of the Seven Lucky Gods. Some say he's Fukurokujū's grandson; others say he's actually the same spirit as Fukurokujū, just in a different body . . . but no one knows for sure. He's a scholar, he likes a drink every now and then, and he carries a staff and a scroll. Some say the scroll contains all the wisdom in the world; others say it tells how long each of us will live . . . but no one knows for sure. He's got a lot of secrets.

Middle Lands Earth. Where we humans live. The official Shintō term is actually "Central Reed Plain," but that sounded weird to me, so I changed it.

Mizaru (mee-zah-roo), **Kikazaru** (kee-kah-zah-roo), and **Iwazaru** (ee-wah-zah-roo) Their names mean "see not," "hear not," and "speak not," and they are famously carved into the gate over the Sacred Stable at Tōshōgu Shrine in Nikkō, Japan. Most people believe they're just a reminder not to watch, listen to, or say anything evil, but some believe that they are like little spies that keep track of everyone's good and bad deeds.

Mizumaki-no-kami (mee-zoo-mah-kee-no-kah-mee) A kami of watering and irrigation.

Mochizuki Chiyome (moh-chee-zoo-kee chee-yoh-meh) Some say she was a samurai's wife from way back in the 1500s and that after his death, she was recruited to do some spy work for her dead husband's lord. Back then, most men thought women weren't smart enough to understand or remember complex political and military plans, so the men blabbed about everything in the presence of these ninja women, who then acted on the information. Mochizuki is said to have commanded more than three hundred female ninja by the end of her life. Is any of this true? It depends on who you ask—but if no one knows whether she really existed, maybe that just proves how good she was.

Momotarō (mo-mo-tah-roh) One of the most famous, most beloved heroes of Japanese folklore. He was born from a peach (a symbol of life) and grew into a strong, cheerful young man. When oni began terrorizing the land, he set off to vanquish them. Along the way, he met a dog, a monkey, and a pheasant; he shared his mother's delicious dumplings with the animals because that's the kind of guy he was. Naturally, they decided to be his friends for life, and together they defeated the oni . . . and everyone lived happily ever after.

ninja (neen-ja) Historical ninja were mostly professional spies and secret messengers who were so good at their jobs that ordinary people thought they had magic powers. There may have been a *few* ninja who could see the spirit realm and used magic to manipulate nature to serve their purposes—you never know! There were real ninja families, like Ryleigh's, who passed down their skills from generation to generation, and they lived in ninja villages hidden deep in the mountains. But once they entered a non-ninja town, they blended right in with the townspeople. As Ryleigh says, the whole point of being a ninja is that no one *knows* you're a ninja.

Niwataka (nee-wah-tah-kah) His formal name is Niwataka-tsuhi, and he's one of many minor kami who are associated with houses and homes.

nure-onna (noo-reh-on-nah) Her name means "wet woman," and she appears on beaches and riverbanks, soaking wet and carrying a baby. Who wouldn't help a poor soul like that? But watch out—this is what the nure-onna is counting on! Take her sweet little baby from her, and you'll find yourself holding a sweet little baby that weighs a hundred pounds. While you're staggering around with a freakishly heavy infant in your arms, the nure-onna will regain her true form (a sea serpent with a human face) and suck your blood dry.

nurikabe (noo-ree-kah-beh) These yōkai aren't technically scary or dangerous, but they can cause a lot of trouble. A nurikabe is just a wall that unexpectedly appears in front of you, often in the middle of the night. You can't get over or around it, because nurikabe can grow and stretch as long as they want. They're best known for planting themselves in front of travelers, who suddenly discover that they can't go any farther on the road they thought they were supposed to take and are forced to stop, turn back, or continue walking next to the wall . . . possibly forever.

Omopikane (oh-moh-pee-kah-neh) The kami of thought. After Susano'o destroyed Amaterasu's palace and killed her favorite handmaiden, she hid in a cave, thus plunging the world into darkness. It was Omopikane's brilliant idea to gather all the kami outside the cave and have Uzume do a wild dance on top of an overturned rice barrel (thus inventing the world's first drum). That made the kami laugh and cheer so much that Amaterasu wondered what the heck was going on. When they told her they were cheering for a new goddess of the sun, Amaterasu couldn't resist the urge to check out the competition—and saw herself in Yata-no-kagami, the mirror that Omopikane had hung directly across from the mouth of the cave. For some reason, ancient gods and people in fairy tales always fall for the old "Is it someone else or is it just my reflection?" trick, and Amaterasu was no exception. She stepped partway out of the cave to get a better look at this gorgeous woman, and Tachikara'o, the kami of strength, pulled her all the way out and shoved a boulder in front of the cave so that she couldn't go back inside.

oni (oh-nee) Demons. Devils. Horns, fangs, bad hair, multicolored skin. . . . You get the idea.

onibi (oh-nee-bee) Little blue floating lights that appear over swamps and in forests, often luring passersby farther into these dark and dangerous places with their luminous beauty. Some legends say that if you get too close, they will suck your soul out.

Palace of the Sun It's not named in Shintō texts, but we do know that Susano'o destroyed it after he lost (or won, depending on who you ask) a kami-making contest with Amaterasu. I loosely based its layout on that of Heian Palace, which was the official residence of the Japanese imperial family for most of the Heian period (794–1185).

Rabbit in the Moon He once offered to sacrifice himself to give Tsukiyomi something to eat, and Tsukiyomi was so moved by the rabbit's devotion that he brought him back to live on the moon. If you look carefully at the full moon, you can see the rabbit in profile, facing right.

sazae-oni (sah-zah-eh-oh-ni) A sazae is a type of shellfish (a turban snail, if you want to get technical), so I guess you could say that a sazae-oni is a . . . shellfish demon? Sazae-oni have long arms and giant snail shells for heads, and they enjoy terrorizing sailors.

Seven Lucky Gods I love them so much. They come from a mix of the different religious and folk traditions in Japan, but they're literally all in the same boat. (*See also* Takarabune.)

shinobi (shee-noh-bee) Another name for the ninja; it's an alternate way to read the first character of "ninja" (nin = 忍 = "secret"; ja = 者 = "person who ___").

shuriken (shoo-ree-ken) Most of the world knows these weapons as ninja throwing stars, but they were originally used by samurai. In English, the word means "hand-hidden blade."

Sky Kingdom The official Japanese name is "Heavenly Reed Plain," and it's where all the kami hang out who aren't assigned to be elements of nature in the Middle Lands. Amaterasu lives there and is the queen. Susano'o and Tsukiyomi also lived there until they got kicked out for doing murders. Aren't you glad you're not part of that family?

suiko (soo-ee-koh) Remember Uncle Kappy, the kappa from Momo's last adventure? Suiko are like kappa—vaguely humanoid aquatic creatures—but smaller, meaner, and more deadly. They have scales instead of froglike skin, and sharp claws and teeth. And they're not much for talking—just sucking the blood and souls out of their victims.

Susano'o (soo-sah-noh-oh) The kami of the sea and its storms. He has a terrible temper and very bad manners, which got him kicked out of the Sky Kingdom, where he used to live with his older siblings, Amaterasu and Tsukiyomi. He spends most of his time underground in Ne-no-kuni, the Land of Roots.

Suzaku (soo-zah-koo) The Vermilion Phoenix of the South and guardian of the Vermilion Phoenix Gate. Why "vermilion"? Why not just "red"? I don't know. That's just what every single source says. Suzaku is associated with summer—and with fire. Some accounts even say the bird is made of fire. Full disclosure: I called the bird a phoenix in the pages of this book, but the actual type of bird isn't named in traditional literature. Why is everyone so particular about the color and not the bird species? Beats me.

Takarabune (tah-kah-rah-boo-neh) Literally, the Ship of Treasures. The Seven Lucky Gods sail it down to the Middle Lands on New Year's Eve to deliver good fortune to us humans.

Tamamo-no-mae (ta-ma-mo-no-mah-eh) One of the most powerful and most feared demons in Japan. She was an evil nine-tailed fox who first appeared as the wicked wife of a Chinese king over three thousand years ago. She made him do such terrible things that the people eventually rebelled and overthrew him. She fled to India and married a king there—and under her influence, he beheaded a thousand men. A couple thousand years (and horrific tragedies) later, her spirit was finally trapped in a boulder in Japan. In 2022, the boulder split open and released her back into the world. For real! You can look it up! Some say she repented long ago and is at peace, so we have nothing to worry about. I'm not so sure.

By the way, I have questions about those age-old stories of beautiful women tricking good men into doing bad things. Even now, studies show that "beautiful" women tend to rise higher and faster than their "regular" female colleagues—but the more powerful a beautiful woman becomes, the less people trust her! And identical behaviors are interpreted differently in women (rude, aggressive, sneaky) and men (honest, assertive, strategic). Where did all of this start, and when will it change?

tengu **(ten-goo)** Flying chaos demons, basically. They're not exactly evil (sometimes they're even on the side of good), but they do tend to cause trouble. Full disclosure: I gave them bat wings in this series, but in real life, they're related to crows and have feathered wings.

Tsukiyomi **(tsoo-kee-yoh-mee)** The kami of the moon, Amaterasu's younger brother, and Susano'o's older brother. Some people also associate his name with Yomi, the land of the dead. One time, Ukemochi, the kami of food, invited Tsukiyomi to dinner. When he saw that the food was coming out of literally every hole in her body, he killed her in a fit of rage and disgust. (I mean, I get why he was grossed out. But murdering her was a *tad* extreme!) Amaterasu was so upset with him that she refused to allow him in her presence ever again. (Some stories say it was really Susano'o who killed Ukemochi—and to be honest, that tracks, don't you think?)

Ukemochi (oo-keh-moh-chee) The kami of food and one of Amaterasu's favorite little sisters. She was killed by either Tsukiyomi or Susano'o, depending on whose story you believe. I think the whole "food coming out of her holes" thing is supposed to show that it came from inside her—just as food comes from inside the earth, out of the dirt.

ushi-oni (oo-shee-oh-nee) Half bull, half spider, all aquatic creature. I know. It makes zero sense that a bull-slash-spider would hang out at the beach, but guess what? Not everything has to make sense. There are too many stories associated with the ushi-oni to list here, so if you're interested, I encourage you to look them up!

Uzume (oo-zoo-meh) She's the kami of drums, dance, laughter, and the dawn, and she's one of my faves, to be honest—she just seems like a fun hang. She was part of the successful plan to lure Amaterasu out of her cave when she went into hiding (*see* Omopikane).

Yata-no-kagami (yah-tah-noh-kah-gah-mee) Literally, the eight-sided mirror. One of the Three Sacred Treasures that Amaterasu gave to her grandson as a symbol of his right to rule the Middle Lands. I made up all the things it can do, but you never know—maybe I'm right! See the entry for Omopikane for the mirror's origin story.